HER MAJESTY'S BOY SCOUT

AT HOME, BEHIND ENEMY LINES

by Guy Simonis
edited by Joanne Simonis

Copyright © 2010

All rights reserved

ISBN 9781450550550

ABOUT THE AUTHOR

Guy Simonis was born in 1931 in the city of Leiden, near The Hague in the Netherlands. When Hitler's Nazi forces invaded Poland in 1939, Guy was an eight-year-old child. When VE day was declared, he celebrated his 14th birthday. Many of the characters and colour of this story are based on his experiences throughout the German occupation. Following the war, Guy spent two years in the service of the Royal Netherlands Air Force, stationed in Fontainebleau, France. In 1954, he married his long-time sweetheart Ina Blaauw and emigrated to Canada.

After a successful career in the world lottery industry and a subsequent retirement career in consulting around the world, Guy has 'slowed the pace' somewhat and taken up writing. His first effort was a lottery insider's guidebook called *Dissected and Reassembled*, co-authored with Jean-Marc Lafaille. His second effort – a detailed, but amusing family history – is entitled *It's a long story, kids, and at times interesting*. Tired of telling the truth, Guy has turned his hand to historical fiction with "Her Majesty's Boy Scout" a tale of Agent Mark Zonder from Leiden.

ACKNOWLEDGEMENTS

A great deal of thanks to my daughter Joanne for taking my manuscript and applying her sceptical view of the world, testing the boundaries of fact and fiction, as well as the innocent view of a child who grew up without war and without ever knowing mandatory blackouts and ration coupons. She said she enjoyed the book. I choose to believe her.

My thanks also to the friends who provided me with inspiration for the many fictional characters in this story. Here's hoping they don't mind me using their names and the fun I had imagining them in these situations. Although almost all of the characters are fictional, the events and background of the war surrounding them are real. I would hasten to explain that the events befalling Princess Juliana are purely figments of my imagination.

I also need to express gratitude to the Google search engine, which helped me keep my dates and events factual.

Many readers may think that Holland is the official name of a country. It is not. The Netherlands has several provinces. Only two of them are named Holland – South and North. Because the action of this story swings between various provinces and in a wish to avoid confusion, I have used the local name of the country: Nederland rather than Holland or The Netherlands.

After reading many superb spy novels, I arrogantly thought, "I can do that." Reading this book will attest to my failure to come even close.

In developing the plot, I've grown an appreciation for Tom Clancy's quip: "The difference between fiction and reality? Fiction has to make sense."

1

1927
WEDNESDAY, JUNE 8, 5:30 PM
BOULEVARD
KATWIJK AAN ZEE, NEDERLAND

The North Sea waves crashed wildly on the wide sandy beach of Katwijk-aan-Zee. Sudden thunderstorms were normal this time of year. The storm had cleared and the weather was calm but close to the water's edge, the noise of the sea was still thunderous.

At the first rumble of thunder, the beach-goers had begun to disperse. Sunburned and tired they carried their heavy trappings to the *Blauwe tram* – the blue streetcar, for the half-hour, standing-room-only trip to the city of Leiden in the province of South Holland.

Over the years, beautiful villas had begun to replace the simple fishermen's homes along the boulevard. One of the most majestic homes was *Huyze Ten Cate*, owned by the Heineken family. Each of its 20 windows provided a panoramic view of the ever-rolling North Sea. The Heinekens were the richest commoners in the country. The profits from their renowned brand of beer had allowed them to work their way into the circles of aristocracy who – in these, the Roaring Twenties – still stood on noble pedestals, far apart from the hoi polloi.

When the Royal Family wanted a residence in Katwijk for Princess Juliana to study at the nearby Leiden University, the Heinekens had immediately volunteered their mansion.

Few of the departing beach crowd paid much attention to the Marechaussee corporal standing guard in front the imposing residence. They knew the state police force – in blue uniforms, kepis and white lanyards – was always there to guard the Crown Princess Juliana.

This June evening of 1927 was one of those memorable times when – once the thunderstorms had pushed their way inland and the sky had cleared – the world smelled brand new again.

A black limousine drew up along the sidewalk. The chauffeur walked around and opened the door for a tall, immaculately dressed man in morning suit with grey vest, wearing a black homburg. A big handlebar moustache made him look older than his 44 years.

"Everything alright, corporal?" the man asked in an authoritarian voice.

"No trouble, Chief van Zandt. The Princess insisted on a walk before dinner. Corporal de Boer is nearby."

"It'll be easier when she starts university next month," van Zandt said. "Hanging around the beach, shopping and bicycling may be attractive to the Princess and her school mates but it makes it more difficult for us."

Francis (Frans) Lodewijk van Zandt, in his function as the Chief of Police of The Hague, had no jurisdiction over the Marechaussee, nor did his responsibilities include protection of the Royal Family. Yet, no matter how much the top brass of the Marechaussee complained, his power to intercede came directly from Queen Wilhelmina who trusted him completely. During the Great War of 1914, van Zandt had served as Chief of the Harbour Police in Rotterdam where, in spite of Nederland's neutral status, he worked closely with the British. His painful limp was a constant reminder of having found trouble in places that were none of his business.

Wilhelmina herself had been tutored at the palace and had hardly ever set foot outside before she became Queen at age 18. Juliana had the kind of freedom no royal princess had ever enjoyed; the Queen expected her to experience how the people live day to day. However, she had asked Chief van Zandt to keep an eye on her.

Wilhelmina liked van Zandt because he volunteered to undertake 'special services' such as paying off the Palace's linen maid who became pregnant by Prince Hendrik, her husband. In such cases, the Crown appreciated his sometime neglect of the law.

He had made the 20-minute drive from The Hague for no other purpose than to make sure all was well. He was about to depart, when Princess Juliana and Jonkvrouw Mieke de Jonge returned from their walk accompanied by a dark, handsome young man.

Juliana was no classic beauty in anyone's view but a pleasant, solidly built Dutch girl. Critics abroad – especially in England – frequently commented on her looks. *The Times* snarled that she would "not stand out in a crowd of a thousand *Frauleins* of her age." Leave it to the British press to mistake the German for Dutch. Her engaging smile and unpretentious ways didn't go over well in staid old England, but the Dutch adored her.

The Chief clambered out of his car and ceremoniously greeted the Princess with a formal bow, doffing his homburg so flamboyantly, it nearly scraped the sidewalk.

"Oh, Chief van Zandt, how nice to see you. Maman must be quite worried about me to send you on a lovely summer evening," she chided.

"Not quite, Your Highness," he said smoothly. "I happened to be in Katwijk and thought I would introduce myself to the young gentleman."

Juliana answered with just a hint of petulance in her voice. "Chief van Zandt. I waved at Mr. Ferenc Kolmar as he walked along the boulevard and Corporal de Boer rushed immediately to my side. He checked Mr. Kolmar's passport and confirmed that he is a talented pianist who played a Command Performance last month at the Palace. I find him a charming young man. I asked him to walk back with us to the villa."

If van Zandt was concerned about this surprise encounter, he did not show it. He was an old intelligence man who did not believe in co-incidences. Any stranger with a strong accent aroused his suspicions.

"Your passport, please," van Zandt demanded curtly. Kolmar, as a foreigner, was accustomed to officious men and handed over his papers.

Ferenc Buda Kolmar, 20, was born in Budapest in 1907. His religion, a requirement on most European passports, was Jewish. His dark wavy hair and brown eyes reminded van Zandt of Rudolph Valentino, a new movie idol of silent films.

Ferenc was happy to provide complete information. "I have earned a bursary at the Royal Conservatory of Music in The Hague. I have a flat there. Tomorrow I will be performing at the Katwijk Pavilion with the Residency Orchestra of The Hague. Tonight and tomorrow evening I am staying at the villa of the Wernink family, here in Katwijk."

Juliana turned to van Zandt. "I shall attend that concert along with Mieke and of course our ever-present Corporal de Boer, dressed in his finest formal uniform."

Van Zandt responded as a father with a recalcitrant daughter. "Has this been cleared by the Palace?"

"Not yet, but you will do that for me, won't you Chief?"

Ferenc Kolmar, visibly nervous at this sassy display by the future queen stumbled for words, "I must go now. I must rehearse for tomorrow and my host is waiting for me."

"We'll be there tomorrow," Juliana sang as she watched Kolmar walk away. She nodded coolly as van Zandt made yet another flourishing bow, hat in hand.

The following day, the Heineken home was atwitter with what Juliana and her courtiers should wear to the concert. Finally, light, colourful summer dresses were judged appropriate and the discussion turned to what type of hat was proper for an outdoor concert. The white straw hat with the extra wide brim won out.

A stage, erected on the boulevard in front of the White Church, housed the Residency Orchestra. The Heinzmann Concert Grand on which Ferenc Kolmar would perform reflected the rays of the setting sun.

The beach was crammed with folks sitting on blankets or reclining in folding beach-chairs. Special guests and dignitaries, unwilling to plod through the sand were assigned metal folding chairs on the boulevard. Juliana sat in the front row between her friends. Corporal de Boer sat directly behind her.

After the overture, Ferenc Kolmar was introduced as the talented interpreter of Franz Liszt's works. The crowd fell silent as he sat down at the piano and fussed with his coattails. The opening stanzas drowned out the cawing of the soaring seagulls. The music flowed across the sand and sea and wafted toward the setting sun. The young pianist received a prolonged standing ovation from the hundreds of spectators.

"Isn't he gorgeous?" Juliana whispered as she stood to applaud.

Mieke hushed her, put her index finger to her lips and nodded in agreement. Back at the villa, Juliana exclaimed excitedly, "I shall invite him for dinner tomorrow and then he could play for us afterwards."

Ferenc was generous in his after-dinner recital. In spite of his difficulty with the language, he was an interesting raconteur and good actor. Whenever he failed to find the right word, his hands and expressions translated for him. Juliana was smitten.

Brought up with the notion that dinner table was a stage for serious debate, she engaged her guests in the discussion of the difficulties facing the Weimar Republic with its pitched battles between the Communists and Adolf Hitler's Nazi goons. Ferenc talked about the fall of the Austro-Hungarian Empire and its effect on Eastern Europe.

The evening weather was balmy and the discussion soon turned to more youthful matters: the jazz music coming from America and the popular black performers now being featured in Paris and London.

The servants brought out the gramophone to let Jonkvrouw Mieke and Baroness Elisabeth demonstrate the Charleston, the current dance craze. Ferenc surprised all by his rendition of the *Tiger Rag*, ripping the keyboard with his thumb to create the roar after *Hold that tiger!*

When the evening ended, Juliana gave a not-so-subtle hint that she wanted to see Ferenc out without anyone else present. De Boer followed the Princess at a discreet distance and tried not to listen to the small talk. He smiled to himself and thought about his girlfriend Emma.

Juliana interrupted his reverie, "It's all right Corporal de Boer; you may stand down for the evening." He moved across the hallway but never lost sight of his charge. Juliana took the young pianist's head in her hands and placed an inexperienced hard kiss on his lips. Ferenc was startled but regained his composure and returned a much gentler good-bye kiss. De Boer smiled as he heard Juliana tiptoe up to her room, humming a melody; Liszt he supposed.

The corporal was not a cultured man. He was the perfect officer to protect the Princess. Easy-going and game for any of Juliana's caprices, he was also alert to any danger. He enjoyed his assignment; his colleagues guarding Juliana at the University had a boring task, sitting through interminable lectures on religion, parliamentary history and constitutional law. He preferred the summer assignment.

As the summer of 1927 rolled by, the informal dinners became more frequent. Ferenc Kolmar was an ever-present dinner guest.

De Boer made an entry in the log, "Goodbyes taking longer."

In the year since the summer of 1927, Juliana and Ferenc had exchanged many letters. In December, they had managed to meet in his dressing room at the Scala Theatre in The Hague at a

Christmas concert by the Royal Conservatory students.

During the 1928 Olympics in Amsterdam, Ferenc had taken up residence in Katwijk again and was often a dinner guest at *Huyze ten Cate*.

Juliana expressed the wish that Ferenc should join her at the Olympic Games. She knew that seating Ferenc in the Royal Box was out of the question. However, the Queen had given permission for Juliana to attend several competitions incognito, meaning she would move among the public without any formalities.

The Queen asked van Zandt to secure tickets for Juliana's entourage consisting of her three girlfriends as well as Ferenc Kolmar and, of course, Corporal de Boer.

Juliana liked the corporal because he quietly withdrew at the close moments with Ferenc. She was confident he wouldn't tattle, because if Maman found out about her amorous thoughts, she would find herself in a golden cage at the Palace. Yes, de Boer would allow her some freedom.

Van Zandt, as Chief of Police and his 'special' attention to the royal family, had a V.I.P. suite at the Olympic Stadium. He and his wife used the opportunity to host Juliana's party and thus keep an eye on things. A four-car convoy left Katwijk in the morning to attend the event, a mere 30 minutes away.

The group threw all regal decorum to the wind as they celebrated achievements by the orange-clad Dutch athletes.

During the latter days of August, Ferenc continued his frequent visits to the villa and spent a lot of time alone with the Princess. The household staff adored him because he was considerate and fun to be around. They spoiled him by catering to his taste in Hungarian spicy food, something the Princess abhorred.

By his constant presence, Corporal de Boer had become part of the scenery. He was careful but considerate in affording the Princess as much privacy as possible. Their little trysts had become more physical. He knew it but he was not about to interfere in a love affair.

As summer ended, Juliana was determined to spend an afternoon with Ferenc without being observed. She chose the dunes at the south end of the Boulevard where public access was restricted. The fragile ecology of the dunes that protected the country from the sea could not survive the trampling of the masses. Juliana expressed the wish to pick a few baskets of the delicious blackberries that grew abundantly in the wild.

"Can you secure access to the restricted area?" she asked De Boer.

"I think I can Ma'am." He did not explain that he would be snipping the barbed wire fence.

Her friends offered to come along but Juliana discouraged them. She put on sunglasses and a wide brimmed straw hat decorated with a sheer blue scarf and strolled hand-in-hand with Ferenc to the end of the boulevard. Turning into a fenced-off path, they watched as de Boer snipped the wires.

Juliana hesitated for a moment but said, "Corporal de Boer, I am going to spend some time with Ferenc. I wish to have some privacy. Stay in the area if you must but give us these moments together."

De Boer thought of his girlfriend Emma and their schemes to find a place, any place, to be alone.

"I'll be at my post Your Highness and I understand your need for discretion." He watched them walk barefoot, shoes in hand, into the soft sand. He followed at a distance and took up a position behind a sand hill. He thought he should bring Emma here someday and make love to her. He took off his blue tunic and kepi, laid down and basked in the sun. No one could approach the couple without getting past him.

He did not hear the passionate moans, did not see the hot embraces, the hands, feverishly searching. He laid on the gentle rise and imagined Emma in his arms. He felt the gentle breeze, heard the roar of the surf. He was in his own world.

2

1928
TUESDAY, OCTOBER 3, 2:00 PM
PALACE NOORDEINDE
THE HAGUE, NEDERLAND

The 1928 Buick 47 slowly made its way through the rainy October streets of The Hague. Lounging comfortably in the back, van Zandt lit an expensive Willem II cigar. He always carried a supply of his favourite smokes in a silver container carefully stashed in the inside pocket of his formal dress-jacket. He always dressed formally for an audience with Queen Wilhelmina.

"Off to the Palace then, Sir?" Loek Mol, his long-time driver, asked.

Van Zandt merely nodded. He was a stern, tight-lipped taskmaster, but he did confide in Loek from time to time. Not state secrets of course, but a man needed to hear himself talk to get a perspective on his problems.

Loek had been with him since 1917, the days of the Great War. Van Zandt had been Chief of the Rotterdam Harbour Police. He kept an eye on the nest of English and German spies anxious to obtain sailing times of the world's freighters that frequented Europe's major, neutral harbour.

A look through the rear view mirror told Loek that something was eating away at the Chief. "You've solved many problems before, Sir," he said looking straight ahead.

"Yes, but this one won't be easy."

The rain splattered against the windshield of the American automobile with its chrome spokes, yellow trim and spare wheel mounted on the running board. Van Zandt loved the perks of his position. He and his wife lived in an opulent villa in the ambassadorial enclave of Wassenaar. The couple were regular invitees to many government and social functions.

As the impressive Buick pulled up to the pillared entrance of the Noordeinde Palace, tourists clustered under umbrellas in anticipation of the changing of the Marechaussee guards, a scene straight from an operetta by Franz Lehar.

"Better go around to the side entrance, Loek," he said, "Too many eyes here." He acknowledged the salute of the sentry and entered without any identification.

Inside the atrium, he greeted Prime Minister Ruys and Professor Pronk, the personal physician to Her Majesty. Van Zandt turned to the third man seated in one of the fashionable Queen Anne chairs. "We haven't met. You must be Rector Kolkman."

The cadaverous figure rose from his seat to shake van Zandt's hand. He was an intolerant cleric forever railing against the moral depravity of the postwar culture. As head of the Netherlands Reformed Church, he saw it his duty to maintain the values of a god-fearing nation. The prime minister, his nose in the air as if he smelled something unpleasant, stepped forward.

"I presume Chief van Zandt, that you know why Her Majesty called us into her presence?" he asked in his imperious manner. Before the Chief could answer, the Master of the Royal Household formally called the four advisors into the Princess Emma Salon.

The Master, a throwback to the Napoleonic era, was dressed in a metallic coat complete with bow-tied slippers over white stockings. The Queen received them in the centre of the cavernous room. She was a dumpy looking woman in a dark blue dress, the ever-present handbag dangling from her wrist. Her private secretary waited at her side.

She greeted each of the officials by name and sat down in her ornately carved chair – a half-throne. Its straight back was topped by a carving of an eagle in attack mode, its beak pointed at the back of the Queen's head. It created the impression that the bird might peck at her at any moment.

Queen Wilhelmina was among the last of the truly regal Royals. She had become Queen at the age of ten. Her mother, Princess Emma governed in her place until she ascended the throne at age 18.

At the end of the Great War at age 28, she had seen many of her royal relatives removed from power: the Tsar of Russia and his family killed, the Kaiser of Germany exiled, the king of Italy deposed. She vowed, then and there that the House of Orange would become closer to the people. Governing in this new age was an obligation, not a privilege to be abused. Yet, she found it difficult to depart from the formal life for which she had been trained. The Netherlands Reformed Church was her strength and her beacon. She was a devout Protestant.

Van Zandt was impressed, as always, by the ornate decor of the room. The huge paintings, the gilded wall coverings, the golden clock ticking on the mantelpiece all spoke of tradition and power.

Wilhelmina formally addressed her gathered advisors. "As some of you are aware, Professor Pronk's examination of Princess Juliana shows that she is with child and is expected to deliver in May of next year. The child is the product of a liaison with a pianist, a Mr. Ferenc Kolmar, a Hungarian national," the Queen sighed with heavy heart. "She has not told anyone else of her situation, least of all Kolmar. The circle of knowledge is limited to this group and Jonkvrouw Mieke de Jonge."

Prince Hendrik walked in unannounced. A glance of disapproval crossed her face, a slight cough her only reprimand. "Rector Kolkman and I agree that the pregnancy must be carried to full term. Any other solution is repugnant. Yet, my fear is that the people would strongly disapprove if this pregnancy were to become public knowledge."

Queen Wilhelmina looked mournful but steely-eyed. "This, therefore, is an issue of national security."

The prime minister who had not been aware of this delicate situation addressed the Queen. "Your Highness, while this development comes as a shock, I fully concur with the sentiments you have expressed. News of this pregnancy would have a destabilizing effect on the country. I would recommend that a solution be found that will keep this situation from becoming public knowledge."

The Queen acknowledged him with an appreciative nod and turned to van Zandt. "Chief van Zandt you were charged with the responsibility of observing Princess Juliana."

"Majesty I have the reports of the Marechaussee. They met in Katwijk last summer. The Princess invited this young man to her villa on several occasions to perform impromptu concerts attended by her friends."

"You know this Mr. Kolmar?" the Prime Minister asked.

"He is a student at the Royal Conservatory here in The Hague. His father, now deceased, was a Conductor of the Budapest Symphony and his mother is a well-known opera singer, who is much in demand as a vocal coach," van Zandt offered. He added for effect, "The music critics are unanimous in their praise of Mr. Kolmar's performances."

"Did you have any idea that my daughter had any romantic feelings for this young man?" the Queen asked.

"I relied completely on the services provided by the Marechaussee. The officers were asked to find a balance between protecting the Princess and allowing her sufficient privacy."

The Queen allowed herself a grim smile and a barely noticeable shrug of her shoulder. She rose, causing the others in the room to rise as well.

"Prime Minister, I would ask you to immediately convene a meeting with the advisors present here and discuss options to resolve this issue in the best interest of the Princess and the country."

Three hours later Prime Minister Ruys and van Zandt met again with the Queen and her husband in her study. An enclosed coal-burning hearth glowed under a mantelpiece crammed with small portraits. Two floor-to-ceiling bookcases covered one wall. A centuries-old, leather-covered bible with a small, brass lock rested on the reading table. On the opposite wall two paintings of Dutch landscapes were tastefully lit. The Royal pair sat in the 'discussion corner', four enormous leather club chairs placed around a low, round table.

"Your Majesty," the Prime Minister began, "Your advisors are of the unanimous opinion that should the situation with the Crown Princess become public knowledge, the Government will fall. The Communists and Socialists who are innately opposed to the Monarchy will side with the religion-based parties in a vote of censure. This in turn may result in a massive agitation to establish a republican form of government."

Prince Hendrik coughed and raised his hand. Ruys ignored him and continued, "We recommend that the Crown Princess should live, incommunicado, at the Palace at Soestdijk until the birth of the child. Professor Pronk's staff will see the Princess through to full term."

Since the prince sat quietly, Ruys carried on, "Government Information Services will announce that Princess Juliana will study Islam at the Batavia University in the Dutch East Indies because 80 million of her future subjects are Muslims."

Queen Wilhelmina nodded thoughtfully and asked, "What is to be done about the Hungarian pianist?"

"Ma'am, your advisors recommend that Mr. Kolmar should not be informed of the pregnancy. Chief van Zandt will arrange a scholarship at an American music academy. It will include transportation and living expenses for the entire period. It will be impressed upon Mr. Kolmar that he must take up this position without delay."

"What about the child?" Prince Hendrik asked.

"Obviously, Majesty," the Prime Minister refrained from responding to the Prince and continued to address the Queen, "A normal adoption process is unacceptable. The Princess would have to register as the birth parent. That is the law of the land. However, it would be in the interest of all concerned if the child were registered as being born unto the designated parents. The Princess should be discouraged from bonding at birth but rather surrender the child immediately to the parents who will register the newborn as the fruit of their marital union."

The Queen looked relieved. "Your advice is welcome and appreciated," she said. "The Prince and I must now comfort our daughter. She will be distressed; however she will do what is expected of her." Wilhelmina nodded at her husband, a clear signal for him to jump into the conversation. He fished his monocle from his vest pocket and unfolded a typed sheet of paper.

"I have made some discrete inquiries and I have a suggestion for potential parents." He fixed the monocle in his left eye and began to read, "Baron Alexander von Becke, a member of my extended German family in Mecklenburg is a promising young architect. He came to Nederland ten years ago to study architecture in Delft. He graduated and accepted a position at the Ingenieurs Bureau, a consulting firm in Leiden. He is a naturalized Dutch citizen, 31 years of age and has been married for four years to Paula von Becke, 29, born in Delft. The couple is childless. They are infrequent guests at this Court and in my view are excellent prospects."

The Queen, in icy composure, said, "Prince Hendrik will approach the couple to determine their willingness to act as surrogates. Chief van Zandt please check into the background of the von Beckes and assess their ability to rear the child in circumstances commensurate with the dignity of the Royal Family."

With that, the audience was over. Van Zandt bowed to the Royal couple, more optimistic now that the dreadful situation might have an acceptable solution after all, albeit not quite in keeping with – as he would put it – the law of the land.

With her eyes puffy and red-rimmed, Juliana sat curled against her father on the settee. He stroked her hair for comfort. Queen Wilhelmina sat stern-faced behind the table, the ancient Bible opened at Deuteronomy.

"Now then, my dear," Wilhelmina said in a strong voice, "Papa and I have had some time to assess the situation. We must be practical."

"This is not the time to reproach you, my daughter," Prince Hendrik added, "We must consider your needs but also the needs of the Monarchy. Your child will be welcomed into God's care but to be blunt, Juliana, it cannot be recognized as yours."

"What about Ferenc, what will he think?" Juliana asked tearfully.

"Mr. Kolmar must not know of this," the Queen asserted. "The Monarchy cannot withstand a stain on the House of Orange that might be used as a rallying cry for a republic."

"Maman," the Princess sobbed through her tears, "I am so sorry to have caused such problems. I hoped for a while that you might confer a title upon Ferenc so we could marry but it would not work for he is not a Protestant as the Constitution prescribes. He is Jewish."

Prince Hendrik hugged his daughter. "Juliana, my dear," he whispered softly, "Mr. Kolmar has been awarded a scholarship at the Juilliard School of Music in New York. He will be leaving tomorrow."

The Queen interrupted sharply. "The National News Service will announce that you will terminate your studies at Leiden in favour of studying the religion of Islam at the University of Batavia. Chief van Zandt gives assurances that the press will not make further inquiries."

"Will I be staying here in The Hague?"

"You will move tomorrow to the Palace at Soestdijk ," Wilhelmina stated matter of factly.

"You will not be alone Juliana," the Prince assured her. "Maman and I will visit frequently. Mieke de Jonge has agreed to be your Lady-in-Waiting. She will be with you throughout your stay."

"What will happen to my baby?" Juliana asked.

"The family Papa has arranged to care for the child are excellent people who will provide loving care; we will see to that," the Queen continued. "The couple has been married for a number of years and is childless. They have agreed to register the birth as their own and take care of the child."

"When will I meet them?" Juliana asked defiantly. "I want to approve the parents of my child."

"You will neither see the child nor will you meet the parents. You should only know that all will be well. The child will be born as a Dutch citizen and will live in the province of South Holland."

"I hate these arrangements," Juliana wailed.

"We must do our duty," Wilhelmina said.

Juliana turned and buried her face in her father's chest, crying inconsolably.

The Queen rose. "It has been decided," she said sternly. "We shall proceed."

Van Zandt paced up and down the marble hallway of Soestdijk Palace like an expectant father. He had been banned from the hospital wing by Juliana's caregivers. Van Zandt had objected at first, but lost out. He was on edge. If anything went wrong with the delivery, the Princess would be rushed to Leiden's Academic Hospital. In that case, the illegitimate birth would become public. It would bring vast consequences that he could not fully foresee.

He decided to lecture the new parents again. Alexander von Becke and his wife Paula were waiting anxiously in the library. "Let's go through this one more time, Alexander," van Zandt said. His voice sounded raspy.

"As soon as the child is born and ready for travel, you and Paula will take the child to your home. You will receive a signed birth certificate from Professor Pronk that the child was born at your home. Tomorrow, you will proceed to the Civil Registrar at City Hall in Leiden and formally register the birth. You are free to name the child except for any reference, however vague, to the Princess."

"Yes, we understand," Alexander, responded huffily. He was a sombre looking man with intense dark eyes. His brilliantined hair parted to the left appeared glued to his head. While his Dutch grammar was excellent, his German accent was noticeable. To pronounce the scraping sound of the letter "G" was beyond him; it would forever mark him as a non-native.

Baron Alexander Wilhelm Gustav Berndt von Becke was born in 1898 in Rabow, Mecklenburg, a Duchy on the shores of the Baltic Sea not far from Hamburg. His father was a minor landowner who had suffered serious lung injuries during a British gas attack in Flanders in the Great War. A huge photograph of his father, Major Gustav von Becke, wearing his gleaming, spiked Prussian helmet still dominated his study at home.

His uncle, Prince Hendrik von Mecklenburg, Queen Wilhelmina's husband, had sponsored him to study architecture at the Technical Institute in Delft where he received his degree in architecture in 1922.

Paula's father, Harry Meunier was a photographer who operated his own photo printing and developing shop in Delft. Studying nursing during the week, Paula worked in the store on Saturdays. One day Alexander had come into the shop. She noticed that instead of snapshots of girlfriends or family, he had photographs of buildings. He told her that he studied architecture. She liked him. They met often.

After several years of dating and waiting until Alexander graduated, they married on June 8, 1924. When he married Paula Meunier, he stopped using his title 'Baron'. His friends and colleagues knew him as Alexander. After five years, the marriage was childless.

The sound of footsteps made them sit up. Professor Pronk walked in, his face inscrutable. "Mr. and Mrs. von Becke," he said in an official voice, "The Princess and child are fine. She has delivered a healthy boy, weighing 3.2 kilograms and 56 centimetres in length."

Paula cried as Alexander helped her to her feet.

Van Zandt could not resist one more parting instruction. "Our contractual agreement states that your annuity is intended to provide for the proper care and education of the child, appropriate to his heritage. You may meet Princess Juliana in the years ahead. If you divulge the parentage of the child, you will be in violation of the contract and the annuity payments will cease." Both Alexander and Paula were too enraptured with the thought of a child to respond.

When the baby was brought in, Paula clutched the bundle of new life to her bosom. She pulled the small blue blanket away from the newborn's face. His abundant black hair topped off a grumpy, beautiful face.

"Hello," Paula whispered, "Welcome to the world, Wilhelm James von Becke. Say hello to your Papa." Alexander put his arms around Paula and kissed the boy.

"Wilhelm will be his formal name but we shall call him Willem. Right Willem?" he said as he gently gazed into the baby's eyes.

Van Zandt watched as the couple departed for their home in the suburb of Oegstgeest, near Leiden. He felt no relief; rather, a heavy load had been placed on his shoulders. This deception was fraught with danger of exposure. It was bound to come back and cause pain for all involved.

3

1937 (NINE YEARS LATER)
WEDNESDAY, AUGUST 4, 10:00 AM
RAILWAY STATION
VOGELENZANG, NEDERLAND

The temporary platforms of the small railway station at Vogelenzang were packed with hundreds of Boy Scouts. They were passengers on the first three of 40 trains that would disgorge 28,000 scouts from 45 countries in the next couple of days. The tiny station had never seen that much activity. Located only six kilometres from the city of Haarlem, it usually handled only a few local trains per day.

"My troop must be accommodated immediately," the man in a German Boy Scout uniform shouted at a young woman in a nurse's uniform. He had a thick Bavarian accent. "We have no time for incompetents. We have travelled 20 hours from Munich and my men are tired." The girl was not to be intimidated.

"The Boy Scouts from India travelled for three-and-a half weeks and they were strong and spirited," she retorted.

"I do not care about those brown people; they know no better."

Jenny Bos blanched at this racist comment. She was an 18-year-old nurse's assistant, eager to be part of the 1937 Boy Scout Jamboree.

Kurt Streicher, the Scoutmaster of 400 Munich-based scouts continued to demand special attention. "Our section is Zone Two," he shouted. "Show me the route and we will depart at once."

Standing at the back of the platform, Mark Zonder overlooked the melee. Tall, blue-eyed with a mop of blond, ever-tousled hair, the 19-year-old stood a head taller than the younger scouts did. He had just graduated a few weeks ago from high school and volunteered to begin his summer by working with the Jamboree's security team.

He noticed the unpleasant exchange and approached the belligerent German. "My name is Mark Zonder. I am the Senior Scout in charge of security for Zone Two," he said, nodding at Jenny to let him take over. He gave the German a hard stare.

"Miss Bos here will assist you with any medical problems your troop may have. If there are questions with respect to your camp assignments, there are scouts in your zone ready to assist you. To make our job of welcoming you more effective we ask you to respect the Jamboree's rules." The German looked at him with a sneer.

"I would obey your Dutch rules but the organization is not good. Just look at the confusion," Streicher said, gesturing at the mass of new arrivals as yet another train was unloading.

"But let me introduce myself. I am Gruppenfuehrer Kurt Streicher." Somewhat surprisingly for a Boy Scout, he bowed from the neck and clicked his heels in German military fashion. He spoke much louder than necessary. In his mid-thirties, Streicher was one of the oldest scoutmasters at the Jamboree. His fancy German title, derived from the military rankings of the SS, meant no more than Group Leader. Streicher had emphasized the fuehrer part, probably to identify himself with Adolf Hitler.

Six years earlier, Hitler, a corporal in the Great War had declared himself "Fuehrer of the German Reich." He was the Leader of the *Nazionalsozialistische Deutsche Arbeiterspartei*, the NSDAP, generally referred to as Nazi, the first four letters of that long name.

Streicher looked the typical Prussian leader, a lanky rigid frame, close-cropped hair, and a fair complexion. His face showed a permanent sneer as if his lower lip tasted something so bad that his upper lip was unwilling to touch it.

In training, Mark had been warned that some scouts would be difficult and that he should remain calm and polite. "As a leader, you know that in difficult situations conforming to the rules is paramount. Please line up your troop so I may lead you to your bivouac."

The German, unused to being ordered about, clicked to attention in front of his eight platoons of 25 scouts each. To Mark's eye, the boys' red armbands with the black Swastika stood out like bloodstains against their khaki uniforms. The warlike impression was somewhat softened by the grey felt mountain hats with the green feather on the side. They carried *Alpenstocken*, the spiked walking sticks used by mountain hikers.

Mark sounded more confident than he felt. His assigned territory, Zone Two, housed a campground for 2,000 scouts from Scandinavia, Nederland, Germany and Belgium. The scouts were largely self-sufficient. The host country provided a support group of 500 people consisting of parents and volunteers from the surrounding communities.

When his troop stood at attention, ready to march, Streicher pompously relayed his order to his deputy who – in turn – barked out the command to the boys. The scouts looked stern; the canes went up and down in lockstep with the march. Mark wondered how many months of training it had taken to instill such a military cadence.

The normally seven-minute march from the railway station to the tent city went much slower than Streicher would have liked. A large Scottish troop, led by drums and bagpipes, preceded them. The slow march by the kilted scouts lit the flame of rage in him again. "Tell those damned skirts to walk like men," he yelled. Mark ignored him.

The gravel path cut through the forested estate of Count Edward van Edelsteyn who had volunteered the venue for the international event. Even Streicher could not hide his awe when the path widened into the vista of a square kilometre of tents. Sixteen streets of tents radiated from the central ceremonial complex. The camp housed movie theatres, a full-fledged hospital, first-aid posts, mess halls, a telegraph and post office. The main security building even held a number of jail cells.

Each pad was equipped with an open fire pit. An exotic aroma wafted from the direction of the scouts from India and filled the German nostrils. Streicher's sneer seemed to grow.

Henk van Weeren, a scout from Groningen, a northern province of Nederland was in charge of settling the Germans in their assigned tents. Van Weeren was a gangling 18-year-old with a chip on his shoulder. His straggly hair, sallow features and slouching posture made him look out of place in this aggregation of sturdy young men.

He ingratiated himself with Streicher by helping to settle the Bavarian group and watched the German scouts salute the Nazi flag as it rose up the flagpole. They sang *Deutschland Über Alles* with gusto, to the rude taunts of the Dutch troops in the adjoining section. Van Weeren ran over to silence them but was heckled mercilessly for his efforts.

Walking back to the security building, Mark noticed nurse Jenny Bos sitting at a corner table chatting with her colleagues. He went over and apologized for the treatment the Germans had dished out. She laughed.

"I live in Groningen – close to the German border. We see Germans all the time shopping. They always act so arrogant. I'm used to it."

Jenny had short-cropped blonde hair that accentuated her open, clear-skinned face. She looked confident and walked with a natural grace. He noticed she had nicely tanned, strong legs. He liked her. She looked far more interesting than the few girls he had met before.

Talking to Jenny was easy. She was eager to absorb the atmosphere of the Jamboree with its many nations and cultures. The discussion inevitably led to the headlines of the day: whether or not Germany under Hitler would honour Nederland's centuries-old neutrality.

"I sometimes wonder if some morning we will wake up and the Germans will be marching in," Jenny said, "My father fears that German troops would take Groningen in 20 minutes. I am more optimistic. Look at all these scouts together here from all parts of the world, singing, laughing and playing. I find it hard to believe that they could try to kill each other."

Mark was more pessimistic, "Yes, but Hitler did march in the Rhineland two years ago and annexed Austria and the major part of Czechoslovakia and that will not be the end of it."

Mark wanted to know more about Jenny. "What do you do in Groningen?" he asked, afraid she'd tell him it was none of his business.

"I am a kindergarten teacher," she gushed, "I have already done one year as a trainee and in September I will get my own class."

Jenny asked him how he got his assignment at the Jamboree.

"My scoutmaster for the last ten years is the Chief Scout in charge of security for the entire Jamboree. Dirk Vreelink. You'll meet him one of these days. He's a good guy," Jenny got up to leave. Mark saw his chance.

"Would you like to come with me to the official opening on Wednesday evening?" Jenny hesitated so Mark added quickly. "It isn't a formal date. We just sit on the grass with thousands of others while the scouts march past."

"Okay, pick me up at the first-aid post," she said in a singsong voice as she skipped out the door. Mark was in heaven.

As the Boy Scouts passed the Royal reviewing stand, the discordant drums, bugles and bagpipes drowned out the peaceful sounds of the beautiful summer evening. Her Majesty Queen Wilhelmina took the salute and waved her peculiar Royal wave. The Dutch loved the strange greeting that had become her trademark over the decades. Her outstretched hand – palm up – looked as if she was about to receive change from a grocery clerk. She then appeared to motion some imaginary spectator with a movement best described as "come here, please!"

"My father told me it means *you owe me money*." Mark laughed.

Jenny had found a spot for them in the grassy clearing near the dais and spread the blanket she had brought.

To see Queen Wilhelmina receiving the salute of the parading scouts was a thrill; both he and Jenny were brought up to revere the Queen. Princess Juliana looked happy with Prince Bernhard, her new husband, by her side. They had met at the 1936 Winter Olympics in Bavaria and married one year later.

"Who is the man next to the Queen in the formal suit?" Jenny asked.

"He is Frans van Zandt the head of the scouting movement. My father knows him. He used to be Chief of Police in The Hague," Mark said.

"You mean he is not the chief any more?"

"At the time, the papers said there were questions about him blackmailing an Ambassador or something but – you know – people that high-up never get into real trouble. They just move on."

"So what is he doing now?"

"I heard that the Queen engaged him to be her personal advisor for National Defence. The bureaucracy is not very happy about it, but the man seems to have her complete confidence. It was also Wilhelmina who proposed him to head the Jamboree."

"So he can keep an eye on the foreigners?"

"Don't laugh. Dirk Vreelink, our supervisor here, says van Zandt spoke at a meeting of the camp supervisors and asked them to be alert for any suspicious behaviour."

"Hey that reminds me," she said laughing, "Henk van Weeren bragged that he is taking Kurt Streicher on the Sea Scouts tour of the Port of Rotterdam. Do you think that's suspicious?"

"His entire troop of 400?"

"No just him and his deputy, Beitz."

"Why would a mountain scout from Bavaria want to leave his troop to see a harbour?" Mark wondered.

"That's what I asked him," Jenny said. "Henk told me it was none of my business. He is a bit of a creep. My mother knows his family. He is always after me for a date but I don't want to listen to his raves about Hitler. His father is a member of the NSB, the Dutch Nazi Party."

"What else did he say about Rotterdam?" Mark asked.

"They want to be on the train to Rotterdam but they don't want the regular scouts' tour. They want to see the harbours from the shore. So they will separate from the tour at the train station and make their own way."

"That does not make sense, Jenny. There is no better way to see the harbour than from the tour boat."

They returned their attention to the ceremony. They had been talking during van Zandt's speech and had missed most of it. The huge campfire was lit. The scouts of South Africa in their Afrikaans/Dutch language opened the evening with a stirring rendition of *Sarie Marijs*, a song that every Dutch schoolchild knows. Even Juliana joined in the singing. The Queen's entourage left soon thereafter but the scouts' march-off with songs and flaming torches took a long time. It was a magical night.

Mark walked Jenny to the first aid post. It was an awkward moment. He had taken a girl out once or twice but after a long evening like this, he worried whether should he kiss her? They stopped at the first aid tent and looked at each other. Jenny took a step back and extended a straight arm, negating any worry about a kiss.

"It was a wonderful evening, thank you."

"For me too," he said, both relieved and disappointed that the dreaded kiss had vanished so quickly. "I am going to follow up on that Rotterdam business. I'll see you tomorrow." Any excuse to see her again, he thought.

He walked back to his tent with a spring in his step. Moonlight cast shadows on the path through the pines. He passed by the German camp and could see Streicher and his deputy Joachim Beitz talking with Henk van Weeren. The scouts in the adjoining campsite had retired for the night and Mark decided to take a seat and listen to the conversation. The three men were focused on the fire and would not be able to spot him.

Streicher poked the fire with a long stick and watched the little embers float in the air. He spoke a much gentler German than the harsh Gruppenfuehrer's stentor earlier in the day. He studied van Weeren intently. "So many of your countrymen resent Germans and yet you are so willing to assist us. Why is that?"

Henk was sipping from a bottle of *Cassis* he had bought at the canteen. He rested both elbows on his knees and looked into the fire. "The Hollanders treat us in the East as colonials. We must buy their expensive products but they will not buy our peat. They prefer coal from the south.

During the Great War, Germany bought our peat to stoke the factories in Hamburg and Bremen. Those were the good times for us."

Streicher nodded his understanding, pulled a cigarette from a case in his tunic pocket, and offered one to Beitz. He lit their cigarettes with the burning end of his stick.

"I gather your family is in the peat business?" Streicher asked.

"My father has a license to harvest a few hectares but business is bad. The Germans are still buying but we have no business in Nederland."

"And your father supports the national socialist movement?"

"Oh, absolutely. He is the head of the local NSB unit and he admires the Fuehrer for revitalizing Germany's economy. He wants the same strong leadership in Nederland. All economic policy in Nederland is formulated by the Jewish bankers and aimed to benefit the West at the expense of the peat colonies where we live."

Mark decided he had heard enough and slinked out of the camp area back to the path.

"Why do you think that Streicher is up to something?" asked Scoutmaster Vreelink with a mouthful of jam sandwich. He was eating his cafeteria breakfast. The head of security of the Jamboree was, as nearly everyone else at the Jamboree, a volunteer. In his professional life, he was a sergeant in the Fourth Regiment Infantry, under the command of Mark's father. Years ago, Major Pieter Zonder had asked Vreelink to take his son under his wing and had him join Vreelink's scout troop.

"It seems strange to me that he wants a tour away from the organized excursion when he could see everything from the boat," Mark said.

You look for conspiracies when there may be simple explanations," Vreelink said. "Could be curiosity," he added, taking another bite. "There are no harbours in Bavaria."

"Yes, but he is scoutmaster of a mountaineer group that is scheduled to go on a trip to the Veluwe, the heaths far way from Rotterdam."

"He must have delegated someone else to supervise the Veluwe tour?" Vreelink could play devil's advocate with the best of them. He took a slug of the coffee.

Mark was not to be deterred. "Perhaps I didn't make myself clear. Streicher and Beitz don't want to join the main harbour tour; they want Henk van Weeren to guide them on a special private tour."

"You are very clear," Vreelink said as he ripped a page out of his note pad and wiped up a blob of strawberry jam that had fallen onto his desk. He crumpled it and threw it at the metal wastebasket. "Rotterdam is a strategic harbour," he said, attacking another jam-laden sandwich. "In case of war, Germany would need access to the North Sea. England would want to deny that access for the same reason. There are defence installations and warships in the Navy portion of harbour. The Sea Scouts will not see any of that on their tour or even hear about it."

Vreelink took a bite and continued, "I think the bastards are after information about our naval installations," he sniffed before he acquiesced, "Okay you can join the harbour tour. Follow them and see where they go, but don't cause any international incidents."

Mark got up to leave and said, "Jenny Bos of the first aid contingent knows van Weeren. She's the one who told me about Henk's activities. I'd like her to come on the tour with me." Vreelink ran his lips around his mouth removing the last bit of jam.

"Don't cause an incident with her either," he laughed.

The train taking the hundreds of Sea Scouts to Rotterdam looked like an exhibit in the Museum of Transportation. The Dutch Railways must have hunted high and low to find the carriages whose glory days were likely in the 1880s. Folks who travelled third class in those days could not have been overly demanding. The black carriages had been enlivened by painting the words 'JAMBOREE 1937' in colourful letters on each side.

Each outside door gave access to a single compartment where two wooden benches stood across from each other. There was no hallway, so the passengers, four on each bench, had to look at each other for the entire trip. While the train was in motion, any passenger in need of a bathroom had only one option – and that window was not easy to open. With all eight seats occupied, the struggle of 'whose feet would go where' was an ongoing game.

Mark waited for Jenny in the corner of the tiny passenger terminal. He wore the standard Boy Scout dress of khaki shorts with numerous pockets, thick grey woollen socks right up to the knee and brown hiking boots. The standard green jersey carried many badges of achievement earned over the last five years. A red neckerchief was bunched under his chin with a leather knot holder. His Sam Brown hat, sometimes referred to as a 'Smokey Bear' hung on his back, secured by a chinstrap. His haversack hung over his right shoulder. The canvas bag was just big enough to carry a half dozen sandwiches and his water bottle.

Jenny appeared at the last minute, dressed in her white apron and Red Cross nurse's cap. In deference to femininity, her canvas haversack was blancoed. Inside were more sandwiches and a small thermos with coffee. She looked cool, competent and gloriously healthy. She found Mark in the arrival hall and squeezed his hand in excitement.

"There is Streicher, with his deputy and Henk," she whispered.

The Germans were dressed in khaki shirts and shorts but the swastika armband had disappeared in favour of the blue and white band of Bavaria. They looked quite smart in their green alpine hats. Henk hung around the Germans like an anxious puppy.

"Following the three of them will be difficult," Mark said, "Vreelink told me that the Navy Yard is across the river from the tour embarkation point. To get there they must take the public ferry."

They managed to settle in the second-class compartment reserved for medical personnel and support services. The benches were softer, there was a connecting hallway and even a toilet. At every railway crossing along the route people cheered as the scouts hung out of every possible window waving at anything that waved back. They passed through Leiden, The Hague and Delft before the train rumbled to a halt in Maassluis, the nearest location to the Rotterdam harbours. The stationmaster, a pompous little man, attempted to shoo the trainload of Sea Scouts in the direction of the tour boat. That he was largely unsuccessful was due to the many cross-legged scouts lined up for the men's toilets.

Mark watched as Henk led Streicher and Beitz away from the tour toward the public ferry terminal for Rozenburg. The small ferry was really a large flat-bottomed scow with a super structure that held the wheelhouse. The open-air car deck would hold perhaps eight automobiles. An indoor seating section provided room for 30 people at most.

Mark said, "We will never get on that ferry without them spotting us."

Jenny was more optimistic, "If we join the foot passengers, they'll see us. But, we can hide behind one of the cars."

The Germans and Henk elbowed their way to the front seating area while Mark and Jenny remained behind the last car in line. A brand new 1937 Citroën, pulled up behind them. Jenny smiled and made a circular motion that the driver, an elderly man, should roll down his window.

"Are you youngsters with the Jamboree?" he asked with a broad grin.

"Yes we are," Jenny said, "We are on our way to visit my uncle at the Navy Yards. My mother insisted I should see him if I got the chance." In his excitement, the man leaned too far out of the window knocking his hat onto the seat behind him.

"I was in the Boy Scouts when Princess Wilhelmina was crowned Queen and I participated in the parade," he said proudly. His wife leaned over his ample body and said, "It'll be another ten minutes before the ferry sails. Come join us in the backseat and tell us about the Jamboree."

Jenny, with a quick 'I-told-you-so' glance at Mark, opened the door, and they both slid quickly into the back seat. The Citroën glided smoothly onto the car deck, well out of sight of the seating area. The elderly couple explained that they preferred to stay in the car for the 20-minute crossing because the passengers' seats were unforgiving wooden benches.

The scouting festival fascinated their eager hosts and Jenny was happy to fill them in on details. As the ferry approached the landing pier, Jenny suddenly asked for a ride to the gate of the Naval Yard to meet her uncle. The couple happily obliged. As the ferry slipped into her berth, the Germans and van Weeren pushed their way forward to make sure they were first off the boat. By the time the Citroën came down the ramp, the trio was lined up at the taxi stand.

Ten minutes later, the Citroën pulled up at the unimposing gate of the naval installation. There was some initial doubt that this was the place, because the buildings lacked any signs of identification.

They stepped out of the vehicle and Jenny gave effusive thanks for the ride. The Citroën drove slowly away but stopped at the corner waiting to see if the young couple was all right. Jenny waved at them indicating they were just fine. Finally, the car drove off.

"Okay, what do we do now?" she asked.

"We are just improvising now," Mark was beginning to feel uncertain about this adventure.

Jenny was more resolute. She walked up to the sentry. "We are with the Jamboree tour for the international Sea Scouts. They are cruising the harbour today." Mark expected the sentry to give them the official brush-off but the white-belted seaman with his revolver peeking out from its holster immediately morphed into an eager visitor's guide.

"How come you are here rather than the tour boat?" the sentry asked. He was a good-looking lad, with a ready smile, maybe 20 or so.

Jenny embroidered the story. "When we got off the train we took the exit to Rotterdam instead of the tour boat dock. They left without us. The nice people who dropped us off believed the tour would end up here."

"Not likely," the sentry said, "Access to the Navy Yard is forbidden."

"Is there someplace we can just sit and have a look?" Mark asked.

"There is a children's playground and picnic area for the Navy personnel about five minutes from here," he said pointing west. "Visitors are not allowed, but the gate is not locked."

A mother with two girls played on the seesaw, but otherwise the place was deserted. On the levee, they found a perfect view of the waterway. Less than half a kilometre away, they could see five or six destroyers and two frigates moored along the quay; too far to see any real detail.

"Good thing you brought sandwiches," Jenny said. She opened Mark's bag and spread the goodies out on the bench. "We've got enough here for lunch and supper too," she said as she bit into a ham and cheese sandwich.

They sat and watched the harbour activity when, suddenly, they heard voices. Streicher and his mates approached. They were arguing about something. Van Weeren hopped sideways beside them. He seemed anxious to make a point. Beitz appeared uninvolved. He carried a brown leather case and looked toward the ships.

"Down to the river! Quickly!" Mark instructed. "We'll hide behind that clump of willows there."

"They'll spot us," Jenny protested.

"Perhaps, but if we stay here they will see us for certain."

Jenny half walked, half slid down the steep slope and crouched behind the bushes. Mark followed.

"You look a fine mess," Mark giggled, finding humour in the situation. "How are you going to explain those grass stains on your white skirt? Matron will have a fit." She slapped him lightly on the arm but smiled.

They saw Beitz move over to the park bench where he took an expensive-looking camera from the case. He attached a zoom lens and focused in the direction of the warships at anchor. Mark cursed, "Jenny you were right. Beitz is photographing the layout and the ships."

"We should go now," she urged. "We know what they are up to and that should be enough." The thrill of adventure was lost; she wished the affair was over. Just then, Henk jumped in front of them.

"What the hell are you doing here?" Henk shouted, struggling to keep his normal voice. He threw his hat and haversack on the ground and lunged at Mark who tried to duck, but the punch knocked him off balance. Mark fell backward and slipped down the embankment. Henk dove after him to keep him pinned down but the dike's clay was greasy and he too slipped. They both got up slowly; Mark regained his footing first. The split second advantage let him tackle his nemesis. Henk fell back into the river's muck. His shoes made belching sounds as he tried to extricate himself from the mud.

When he got back on his feet, Henk smiled disarmingly, bent forward apologetically, only to rise and viciously smash Mark on the temple. Mark bent over in agony. A cut above his eyebrow bled and ran into his eye.

By now, Streicher had made his way down the dike careful not to lose his alpine hat. "Why are you following us?" he bellowed at Mark.

Jenny decided to go for help. Streicher's feet slipped as he watched her run away. He secured his hat first before stabilizing himself. On top of the dike, Beitz kept shooting pictures, indifferent to the fisticuffs below.

At the water level, Streicher now stood over the two grappling scouts. *"Ach, Herr Zonder,"* he said in an unpleasant voice. "Are you spying on us?"

Mark undid his neckerchief to stem the bleeding above his eye. Had he been more experienced he might have concocted a reasonable lie, instead he resorted to the truth. "The Chief of Security asked me to follow you."

"How did you know we were going to Rotterdam?" His sneer was nastier; if that was possible.

"Henk told me," Mark improvised.

"No, I didn't, I only told Jenny," Henk answered.

For a moment, Streicher must have imagined that he was in Nazi Germany. He slapped Henk across the cheek with an open hand. "You fool," Streicher bellowed, "And you want to serve the German Reich?"

Henk stammered, "She is only a girl." This might have been enough for Streicher to increase the level of invective but Henk pointed to the top of the dike. Two Navy MPs looked down on the three men. More precisely, one MP looked down while the other had his Smith & Wesson buried in Beitz's ribs. The other Navy cop rotated his gun in small circles, indicating that the men should come up. Mark and Streicher obeyed immediately, while Henk looked around for an avenue of escape. Not finding any, he picked up his haversack and hat slowly made his way up the dike.

"You will come with us to the guard house," the taller of the MPs said. He did not look as authoritarian as he tried to sound. However, his Smith & Wesson was the decisive factor in Streicher's decision to go along quietly. Beitz, looking guilty, carried his camera in one hand and the leather case in the other.

The Germans walked ahead of the tall MP who kept his gun trained on them. Henk and Mark were guarded from behind by the younger MP. When Henk stopped to tie his shoelace, the young Navy corporal made the mistake of allowing his charge to get behind him. Henk reached into his haversack and pulled out a Luger handgun.

"Drop your weapon," he yelled as he stuck his gun in the back of the hapless corporal. The Smith & Wesson fell to the ground. Henk kicked it away but not far enough. "Do anything funny and your buddy will get it," he screamed at the lead MP, who lowered his gun. "Run for it!" Henk shouted at Streicher and Beitz. "You've got the pictures, now run for it!"

Streicher regained his composure. "*Sie idiot. Sie verrückt täuscht. Sie werden uns alle getötete erhalten,*" he shrieked, "You'll get us all killed, you idiot."

Mark used the brief distraction to dive for the MP's gun lying on the ground. Henk spun around to see what happened. As he did, the MP tackled him. Luger in hand, Henk fell down and fired a shot that went astray. Both Mark and the tall MP jumped on him and shoved their Smith & Wessons in Henk's face. His rage turned into a wailing sob.

"Give me the gun, Henk," Mark yelled. Van Weeren shook his head 'no' but dropped the Luger beside him on the ground. Mark picked it up and handed it to the lead MP.

The three would-be spies walked side by side toward the guardhouse followed by the gun-toting MPs; Mark straggled behind.

The same sentry was still pacing his beat in front of the guardhouse. Inside, it looked like a small police station. Two wooden benches stood against the wall. The focal point was a large counter, behind which stood an enormous black walrus moustache, attached to an amorphous face and body, tightly wrapped in a Royal Navy tunic. Master Corporal J. Otto, whose body suggested terminal lethargy, confiscated Beitz's camera and Henk's Luger with alacrity and locked them in the old-fashioned vault behind him.

"Better lock him up too," the senior Navy policeman suggested, nodding toward Henk.

"You there," the walrus pointed at Henk, "Come with me." He produced a large key ring with huge keys from below his desk, marched Henk into one of the two cells, and clanked the door shut behind him. Henk wailed and threw himself on the cot as a frustrated kid sent to his room for refusing to eat his broccoli.

"You," this time he pointed at Mark, "Go to the head and clean yourself up." Mark assumed the 'head' was navy talk for washroom. A look in the mirror showed that there wasn't much bleeding. In fact, it had almost stopped but his right eye was closing. He cleaned his face and hands. He dabbed at the blood spatters on his uniform but to no avail. He joined Jenny back on the bench.

"Has anybody been called in?" he asked.

"After he took their passports, he locked both of the Germans in the cell next to Henk's." Jenny said.

Busily fussing with a mass of paperwork, the walrus motioned for Mark and Jenny to remain seated on the bench. The clock ticked the minutes away. No one spoke. The office door suddenly opened. A navy lieutenant walked over to desk to collect the paperwork left by the Corporal.

"Mark Hendrik Zonder and Jennifer Martina Bos." Mark's stomach tightened at the calling of their names. His thoughts raced from his father's strong disapproval to dishonourable dismissal from the Jamboree. The lieutenant led them into his office. He glanced at Mark's swollen eye.

The lieutenant was a handsome man in his mid-forties. His neatly cut silver hair suited his square face and his imposing height added to the impression of strength. The plaque on his desk identified him as Lieutenant J. Raamsdonk. He came straight to the point.

"Miss Bos came to the guard post and told us how the two of you entered the recreation area. Your actions contravened the laws restricting access to defence installations. If convicted, the penalty ranges from two to ten years in prison." Jenny squirmed at this legal recitation.

"We were here on a visit sanctioned by Jamboree officials," Mark said.

"So why not start at the beginning," Lieutenant Raamsdonk said. He pulled out a gold fountain pen and began to write in a green, government-issue record book that looked like a spiral-covered school scribbler. Mark knew honesty was the best policy although he had often thought about what the second-best policy might be. He explained their respective positions at the Jamboree. He managed to slip in 'Major Zonder', his father's army rank a few times. He told how Jenny's suspicions had led him to tell his story to Scoutmaster Dirk Vreelink who just happened to be a sergeant in Major Zonder's command.

"How did you gain access to the recreation area?" Mark thought of the genial sentry who had given them the chance to see the waterway.

"We found the gate. It was open so we went in." Lieutenant Raamsdonk glanced at Jenny who sat with her head bowed. Mark knew she had ratted on the sentry but the lieutenant did not follow up.

"It was you, Zonder, who retrieved the Smith &Wesson? You were foolish to put yourself in danger but you likely saved the situation," Raamsdonk said. "Tell me why you think van Weeren did what he did?"

Lieutenant Raamsdonk busily transcribed the story of Henk and his NSB sympathies. He used his gold fountain pen to slam a soul-satisfying punctuation mark behind the last sentence.

"There," he said and realized that a blob of ink had stained the page. He picked up a blotter to soak up the offending blob and smiled apologetically. He closed his scribbler with a flourish. "I must ask you both to remain in the waiting area; we may have some further questions."

The reception area was empty except for a civilian who waited to collect Beitz's film for developing. Streicher was pacing in his cell. There was no sound except for the huge clock that clicked the minutes away. Jenny ate her last sandwich and finished the coffee in the thermos.

After what seemed like an hour, the silver-haired Lieutenant summoned them into his office once more.

"Zonder, I have spoken to Sergeant Vreelink, your Scoutmaster," he began. "He is not very happy that you broke the law but he confirms that he asked you to follow the German Scouts. The Navy will not lay charges against either of you for illegal trespassing. Master Corporal Otto will arrange to get you back to the Jamboree site. That's all."

Mark was relieved but asked, "What about the Germans?"

"The German Embassy will collect Streicher and Beitz. They will be dealt with by their own authorities."

"And Henk?" Jenny asked.

"Van Weeren will be turned over to the civilian police. The Boy Scout Movement will be made aware of Mr. van Weeren's opinion of the Dutch political system. Our intelligence people are aware of his aggressive tendencies and will monitor his future actions."

"What about the photographs?" Mark asked.

"The photographs will remain the property of the Navy. That's all," Raamsdonk said, shooing them out of his office.

Mark felt let down. Henk was in custody for anything from treason to attempted murder but the Germans who had photographed Navy installations would only receive a slap on the wrist?

On the train ride back to Vogelenzang, neither of them spoke much. It was dark when they entered the gates of Jamboree City.

He walked Jenny to her dormitory tent. Then she caught Mark off guard by reaching up, pulling his head down towards her and kissing him. Not one of those puffy, wimpy dry pecks either, but a wet lingering one. She pressed her body against his. He froze.

"I should apologize for all the trouble..." he mumbled.

"Hush," she said and kissed him again. Only this time he pulled her towards him and all the curves and hollows fit together.

"Don't worry about tomorrow," she whispered. Mark was on cloud nine. He was 18. He was in love. Life was wonderful.

4

1937
THURSDAY, AUGUST 6, 6:00 AM
JAMBOREE CITY
VOGELENZANG, NEDERLAND

The damned bugle call made him jump upright in his cot. The wake-up troop took its daily revenge on those who were permitted to sleep a bit longer. The cheap mirror fastened to the tent pole showed that his right eye was turning an angry purple. His head had grown twice its size; it felt like that, anyway. A message pinned to the tent flap informed him he was to report to Scoutmaster Vreelink at 7:30 a.m. Outside, at the communal pump, a helpful scout pumped water over his head. The ice-cold water on the bruise made him wince.

He timed his arrival for the precise minute. Vreelink, who always managed to look as if he slept in his uniform, was waiting for him in his office tent. Sunlight could barely penetrate the mica windows. The tent smelled like a wet raincoat.

Vreelink's desk was a small folding table covered by a green tablecloth with a cigarette burn in the corner. "I asked you to follow them, not to create an international incident and what's with your eye?" Vreelink didn't believe in small talk.

Dirk was a tall man, 27 years of age who had the quaint habit of walking very fast and swinging his arms from side to side, leaving the impression that he might be late for an appointment. His bulging lips were the focal point of his face, which resembled an unmade bed. Any situation that struck him funny would unleash a bellowing roar that caused the creases to unfold and reveal a boyish smile. A curly mop of reddish hair refused to be restrained by any headgear except perhaps a steel helmet.

He was a born Amsterdammer, a breed unto itself, with a humorous accent that sounded so different from the harsh Leiden inflection. Another peculiarity was that during a conversation he would turn his head to the left while inhaling through his nose.

"Did you talk to anyone about yesterday?" Vreelink asked.

"I haven't spoken to anyone since we left the Navy Yard but I sure would like to know what happened to Streicher and Beitz."

"It is complicated," Vreelink looked away. He twirled the glass ashtray on the metal table. It had three grooves to rest cigars. Vreelink had the habit of putting one groove pointing to 12 o'clock and the other two at four and eight.

"It is neither in my hands nor in the Navy's. The case has been taken over by Centrale Inlichtingen Dienst," said Vreelink. The CID was Nederland's central intelligence group. "You and I will report to Director General van Zandt, at 9:00." He twirled the ashtray and re-aligned it again.

"Is that the man who spoke at the opening, the president of the Boy Scout movement?"

"That is his community service as requested by the Queen. His full-time job is boss of the CID."

In 1936, at the Queen's request, van Zandt had left his post as The Hague's Chief of Police and resurrected the CID. The Queen, perhaps more than any of her ministers, was alarmed by the growing German threat. She trusted van Zandt because he shared her conviction that the country's vaunted neutrality would mean nothing to Hitler.

Mark and Vreelink were quickly ushered into the posh waiting area of the Jamboree administration building. No smelly tent here, just deep carpeting and red leather club chairs clustered around teak coffee tables. Scouting magazines and the latest edition of *De Telegraaf* were spread out on the reading shelves. Mark was nervous. He didn't know what to expect.

A young busty woman slightly older than Mark, with her hair done 'up' in a bun came out of the office. "Mr. Zonder please," she said, indicating with an apologetic look that Vreelink shouldn't expect to be asked in.

Van Zandt sat behind an impressive desk in a room decorated in the style of the colonial Dutch East Indies. An elaborately carved smoking set with ashtray, cigarette holder and pipe rack stood to one side. The walls were hung with a display of exquisite Wayan puppets. High-backed rattan chairs with batik cushions completed the image. Van Zandt noticed Mark's glance around the room.

"Not my room, my young friend," he boomed. "It's just some decorator trying to impress the visiting Pooh-bahs." The self-deprecating tone made Mark feel immediately at ease. In a tent city of thousands of boy scouts, van Zandt stood out in his immaculate grey-striped morning trousers, starched collar, vest and expensive, well-tailored jacket. The bushy black moustache looked like a junior version of Corporal Otto's.

"Sit down, young man," van Zandt said pointing to an enormous high-backed, rattan seating cocoon. It felt like an open sarcophagus.

"Sergeant Vreelink informs me that upon his request you and a young nurse followed the German scout leaders Streicher and Beitz to the Navy Pier in Rotterdam. One of our scouts, a fellow named van Weeren appeared to assist them in taking photographs of navy activity.

"Yes Sir." This was going well, Mark sensed. No recriminations, no accusations; it sounded like a compliment.

"I must congratulate you on being alert to a threat to our national defence. Most of our fellow citizens are asleep and think they can rely on our neutrality to keep us safe."

"I am glad we caught them red-handed," Mark said with some pride.

"Well that's what we must talk about. You and Jenny did a fine scouting job and fortunately it turned out to be nothing."

"Nothing, Sir? The German scouts were in a restricted area. They were photographing military objects. You have the film to prove it."

"Yes, we have the photos but they show images of a busy harbour, freighters, tug boats and the like."

"Sir, I saw them shoot photos of destroyers and frigates."

"Did you see any of those ships, Mr. Zonder?"

"I did not see the ships up close but I could read H93 on the side of one destroyer. With his expensive camera Beitz could have zoomed right in."

"What kind of camera?"

"A Zeiss camera with a long, zoom lens. I saw it at the guard house."

"Very observant. I will now tell you why nothing happened at the Navy Yard." Van Zandt moved from behind his desk and sat in the rattan cocoon facing him. "You must understand that not all intelligence can be revealed publicly. You and Jenny were witness to something that our government cannot acknowledge."

A young woman in a blue apron interrupted to place a tray with a coffee service complete with cookies on his desk.

Mumbling his thanks van Zandt continued, "Some of the younger ministers in Her Majesty's government believe that Hitler's aim is to conquer all of Europe including our country. Common belief is that Hitler can just attack a country at will but he must convince the German public that the countries he attacks are a threat to the Fatherland."

"He personally doesn't care what the world thinks of him but he must have the German people's support in a war." He pushed a bell on his desk. When the coffee lady looked in, he ordered her to pour two cups.

"The Abwehr, our counterpart in Germany is looking for evidence that Nederland is not neutral. They look for proof that we are preparing to facilitate an attack on them by either Britain or France. They would use this evidence to sway the German people that we are the threat next door."

"They wouldn't find anything!" Mark said indignantly.

"That is a matter of interpretation. The German public doesn't need much persuasion. Some startling photographs would do the job but they don't want to be caught spying during the Jamboree. That is their dilemma." He got up, put extra spoonfuls of sugar in his prepared cup, and motioned for Mark to drink his coffee.

"Our problem in Nederland…" he said balancing the cup on his stomach, "is that our older politicians demand absolute neutrality while the new breed sees the danger posed by Hitler and would like to be 'neutral'…but on the side of Britain." He took a sip and smacked his lips a couple of times.

"Last week Minister Bracken of Defence authorized two British Royal Navy destroyers to enter the Rotterdam Navy Yard. Under cover of darkness, they slipped into the Navy Yard three days ago. That H93 you saw painted on the hull is the HMS Hereward, one of Britain's newest war ships. The other destroyer – lying alongside – was HMS Havock, marked H43. Both ships have been assigned to guard Nederland from the sea."

Van Zandt paused to gauge Mark's reaction. He placed his coffee cup back on the table.

"And Kurt Streicher is not a Boy Scout either. He and Beitz are members of the Abwehr. Their boss in Berlin is my counterpart, Admiral Wilhelm Canaris. They were sent here to document that British warships are training with the Dutch Navy."

"You told me that their photographs were typical tourist pictures."

"Exactly," van Zandt winked. "You followed some German scouts. They took tourist pictures. End of story. Nothing happened."

Van Zandt paused to ensure that the message had been received, then continued, "Van Weeren is in custody in the Marechaussee barracks in

Haarlem and will be charged with possession of an illegal weapon and discharging it in a public place. He'll likely be put away for a year or so."

"How can Henk can be trusted to keep the story quiet?" Mark asked.

"Off the record, he will be charged with espionage, an offence that carries a jail sentence of 30 years. The charge will be stayed for now, which means that it can be resurrected any time. The incentive for him to keep quiet about espionage is obvious. If he opens his mouth, he goes to jail."

"But then there are still the photographs, Sir. They are evidence."

"The photographs will stay under lock and key and will not embarrass the Minister of Defence. The Abwehr will not be accused of using the Jamboree for espionage. And Cabinet is happy that our neutral status is maintained."

"That's it?" The whitewash of the entire episode stunned Mark.

"Well not quite," van Zandt said. "There is that black eye of yours but you will explain that away somehow, I'm sure." Van Zandt got up and walked to the door, indicating the interview was over.

Vreelink was waiting for him in his club chair looking rumpled. They walked back in silence.

Jenny was waiting for him at the first aid tent. "I have packed sandwiches," she said and added a couple of apples and oranges to the simple lunch and pronounced it fit for a picnic in the dunes. Mark filled their hipflasks with *Ranja*, the popular orange-flavoured drink. The beach was only a 15-minute walk through the dunes.

Along the gravel path, they saw a sign that threatened anyone stepping outside the path with some unspecified but severe penalty. They ignored it, stepped over the barbed wire and climbed to the top of the highest dune. The waves of the North Sea broke onto an immense sandy beach that stretched as far as the eye could see. The gusts of wind blew sand at their faces and they soon settled in a hollow, away from the wind. The August sun was warm and soothing.

Jenny spoke first. "How did your meeting with van Zandt go?"

"He explained at length that nothing happened in Rotterdam."

"You must be joking?"

"No I am not. If questioned we are to say that we followed the German scouts on a sightseeing tour of Rotterdam. They took some innocent pictures of harbour traffic. They were sent home to Germany because they neglected to properly supervise their troop." He related the gist of what van Zandt had told him and the reason for suppressing the story.

"I never thought we'd be part of a political intrigue," she said, and they both fell quiet as they pondered the implications. Jenny suddenly said, "Let's forget it. It is summer and we are having a picnic." She spread the blanket over the hot sand and put out the sandwiches They ate their lunch, each being very much aware of the other's physical presence. Jenny finally initiated the contact, sensing that Mark would not. She took his hand, brought it to her lips, and gently kissed it.

"Just three more days and then it will all be over. We'll each go our different ways but I will always remember this week," she said.

"It's not over yet. There is still a lot of fun ahead." He laid on his back, gazing at the white clouds racing by. Jenny turned to look at him.

"I have thought about doing this all morning." She bent down and kissed him gently. He pulled her on top of him in a smothering bear hug. They rolled over and changed positions. He was on top and looked at her.

"Jenny Bos, you are wonderful," he said planting a small kiss on her lips. He hoped his horniness would not manifest itself too obviously. Mark rolled off onto his back again and looked at the sky. Jenny lay beside him uncertain if her intimacy had offended him until she noticed the bulge. She brushed by it gently, almost accidentally. He reacted with a sudden start. She laughed.

"Gee, you are sensitive, I hardly touched you," she said brightly, as if she had accidently bumped into him. She stroked him there again and then rolled on top of him.

"I can feel you now," she said.

"That's not fair," he said and rolled her on her back and began to massage her breasts through her white apron.

"Do those all those buttons have to be undone to get where I want to be?" he asked. He was not good at undoing buttons and Jenny had to help him but finally he reached the whiteness of her skin and the glorious nipples standing at attention. They kissed and fondled. Jenny had started it and knew when to end it.

"There will be another time," she said straightening her uniform. They walked back, arms over each other's shoulders.

Back at the camp, a message informed Mark to see van Zandt. For the second time that day, he walked into the luxurious lounge. The Chief wasn't there. His wife was hosting a reception for the spouses of the senior scouting entourage. Kirsten van Zandt was a very attractive woman, much younger than her husband, perhaps 35 or so, Mark guessed. Her light blond hair was cut in a bob style that framed her Nordic features like a helmet. Her light blue eyes lit up when she spoke. She must have spent hours in the sun as evidenced by her tanned face and bare athletic legs. Mark caught himself wondering if she was tanned all over.

A scout from the communication troop approached and said the Chief would see him now. This time he was led into a far more utilitarian office furnished with a desk and chair. On this nice summer evening, the spymaster was dressed in Boy Scout regalia, khaki shorts, shirt and neckerchief. This van Zandt looked far more approachable. If clothes made the man, this was a perfect example.

He sat down and tugged at the imaginary crease in his shorts as if he sat down in his dinner costume.

"Young man, your initiative has not gone unnoticed. I have spoken to your father and he is proud of your role in the Rotterdam affair. In two years, you will be called up for compulsory military service." He made a movement with his right hand across his heart that could be mistaken for a sudden pain but actually was a reach for the non-existent cigar case in his absent jacket pocket.

"Looking for a smoke," he said apologetically. "Now, as you know, raw infantry recruits are destined to slog through mud and march hundreds of kilometres a week, never mind the latrine and kitchen duties. If you want to avoid that, I suggest that you make yourself promotable."

"Promotable, Sir?" Mark was suddenly leery of the conversation.

"To join the CID. Of course, not everyone who applies will be accepted but your father will guide you if you are interested. You'd make an excellent candidate. You have initiative, are athletic and you assume leadership when it's called for. If you spend time immersing yourself in languages, you could be too valuable to leave among the ranks."

"What does CID actually do?"

"We keep the bad guys from stealing our secrets while we steal theirs. That is not the official description of course, but it's clearer than the brochures. For one thing CID is becoming concerned about the treasonous behaviour of the NSB; your incident with van Weeren is a case in point."

Van Zandt appeared anxious to be off to another function. This time his thumb and forefinger pinched his scout's jersey in the area where his pocket watch would normally be, but it wasn't there. Without uttering a word he walked to the door and held it open, his way of indicating the interview was over. When Mark was almost through the door he said, "I would like you and that Jenny to join me at the closing ceremonies."

D rums and bugles clashed as thousands of scouts marshalled for the closing ceremonies. Mark and Jenny entered the deep-carpeted VIP lounge conscious of the fact that they were minor players in the event among the hundred or so elderly bigwigs of the international scouting scene. Dressed in their scout get-ups, a sea of white, bony knees protruded from khaki shorts. The color-clashing display of merit badges, most of them unearned, hung from sagging jerseys like overripe fruit. The scene was made more ridiculous by the fact that their wives accompanied them in splendid evening attire.

A quintet of piano, harp and strings played light classical music made popular in the late 1800s. To judge by the lightly swaying bodies, the occasional waltz by Strauss visibly lightened the overly formal spirit of the room. But it was still early. Female catering staff dressed in light blue aprons pressed glasses of champagne in every willing hand. Jenny barely repressed a gesture of disgust after her first sip of the bubbly. "Oh, I always thought it would taste nice," she coughed into her serviette.

As official host of the fifth Jamboree, van Zandt was busy glad-handing all around. He had wisely chosen to wear his diplomatic togs in preference to khaki shorts. He spotted Jenny and Mark and immediately walked over to greet them. He introduced them to his wife who was delighted to have someone to latch onto while her husband did all the politicking.

"You must have done something special to cause my husband to invite you," she warbled in her Swedish accent. Both Jenny and Mark demurred and said they were just happy to be present. "I hear you may join my husband's unit," she told Mark saucily. "Won't that be fun?" Van Zandt pulled her away for the opening of the parade before she could say more.

A tinkling of glasses interrupted their discussion. A spokesman for the organizing committee told the guests to consult a layout of the grandstand to locate their seats in the VIP section. Mark and Jenny's were four rows behind Mr. and Mrs. van Zandt. Although darkness was falling, the temperature was still a balmy 22°C. The entire party had barely settled when the electric lights dimmed and thousands of flaming torches held by the massing scouts provided light with eerily shimmering shadows. The Marine Corps band next to the grandstand struck up the Jamboree March.

One by one, the scout troops of the marching nations dipped their national flag in salute as they passed by the reviewing stand.

They entered in reverse order of their position in the opening ceremony. The delegation of Venezuela was followed by the 2,000 scouts of the United States interspersed by their five drum corps. Van Zandt took the salute on the raised platform. He waved without pausing, his face a mixture of bliss and excitement.

Many national troops marched to the rhythm of their own drum corps. The scouts of the Dutch East Indies dressed in sarongs and sandals, and pounding their gamelan drums, received the greatest applause. Jenny bounced up and down as she clapped along with the beat.

The noise was deafening as each delegation's drum corps tried to outdo the other. The huge French *peloton* hobbled by; their front column marching briskly to their own drums while the rear kept pace with the slow bass-beats of the Finnish troop behind them.

They sang the anthem as the Dutch flag was lowered. The Jamboree flag was presented to the United Kingdom, host of the next Jamboree in Scotland in 1941. Only the flag bearer of each nation remained before the grand stand. Van Zandt made a brief farewell speech and declared the fifth Jamboree closed.

The event had taken nearly three hours. It was late. He had looked forward to some stolen moments with Jenny but they walked arm in arm to her dorm tent and said good night. Mark suggested they meet tomorrow after most of the scouts had departed. They, as most of the support staff, would remain in camp for an extra day to clean up. The Germans, he noted, were packed for an early departure. He slept soundly.

The Vogelenzang station had turned to bedlam again. For the railways, the logistics were akin to planning a major battle. Trains were marshalled in the yards of Amsterdam and sent to Vogelenzang in 20-minute intervals. More than 7,000 scouts would be on their way by noon. The discipline, drills and exercises during the Jamboree paid off as the schedule ran like clockwork.

Mark went to meet Jenny at the now-calm first aid post. They talked enthusiastically about the closing ceremonies and the day's events.

Later, in the gathering dusk, they sat on Jenny's blanket among the tall pines. He talked about his childhood: his home, his sisters and his father's military barracks as a special playground.

"What do you want to do in life?" she asked.

"As a kid I always wanted to be a sailing instructor with my friend Brenner Zijlberg but that's hardly a profession. My father assumes that I will follow in his footsteps and become an Army officer. Van Zandt said I should attend classes in the military college and then volunteer for the CID. I think our experience in Rotterdam impressed him somehow."

"What about the future?" she asked.

"I don't know. All I see right now is the military. My father is convinced that Germany will invade us sooner or later and if so, life will change. What do you want in your future?" he asked her.

"I am going to do what neither my mother nor grandmother ever did. I will earn my pay at a job and I will see what happens after that."

They laid down on the blanket but their kisses were tentative as if showing passion would mean commitment. It had been less than a week but Mark was certain. He wanted to see her again. They talked of meeting again but the reality of a five-hour train ride between their homes came in between. Mark had no job; she would earn little. Each promised to write.

The next morning they held hands as they waited for their respective trains to take them home. Jenny north, to Amsterdam and beyond. Mark south, to Leiden.

Suddenly they were back in that embrace where everything was warm, the hollows and curves fit perfectly again and the long, passionate kiss promised much.

He waved as the train to Amsterdam pulled out of the little station of Vogelenzang. It must have been the smoke from the locomotive that made his eyes water, he thought.

5

1938
THURSDAY, FEBRUARY 3, 4:00 PM
GLADSTONE APARTMENTS
NEW YORK CITY, USA

On warm summer days, New York's Central Park is a happy place filled with smiling people but on this miserable February afternoon, it looked deserted. From the eighth floor of his Fifth Avenue apartment, the scene matched Ferenc Kolmar's mood.

In the decade since he had immigrated to New York his career as a piano virtuoso had rocketed.

He was a celebrity now, part of wealthy America. His sold-out concerts no longer thrilled him. Life on the road and endless cocktail parties had taken their toll. He longed to be in one place long enough to feel at home.

The expensive apartment had been Margot's idea. She wanted a prestige address to roost between the exciting whirls of concert tours. They'd been together for only a year. Margot was actually no more than a classical music groupie – forever waiting at the proverbial stage door to bask in the performer's glory. She loved the rush of travel, seeing new things, meeting new people. He hadn't really loved her. She was good company on the road, fun in bed. Now she was gone.

In his downcast mood, he didn't feel like preparing for this Saturday's concert, a benefit for B'nai B'rith. He had never been too deeply involved in his religion but being a Jewish celebrity and living in New York brought a special burden of responsibility.

He was concerned with the plight of the Jewish people so ruthlessly persecuted by the Nazis, hence his agreement to perform at this gala.

The rainy afternoon reminded him of The Hague where this kind of weather was common at any time of the year. Had it really been ten years? The gift of a scholarship had come as a complete surprise to him. He had no idea that Queen Wilhelmina had been so impressed with his talents.

He had written many letters addressed to Juliana at the Palace but they remained unanswered. He had never entertained any thought that he could have ever been anything more than a summer romance for the vivacious princess. Over the years, he had sent clippings of the reviews of his performances just so she could keep up with his growth as an artist. He had made it a point to follow her development. Her sudden departure to study Islam in the Dutch East Indies had surprised him; she had never mentioned any interest in the subject. He had read about her engagement to Prince Bernhard – a royal stud, he thought – at the Olympic Winter Games in 1936. The Times had carried a full supplement of her marriage in 1938. He had been surprised by a twitch of jealousy and a sense of loss.

He looked down on the scene below. It was beginning to darken. The glow of red taillights provided an odd illumination as the parade of cars sloshed through the avenue below. He settled down on a sofa.

The Arts section of *New York Times* noted his appointment as a guest tutor at Juilliard. The writer had done a good job of piecing together the details of his career.

> *Ferenc Buda Kolmar was born in Budapest, Hungary. He received piano instruction from an early age, initially from his mother, who was herself a competent pianist. In 1927 at age 20, he entered the Royal Conservatory of Music in The Hague. His first solo recital was in May of 1927 at the Court of Queen Wilhelmina of the Netherlands. In 1929 his outstanding performance of the Rachmaninoff Piano Concerto No. 3 in D minor led the Queen to arrange for a generous four-year bursary to allow the artist to further his studies at the Juilliard School in New York City. During the 1934-1935 season, he performed 23 concerts of 11 different programs in New York City alone. Kensington Downes, writing for the New York Times, credited Kolmar with both a tremendous technique and a beautiful tone. He has performed on a regular basis with the London Symphony Orchestra, the Toronto Symphony and the Los Angeles Philharmonic.*

He found it all boringly correct. He poured himself a glass of wine and read the story again. Not a word was said about his real life. Nothing about a spouse, children or even a lover. He was a commodity, not a person. He dumped the Arts Section and picked up the front page.

His eyes were drawn to the headline 'Dutch Royals Welcome Heir to the Throne'. The article announced the birth of a daughter to Princess Juliana and Prince Bernhard. Princess Beatrix is second in line to the throne and she continues the long line of female heirs to the Dutch throne. The last male heir of the House of Orange was William III in 1827.

He decided he should try to contact Juliana again and convey his congratulations. He headed for his study. The gold-embossed stationary would impress her he hoped, although at the same time he doubted if it would ever reach her.

6

1938
WEDNESDAY, MARCH 24, 2:15 PM
RAILWAY STATION
LEIDEN, NEDERLAND

He had re-read her letters a dozen times. In the seven months since the Jamboree, they had written every week; with each letter, the longings of love and lust had become quite graphic.

The train was on time. Passengers were piling out. Suddenly he saw her. She wore a tailored coat with a red alpine beret that clung to her close-cropped blond hair. Her well-shaped legs attested to regular exercise.

They kissed warmly. She tasted good and smelled so wonderful. He remembered all the curves and hollows. Some passersby stopped and smiled as they watched the iconic picture of a boy and girl in an embrace with a train in the background.

Both had been summoned to testify at the trial of Henk van Weeren in The Hague. A panel of three magistrates would decide his fate.

The trial was expected to last only one day. The Court had provided for Jenny to stay at a small hotel in The Hague but Mark had persuaded his mother to let Jenny stay at their Leiden home, only ten minutes away.

"I hardly recognize you," Mark said, "You look like a movie star; you're beautiful."

"You look great too. It's the first time I've seen you in a suit. Those Boy Scout shorts are what I remember."

"It's a little cool for shorts," he laughed.

Jenny chortled happily and hooked her arm into his as they walked to the Zonder home on the Morssingel, one of the prettiest canals in Leiden.

Mother Zonder took charge of Jenny's suitcase and showed her to her room.

It had not been easy for Jenny's parents to approve their daughter's stay at the home of a boyfriend she had only known for a few months. Mark's mother had written a post card to the Bos family in Groningen saying that Mark's father was a Major in the Army and that they had raised two daughters and a son. She offered to welcome Jenny and treat her as one of her own daughters; in fact, she could use the room of her oldest daughter, Trees, who was away from home.

Hubert Bos, a Dutch Reformed conservative man had given his grudging approval. This alternative was better than Jenny staying alone in a hotel in a big city, he decided.

Jenny felt at home immediately. She chattered away and helped in the kitchen. After supper, Mark's mother decided that she must visit a neighbour, most urgently. "You two have a lot to talk about, so I'll be off."

They talked about the concern by their respective family and friends that war would come to Nederland and speculated what would happen to the country and their lives.

"The German border is only an hour bicycle ride from Groningen," she said. "A barbed wire barricade stands in the middle of the street. Soldiers shove it aside to allow traffic to enter from Germany. On the German side, the *Moffen* pace up and down. It is scary."

Mark smiled at her use of the pejorative word *Moffen*. Most of the Dutch could not bring themselves to say "German" when referring to Nazis. The word German evoked images of happy, red-cheeked people who liked beer and singing. *Moffen* expressed an immense dislike of their neighbours. The word was not in any dictionary, yet its use was universal.

Mark was more optimistic about the situation in Europe. If there were an attack, it wouldn't be just Nederland. He was sure that Belgium and France would be invaded at the same time and then England was sure to come to the rescue.

The return of Mother Zonder from her neighbourly visit interrupted their discussion as she brought in cups of coffee, ready-made from the kitchen. Jenny talked about her family, and her first year as a kindergarten teacher. Mother Zonder embarrassed Mark with stories of the days when he was in kindergarten. Jenny loved it.

Around ten, she announced that it was time for all to retire. Mark objected, "Oh mother, let us stay a little a little longer. We have not seen each other for so long." In an exaggerated gesture, she pulled her glasses down on her nose peered at him with faked disdain and then motioned for Jenny to follow her upstairs. In disappointment, Mark gulped down his now cold cup of coffee. He was about to go to his room when heard footsteps on the stairs. It was Jenny, wearing a bathrobe. She carried a glass of water.

He might have been imagining things, but he could swear that she had brushed her hair and applied a dab of lipstick. She grabbed a chair and sat down facing him. She put her slippered feet in his lap. She had great legs, he noticed again. Her robe slid slightly open. He noticed that she was not wearing a bra underneath her silky nightshirt. The cute globes jiggled a bit and the robe revealed a good portion of one thigh. She appeared to be unaware of the effect she had on Mark. He fought gallantly to keep his eyes on anything except Jenny. The eyes weren't winning, especially once Mr. Humongous joined in.

"So tell me what will happen to us once the trial is over," she asked.

'Lie in bed and make love all day,' Mr. H. whispered in his ear, but Mark did not say it. He told her instead that he would show her the old city of Leiden and if it was a nice day, they might go sailing on the Kagermeer where his friend Brenner kept his small sloop.

"If you think we should keep seeing each other I could try to find a job at the Montessori school in Leiden," she said tentatively. He hesitated.

"Well, I... ahem... um. Yes, Good idea. I don't have a job yet. I am still studying languages hoping that the CID will accept me..." He was rescued from further fumbling by the front door opening. His sister Jo walked into the living room. After the introductions and small talk, both girls retired to their rooms. Mark felt relieved. Mr. H. had retreated. He could think rationally again.

The trial of Henk van Weeren took place in Court Room 5 of the Gerechtshof located on The Hague's historic Korte Voorhout. As the lawyers had predicted, the prosecution and the defence had worked out how it would unfold. The participants would merely be actors in a staged play.

Mark was one of the first to testify. He responded to the question as to what he did after Henk was knocked down and whether he knew why the accused took out a gun and fired it in the air. The judge told him not to speculate. Mark said he didn't know. Jenny's testimony was over within five minutes. Henk did not testify. Lieutenant Raamsdonk's testimony was read into the record. The gist of the statement was in line with the overall suppression of the story. The defence rested.

The NSB party did not do Henk any favours by filling the gallery with supporters dressed in Nazi brown shirts. The German Embassy had sent an observer leaving many to wonder why Germany was so interested. When the President of the Court rendered the verdict of guilty, Henk was sentenced to "two years in jail to think it over."

Over a plain but nutritious meal at the Zonder home they discussed Mark's studies at the International Language School in Wassenaar. Mother Zonder announced she had a headache and left the two of them alone.

"The way things are, I don't know when we will meet again but perhaps I can call you by telephone?" Mark suggested hopefully.

"My parents do not have a phone nor do any of their friends," Jenny said, "But there is a phone at the Post Office," she said, "You can send me a post card on what day and time you will call and I will be there." She snuggled against him.

He reached around her waist and gently lifted her out of her seat. They stood and kissed. He could feel the swell of her breasts. They clung together so closely that it was impossible for her to avoid becoming more acquainted with the ebullient Mr. Humongous. Jenny rocked herself gently against him. She moaned softly and felt around to find out more about the cause of the bulge. He buried his tongue in her mouth, while kneading her breast in his hands.

Mother Zonder noticed the absence of talk and descended the stairs, stomping her feet as loudly as seemed reasonable. Jenny pushed Mark away and straightened her hair and dress.

"I had a little snooze and feel better now. I think I'll make some coffee and cake," she said, smiling benignly. They enjoyed a warm, pleasant evening, talking of everyday life and little things.

The short court case gave them a free day. Mark was up early. "I promised to take you sailing someday," he said pouring her a coffee. "You should meet Brenner Zijlberg, my high school pal.

His father owns the marina at the Kager Lake. He'll lend us his sail boat."

"It doesn't feel all that summery today," Jenny said.

"Oh, come on. It will be warm enough with the sun. We'll dress for it. The lake will be beautiful and we can be alone with no one around."

Jenny borrowed Mother Zonder's bicycle and after a brisk one-hour ride, they arrived at the marina. They found Brenner Zijlberg tarring the hull of a client's boat. The hot tar made the place smell like a highway.

"Can't leave this now," he yelled, "Must finish it." When introduced to Jenny he bowed with tar brush in hand and promptly spilled the hot stuff on his pants. "Go ahead. Take the boat. We'll talk when you come back."

Mark deftly rigged the boat while Jenny watched. "You have done this before," she said admiringly. They set off just before noon.

On a hot summer day, the Kager Lake would be crowded with sailboats, but March was chilly and the lake was entirely theirs. The sun played hide-and-seek with the bits of white clouds. The wind was growing stronger, pressing upon the sail so that the hull cut through the water with a loud hiss, leaving a wake of foamy white trimmings.

Jenny sat well forward. Huddled in her bright yellow hooded jacket, a sweater and scarf, she still she shivered. She let Mark do the tacking, jibbing and trimming. He didn't seem to feel the cold.

Mark sat lounging, knee-bent at the stern, head turned, arms outstretched, elbow and fingers resting on the tiller. "I am very happy," he said. He beckoned to her and she moved to sit close beside him.

"Why can't we always be like this?" She asked in that forlorn way that children sometimes pose silly questions.

"Shall we tie up in a little cove and try to finish what we started last night," he said in his best Groucho Marx imitation of a lecherous old man, tapping the ash of an imaginary cigar.

"You couldn't find me in this mass of clothing," she said jabbing his arm playfully. She was right. Even Mr. H. thought it was too chilly to rise.

Back at the marina, Brenner bought them dinner. The meal was simple and delicious. The boys told stories from their years at school together.

"Will you take over the marina after your parents, retire?" Jenny asked.

"A lot of guys like Mark and me don't know what we will be doing after our military service," he said scooping up the last bit of gravy and roast beef with his potatoes. "The older folks have a lot of faith in that ever-repeated claim of neutrality. But if they are wrong, it is guys like Mark and me that will have to do the fighting." He asked the cute waitress for the bill and a date for a movie on Saturday at the same time. The girl giggled and assented if she could pick the film.

"Hope you don't mind?" he said with a wink to Jenny, "I am not as lucky as Mark with a beautiful girlfriend."

The following morning at their goodbye at the Leiden station, much remained unsaid. The wonder of their infatuation perplexed them. They were too Dutch, too reticent to dare call it love. They kissed goodbye not sure when or whether they would ever meet again.

Desire was their master but distance was their enemy. A five-hour train ride separated them; it was not something that could be undertaken on a kindergarten teacher's salary, nor a student's stipend. Their relationship was confined to weekly letters with kind words and stories of their everyday lives.

She looked forward to coming home from school each day, hoping that there would be word from Mark. She read and re-read each card, letter and greeting from him. She eagerly replied, but time began to wear heavily on their relationship.

Mark wondered if Jenny had other suitors in Groningen. He was relieved that Henk van Weeren was in prison and out of the picture – at least on that front he was safe. For his part, there were several pretty girls in his language classes, and he occasionally felt eyes of admiration upon him. He felt it would be dishonest to engage any of them in more than polite conversation. He hoped Jenny would do the same.

Special occasions were marked by moments on the telephone – she in the Groningen Post Office and he in the hallway of his parents' home. Those conversations, however mundane the topic, were the glue that held them together through his nineteenth birthday, the Christmas of 1938 and her twentieth birthday in spring of 1939.

Jenny – always the one to initiate – talked to her parents about a teaching post in Leiden. The thought of their daughter living that far away did not go over well. Hubert said no and thought the argument was settled. Jenny let it rest. For now.

7

1939
THURSDAY, JUNE 8, 9:00 PM
MORSPOORT BARRACKS
LEIDEN, NEDERLAND

On April Fool's day of 1939, the formal conscription notice declared that Mark Hendrik Zonder – on his twentieth birthday – was to report to the Morspoort Army Barracks in Leiden to serve in the Fourth Regiment Infantry under his father's command, about 500 metres from home.

Sergeant Dirk Vreelink was the leader of the brutish group of instructors that had been the bane of his existence for the last six weeks. If he had expected lenience, he was quickly disabused of the idea. If anything, the sergeant had taken delight in pushing him harder than the others. Mark couldn't fault him though, for whatever he asked his recruits to do, he did double himself. The man was indestructible.

Dirk had asked to meet him in the canteen after the evening meal. Mark had arrived early, knowing Dirk was always on time. The canteen was only half full. Most of the company was out on a war game in the Katwijk dunes.

Vreelink sat down and came straight to the point. "Do you want to get out of the infantry? You've had six weeks of it!"

"Anything would be easier than this," Mark sighed.

Vreelink leaned in a little closer. "Chief van Zandt, remember him? He is now the Director General of the CID and he wants us in The Hague."

"You mean he wants us to volunteer for the CID?"

"Van Zandt needs to strengthen military intelligence. He has been given the green light to expand his field of operation. We have been summoned to go and see him tomorrow morning at 10:00."

Mark went to his bunk but couldn't sleep. He read Jenny's birthday card again. *'With love forever yours,'* the card read. The card smelled of her. He re-read her wish of coming to Leiden to teach. Life would certainly be a lot more exciting! A tour of duty with the CID sounded also stimulating. More exhilarating than standing four-hour guard shifts or digging latrines. He had no idea what he would do at the CID.

The Centrale Inlichtingen Dienst Building on Zeestraat 39 in The Hague was not overly impressive. It was a large three-story house that at one time belonged to one of the city's more affluent residents. It still looked like a house, outside and in.

The first and second floors held cubbyhole offices, former bedrooms, with name plates such as *Harbours, Borders, Industry* and *Aviation*, encompassing the core of the Dutch counter-espionage efforts. Van Zandt's third floor office had once been the master bedroom. Glass doors behind his desk opened onto a balcony that overlooked a garden in dire need of attention. Inside, hideous green-patterned wallpaper clashed with the plain, government-issue furniture.

A gloomy painting of a seventeenth century sea battle between valiant British ships and the glorious Dutch navy hung on one wall. The Dutch must have been winning because the cannon-battered British ship in the foreground was sinking.

On the way over, Dirk and Mark had spoken little. They rose in unison as van Zandt clomped into the room, muttering excuses about letting them wait. He was dressed to the nines: grey striped trousers, expensive jacket and a watch fob on his tailored vest. His moustache looked as if a swallow had flown up his noble nose and become stuck there.

"How are my favourite scouts today?" he jollied. "I've asked you to come here because the CID is in need of good men." He put both hands, palms down, on the desk. He appeared to study them for a while before he looked up. "Let me be direct. Our nation is naïve with respect to today's world conflicts. When Hitler thinks the time is right to secure the entire Atlantic coast from South to North, he will do so. He has said as much. Our security depends on an alliance with Britain." He opened a drawer of his desk and fished through it but when he couldn't find what he was looking for, he slammed it shut.

"The conundrum we face is that we cannot be allied with Britain and neutral at the same time. Her Majesty, with the knowledge of only a few cabinet ministers, has charged CID with providing covert support to

Britain." He looked toward the ceiling as if trying to remember something, then opened the top drawer on the other side of his desk. After fumbling about he found a small tin, placed it on the desk, and attempted to slide the lid open. He glanced at his guests.

"We suspect that the NSB, secretly supported by Germany, is training an underground army in this country. When Germany attacks, they will spring into action by guiding the enemy and creating panic among the population." He now had the lid off and poured some of what seemed like peppercorns in his hand. He popped the handful into his mouth.

"An objective of the CID is to keep our weak-kneed, neutrality-afflicted politicians informed of incidents that undermine our security now, before a single shot has been fired." He chewed loudly on the kernels.

He took a deep gulp of air as if he had expected something quite different from what he had been breathing all along. "Both of you are candidates for CID's branch charged with Internal Security. It encompasses the off-the-record liaison with the British and the underground activities of the NSB. I selected you because you are self-reliant and possess skills that may prove valuable." He held the little tin up, offering to pour some kernels in Mark's hand. "Menthol," he said.

Mark declined politely and asked, "Do we have any choice in the matter, Sir?"

"Of course you do. For example, you could decide to flunk the test. You'd be dismissed and returned to your infantry unit where kitchen patrol and latrine cleaning awaits you for the rest of your service."

"If we accept will we still be in the army?" Vreelink asked.

"Yes, but on the reserve list. It means that you can be pulled back into service at anytime. You will wear civilian clothing and receive special field training. Should you fail, you will return to your rank and unit. And finally, you will sign the Official Secrets Act which makes it a criminal offense to divulge any of CID's operations." He put the tin in the proper drawer where it should have been in the first place and slammed it shut.

"Will I keep my rank as Sergeant?" Vreelink asked.

"There are no ranks in Operations. You are all agents at the same rate of pay, which, by the way, is higher than a sergeant's pay. You may keep your uniform at home but you will not wear it on duty or otherwise. To all intents, you are civilians now. If you accept, you can proceed to the Quartermaster's office and sign in. On Sunday evening at 18:00 hours, you will report to the training camp in Oirschot near Eindhoven."

"Great!" Vreelink sniffed, "More basic training."

8

1939
SUNDAY, JULY 2, 2:00 PM
THE VON BECKE RESIDENCE, JULIANALAAN 45
LEIDEN, NEDERLAND

On the chestnut-lined streets of the Leiden suburb of Oegstgeest, the von Becke house did not stand out among its prosperous neighbours. It was a large, inviting home with huge picture windows, typical of the managerial and professional homes in the area. Alexander and Paula von Becke had lived there for 14 years.

Wilhelm James (Willem) von Becke was a good-looking lad with curly black hair and beautiful dark eyelashes and eyebrows. He was a good student in his fourth grade class.

His mother Paula was a vivacious dark blonde, 39 years old with a trim body and an ever-present smile. Her optimistic can-do spirit was largely responsible for Willem being a well-adjusted child.

Money was not a problem for the von Beckes. Alexander's income as an architect was more than sufficient to lead a solid middle-class existence with Paula as the stay-at-home helm of the household. Their income was substantially enhanced by the secretive annuity payments transferred to their bank account each month.

Willem's grandparents on his mother's side visited almost every Sunday. Old Harry Meunier had instilled in Willem a love of photography. For his seventh birthday, he had given Willem a used Hasselblad camera, a complex instrument that took time and skill to learn. Young Willem spent weekends photographing anything and everything. Harry Meunier developed the photos in his shop and critiqued them regularly.

Alexander's nature was the complete opposite of his lively wife. He was a taciturn man, given to sombre introspection. He loved Willem dearly but found it difficult to express his feelings. He did well in his profession but wasn't particularly liked by his co-workers. Alexander sensed a latent hostility towards him. He guessed it was because of his German accent or perhaps his admiration for the NSB, the national socialist party.

Alexander detested both social democrats and communists. He had no sympathy for those who wanted the workers to own the means of production and control the banks but he identified with the strong Nazi ideology of law and order, private ownership and maintaining the purity of races – a code name for excluding Jews.

When Queen Wilhelmina took a strong position against Hitler's New Order, he began to reconsider his support of the Monarchy.

This was to be a proud day for Alexander von Becke as his son Willem was marching in his first public parade in the *Jeugdstorm* or Youth Storm – an organization allied with the Hitler Youth in Germany and dedicated to the immersion of young people in the benefits of National Socialism.

The lad was dressed in black shorts and light blue shirts with the NSB logo on the sleeve. The orange neckerchief suggested an allegiance to the House of Orange but they were generally known as children of Nazi sympathizers.

Young Willem was not that thrilled. His German surname and his father's open avowal of the Nazi philosophy had made him the butt of jokes and name calling by his schoolmates. His one-time friends did not want to visit his home. His mother's heart ached to see him so disliked.

Paula's father, Harry Meunier berated her for letting Alexander 'poison' his grandson. Paula was torn but told herself that the Jeugdstorm was just like scouting.

The strongest voice of disapproval for Willem's Jeugdstorm activity had come from Frans van Zandt. Late one evening when Willem was asleep, he came over and delivered a stern note of displeasure from the Palace. He reminded the von Beckes of their commitment to rear the child befitting his heritage.

"Nonetheless, the Queen wants Willem removed from any political associations, whatsoever," van Zandt stressed. The issue of the monthly payments was not raised but understood by both sides.

The Palace can't do anything anyway, von Becke rationalized. They dare not make this a public issue; revealing the subterfuge would bring upheaval to a country already under stress.

9

1939
FRIDAY, SEPTEMBER 1, 5:30 AM
CAMP OIRSCHOT
BRABANT, NEDERLAND

"For God's sake, let me sleep," he mumbled. His teary red-rimmed eyes looked at his interrogator.

"Just a few more questions, Mark. Answer me and you will have the best sleep ever." The bully's foot prodded the form slumped on the tiled floor. "C'mon, boy, let's talk. What's his name?"

"I don't know, I told you, I don't know. He was just a..." his voice slurred and his head fell down.

"Oh, don't give me that shit. Wake up."

A voice from the back of the room asked. "How long has it been, Tim?"

"Thirty-nine hours, Sir." At 185 cm weighing 124 kg, "Tim" Timmerman was an imposing specimen. He was not a cruel man; he had a job to do. He was a CID instructor training recruits to withstand sleep deprivation – a favourite tool of questioners to extract information from detainees.

"I think he's had enough," the voice said, "He's over the 35 hours required to stay in the program. Take him to his bunk and let him sleep. Mark groaned when Timmerman picked him up in the fireman's hold and dragged him to his bunk in the barracks. It was Friday, September 1, 1939.

The voice was that of Stolberg, no rank or first name please. Stolberg converted decent young men into thieves, lawbreakers and skilled killers – all on behalf of the law-abiding government of gentle Nederland. He was a communist sympathizer who had fought against the fascists in the Spanish Civil war. CID had overlooked the fact that he was a 'Red', because the man practically wrote the book on covert warfare. Interrogation techniques, sneaking unseen through enemy lines or trapping vulnerable bureaucrats into spying for his side were his specialties. The bonus was that he hated Nazis from the depths of his scarred soul.

He was a huge man of mixed Dutch/Indonesian blood. He was able to maintain an inscrutable expression in all circumstances. Just when any reasonable person assumed that he had no other expression, his face would transform into a wide, happy-go-lucky grin – that is if he wasn't busy breaking someone's arm at the time.

Mark dreamed of Jenny. He remembered their last meeting two weeks ago when they had attended the celebrations of the birth of Princess Juliana's second daughter Princess Irene. CID had sent him to The Hague to mix among the massive crowds to spot any potential security threats to the Royal Family. Jenny was there as part of the first aid contingent; volunteers, drafted from far and wide.

He forced his fevered brain to concentrate on the happy moments during that visit, the evening in the haystack on the farm. He banished the erotic images from his mind. In his daze knew he had done something right today, but what? Slowly it came back to him – the interrogation. He hadn't broken. He had outlasted the bastards who had kept him under those bright lights asking the same questions over and over again.

When he didn't answer or gave them false answers they had locked him up and kept him awake with ear shattering noises emanating from a stack of loudspeakers. Then they hauled him back in for the same questions. He wondered how Vreelink had made out. They'd become mates in spite of the ten years difference in age.

The set-up for his interrogation was complex. The trainees had been shown a film of a fictional bank robbery. The names of the holdup men were clearly heard. Suddenly one of them fired point blank at the bank manager who appeared mortally wounded. Stolberg said experts would interrogate them. The interrogators were not aware of the details, only that there had been a bank robbery.

The questioners' task was to learn how the job was carried out, the names of the gang members and specifically, the name of the shooter. The job of the recruits was to withhold as much information as possible. The trainees had some leeway in revealing parts of the operation but giving the name of the shooter was grounds for dismissal from the program.

He remembered how close he came to telling all. He needed sleep. It was only a game. Who wanted to stay in this damned program anyway? Why suffer? But, damn it all, he had stuck it out.

His brain was too active to let him sleep more. He got up. He looked at his watch on the ledge behind his cot, washed his face, put on some clean skivvies and poked Dirk Vreelink who was sound asleep in his bunk.

"Go away," Dirk sniffed, "Get lost." Yet, he threw his blanket off and sat on the edge of his cot, his head in his hands. He sniffed a few more times. He finally woke up enough to ask, "Did you tell him to stick it up his ass?"

"Told him nothing much. I'll go and see if there is some coffee. Have a shower and put on a clean shirt," Rather than watching Vreelink dress, he made his way to the canteen. The place was empty. Most of the chairs were upside down on the tables. Nelis, the cook was busy laying out the bread and sausages and glad for the early company.

"You got up early," Nelis said. "Most of them are still recovering. You look pretty good though."

"Maybe after a few cups of coffee I will feel like a human being again," Mark said. He poured a cup of coffee for Dirk and one for himself and asked Nelis for some *beschuitjes*, the crumbly rounds of rusk. He slathered them with margarine and sugar and carried them to a table where Dirk joined him. "That damn shower is like ice," Dirk said clasping his hands around the warm cup. He shivered as he put three spoons of sugar in his coffee. They reminisced about their training over the past few weeks.

One of their first classes had been learning Morse code, using the telegraph keys, and trying to decipher a message from dots and dashes. They understood its importance in the spy game but to listen to the clicking machine and decipher the message by just listening to the taps was difficult.

They were taught how to drive a car. Very few people owned cars and Mark had neither the need nor the opportunity to learn. The standard driving lessons were easy and he quickly mastered them. The ins and outs of high-speed chases and how to use evasive action had taken a lot of practice. They agreed that standing on the brakes to cause the car to spin 180 degrees was a most satisfying experience.

Vreelink smiled and gingerly picked up his beschuit but the rusk broke as he moved it towards his mouth. The breakaway piece first covered his tunic with sugar and then dropped onto his lapel. He cursed under his breath. He cleaned himself off, pretended that nothing happened and said, "I thought I'd never live to see the day that you would become an expert at handling small arms and hand-to-hand combat. Your Dad would be impressed."

"He would not be impressed by breaking the law," Mark said, reaching over to brush the last bit of sugar off Dirk's chest. "Tapping telephones, opening other people's mail and stealing cars are skills that are of little use in civilized society."

"You are assuming of course that we will be operating in a civilized society. But someday we may find ourselves in a situation where we have to outdo the bad guys in dirty tricks." He daintily steered his second rusk to his mouth avoiding any undue pressure or imbalance. A fleeting smile crossed his face as he managed to take a delicate bite and put the remainder back on the plate where it promptly broke into three pieces.

"I've got to tell you though," Mark said, "In the beginning, I was quite nervous about these illegal activities. It was always hammered into me that breaking the law is never acceptable. I was really nervous when I was ordered to break into a house."

Corporal Nelis had been listening in; without being invited, he pulled up a chair and joined the discussion. Mark expected Vreelink to be annoyed but Dirk hardly ever pulled rank in social settings.

"These stories about being alone in the field are always good," Nelis said eagerly. "What did you have to do?" he asked Mark.

Mark looked at Vreelink, who leaned back in his chair. "Yeah, I'd like to hear it too," he smiled.

"My briefing said that a cache of German weapons was hidden in a house on the Spijkerstraat in Eindhoven. It was supposed to be an arsenal for an attack group of the NSB that might spring into action if Germany invades. My task was to find out if it there were actually weapons there. An Army truck dumped me in the neighbourhood. I didn't know the number of the house but they gave me a name – Steenburgen – and that the Steenburgens were expecting a baby."

"The street was full of identical rowhouses with small front gardens, so I went around the back where I could see most of the back doors. The first house had a neatly kept garden but there was an old woman pulling weeds. Too old for a baby I figured."

"The back door of the third house opened. It was a grey-haired man, carrying a leather briefcase. He looked like an accountant. Too smug to be a Nazi activist. Nothing in any of the backyards gave me a clue so I went back to the front street."

"I rang the doorbell of the first house. The name on the doorjamb read Bakker and this querulous old hag answered the door. She told me she'd seen some people go into number 51. She called them 'brownies from the Indies'. She said maybe the woman could have been pregnant."

"Number 51 looked just like all the others. A damaged 1935 Ford sedan stood in front. The front garden was ill kept. I pulled the doorbell. No answer. I stepped into the garden and looked though the bay window. The living room was empty. No furniture. I pulled the bell again. No response."

"The lock was a standard Yale, a tongue on the door side and a socket in the jamb. I had to get in. There was a small window next to the door. I figured I could break it and open the door from the inside but that would leave a mark."

"I needed a tool of some kind. The Ford on the street was one of those slanted-back Fords with a horizontal trunk lid. All those kind of Fords have a tool kit. I had a paper clip in my pants pocket. It took about 30 seconds. Click! There was no hammer but I figured a big wrench and a screwdriver would do the trick."

"I put the screwdriver between the jamb and the door and hit it with the wrench. After two tries, I was able to wriggle the screwdriver back and forth and the door opened."

Nelis, the cook, was getting antsy. Several trainees had come into the canteen and demanded service. "I'll be with you in a minute. Help yourself to coffee," he yelled, "Go on. Go on."

"Well, I looked around; still no one in the street. I entered the hallway, it was dark in there and I stumbled over a couple of bicycles parked against the wall. The living room was bare except for a wide sofa with a small table next to it. An unopened letter on the floor was addressed to a name that was not Steenburgen. After inspecting the kitchen and bedroom, I opened a door leading to a cellar. Then I heard the voice."

"It was Stolberg, standing behind me with his hands on his hips."

"Ah shit," Nelis exploded. "Is that it?"

"He told me the place was a CID safe house. He said he could have killed me because I never heard him coming in through the back door using the regular key."

Nelis was disappointed and left to attend to his customers. He had expected blood on the floor.

"So how did you feel breaking the law?" Dirk asked.

"I have to admit that it was kind of thrilling. I can see how criminals might become addicted to the adrenalin rush."

"I'm going for a walk," Vreelink announced. As he reached for the door handle, Timmerman simultaneously opened it from the other side.

"Hold on boys. Commandant Byers wants you all in his office pronto."

"Maybe they will move us out of here," Mark said, hoping to return to a normal life.

The commandant's office was barely big enough to seat the ten recruits who had survived the course. The cadre of six trainers sat along the wall in a separate row. Commandant Byers looked ashen.

"Men," he began, "A serious development. A few hours ago, the German Army invaded Poland. France and Britain are expected to declare war on Germany later today. The Dutch Armed Forces are now on full mobilization. Later today, you will receive assignments to your new posts. You will perform your duties in civilian clothing. You will not wear uniforms unless ordered to."

"Your training is now complete. Sorry, men, but this brief announcement will serve as your graduation ceremony. Your training has provided you with skills that our country will call upon when needed."

Commandant Byers rose. The men stood at attention.

"Long Live the Queen," he yelled. His eyes had a distant stare.

Vreelink was one of the first to be called in for an interview. He was assigned to the barracks in Leiden, attached to the command of Major Pieter Zonder.

It was early afternoon when Mark received his briefing. It didn't take more than five minutes. He was ordered to serve at the CID offices in The Hague as the personal adjutant of Director General Frans van Zandt or the "DG." as he was referred to on the memo.

10

1939
TUESDAY, SEPTEMBER 19, 2:30 PM
ABWEHR HAUPTAMT, TURPITZUFER 76/78
BERLIN, GERMANY

Abwehr headquarters was a sombre looking edifice – functional but bland – located on the banks of the River Spree. Built in the 1880s, it was originally an elite school for boys. Admiral Wilhelm Canaris, Chief of the Abwehr for five years now, waited impatiently in his large fourth floor office that once housed an entire class of students.

His rival, Heinrich Himmler, leader of the Schutzstaffel – the SS – had demanded an appointment. Canaris secretly detested the pasty-faced little man with his round, granny glasses. He was a ruthless man who had 'taken care' of Hitler's opponents when the Nazis were striving for power.

Admiral Wilhelm Canaris was a tall man in his mid-fifties with grey hair and a posture that spoke of military discipline and an ascetic lifestyle. He never appeared publicly in civilian clothes and took great pride in wearing the uniform of an admiral of the Kriegsmarine. He had been a loyal follower of Hitler since 1933 when the Fuehrer entrusted him with running the German spy agency. He kept his political views to himself but he detested the latest focus on the elimination of those whom the leader considered *Untermenschen,* the less than human.

The Gestapo was under Himmler's command and Canaris expected that the reason for the visit was to announce another encroachment of his intelligence agency. He was not mistaken. Himmler made a big show of taking off his officer's hat, removing his leather gloves finger by finger and carefully depositing his silver tipped officer's baton on the desk.

"Herr Admiral Canaris, I have come to see you on a matter of great importance to our Fuehrer." Invoking the name of the leader was a sure sign that Himmler didn't think his case would stand on its own.

"The Abwehr has failed to respond to the Fuehrer's demand to destroy or undermine the credibility of the regime in the Low Countries. The

Fuhrer's strategy for a Greater Europe foresees that the Atlantic Coast from Norway to Spain will be under the Reich's control. This will naturally involve the peaceful occupation of Nederland." He removed his granny glasses and held them up to the light – a stalling technique he used to let his words sink in.

"You have failed to deliver evidence that English warships are guarding the waterways of Holland. And now we know that British MI-6 agents roam about freely. The Fuehrer demands action on these important issues." With a lesser man than the Admiral, he would – at this point – have lifted his officer's baton and slammed it on the desk.

Canaris listened to the diatribe in silence. "My dear Heinrich," the use of Himmler's first name was a subtle reminder that he outranked him. "Your busy schedule may have prevented you from reading my report with regard to exposing the British presence in Nederland." He had not sent a report, but he knew Himmler was the kind of person who hardly ever read any lengthy documents. He survived mainly on instinct.

"I was coming to that," Himmler bluffed, "I want more details."

"The Abwehr is not interested in merely exposing MI-6 agents," Canaris said, "We have infiltrated MI-6 and established a deep contact within the agency."

He got up to walk to the corner of his office and painstakingly selected a cigar from the humidor. He didn't offer one to Himmler. He knew that he would decline. Canaris let his guest watch as he retrieved a cigar clipper from his desk and mutilated the end of it before lighting it. Once lit, he passed the cigar under his nose and blew the smoke in the direction of his adversary. The ceremony was a deliberate show to demonstrate Canaris was in control.

"One of our best agents, a Dr. Jakob Franz has established himself with MI-6 over the years as a Jewish refugee from Germany. He is a psychologist at St. Pancras hospital in Amsterdam. Through one of his contacts in London, he has led MI-6 to believe that he is in touch with a group of German Air Force generals, plotting to overthrow the leadership of the Reich and sue for peace with Britain. A fictitious General Semmel is supposed to be heading this group of dissidents."

"My God, Admiral!" he scolded. "You are betraying our Fuehrer's leadership. How dare you plant such a scenario with the enemy!"

Canaris assumed an even more familiar tone. "My dear Hein, the words spy and lie are interchangeable in intelligence circles. The story must be believable for the British to take the bait. They already believe that there is great opposition to the Fuehrer's direction for Germany. They are naïve."

Himmler seemed to relax. "So what are you planning?"

"Dr. Franz will convince MI-6 that his German contacts can deliver the fictitious General Semmel to a German/Dutch border town to initiate peace talks with MI-6. Initially, the Englanders will only meet a low-level officer who will give some information. He will suggest a second meeting with a higher ranking officer, perhaps even General Semmel himself – an actor of course," he quickly added.

"And what will that accomplish?"

"We will have proof that Nederland harbours MI-6 agents and even more important, we will obtain details such as the hierarchy of MI-6, their modus operandi and names of operatives."

"Good progress, Admiral. Keep me informed." With that, the little weasel got up, put on his hat and gloves, clicked his heels and picked up his baton. Then, with great ceremony, he raised his arm in the Nazi salute, bowed from the neck and shouted "Heil Hitler!"

Creepy showboat, Canaris thought, but didn't say it. He lifted the telephone. "Tell Oberleutnant Walter Schellenberg I want to see him."

11

1939
MONDAY, OCTOBER 2, 3:00 PM
VAN ZANDT RESIDENCE, KIEVIETLAAN 22
WASSENAAR, NEDERLAND

The meandering roads to the posh community of Wassenaar allowed for a most enjoyable bicycle ride for an early October afternoon. The stately chestnut trees were beginning to shed their leaves. The van Zandt residence, a grand mansion on the Kievietlaan, stood well back from its gated entrance.

Mark had received the notice at noon that Lieutenant General van Zandt had summoned him to meet at his home. Queen Wilhelmina, over the objections of the Chief of the General Staff, had promoted her trusted advisor to the rank of Lieutenant General in charge of the CID. It was a distinction he had asked for. He had found it difficult to work his way through the bureaucracy with the civilian title of Director General. The two gold stars on his brand-new uniform would silence many military men who otherwise might object to his orders.

The half-hour ride from The Hague had made him squirm in the hard saddle. The bicycle, a heavy government-issued machine, one of tens of thousands in the Army, had only one gear. Its only amenity was a bell that needed a flick of the thumb to create a tinny warning sound.

The gate to the big house stood open. He parked his bicycle and undid the ankle clasp on the trousers of his dark suit. The cool weather had prevented perspiration from darkening his white shirt. As he walked past the tennis court, he heard a woman's voice call his name.

Kirsten van Zandt waved her tennis racket, "Yoo-hoo, Mark?" She had just finished a few sets with a neighbour and was on her way back into the house. She looked flushed and full of energy. She wore a white V-neck sweater and a short tennis skirt that would have shocked the matriarchs of the Wassenaar elite had she dared to wear it in public. *She must notice me looking*, he thought, averting his eyes. She smiled a knowing smile.

"The General is delayed; he'll be an hour at least. I'll just clean up a bit and then let's have coffee in the gazebo; it's such a lovely day."

The gazebo was an octagon structure covered in vines, the Centrepiece of a professionally tended garden with an immaculately groomed lawn. Here and there, sparse fallen leaves hinted that autumn was in the air.

The inside of the gazebo looked more like a living room than a garden shelter. Four plush velour-covered easy chairs surrounded a low table.

Kirsten came back, still wearing the short skirt but a silk blouse had replaced the sweater. A red bolero jacket hung over her shoulders. A maid brought in a pot of coffee and set it on a tray on the hutch.

Kirsten, never unaware of the effect she was having on men, burbled girlishly, "Mark you must come and play tennis with me sometime." He recognized the invitation for what it was. She must have picked up the expression during her visits to Britain where it was quite common to be invited 'sometime'. However, should anyone ever follow up and expect to visit, he or she would be deemed to be utterly devoid of civilized manners.

"Tell me about your new career," she said, as she sat on the armrest of his chair pouring him a cup of coffee. Mark expected her to get up and sit in one of the other chairs but she stayed beside him. He turned sideways to speak to her and found her face close to his. He sensed her body and smelled her perfume. He choked a bit and told her how exciting it all was.

"You are so strong to survive that training," she cooed. "Did the girls ever tell you that you are a very handsome man?"

"Not really, Ma'am."

"You must not call me Ma'am unless it is a formal occasion where the General and his coterie are around. Call me Kirsten," She pronounced her name with that lilting Swedish inflection on the last syllable.

"I don't think I can do that; you are the General's wife," Mark objected.

"Nonsense. In Sweden, it is quite proper to be good friends in private but we must be formal when the occasion demands it. I would like to think that on some fine afternoon you could sneak away from the office and come by to play tennis. I am running out of male opponents and the women are too easy to beat. Really, you must come." She nudged her shoulder against his body and let her hand linger on his arm. "You have the body of a strong player." Mark sat transfixed.

The maid entered to announce that the General had arrived with a guest and Mark was expected to attend in the den.

"Who's the gentleman with the General?" Kirsten asked. The maid said she didn't know but he looked "very English."

The den was a cozy place – the kind of place where you could either relax all by yourself or sit and have a drink with a good friend, in the secure knowledge that the outside world not intrude. One wall of shelves was filled with books all the way up to the ceiling. On the opposite side, a big painting dominated the room. It was a typical eighteenth century battle-scene: handsome officers in bright uniforms on prancing steeds waved swords, while far away in the background anonymous figures were killing each other in the smoke.

The guest rose as Mark entered. The man looked English indeed. Van Zandt stayed in his leather club chair and waved at Mark to come closer.

"Director General Menzies," he intoned, "I would like to introduce my aide, Agent Mark Zonder." Menzies, wearing gray slacks and a blazer with the required club tie remained firmly erect as the General continued. "Mark Zonder, please meet my counterpart in the United Kingdom Director General Stuart Menzies of MI-6."

He looked at DG Menzies, the well-known English spymaster he had heard about in his training course. "I am honoured to meet you, Sir," he managed to say.

Menzies was a stern, mournful looking man with a hairline that had receded halfway up his skull. His moustache resembled two detached black eyebrows slanting down toward the corners of his thin lips.

"DG Menzies has come here to discuss confidential matters," said van Zandt. I asked you to come because will be part of an operation planned by MI-6." He turned toward the liquor cabinet and lifted the crystal decanter that held the Johnnie Walker Blue. For a moment, he contemplated offering his visitors a drink but decided against it and sat down again.

Menzies appeared slightly disappointed but began to relate how Dr. Jakob Franz, a German refugee based in Amsterdam had relayed information – obtained through family sources – that a number of Luftwaffe generals were planning a military coup to depose Hitler and then negotiate a peace settlement with Britain.

"We brought Dr. Franz to London and checked him out. His story stands up; the plotters have put out feelers to open discussions with MI-6. The purpose is to determine the terms of an eventual peace agreement." He looked at van Zandt for an indication whether or not he should continue. The General nodded a paternal yes.

"The conditions for talks include that the MI-6 agents must be fully empowered to negotiate." Menzies paused again, produced a cigarette case from his jacket, and offered Sweet Caporals all around. No one took him up on it. He lit the cigarette, inhaled deeply and continued.

"MI-6 has selected two experienced agents for initial discussions." Menzies' clipped accent sounded cold and aggressive. "At first we planned to land them here without the knowledge of the Dutch Government. But, since our men need support, we decided to approach CID." Van Zandt got up and held out the bottle of Johnnie Walker Blue in his direction but Menzies waved him off.

"Your official neutrality would be jeopardized if British operatives were found roaming around your country. We are fortunate to have such great support from General van Zandt who tells me Queen Wilhelmina and the Minister of Defence are aware and approve."

Van Zandt added, "I have assigned Agent Zonder to assist your agents. Knowledge of this operation is on a need-to-know basis. It is a covert operation not sanctioned by cabinet as a whole. The MI-6 officers do not report to Agent Zonder but Zonder will ensure that they do not engage in activities detrimental to the interest of this country." Mark still hadn't spoken; he was staggered by the role suddenly thrust upon him. Van Zandt looked at him and slightly lifted his chin; an unspoken order to respond.

"I am honoured to be chosen, Sir, but why me?"

"Stolberg rates you the most able and qualified operative. Your skill in languages will be at play in this operation and you are fluent in four."

Menzies and the General discussed the potential success of the negotiations. Van Zandt was still somewhat uneasy, cautioning that the operation might be a trap by the Abwehr. He quizzed Menzies about the reliability of Dr. Franz and his family connections.

Menzies said he was very confident and added that the opportunity for peace could not be ignored. "MI-6 will get a good handle on the Abwehr's presence in Britain. We will get more out of them than they will get out of us," he declared confidently while beckoning for the bottle of Johnnie Walker Blue.

12

1939
MONDAY, OCTOBER 29, 1:00 PM
FERRY TERMINAL
HOEK VAN HOLLAND, NEDERLAND

Agents Peter Best and Jeffrey Sangster were scheduled to arrive at one o'clock at the Hoek-van-Holland ferry terminal. Mark had little difficulty picking them out of the crowd. Peter Best was a trim looking, immaculately dressed 35-year old, with stylishly cut, curly hair and a Clark Gable moustache. His Oxford English enunciated every syllable precisely, quite the opposite of Jeffrey Sangster whose Liverpool roots frequently betrayed him. He was an imposing silver-haired giant, mid-forties or so, exuding an air of bonhomie that might be deceptive.

After a perfunctory introduction, the pair settled in the back seat of van Zandt's '38 Buick Century on loan to Mark. They ignored Mark and talked about hot spots in Amsterdam.

The doorman at the Panorama Hotel hustled their baggage into the lobby. Sangster smiled, "Let's have a drink in the lobby before you go. Best and I will be down in a jiffy."

Mark's *Hero* pineapple drink was almost finished when the agents finally joined him. "Flight Lieutenant Albert J. Formby, I presume," Jeffrey Sangster appeared to be in a jolly mood. Peter Best smiled benignly.

"I'm not sure what you mean, Sir."

They ordered J&Bs with soda and another *Hero* for Mark. Peter Best handed Mark a genuine looking document that identified him as an officer of MI-6. It was a surprise to see his photograph among the English words.

He half listened to Best who rattled on. "The brass didn't think it was a good idea to have a Dutch officer along on peace talks between Britain and Germany. If the three of us get caught your government can claim '*Neutral, Neutral*' and say that they knew nothing about us."

Sangster took a sip of his scotch, held it in his mouth as if to test it for impurities before swallowing it, and said, "So, presto, you are Flight

Lieutenant Albert J. Formby, born in Cardiff, Wales." The first sip must have been okay for he tried another one and put his glass down.

"One more detail, Albert," Best said, "If the Germans ask you why your accent is different from ours, tell them you come from Wales. The Jerries cannot distinguish between English accents. Of course Australian doesn't count; no one can understand them," Best said, laughing at his own joke.

Mark reached to put the MI-6 identity card away. "Better sign it first," Sangster suggested. "Now tell us, what's happening tomorrow morning?"

"We will leave here to meet Dr. Franz at General van Zandt's home at eight in the morning."

After ordering a second round, Sangster leaned closer and said conspiratorially, "I am not as convinced as DG Menzies is. A mind-spook who knows how to arrange world peace – it just does not ring true." He was animated now. The scotch made his Liverpool accent thicker.

Peter Best declared he was hungry. The Brits went down to the dining room. Flight Lieutenant Albert Formby declined and went back to the CID barracks to finish work and write a letter to Jenny.

The Brits were difficult to separate from their breakfast. Hoping for kippers, eggs and sausages, they bitterly maligned the jams and jellies of the Dutch breakfast.

They were more subdued on the drive to Wassenaar. Van Zandt wasn't quite ready to receive them so the maid showed them into the salon.

"Quite the place for a servant of the people," Sangster said, inspecting the expensive furniture, "Unless the Dutch are more generous to their generals than Britain, he must have married into money."

"It is so amusing that the British are always ready to measure people by their wealth, isn't it?" Kirsten van Zandt's voice sounded more teasing than reproachful as she swirled into the room.

Peter Best tugged at the tip of his moustache and, in lecherous appreciation, said, "Well, Hel-l-l-l-l-o-o-o," as he bent to kiss her hand.

Kirsten looked lovely this morning, Mark thought. Her form-fitting dress reached just below her knees providing a full view of her shapely longs legs. Its vermillion colour offset her flaxen hair. She extricated herself from the fawning MI-6 agents and kissed Mark lightly on the lips. Best's gasp of surprise was audible.

"Hello Mark, how are you this lovely morning?" So much for official behaviour when there is company, Mark thought.

Kirsten withdrew from the room when van Zandt entered. Once again, he was dressed as if he was about to attend an ambassador's ball: a beautifully cut dark suit, grey vest and watch fob. He led the men to his den. They settled in the huge upholstered easy chairs and listened to van Zandt's opening monologue.

Cabinet approval for participation in the British mission had not been forthcoming but the Minister of Defence was completely on side. He lit a cigar and invited the British agents to "smoke them if they had them."

"About the meeting today," van Zandt continued, "You have the background on Dr. Franz. MI-6 is confident that he has important German contacts. Nevertheless, I think you should remain alert to entrapment."

The maid entered to announce their visitor.

Jakob Franz was a heavier version of Charlie Chaplin. His black suit looked like it was bought at a flea market and it was at least a half size too small. His black square moustache looked pasted on.

He bowed from the neck and nearly clicked his heels as he was introduced. Mark responded naturally to his introduction as Albert Formby. He felt as if he had successfully passed some kind of test.

Van Zandt made Dr. Franz walk through the scenario again. How did he become aware of the intent of the Luftwaffe generals? Did he know their leader General Semmel? When was the last time he had heard from his German contact?

Franz answered matter of factly, "Yesterday I told General Semmel that I would meet the British agents today. He suggested an exploratory meeting this afternoon at the border in the town of Dinxperloo."

"Who are we meeting with?" Sangster asked, surprised at the timetable.

"Hauptmann Walter Schellenberg, a nephew of General Semmel."

"Does he have any authority?" Best wanted to know.

"Not really," Dr. Franz sighed in frustration. "He is authorized to listen to a proposal for peace talks, that's all." He added, "If I may use your telephone I can let Schellenberg know you will meet him today."

Van Zandt didn't like this at all. "You can tell him that there will be a meeting but not in the ten-houses-and-a-bar village of Dinxperloo. We will meet in the city of Zutphen, 15 kilometres from the border, a four-hour drive, given the checkpoints. It is almost ten o'clock. Make it for three o'clock at the Aster Hotel." He looked at Mark, "It's a safe place."

When Franz came back with confirmation, Sangster phoned London and got an enthusiastic endorsement from Menzies.

After a few last minute arrangements, they went outside to the circular driveway to find that van Zandt's Buick had gone. Instead, there was a luxurious 1938 Lincoln Zephyr, license plate G1443 indicating that the car was licensed in the province of Gelderland. There was no way a car licensed to CID would be used.

The car smelled of new leather. Mark opened the glove box and found a chamois pouch containing a Colt single action revolver and a box of ammunition, but no holster. He locked the glove box. Peter Best wanted to ride beside him. Sangster, who spoke passable German, sat in the back seat with Dr. Franz.

Sentries along the route had been alerted to a Lincoln Zephyr whose passengers were racing towards a rendezvous of international importance. However, the very first sentry didn't speak English and had not heard any of the CID alerts.

Agent Albert Formby switched into perfect Dutch and slipped him both the CID pass and the MI-6 identity card. The sergeant told the sentry to raise the barrier. Sangster confided to a surprised Dr. Franz that this MI-6 team had many surprising talents.

"Just as I speak German with a Liverpool accent, Agent Formby speaks Dutch with a Welsh accent," he said pleasantly.

They endured at least a dozen more stops along the 120-kilometre route to Zutphen but van Zandt seemed to have worked his magic because they cleared most barricades quickly.

It was a relatively nice day for the end of October. Mark parked the Lincoln in a side street by the Aster hotel. They were an hour early. The smell of coffee brewing and beer on tap made Mark feel more at ease. He chose a place near the front window to spot any approaching cars.

A green and white striped canopy covered the outdoor terrace. The four tables with matching rattan chairs were unoccupied. A couple of well-fed farmers in coveralls and mud on their boots nursed a beer while chattering in their local dialect.

At ten minutes to three, a Daimler bearing Münster licence plates parked at the curb across from the hotel. Captain Schellenberg looked around, walked across and sat down at one of the tables under the canopy.

The captain was a broad-shouldered, athletic looking man in his late 20s with an aristocratic bearing. His face had a nervous look as if he was constantly alert to an unpleasant surprise.

He took his gloves off and placed them on the table – a sign for two men to step out of the Daimler and join him. They were a couple of rough-and-tumble guys. Mark wished he'd taken the Colt out of the glove box.

Sangster rose and said, "The show is on, lads." He walked onto the outside terrace followed by Best and Dr. Franz who shook hands with Schellenberg. The doctor must have said something comforting because suddenly Schellenberg looked a lot more relaxed.

After courtly introductions all around, Dr Franz, Schellenberg, Best and Sangster sat at one table while Mark sat with the burly types at another. He had missed the older man's name. Knost, he thought or perhaps Knaust. He decided on Knaust because it sounded uglier. His figure, complexion and demeanour suggested a manual labourer or maybe an infantryman. However, he was not in the right physical shape to be either; his face was red – the sort of complexion that comes with high blood pressure, aggravated by smoke and alcohol.

The pair was likely from the SD – the Sicherheitsdienst, Hitler's goon squad providing the official strong-arm.

The café owner placed Heineken beer felts in front of everyone and asked for the order. Not surprisingly, the orders followed cultural lines: beer for the Germans, tea for the Englishmen. Mark was about to order coffee when Sangster interceded. "Albert? Tea?" Mark hastily agreed. He didn't care for tea but was glad Sangster had caught him in time.

When the refreshments arrived, Schellenberg started by giving a clear and convincing overview of conditions in Germany and the degree to which the army had suffered in the Polish campaign. Losses had been high and the present military and economic conditions made it imperative that the war be brought to an end quickly. Hitler though, did not listen to the advice of his general staff and allowed nothing to stand in the way of his ambitions. Therefore, he had to go. Assassination was out of the question, as it would lead to chaos. The intent was to imprison him and then a junta of officers would sue for peace with Britain.

Schellenberg added, "We have to put the interest of our country first. Before we take any steps against Hitler we want to know whether England is ready to grant us a peace which is both just and honourable."

Mark was taking notes, but when he realized he was writing in Dutch, he quickly turned the page and began scribbling in English. Up to this point, neither Best nor Sangster had said very much. Dr. Franz suggested that the British side list their terms for a negotiated peace.

Sangster took the lead. After complimentary words for the 'enlightened' German officers who so nobly cared about their country, he launched into a well-rehearsed set of demands. Germany must depose Hitler, disband his cabinet and withdraw German troops from Austria, Czecho-Slovakia and Poland. For their part, Britain would return the former colonies in Africa to Germany.

Schellenberg, who had remained expressionless throughout, said he would relay the demands to General Semmel.

"He will no doubt prepare a response for a next meeting," Schellenberg said. "The General also has some conditions. First, the British must supply a radio transmitter by which negotiations can be conducted directly with London. Second, the next meeting must be at a border point eliminating German travel in neutral territory. Lastly we must be assured that we are negotiating with authorized representatives." He handed Sangster an envelope containing a sheet of paper with the conditions. He took a sip of his beer and licked a flick of foam off his lips before he rose, "Gentlemen, we shall contact you through Dr. Franz as to the next meeting."

After the obligatory handshakes, Schellenberg and his men took off in the Daimler towards Germany. Mark had not touched his tea. No great loss. It was almost four o'clock. If they returned to The Hague now, they would be back by eight. However, Sangster and Best wanted to "have tea" at the Aster before returning.

"You have already had tea," Mark suggested.

"Tea means food, Albert," Best said, indignantly.

The owner had no concept of 'tea'. He served cheese sandwiches, with awful tasting coffee. Sangster must have been hungry. He didn't criticize. Dr. Franz nodded off over his sandwich. They left at five.

The route back was a tiresome exercise of barricade after barricade. The complete blackout, combined with what little light that the shaded headlamps were allowed to emit, made the rain-swept road nearly impossible to see.

Dr. Franz was sound asleep in the back seat. Mark didn't listen to the conversation of the Brits. He replayed the day's conversations in his mind. He mused about the ordinariness of it all. It might be an opening for peace in Europe but it felt more like an afternoon chat over a cup of tea.

13

1939
MONDAY, NOVEMBER 6, 8:00 AM
CID BUILDING, ZEESTRAAT 39
THE HAGUE, NEDERLAND

A week had passed since the exchange in Zutphen. Van Zandt had not called for his report until this morning. He had his back turned and was looking out the window behind his desk as Mark entered.

Van Zandt looked tired as he turned and reached for the pen on his desk. Whenever he had not quite formulated his thoughts, he would juggle his fountain pen between his fingers like a cheerleader marching in front of the school band. He was fully engaged in the performance now.

"I am concerned about our politicians," he said watching his own hands. "They are uncomfortable about CID's shift toward cooperation with Britain. I have had to step back from the Menzies affair."

"You will have to be CID's eyes on these discussions. We will not be able to help you if anything goes wrong, but we will watch over you. I can no longer ensure you unhindered passage, although Evert Bracken, the Minister of Defence will try to clear the way."

"Is there a time set for the next meeting, General?"

"Dr. Franz says Schellenberg wants a meeting the day after tomorrow, at four in the afternoon. The meeting will be at the Backus café at the border at Venlo, on the Dutch side of course. Menzies says Best and Sangster are crossing to Nederland tomorrow. However, Franz wants out. He does not want to be involved any more."

"That's what he told us at Zutphen too."

"I don't like it that he suddenly wants to bail out. You must take him along. He might give us some cover."

"What if he refuses to go?"

Van Zandt wasn't smiling when he said, "Make him believe it's in his best interest." The pen was really travelling now. "One more thing, if Schellenberg brings General Semmel, there is a problem. Semmel doesn't have a passport, so you'll have to convince the Marechaussee detachment in Venlo to let these German officers cross."

"I'd better check today what that café looks like. When will Best and Sangster arrive?"

"Tomorrow at four in the afternoon. You should meet them and become an Englishman again." van Zandt chuckled mirthlessly.

Van Zandt put the pen down waved him off. Mark took his coat and a roadmap from his office and descended to the basement garage.

"A luxury car for our agent," van Puffelen, the motor pool dispatcher mumbled. "No cheap car for the General's bum boy." Van Puffelen was close to retirement and determined to make the world aware of his keen assessment of capitalist corruption everywhere.

The old veteran threw him the keys. The Lincoln Zephyr with the G plates stood at the far end of the garage. He checked the glove box; the Colt and ammo were still there. It was going to be a long ride again. There were even more barricades than on his last journey. Most were at roadside level, armed, but some were controlled from an eight-metre high platform with menacing machine guns pointing down.

It was around noon when he pulled up at the tiny Marechaussee office in Venlo and he met Sergeant Janus Hinken, importance incarnate. He had a puffed-up chest like a bantam rooster and he walked like one too, lifting his heels much higher than natural. Like so many others, he sported a Clarke Gable moustache that, combined with his flabby chin and the puffy sacs under his eyes, reinforced the rooster image. Mark told him about the German general without a passport.

"I cannot allow anyone to enter this country without a valid passport," he clucked.

"This is a matter of national importance," Mark assured him, "If you check this morning's dispatch from the Ministry of Defence you will see that your cooperation is sought." This seemed to build-up his ego a bit.

"We have an important post here," Hinken puffed. He walked over to the large map on the wall. "We provide border services for the Venlo area," he said, tapping his finger forcefully on the location on his map. "We staff the border post at the Heronderberg Road." He tapped the spot again to ensure it had not gone away. "We have two men in three shifts of eight hours each plus two shifts of dog patrols patrolling the area at night."

"I can take you into confidence," Mark said. "The day after tomorrow British officials will meet with German counterparts to discuss proposals for peace at the Café Backus. A party of two, possibly three German officials, need to cross the border between three or four in the afternoon. They may not have the required passports since they will be here in an unofficial capacity. We need you to accommodate this meeting by allowing the entry of this party into Nederland for a two-hour period."

"That is impossible." Hinken said as he strutted up and down in his tiny cubicle. "The border can not be opened for unofficial entry."

"It is in the interest of the country," Mark said showing his ID badge. "You can phone Evert Bracken the Minister of Defence directly." Hinken stared at the identity card and considered the pitfalls of insubordination.

Hinken hastily shifted objections. "You can't trust the Backus family," he confided. "They are Nazi sympathizers."

"We have no choice, it's either that or it's off," Mark asserted. "I am going to check out the café. I'll be back."

It was a pretty drive from Venlo to the border – a winding, narrow road through tall pines. When he passed the sign, *'Douane 100 metres'*, he saw the café on his left. Nothing could have looked more peaceful: a red brick building, with a roofed balcony around the front and sides. Behind the café, he could see a large garden with swings and seesaws. The black and white painted barrier across the road was perhaps 50 metres away. A lone German sentry stood; his rifle slung across his shoulder.

Inside, the place looked very much like the typical Dutch café. A large bar – where beer was on tap and coffee was brewed – dominated the back wall. A number of circular tables, covered with white tablecloths were set, ready for the early dinner crowd. It looked just fine for a meeting place.

He returned to the Marechaussee office where Sergeant Hinken had convinced himself that all was well and promised that there would be no difficulty in admitting the 'paperless' General. It was all Mark could do for the day. The drive back to The Hague in the luxurious Lincoln was certainly no hardship for a 20-year old.

It was going to be a long day. He found the Lincoln at the back of the CID garage and checked the trunk to see if the transmitter, promised to Schellenberg, was there. He opened the glove box and checked the Colt automatic. Pressing the thumb release, he drew the magazine out of the handle. He loaded seven bullets into the magazine, pushing them one by one against the spring, then slipped the magazine back into the handle until he felt it lock. He chambered a round.

Sangster and Best waited outside the Panorama Hotel. They weren't pleased with adding 60 kilometres to the trip to detour via Amsterdam in order to collect Dr. Franz at St. Pancras Hospital.

Amsterdam was heavily barricaded and it was slow going. It was after nine when he parked in front of the hospital. He told the Brits to wait for him. The young receptionist plugged in the cord on her console and cranked the handle. Mark quickly put his hand over hers, smiled and said, "I am not a patient, I am his nephew. I haven't seen him for months. I only have half an hour. I would like to surprise him. Can I?" She smiled. "Sure, go ahead. His office is room 310, on the third floor."

Dr. Franz was surprised as Mark burst in without knocking.

"Agent Formby," he said in English, "I informed you that I do not wish to be further involved."

"Sorry Doctor, but General van Zandt requests that you come with us to meet with Schellenberg this afternoon."

"Even if I wanted to come, I couldn't. I have a lecture this afternoon."

"Dr. Franz, I regret this but please come with me now." Franz wanted to argue more but he saw the Colt peering out from under Mark's coat.

"You are forcing me?" he asked plaintively.

"Yes, definitely, I must. Take your coat and hat and let's go."

They passed the receptionist, who waved and smiled.

Sangster recognized the gun-in-the-back scenario. He opened the door and pushed Franz inside. Franz banged his head against the door panel, "Sorry," Sangster said and plopped in beside him.

Franz rubbed his head and demanded to know why he was being kidnapped. "I am a sick man. My gallstones...please let me go."

"Can't do that," Sangster apologized insincerely, "You arranged the party." Franz sighed and appeared to resign himself to his fate.

Peter Best suggested that they have lunch at the foot of the bridge at Arnhem, debating whether it was wise to stop with Franz as a quasi prisoner. In spite of his gallstones, Franz said he was looking forward to lunch and would not make any trouble. Mark reminded him of the Colt's vicinity but Franz appeared more interested in eating than escaping. When lunch arrived, he partook with gusto.

After lunch, they headed south toward the province of Limburg. In spite of the barricades, they made Venlo by three o'clock. They checked in with Sergeant Hinken who had begun to see his role in a new and glorious light. He assured Mark there would be no problem for the 'negotiators'.

Dr. Franz became jittery as they approached the black and white painted barrier on the German side. It was still down, no sentry in sight. Things were eerily silent. Mark parked the Lincoln in the gravel driveway next to the Café Backus. Sangster and Best were on edge; a 30-second walk and they'd be in enemy territory.

"It's not that I distrust Schellenberg," Sangster said, "But it is possible that the Gestapo might have caught on to him. They might bust across the border to catch him meeting with us." They walked around the corner onto the road. Schellenberg, dressed in civilian clothes, stepped from inside the café onto the road, gesturing them to come in. Franz was shaking in fear but Mark pushed him forward.

The dining room was empty. Hein Backus bowed when they came in. He was clad in a white shirt with bow tie, black pants and a stained apron tied around his waist. He led them to a small alcove Schellenberg had arranged. The German officer apologized for General Semmel's absence; he had been held up at the last minute.

"Is it possible for us to meet again tomorrow afternoon?" Schellenberg asked. "The general is anxious to meet because he wants to entrust some secret papers to you for safekeeping. Should the putsch fail, he does not want to lose the record of his work. Also, there are certain issues which he can only discuss face to face."

With a frustrated sigh, Sangster agreed to one more try to meet the elusive General Semmel. Neither he nor Best liked the idea of coming here again. Schellenberg offered beer before they adjourned. Sangster declined. The weather had turned dull and the afternoon light was waning. It was a long way home and they were much too close to Germany.

Mark realized the transmitter was still in the car. He signalled Sangster who picked up on it.

"One more thing Captain Schellenberg, we have the radio transmitter for you to stay in touch with MI-6. It is in the boot of our car. Perhaps you could take it so we need not bring it back tomorrow." Schellenberg looked perplexed. He appeared to have forgotten about it.

"Will you have trouble bringing it across the border?" Best asked.

"No, they will not challenge me."

They agreed to meet at gain at 16:00 hours the next day. Mark moved the transmitter to the Daimler parked on the German side of the café. After shaking hands, Schellenberg got in and drove toward the barrier. It lifted immediately and he raced through unchecked.

Mark shoved Franz into the car while Sangster stood in the middle of the road, swearing loudly. "We are being played for fools. He even forgot about the fucking transmitter. I think we should pack it in."

"Come on, Jeffrey," Best said, "We are so close. If it doesn't work out tomorrow we could leave then." Sangster stomped his feet in anger. "I am not taking that long drive back to The Hague only to do it again tomorrow. There must be a decent hotel in Venlo. Let's stay overnight." Franz protested by knocking loudly on the car window. They ignored him.

The Hotel Wilhelmina was a small country hotel. Over the years, sections had been added, walls knocked out and rooms brought up to the modern standard of the 1930s. A wizened concierge, not a day over 75, announced that he had two rooms on the third floor and two on the second. The Brits opted for the second floor thereby consigning Mark to be a neighbour to the ever-complaining Dr. Franz who had suddenly re-discovered his gallstones.

The old Cerberus fumbled with the guest book and issued their keys, each attached to a huge wooden ball that no pocket could accommodate. After a plain dinner, the Brits opted for Scotch in the bar, Mark for Chocomel and Franz for prayer in his room.

They all slept by eleven.

14

1939
WEDNESDAY, NOVEMBER 8, 23:30 HRS
REICHSKANZLEREI, UNTER DEN LINDEN
BERLIN, GERMANY

As the negotiators in Venlo slept, Reichsfuehrer Heinrich Himmler ordered a complete news blackout as soon as he learned of the assassination attempt on Adolf Hitler. Georg Elser, a German citizen had placed a bomb behind the podium at the *Bürgerbräukeller* in Munich – the famous beer hall where Hitler's political career had started in 1923.

Hitler began his speech punctually at nine o'clock and was expected to finish about 90 minutes later. His usual spirit was not there and he ended early. When he was on his way back to Berlin, the bomb exploded, killing seven and injuring 60.

Himmler ordered air traffic control to keep the news from the Fuehrer. He feared an irrational action by the Leader. The Gestapo's chief officer at Berlin's Tempelhof Airport informed him that the aircraft carrying the Fuehrer had arrived and that the Leader was on his way to the Reichskanzlerei, Hitler's office.

Heinrich Himmler, Reichsfuehrer of the SS, was waiting impatiently.

Hitler knew something was afoot when he saw Himmler pacing in front of the door to his office. He dismissed his entourage and invited him to enter. He hadn't even shed his topcoat before he demanded to know the problem. Himmler tersely described the situation.

Hitler exploded in a furious rage. "We must find the foreign bastard who did this," he screamed tossing his hat across the room. "Jew, pig, gypsy, doesn't matter. Find the mongrel and we'll hang him."

Himmler always saved a bit of good news in his dealings with Hitler, a balm to cool him down. "I have good news, my Fuehrer. The Gestapo has arrested a man trying to cross into Switzerland at Konstanz. He was interrogated. He carried a postcard of the Bürgerbräukeller and has confessed to placing the bomb. His name is Georg Elser, a young cabinet maker from Saarbrücken."

"A German? An Aryan of pure Germanic blood?" screamed Hitler.

"Yes, my Fuehrer."

"That cannot be true," he yelled. "It's a lie. It's a plot by the international Jewry. Hunt for the real assassin. Our enemies would take great comfort from the fact that a German citizen tried to kill his Leader. We must not allow them to tell lies. Find the real bomber and be quick."

Himmler understood his Leader's fear. He had to find a likely perpetrator. The suspect had to be an enemy of Germany.

It was now past midnight. He called Admiral Canaris at home. He explained the attempt at Hitler's life and the need for a quick arrest that would be acceptable to the Leader and believable to the world. "You always have a list of suspects, Admiral. Who could have committed this crime?"

"If we are fabricating a story I have a choice of many," Canaris said.

"We are not fabricating," Himmler yelled. "We must have an acceptable truth."

"I understand the difference," Canaris said but the irony was lost on Himmler. "We have an operation in progress to infiltrate MI-6 but it is far too valuable an asset to break up to find a phony killer. We are close to reeling in the British tomorrow at the Dutch border. We must complete this initiative."

"When is the next meeting?"

"Tomorrow afternoon at 16:00 hours at the border at Venlo."

"Bring them into Germany. These are our murderers. Kidnap them. We'll have a trial. They conspired with agents inside Germany to plant a bomb that nearly killed our beloved Fuehrer."

"My dear Reichsfuehrer that would represent a great blow to the Abwehr's espionage—"

"Herr Admiral," Himmler yelled pompously, "Fuehrer's orders."

Canaris, wide-awake now, phoned Abwehr headquarters and ordered Hauptman Schellenberg to be located and told to report to the Admiral at home. *Schnell*!

15

1939
THURSDAY, NOVEMBER 9, 6:00 AM
WILHELMINA HOTEL, THORBECKESTRAAT
VENLO, NEDERLAND

The lumpy mattress had not given Mark a good night's rest. He grudgingly slipped into yesterday's clothes. He pounded on Franz's door but it was unlocked. The man sat fully dressed on the room's single chair reading the hotel bible. His eyes were red-rimmed. The hands that held the bible trembled. It appeared he had slept on top of the bedclothes, fully dressed.

Mark led Franz down to the breakfast area where Best and Sangster were arguing with the waiter that kippers and sausages were part of any civilized breakfast. The waiter offered boiled eggs and cheese. Sangster asked, "Bloody cheese again?" The waiter pointed at the jar of raspberry jam on the table. Sangster shoved it away as if it offended him.

Franz sat quietly. During a lull in the conversation, he resumed his plea to be excused from the meeting.

The Brits went to find a local barber for a shave. They agreed to meet at three o'clock. Mark decided to take Franz to visit the office of the Marechaussee to ask for additional police coverage.

Janus Hinken was surprised to see him. He had assumed that the meeting was over and done with the day before. Mark explained the delay and confessed his frustration.

"What time is your meeting now?" Hinken asked.

"At four o'clock. Could you provide us with back up? They should stay out of view but come to our assistance if something goes wrong."

"I can let you have two of my mobile patrol men." Hinken was really into it now. After phoning several locations where the patrol might pass, he found them and ordered them to climb on their bicycles and pedal their way to the Café Backus, eight kilometres away.

It was a dull afternoon and much colder than of late; the sky was overcast and rain threatened. After picking up Best and Sangster at the hotel, Mark drove the Lincoln to the rendezvous. Military precautions had intensified and they were stopped twice at roadblocks. The first sentry said his orders were to allow no cars to pass.

Mark showed his CID card but the sentry insisted that he first had to speak to the sergeant in charge. Secretly Mark hoped that the message would be that the team could go no farther but after a few minutes, the sentry returned. "Everything's all right."

A bit farther on, the second sentry did not stop them, but made signs to slow down. He stood at the bend in the road just before the straight stretch that provided a clear view of the border. Somehow, things looked different from the day before. The black and white barrier on the German side that had been down yesterday was upright today. Nothing stood between them and Germany. His feeling of imminent danger was intense, yet the scene was peaceful enough. An unarmed German customs officer lolled in front of the gatehouse and a little girl played ball with a black dog in the middle of the road in front of the café.

He let the car drift slowly in front of the café and then backed into the gravel car park on the Dutch side. Schellenberg stood on the balcony with a brandy snifter in his hand and made a sign that Mark interpreted to mean that General Semmel was inside. He turned off the ignition and watched Peter Best get out.

Mark got out from behind the wheel and followed him. Suddenly shouting and shooting erupted from the German line. An open Mercedes convertible roared across the border. The car was filled with rough-looking characters. Two men stood on the running boards and fired sub-machine guns in the air. Others stood up in the car, shouting and waving pistols. Four men jumped off before the car had stopped behind the Lincoln. They rushed forward shouting, "Hands up!" They were SD men. Mark recognized their leader. It was Knaust, the ugly one from the Zutphen encounter. He reached back into the car and retrieved the Colt from the glove box. It seemed to take forever. Franz was cowering in the back seat, babbling in German.

By this time, Sangster had rolled out of the back door and was emptying his revolver at the posse of SD goons. Peter Best stood mesmerized and whispered to Sangster, "Our number is up, Jeffrey."

One of the thugs tossed Best into the convertible as if he were a bale of hay. Mark fired at the Mercedes. The fold-down windshield shattered. He felt movement behind him. Franz crept out of the open door and ran toward the Mercedes in a zigzag pattern yelling, "*Ich bin Ihr Freund, Ich bin Ihr Freund*, I am your friend."

He looked graceful with both arms outstretched – almost like ballet. Mark realized the betrayal. Franz was a German agent. Franz had set them up. Mark fired in anger. After a few stumbling steps, Franz collapsed into a dark heap of clothes on the grass along the road. One of the SD men scooped him up and carried him to the car. Sangster, now with a German gun to his head, was hauled into the Mercedes. It seemed that the firefight lasted a long time but it had been no more than 90 seconds.

Schellenberg had watched the kidnapping from the veranda. Knaust ran to Schellenberg's Daimler parked on the German side of the café. Mark ran around the back of the building, determined to stop Schellenberg. As he rounded the corner, he bumped into Knaust's Luger pointed directly at his chest. Mark's right arm, holding the Colt, was down.

The blast deafened him. Knaust collapsed, the gun falling from his hand as he dropped. Mark stood frozen. It was not possible. He looked around. Rising from the bushes behind the building was Dirk Vreelink. At that moment, Schellenberg erupted from the building and ran for the Daimler. Mark fired. The rear window shattered but Schellenberg managed to start the car and tore away, spitting gravel. He was across the border in less than ten seconds. The barrier slammed down behind him. Franz – dead or alive – and the Brits were in Nazi Germany. Knaust lay dead in the roadway. Mark was the only one standing. Vreelink, sniper rifle in hand, put an arm around his shoulder.

Just then, the Marechaussee backup contingent came down the stretch, furiously pedalling their bicycles.

H alt. Stop. Police!" Sergeant Hinken's backup shouted as they dropped their bicycles in the middle of the road and ran toward the body of Knaust who appeared quite dead. The senior cop was a corpulent man in his fifties. Still panting from his strenuous bike ride, he bent down to check for a pulse. Finding none, he looked at Vreelink who stood with his rifle in hand. Mark stared at the Colt in his hand.

The younger one looked at the body. "We heard the shooting, I guess we're too late," he said. He was about the same age as Mark and was almost apologetic in his approach to an armed man he didn't know. Turning to Vreelink he said, "Sir, who are you?"

"It's a long story," Vreelink said. He showed his CID identification and handed his rifle to the senior police officer for inspection. "I am agent Zonder's back-up."

The older of the two policemen seemed mollified, took the ankle clip off his pants and introduced himself. "I am Corporal Dool and this is Corporal Linden. Sergeant Hinken sent us here, but we didn't expect a shooting," he said with a tone of exasperation. He beckoned to Mark. "Please let me have your gun!" Mark handed it over but not before Vreelink nodded an okay.

"Can either of you identify the victim?" Corporal Dool inquired in an official voice.

"He's a German," Mark said. "He was the leader of a raiding party that crossed the border to kidnap those British officers."

"Do you know him?"

"I saw him at an earlier meeting last month," Mark said, "At that time he was called Knaust or perhaps Knost. I think he is with the SD."

Dool undid the button on his tunic and produced a small note pad and a stubby pencil. He put the pencil to his lips and licked the lead end before writing Knaust or Knost.

"I must ask you to come inside the café with me. Corporal Linden will call for an ambulance to take the body to the morgue."

Mark spoke quickly, "Please, make no arrangements of any kind. This is a CID operation and it takes precedence over local action. This incident may have international complications. It is not an ordinary police matter. Therefore, the body must remain at this site."

Mark noticed that the little girl, still clutching her ball, was watching them from behind a tree. Two residents from the house across the street watched from behind a tall boxwood hedge. Hein Backus and his waiter stood behind the picture window. Witnesses.

"I'll go and interview the witnesses and take their statements," Corporal Linden volunteered.

"I wouldn't do that either," Vreelink said. "Their statements may not agree with the official version." Dool glanced at him in amazement.

"How can they be different?" he asked.

Vreelink spoke up forcefully, "What we have here is an international incident that is way beyond us. It will be headline news around the world. Our government must be allowed to present the incident from a national perspective. Neither CID nor the Marechaussee should interfere with the official message."

Young Corporal Linden was a practical lad, "We cannot let the body lie in the street until the politicians make up their mind."

Mark was slow in regaining control. "Of course we can't, but we can secure the premises. The border is officially closed. The Marechaussee must block access to the café. Tell the owner no patrons tonight and no talking. Mention national security."

Corporal Linden suggested that the body be stored out of sight. He and Vreelink took the body by the legs and arms and carried it behind the Café. Mark suddenly felt more confident in leading the chaotic scene. This, in spite of the fact that he had lost his British charges, possibly killed a traitor and gained a corpse that was in the wrong country.

Corporal Dool was about to draw chalk lines where Knaust had fallen.

"Don't do that," Mark yelled, "Just make a sketch." Dool looked incredulous but stuck the piece of chalk back in his pocket.

Corporal Linden returned from his undertaker's function.

"Where did you put the body?" Mark asked.

"In the tool shed," he answered matter-of-factly. It was probably the first time he had to drag a corpse but he portrayed it as a prosaic event.

Inside the café, Vreelink argued with old man Backus who protested the closing of his establishment.

"You are on the record as pro Nazi," Vreelink said, "Do you really want to make it worse and have this place closed up for good?" Mr. Backus retreated, cursing under his breath.

"And bring us a couple of your watery beers!" Vreelink yelled after him. Backus looked back and sneered. Mark joined him at the table.

"What the hell actually happened here today?" Vreelink asked.

"I think van Zandt and MI-6 were set up by Franz."

"For God's sake, why?"

"I don't know but both CID and MI-6 believed the negotiations were for real. Sangster and Best certainly thought so. They had been working on it for a long time. What I don't understand is, if they wanted to grab the

Brits, why didn't they do it yesterday? Why take a chance that they would give up and go home?"

Vreelink put his fingers to his lips as Backus approached, put their beers down without a word and withdrew quickly. After a few sips, Mark asked the question although he knew the answer, "Who sent you?"

"Van Zandt said to keep an eye on you. He told me not to show myself. If everything worked out fine, I was to leave without you ever knowing I was here."

Corporal Dool interrupted them and said he was ready to phone in his report. Mark jumped up. "Not until I have made my report." He was surprised at the older man's deference to his commanding tone.

Backus showed him the solid oak telephone booth in the hall. The phone's main body was fastened to the wall. On one side was a little crank to raise the operator; on the other side hung an earpiece with a cord. It was well after five. He hoped van Zandt was home. Since CID had disclaimed any involvement with the British operation, he didn't want to contact him at the office. He lifted the earpiece, cranked the handle and instructed the operator to connect him to van Zandt's home in Wassenaar.

It took five rings before the maid answered. The General was not in but was expected within the hour. Mark stressed the urgency of the call and left the phone number of the Café Backus.

His confidence waned. The Marechaussee corporals would insist on writing their official reports. He didn't know how to delay them. He couldn't allow them to proceed. A truthful account would prove embarrassing. It might affect the reputation of the General who would be crucified by the neutral-leaning press. Mark decided to level with the national police officers.

Corporal Dool, proving to be an understanding and pragmatic policeman, said, "Our superiors must be involved in the way the story unfolds. If we cook up a story by ourselves we'll be accused of obstructing the course of justice."

"But we can recommend a certain action," Mark said, happy, that the older cop had decided to play along.

"Our common problem is the body of this Knaust fellow," Dool said, "We cannot explain him away."

"I have an idea that might work," Mark said, "The Germans will never claim his body; asking for it would admit their guilt. We could repatriate Knaust without the Germans' knowledge."

"How?" Vreelink and Dool asked simultaneously.

"We take him across the border through the forest. I'm sure Corporal Dool could help us with directions."

Dool said nothing but stared at Mark's untouched beer. Mark shoved the beer toward him with a wink. Dool took a hefty swig and sighed.

Hein Backus announced a phone call for Mark. It was Kirsten van Zandt. Vreelink put his head next to Mark and shared the earpiece.

"Mark, my dear," she cooed, "Maid told me you left a number but van Zandt is at the home of Evert Bracken, the Minister of Defence. I have the number if you think it's important." He wrote down the number and clicked the phone hook a few times to alert the operator.

"Operator, would you please..."

"I have the number, Sir, I'll put your call through." So much for the security of phone calls.

"What have you got for me?" van Zandt barked. Mark quickly filled him in on what had happened.

"Damn it, Mark, we lost the MI-6 men, Franz is gone and hopefully dead... and we have a German stiff. And your proposed story is that CID had nothing to do with it? We need a plausible story."

"Sir, Vreelink and I recommend that we return Knaust's body to Germany. If it is ever found, they cannot connect his death to CID. We can say that the British agents acted on their own, only to be kidnapped by Germans, which would make Nederland the aggrieved party. We can't be accused of violating our neutrality." Mark said.

"You sound like a politician, Zonder. I will speak to the Minister. Make sure that German gets back to his homeland. Tonight."

When he returned to the table, Dool announced that he and Linden would return to Venlo but not before Mr. Backus had served them their regular free 'after-shift' coffee.

Corporal Linden handed Mark his Colt. Dool insisted on keeping Dirk's rifle that he strapped across his chest, guerrilla fashion. He gave the signal to mount the bicycles for the long ride into the pitch-black and windy night. Their hooded headlamps threw only a mere sliver of pale light onto the narrow road.

Mark got the map out of the Lincoln and found that a few kilometres south of their position was the Heronderberg, a steep, densely forested mound that straddled the border. There was no road, only a centuries-old smugglers' path that provided a difficult route to Nazi Germany.

"I've got an idea for transporting the body," Vreelink grinned. He took Mark by the elbow and led him to the tool shed. "Voila!" he said, pointing to a big wheelbarrow.

"That'll do," Mark agreed. Once in the wheelbarrow, Knaust looked very much like a drunk being toted home to his wife.

When he took the map from the Lincoln, he had also retrieved his army-issued emergency flashlight that soldiers knew as the 'squeeze-cat'. When the handle was squeezed in a continuous motion, it would produce a beam of light. The noisy thing sounded indeed like a cat in heat. They set out on the road to Venlo, Mark with the shovel in one hand and the cat in the other, while Vreelink pushed Knaust on his homeward journey.

Mark noted that Corporal Linden had done a good job of covering the blood with soil from the side of the road. Dool had shown them where the path began. The two houses they passed were already in full blackout.

Mark walked ahead of Vreelink as they entered a well-trodden path. Vreelink cursed quietly as he tried to keep the wheelbarrow from tipping.

The path ran parallel to the border that, at any point, was no more than a few hundred metres away. Deep into the dense forest, they could barely see. A fork in the road called for a decision. Mark squeezed his flashlight. The sound of the grinding dynamo rasped through the night.

"Well, if they can't see your fucking light, they can damn well hear it," Vreelink whispered, "Muffle it with your jacket." The sound was still too loud. The glimpse of light showed that the east fork in the road was a dead end. Vreelink was becoming edgy; keeping Knaust erect on his wobbly ride took a lot of energy.

Mark was also getting nervous. "We've been gone 20 minutes; I think we should turn toward Germany now."

"No, Dool said this path leads to the border, we should just follow it."

"Yes, but both the German and the Dutch patrols know it too and we don't want to meet either of them."

"Just keep going, Mark. Pretend you are a Boy Scout," Vreelink gasped between breaths. The terrain was rising. The incline was taking its toll. Vreelink put the wheelbarrow down. "I need a rest." Knaust leaned to the side but held on.

They heard voices. Low voices. They couldn't make out any words. Mark drew his Colt. Vreelink wagged his index finger 'No!' They stood stock-still. The voice came from low to the ground as if the man was crawling toward them. Suddenly, a wild boar sniffed and put his forelegs on the wheelbarrow. He sniffed at Knaust and disappeared. Vreelink sniffed deeply and said, "He doesn't like Germans either."

After ten minutes, they came upon a clearing. A ten-metre wide strip of cleared forest crossed their path. Mark assumed it was the no-man's land zone. Vreelink rested the wheelbarrow.

"This isn't fair you know," he whispered. "I am 30 years old and you are 20. How come I have to do all the heavy work?"

"Because you were sent to help me and then you shot him."

Vreelink muttered something and added, "If we are near the border, there should be markers. They stand a hundred metres apart."

"You mean this?" Mark asked, stumbling over a half-a-metre high concrete post. He squeezed the cat and spotted the logo of the standing lion with raised foreleg, the word 'Nederland' underneath.

"Okay, how far into Germany should we go to bury this specimen of pure Aryan manhood?" Vreelink asked.

"Not here, too many patrols pass here every day." Mark walked across the clearing and whispered, "The path continues a bit further down."

They walked another half a kilometre up the hill when Vreelink noted a small trail leading south. "Let's go in here and count the steps as we go. Look for any kind of marker so we can find our way back." He turned the wheelbarrow into the trail that was no more than a rut. It immediately tipped over to the side. Knaust thudded to the mossy ground.

"I guess he's happy he's home," Vreelink said. "We can't get the wheelbarrow through here. I guess it's your turn to demonstrate the fireman's hold." Mark didn't really care for carrying a corpse in the dark but followed Vreelink, who cleared the way ahead as much as possible.

Without warning, Vreelink suddenly hissed 'stop'. He pointed down. As Mark dumped Knaust on the ground, Vreelink started to dig. When Vreelink declared it a proper grave, they lowered Knaust into position, covered him up, stomped the earth down, and covered the grave with moss and leaves.

"Shall we leave the wheelbarrow as a gift to Germany?" Mark asked. "Guess not," he corrected himself.

Mark led the way back, shovel on his shoulder with Vreelink handling the wheelbarrow. The descent was a lot easier. The faint sound of barking dogs caused them to stop suddenly.

"We should have dumped the damn wheelbarrow," Mark hissed and they began to run.

When they arrived at the no-man's-land zone, Vreelink had changed positions. Instead of pushing the wheelbarrow, he was pulling it behind him. He ran with trotting short steps in order to avoid hitting his heels on the carriage. The barking sounds came nearer. Both men crouched down to have a look before they crossed the open space.

"The dogs are about 200 metres to our right," Vreelink whispered. "I hear voices, too." Both listened intently. Two men were talking. It was neither Dutch nor German, something halfway, perhaps. They were in Limburg, a province of Nederland, as well as the name of the adjoining region in Germany. The men were speaking in the dialect common to both sides of the border. The question was, were they Dutch or German locals?

Vreelink whispered, "We are downwind from them. Our voices carry but our scent does not. Let's wait it out."

Mark heard the men say *'Gut nicht'*, good night, but that could be German or Dutch or Scottish for that matter. The dogs yelped as their masters separated. One team went north; the other came toward them. Still they waited, lest the dogs detect them.

Mark decided to cross the strip. Vreelink followed, the wheelbarrow bouncing behind him. As luck would have it, the clouds parted and the moon lit up the landscape. After having been in utter darkness that long it looked like a giant spotlight to them. The dogs spotted their quarry. The handler must have released them for they came tearing down the no-man's-land strip and turned into the smuggler's path. They cornered Vreelink. They snarled around and leaped at him. He put his wheelbarrow down and froze. He knew that continuing to run would cost him an arm and a leg, literally. Mark raised the shovel above his head to smash down the skull of one of the dogs.

"Don't do that," a familiar voice called, "Sergeant Hinken from the Venlo Marechaussee. Don't move. I'll call them off." He called the dogs back and put them on their leash but they kept on barking.

"I see you gentlemen were trying to cross the border. Corporal Dool told me about your scheme. I just spoke with the German customs officer. I told him that Dutch smugglers were doing a run about two kilometres north of here. He took off immediately. He's a good man. We've known each other for years. Anyway, I am happy to have prevented you from crossing the border. It would have been very wrong."

"But we did—" Mark managed to say before Vreelink jumped in with "Thank you, Sergeant."

Hinken guided the CID men back to the Café. "I suggest you put the wheelbarrow and shovel back where you found it. No need to give Hein Backus any ideas." He looked at his watch, "It's about eight o'clock. I think we should stop in and get Backus to fix us something to eat. It's a long drive for you back to The Hague."

They found Backus and his wife in their living room at the back of the restaurant. The owner was a lot more cooperative than before. The shooting and kidnapping must have had a sobering effect. He was almost subservient when he left to fry up a batch of eggs on black bread, a popular late snack in Limburg.

Curfew time for all highway traffic was nine o'clock. In spite of the light rain, it could have been an easy ride to The Hague. Except for the blackout, the absence of directional signs and those damned barricades.

They were too animated to settle into a relaxed driving mode. They rehashed the events of the day. Mark marvelled that Dirk saved him a split second before Knaust would have killed him. Having been so close to death, he would live life differently from now on he vowed to himself.

He dropped Dirk off at the Morspoort barracks in Leiden and drove the few hundred metres to glance at the house of his parents. He slowed down to look at the second-floor window where Jenny would be asleep. He wanted to talk to her and hold her but stepped on the accelerator and drove back through the rainy, darkened streets.

16

1939
FRIDAY, NOVEMBER 10, 10:30 HRS
REICHSKANZLEREI, UNTER DEN LINDEN
BERLIN, GERMANY

Dr. Joseph Goebbels, Reichsminister of Propaganda was not in his office when Heinrich Himmler and Wilhelm Canaris showed up for their appointment.

He had summoned them to report on the hunt for the perpetrators. He was late because Hitler had called him in and subjected him to one of his rages. Goebbels reminded Hitler again that Georg Elser, a German from the area of Alsace Lorraine had confessed to placing the bomb at the Munich beer hall. Hitler demanded that the man be sent to a camp and denied any contact with outsiders.

Goebbels explained that news of the bomb attack couldn't be suppressed; too many had been killed or wounded. He assured Hitler that everything would be taken care of. As Minister of Propaganda, it was his task to spin any issue for the benefit of the Nazi regime.

"There will be no further investigation of this man and no trial," screamed Hitler. Goebbels understood.

Goebbels' usual foul mood had upgraded to a tempest by the time he returned to his office and found Himmler and Canaris waiting for him. He resented being dressed down by Hitler and disapproved of his direction to make Georg Elser, the real perpetrator, disappear.

Himmler and Canaris had already discussed their proposal in advance.

"You are familiar with the situation," Goebbels began, "So let us not waste time. What is your suggested solution?"

Himmler spoke first. "The SD has captured two British agents as they tried to infiltrate Germany from Nederland. They were sent by MI-6 to exploit the chaos in Germany after the assassination attempt on our beloved Fuehrer. Another agent, now in custody, planted the bomb."

Himmler continued, "Admiral Canaris and I recommend that your office should announce that the Dutch government was complicit in the bomb attack on the Fuehrer by allowing two British agents to enter into Germany. These two agents conspired to set a bomb that failed to fell our glorious leader."

Reichsfuehrer Himmler sat down with a smug smile on his face.

Canaris interrupted, "You will recall Herr Reichsminister that as far back as 1937, our agents reported sighting British destroyers in the harbour at Rotterdam, proof that England and Nederland have stood united against Germany for some time.

Admiral Canaris added, "These agents have admitted to the purpose of their mission and the criminal assistance lent by the Dutch government. They will be detained in the re-education facility in Dachau. Foreign affairs Minister von Ribbentrop has agreed to issue a strong warning to the Dutch that their neutrality has been exposed as a fraud and that Germany will take appropriate steps to secure its border from any further Anglo/Dutch aggression."

Goebbels looked pleased. "The Fuehrer will like it. Are you sure there are no traces left in Nederland of our interference in this matter?" Himmler looked uncomfortable.

"We are clean, except for one missing SD man named Knaust, Herr Reichsminister. We cannot ask the Dutch to return him. That would be an admission that arrests were made inside the Dutch border."

"Retrieve the body. It's our weak point," Goebbels said.

Himmler rose and clicked his heels. "Herr Reichsminister, both Admiral Canaris and I are honoured that you have accepted our proposal. I shall provide a solution to the Captain Knaust problem."

Goebbels rose. "The Reich owes both of you its gratitude for the speedy apprehension of the cowards who attempted to slay our beloved Leader. The Dutch will pay for their treacherous behaviour. Heil, Hitler."

Himmler and Canaris raised their arms in salute and walked out in silence. They parted in the hallway.

"What of our principled Germany and its noble aspirations?" Canaris sighed. Himmler did not hear him.

17

1939
SATURDAY, NOVEMBER 11, 7:00 AM
CID BARRACKS
THE HAGUE, NEDERLAND

Mark slept fitfully until the knocking started. He pulled the blankets over his head and sank deeper into the old mattress provided courtesy of the Army. Yet, he was lucky. His status as an aide to General van Zandt allowed him to have a cubicle to himself instead of being bunked in with other soldiers.

The knocking didn't stop. Mark sat up, cursing the morning. The chill when his bare feet hit the ice-cold floor made him shiver. Still wrapped in his blanket, he answered the door. A young conscript in an ill-fitting, mothball-scented uniform stared at him apologetically.

"Message from General van Zandt's office, Sir," the young man said, taking the safe route of addressing the blanket-covered, red-eyed heap of humanity as an officer. "He expects you at his home at ten this morning."

He showered and dressed in grey pants, a black turtleneck sweater and a blue blazer. In the canteen, he helped himself to two slices of bread with cheese. He washed it down with a cup of coffee which featured less 'smell-of-scraped-tarmac' than other mornings. At least it was hot. Regular coffee was still available, but rationing kept it to one cup per day. The military saved its ration for officers and allowed its enlisted men two cups of the real stuff on Sunday morning. With a *Verkade* biscuit, yet.

The Motor Pool refused to let him have the Lincoln Zephyr from the night before or any other car. The yellow streetcar brought him to within a five-minute walk of the van Zandt mansion. Kirsten opened the door and was delighted to see him. She hugged him a bit too closely, Mark thought. He bestowed a polite air-kiss, barely touching her cheeks.

"I heard what happened," she whispered. "You must feel awful."

Van Zandt was in his den, surrounded by stacks of newspapers on the floor and on the filing cabinets. He did not look up or even acknowledge

Mark's presence. He absentmindedly reached for the half-eaten cheese and pumpernickel sandwich from the plate on the side table. A banana rested on one of the newspapers spread on his desk. He eventually did look up but only when Kirsten came in with two cups of real coffee.

"I knew Frans couldn't be torn away from reading about international intrigue, so I thought I would just bring you two some coffee," she said.

He finally spoke to Mark. "The Marechaussee briefing says you and Vreelink handled the fiasco as well as you could but there will be some adverse reactions to the incident. Don't let it affect your work."

"I'm fine, Sir." Mark said.

"Well, let's summarize. The German's body is in the *Heimat* – his homeland – and they can't tie his death to us, right?"

"Yes, Sir, but then there is Hein Backus and the other witnesses."

"Mr. Backus will not rat on anybody. We have enough on his smuggling schemes to put him in jail. The neighbours are isolated between our defensive lines and the German border and no reporter will get access to them. The telephone company has cut the line to the Café and St. Pancras hospital has received a telegram that Dr. Franz has decided to visit an ailing relative in Germany."

Mark asked, "Should we be concerned with what the Germans say about the incident?"

"No need to buy a German paper, you can read the propaganda in our own Nazi rag, *Volk en Vaderland,* published here in The Hague." Van Zandt tossed the paper with its screaming headline towards Mark.

> **NEDERLAND ACCUSED IN FOILED ATTACK ON ADOLF HITLER**
>
> *(Berlin, DNB November 10, 1939) Foreign Minister von Ribbentrop today announced that the international Jewish terrorist ring that masterminded the unsuccessful bomb attack on Adolf Hitler has been broken. The Reich's Sicherheitsdienst, in cooperation with the offices of the Abwehr, arrested two British terrorists as they attempted to enter the territory of the Reich at Niederdorf near the Dutch town of Venlo. The pair has confessed to controlling a third agent who planted the bomb in the Bürgerbräukeller in München.*
>
> *It is clear that this vile attack was made possible by the assistance of the Dutch government.*
>
> *A grimfaced von Ribbentrop added, "Our Ambassador in The Hague has handed a formal protest to Prime Minister de Geer in connection with the hostile position of her Majesty's Government towards its peace-loving neighbour. The Fuehrer has spoken of his apprehension that Nederland may be preparing to invite British Armed forces to enter the country and lay siege to our borders. The Reich shall resist any such aggression with overwhelming force."*

Mark was surprised. He expected some fallout but certainly not the threat of an invasion by Germany. Van Zandt meanwhile had dug into the pile of mainstream papers and found the editorial in *De Telegraaf,* the national newspaper published in Amsterdam.

"Here, listen to this," he roared, "These are our supporters."

> *(The Hague, November 10 1939) This newspaper questions the role of the adventurous General van Zandt in yesterday's failed British operation at Venlo. It is difficult to accept that our own CID was unaware of the presence of the British agents on our soil. If they did not know, we must question their competence in protecting our neutrality. If they did know and indeed assisted in the operation, they put our country in great jeopardy as attested by the belligerent tones of foreign Minister von Ribbentrop who all but affirmed that the neutrality of the Kingdom would not be recognized.*
>
> *This newspaper fears that once the German conquest of Poland is complete the Nazi gaze will be focused upon the West.*
>
> *The reckless alliance of British MI-6 and our CID has contributed to bring us closer to that calamitous day. The Prime Minister should demonstrate that his government strongly disapproves of the cowboy mentality of General van Zandt and dismiss him forthwith."*

Van Zandt's face turned crimson. He shoved the banana deeply into his mouth and chomped off a piece, symbolically emasculating his enemies.

"Will your position be threatened by this, Sir?" Mark asked.

"The ostriches in Cabinet have been after my hide for a long time. They didn't succeed in displacing me because of the support from the Palace but now the appeasers have the sword to slay me with."

"Will Vreelink and I be implicated in this, General?" Mark asked.

"No, you won't. You acted under my command. Look, I asked you to come here to tell you that the Prime Minister will announce my dismissal today. Some hope that this will pacify the Nazis but it won't. Their grand design is control all of Europe. Nederland will not be spared. All we can do is be prepared and eliminate any threats from within."

"You mean a threat from the Nazi party, the NSB?"

"Not the party per sé, but the activists within it. We need to know a lot more about their plans to assist a German invasion. How they train, what kind of weapons they have and where they are hidden. Her Majesty has asked me several times to evaluate the pro-German activists in the country. If I am dismissed from CID, the Queen may want me to take a role in that area."

18

1939
MONDAY, NOVEMBER 19, 9:00 AM
CID BARRACKS
THE HAGUE, NEDERLAND

As expected, Prime Minister de Geer announced that Colonel Willem de Bruyne would replace General van Zandt as Head of CID. De Bruyne was an army man, a strict disciplinarian, who had yet to make an appearance at the CID office. The morale at CID was at a low point. After the Venlo incident, Mark's only assignments had been to write summaries of inconsequential events reported by field personnel.

The violence still haunted him. He wished he could talk to his father to hear him say that maiming or killing a human being was not considered an immoral act if it was in the defence of one's country. He wanted to hear Jenny tell him he was a kind and caring man instead of a murderer. In short, he wanted a normal existence, free of this gnawing guilt.

He got up and looked out the window of his tiny office. Raising its pull-down blind, he saw the dreary rain-sodden patch of grass that once was someone's proud garden. Some potted geraniums in the corner had died without anyone caring. He felt trapped in this cubicle with its green wallpaper and its green metal typist desk and a Ministry of Works chair designed to discourage visitors from sitting too long. The one technical upgrade had been the installation of a new telephone. It sat on his desk and had a horn that contained a mouthpiece and a speaker on the other. There was no crank to ring the operator. After lifting the horn off the hook, all he had to do was to give the phone number to the operator. There had been no incoming calls since his return.

He got back to his desk and picked up the daily newspaper that told of the Nazi conquest of Poland and the displacement of thousands of citizens who wanted only a chance at a peaceful life to raise their children.

The loud ring of the telephone startled him. Alice Hegt, van Zandt's secretary from CID asked him to meet van Zandt at an unfamiliar address downtown. He was surprised to hear from his old mentor. He had practically disappeared in the week since his dismissal.

Carel van Bylandlaan 39 looked like a typical Dutch family home. The front windows featured pull-aside lace curtains and a potted geranium in the centre of each windowsill. Neither the façade nor the door had a nameplate. Mark pulled the brass bell-handle on the doorjamb and heard the loud clanging reverberate through the tiled hallway. A motherly woman, answering the door in her best apron told him, "The gentleman is on the first level up."

Alice was ensconced behind her typewriter in what once was the junior bedroom. She seemed to travel wherever van Zandt was posted.

She smiled and waved him into the former master bedroom. Van Zandt sat behind an enormous highly polished rosewood desk. To get that monster up to the second floor must have inflicted a severe hernia on the movers. The glass doors leading to the balcony were wide open causing the floor-length lace curtains to billow in the draft. The November cold chilled the room beyond comfort and van Zandt wore a heavy sweater.

"Why the breeze, General?" Mark asked.

"This place smells like a house. It smells of tea and soup. I want it to smell like action," he sighed, "And don't call me General. I am Mister Frans van Zandt, soon to be Commissioner for Rationing of Coal and Anthracite." Van Zandt giggled while he closed the doors and put the bulging curtains to rest. A new dial telephone sat on the desk. This morning Mark had been delighted with his new telephone but now van Zandt had topped him with the ability to dial a number himself.

"Are you no longer affiliated with the intelligence sector?" Mark wanted to know.

"Officially, no. This is the Head Office of the national coal rationing system. However, since I have little work to do, I may digress into areas that are of special interest to the Palace. We have a budget to assist such projects. The reason you are here is because Colonel De Bruyne has kindly seconded you to the national coal rationing program, reporting to me."

Mark was amazed at the ability of the man to wield power when it had been so publicly taken away from him. "I know nothing about coal?"

"Don't be naïve, young man. You should know by now how the world works. Yes, I am the Commissioner overseeing coal rationing run by an efficient staff somewhere in the bowels of government. It runs by itself. Whenever my rationing duties do not require my close attention, the Palace has directed me – without the knowledge of Cabinet – to assess the danger posed by activists within the Dutch Nazi party. He selected a cigar from its silver container, ceremoniously cut off the tip with a special cutter and went through a well-rehearsed ritual of lighting it. He leaned back in his chair and blew the smoke toward the ceiling.

"Her Majesty is concerned about the activities of a certain Alexander von Becke, a German-born architect and a distant member of her husband's family. He and his wife Paula, a Dutch citizen, live in Oegstgeest. They have a ten year old son named Willem."

"I am assigning you to nose around the NSB ranks via Alexander von Becke. It will be your job to ingratiate yourself with the NSB and get them to take you into their confidence."

"What should I look for?"

"Anything that reeks of assisting Germany in anyway. Are they talking of assisting the Germans in an invasion? Are they preparing for sabotage? What weapons do they possess, if any? Who are their leaders? In short, assess the dangers these people pose."

"How many regions will be covered like that?"

"Twelve in all and you will be pleased to know that Dirk Vreelink will be working with you."

"How can I get close to von Becke without raising his suspicion?"

"That's your job. I am the Commissioner for Rationing Coal and Anthracite."

"Do I have any choice?"

"Of course. I have told you before. You can be transferred to an infantry unit at a moment's notice." He walked to the door and held it open. You will report to me frequently. If I am not here, Alice, my secretary has my complete confidence. When she makes suggestions that sound like orders, she speaks for me."

19

1939
SATURDAY, DECEMBER 2, 11:45 AM
THE VON BECKE RESIDENCE, JULIANALAAN 45
OEGSTGEEST, NEDERLAND

Paula von Becke often thought about the promise that they would raise Willem in keeping with the heritage of the Royal Family. However, she was certain that indoctrinating Willem with the Nazi philosophy was not what the Queen had in mind.

Paula had listened with increasing unease how her husband filled the little boy with tales of an inept political system in Nederland where unemployment, hunger and political strife were the result of the evil influence of Bolsheviks and Jews. Alexander could reach messianic heights with his oratory and she feared Willem could fall under his spell.

Fortunately, the antipathy of neighbours and schoolmates towards the Nazi ideals was having a stronger impact. Even this morning Willem had created a scene, refusing to go to the Saturday meeting of the Jeugdstorm.

"The kids laugh at me in my uniform. Last week a boy threw stones at me," he yelled but Paula persuaded him that he would please his father if he went. He moped for a while in his room but then reluctantly changed into his uniform, ate his lunch in silence, said goodbye to his mother and made his way to the streetcar that took him to downtown Leiden.

The small meeting room at the *Stadsgehoorzaal*, the city's concert hall, was filled with some 30 raucous boys. Precisely at two o'clock, a heavy-set man in a black Nazi uniform complete with NSB armband and polished boots, shouted the command to rise. In military unison, the boys sprang to attention, clicked their heels and raised a stiff right-arm salute: "*Hou zee*," a Dutch version of the Nazi *Sieg Heil* meaning 'Stay the course'.

It was just a few days before the feast of *Sinterklaas*. Myth or history, no one knew for sure, told that a thousand years ago the Bishop of Myra in Turkey began to leave gifts for the poor children on the eve of his birthday on December 6.

Willem's mind wandered. Today would have been a good day for pictures because Sinterklaas was arriving this afternoon by barge at the weekly outdoor market along the Old Rhine River. But he would miss the arrival because he was stuck listening to this fat man. If it were over soon, he could still catch the tail end of the spectacle. The fat man showed some mercy and after more *Hou Zees*, he let the boys go.

Willem made his way to the decorated barge but Sinterklaas had already disembarked. He never noticed the big man in an old overcoat following him. The crowd was still milling about and he could see the good saint on his white steed heading for the Breestraat. He ran through a narrow alley to catch up with the parade. A hand shot out from a recess in an old building and he was dragged into a narrow gate leading into a small, dilapidated outdoor plaza enclosed by brick walls.

"Your name is von Becke, isn't it?" the big man said pinning the boy against the wall, "You're Willem? Right? Your father is with the NSB, isn't he? You and your father are traitors to our country!" He looked menacing. He shook the boy hard against the brick wall.

"Please don't hate me," Willem sobbed. "My father wants a better country. My grandpa doesn't like the uniform and I don't like it either."

Willem was hauled along, tears streaming down his face. A young man coming from the opposite direction accosted the pair.

"What's going on here," he asked the big man.

"None of your damn business."

"Why are you crying, son," the young man asked of Willem.

"This man," he stuttered, "wants to hurt me." Without a word, the man in the overcoat dragged Willem further down the alley.

"Let him go," the young man yelled. When there was no reaction, the young man turned the big man around. "Let him go, I said." The man again pulled at Willem's arm to drag him along.

The young man reached and smashed the big man in the face causing the man to fall face down. He did not stir. Willem cried harder now.

"Now, now, calm down. It's all right. No one is going to hurt you. C'mon, I'll take you home."

The man in the overcoat lifted his head a bit and saw them walk away. Dirk Vreelink was certain that Mark Zonder had taken Willem under his wing and would take him home.

20

1939
MONDAY, DECEMBER 4, 11:00 AM
OFFICE OF THE COMMISSIONER FOR RATIONING OF COAL AND ANTHRACITE
THE HAGUE, NEDERLAND

Alice took his overcoat and new gray fedora and led him to wait in the office of the Commissioner for Rationing of Coal and Anthracite. "Mr. van Zandt is delayed," she said. If Alice would let her hair down, wear a tight-fitting sweater and a form fitting skirt, she would be quite a dish, Mark thought. She was older of course, might even be 28 or so... but those horn-rimmed glasses would have to go, he mused.

Two potted plants on the windowsill had brightened her workroom a bit and the daffodils on the desk looked natural until you touched them.

"Coffee, Mark?" she purred. He had already had his fill of the hot chicory water mixed with powdered milk over breakfast. "Mr. van Zandt has real coffee," she said, sensing his revulsion. Van Zandt seemed to have access to more than just coal. He savoured the smell of the coffee as Alice leaned over just a little too closely to fill his cup. She smelled nice. He could tell by her smile that she knew she had an effect on him.

The sound of van Zandt limping up the hardwood stairs startled him.

Van Zandt huffed and puffed as he handed Alice his hat and coat and sat down behind his rosewood fortress. "That was a pretty cruel way to work yourself into the good graces of the von Beckes," he grumped.

He adjusted his trousers before sitting down. He checked the cuffs of his shirt and fondled his gold cufflinks. "Now then," he said, "I hope you didn't smack Vreelink too hard."

"It was good exercise for him," Mark smiled.

"How did Willem react?"

"He was upset but he calmed down once we were on the streetcar."

"What about the von Beckes?"

"They had called the police when Willem was late. Alexander thanked me profusely but he was very bitter about the hostility towards his son."

"Did you talk about the NSB?"

"They asked about my family and my job. I said I worked at the CID office as a record keeper and that originally I was supposed to become an investigator but that I was dismissed from the program because I spoke favourably about Germany. Alexander seemed to accept that."

"I said that some people blamed the communists and the Jews for the depression. Those two topics were enough to get Alexander to open up. And—" Van Zandt held up his hand to stop him. Mark realized he knew the spiel by heart. He added, "All I had to do was nod in the right places but his wife was annoyed by his diatribe. She took Willem to his room."

"Do you think the von Beckes have hostile intentions?"

"Alexander is mesmerized by Hitler's strong-arm solutions but I don't think he fancies himself as a fighter."

"How are you going to keep up the contact?"

"I will work through Willem to get invited to the house. I'll hint that I would like to attend an NSB meeting."

"Good work, Zonder, keep it up." With that, he got up and held the door open, indicating the interview had ended.

As he approached his parent's home, he wondered if everything would still feel the same. It had been six weeks since he had seen Jenny even though she was living only 25 kilometres from his posting in The Hague. Since then, his life had been one of turmoil and violence. He had joined CID as a naïve idealist and was coming home as a killer, involved in political intrigue.

As he approached, the door opened and – ignoring the misty cold – Jenny loosed herself upon him and covered his face with kisses. Mother Zonder and Sister Jo joined to make a hugging foursome. Major Zonder stepped outside, shook Mark's hand and proudly welcomed his son.

They gathered around the living room table to hear of his exploits. As Mark described it, his experience had been rather boring. He did mention travel to Limburg and how nice the scenery was. Major Zonder knew what had happened there and admired his son's restraint in telling his stories.

After a long dinner and happy talk, Mark's parents and Sister Jo retired for the night and Jenny and Mark found themselves alone.

"We should talk about our plans," Jenny started matter-of-factly. "I came here to be with you but I haven't seen you for weeks. My mother wants me to come back to Groningen. She says there are teaching jobs available."

Mark looked disconsolate. "I think we should just continue to be friends. We are too young to get married and with war threatening, nothing is certain."

"If we are serious friends, we should be engaged," she countered.

"Even if that means we can't get married for a long time, maybe years?"

"Yes, because it would mean that we plan to be married. In two weeks, I am going home for Christmas. Will you come and meet my parents?"

"Okay, I'll ask for a week's leave. I don't think I can get two weeks."

Jenny fell into his arms. "You will like my family. They are anxious to meet you."

"He's late again," Alice said with a sigh of resignation. "You can wait in his office." Mark thought that having more time to think might not so bad. He would have a chance to rehearse his request for a few days' leave for Christmas in Groningen.

Alice brought him a coffee. She could see that he was pre-occupied and her flirting would go unnoticed; she left him alone.

Mark knew his request was unreasonable. With every available civilian in uniform at stage four of the national mobilization, thousands of families would spend Christmas without fathers, son or brothers present.

He snapped out of his thoughts when he heard the sound of awkward steps on the wooden stairs. It meant that van Zandt was working his way up to the office. His limp had gotten worse since his dismissal from CID.

Alice ran through the ritual of storing his hat, coat, scarf, gloves and cane and putting a cup of coffee in front of him. The biscuit sat on the saucer precisely opposite the handle of the cup, placed at the correct angle for a right-hander. Alice was pernickety like that. He sat down, read the single sheet of paper and eyed Mark who now sat opposite him.

"We are in the midst of mobilization," van Zandt said with a hiss of exasperation. "No soldier gets four days' leave to see his girlfriend at the other end of the country." Mark looked down at his shoes.

"Is there any reason why I should agree to this when a hundred thousand men are stuck in their barracks at Christmas?" he blustered.

"My girlfriend wants me to meet her parents," was all the justification he could muster. Van Zandt rose, held the door open, and told him to go back to work.

At his desk, he played with pencils and paperclips wondering how Jenny would take this disappointment. At noon, the phone rang summoning him back into van Zandt's office.

Alice welcomed him with a smile of insincerity. "Must be some girl," she said. Mark had no idea what she meant. Van Zandt looked serious. He had a document in his hand.

"Perhaps this urgent mission will make you understand why we cannot give agents leave whenever their girlfriend insists upon it." He waved the document in the air, "Remember Henk van Weeren?"

"How can I forget," Mark said, upset that the last vestige of hope to see Jenny was disappearing before his eyes.

"I have a report that his father, Thomas is an NSB activist in Groningen, the one city where CID does not have a presence. I need you to go to Groningen and investigate what his gang of misfits is up to."

"Will I be in Groningen over the Christmas holidays, Sir?"

"Yes, you find that a hardship?"

"Not really, Sir. How many days should I plan to be there?"

"Four days seems enough."

"Yes, Sir. Thank you, Sir."

"Remember Zonder, this is not a holiday. Bring me a full report. You must keep up your cover as a Nazi apologist. Do not take anyone into your confidence. Especially not a good friend, if you get my meaning."

21

1939
THURSDAY, DECEMBER 23, 5:00 PM
BOS FAMILY HOME, HUGO DE GROOTSTRAAT 18
GRONINGEN, NEDERLAND

The train ride to Groningen took nearly seven hours. Troop trains had played havoc with the regular schedule. Jenny welcomed him at the station, jubilant that he had been able to get leave. "It's not leave," he told her, "I am here on CID business," but she hadn't heard. She had immediately taken him home to meet her parents.

The Bos family members were faithful adherents to the Netherlands Reformed Church. It demanded a strict lifestyle that left little room for frivolity. Bedtime was at ten o'clock and not a minute later, or earlier for that matter. Neither alcohol nor smoking was tolerated and singing was restricted to the psalms prescribed by the dominee, their local preacher.

Hubert Bos, Jenny's father was a stoic man with a provincial view of life. He had worked at the Post Office ever since his discharge from the army at the end of the Great War in 1918. He hadn't traveled much beyond his part of the country. His accent and that of his wife Martina or 'Marty', was closer to German than to the 'cultured' Dutch heard on the state radio. For the benefit of the elderly and unschooled, the regional radio station repeated the news in *Gronings*, the local dialect.

Mark did not always fully understand the dinner table discussions. Jenny's brother Fred, 17, and sister Tracy, 16, had an even harsher accent – if that was possible. Mother Marty looked upon Mark with somewhat kinder eyes than Hubert, who took the Neanderthal father's view that evil men intent on deflowering his daughter lurked on every corner. Now, one of those debauched, licentious tomcats was sitting at his table.

The regular weekly letters from Jenny had described Mark as the responsible son of an Army Major. To Hubert that was an asset. Twenty years after his stint in the army, Hubert still had a deep, abiding respect for senior officers. However, this lad was 'from away'.

Mark asked himself if Jenny could really be the offspring of this quiet, devout family. She could also speak in that harsh accent but was able to switch to standard Dutch in a flash – a skill that eluded the rest of the family. If she was restrained by religious dogma, he had never noticed it.

His first dinner was a sombre affair that began with Hubert reading selected chapters from the thick leather-bound bible with brass fittings, an heirloom dating back to 1780.

After dinner, the family moved to the living room and gathered around the radio to listen to a serial play. It was an ongoing murder mystery in 12 weekly instalments and the Bos family was not about to miss one. Hubert's angry stare silenced anyone who dared to speak.

When it was bedtime, Mother Marty did not fear any hanky-panky between Jenny and her boyfriend. Apart from the master bedroom, the house had two tiny bedrooms. Jenny and her sister occupied one room, while Mark shared with brother Fred who was a bit of a nuisance because he was convinced that Mark was embroiled in international conspiracies.

The afternoon of Christmas Eve provided an opportunity for them to be alone. Jenny chose to visit Sterrebos Park, a small jewel on the east side of town. The snow-covered conifers transformed the park into a wondrous Christmas card. Mark cleared a bench so they could huddle together.

"You are disappointed with my family?" Jenny began. An elderly woman with a Pekingese dog on a leash looked on disapprovingly as Jenny nestled against him. Mark couldn't help but smile as the dog's belly dragged through the mushy snow. The animal hopped up and down to rise above the slush but its mistress was too intent on glaring at them to notice.

"No it isn't that. I want to hold you. That's what I was hoping for," he said as he leaned in to kiss her on the mouth. The woman, now thoroughly outraged, dragged the dog through the snow. The poor thing, immobilized, slid behind her.

Thinking it might be the right time to set the stage for his new role at CID, he said, "Jenny, I need to tell you that I have been relieved of field duties because of my sympathy for the Nazi movement."

"You must be joking."

"No, I have befriended a man called Alexander von Becke, one of the leaders of the NSB in Leiden. He has some clear thoughts about the problems facing our country. I asked him to tell me more about their objectives. He said that he would take me to some of the meetings. Van Zandt didn't like that and now I am in charge of counting pencils at CID."

"Mark, this isn't you. It can't be true. I know you too well. Is it just your association with this man or is it something else?"

"There is nothing else but I am willing to listen why they think National Socialism is the way for the Dutch."

"That doesn't make sense. You are talking like Henk van Weeren."

"I do want to talk to them, Jenny. I want to know more about it."

"Well, you picked a good time. Henk's mother is a friend of my mother's and she and her husband will visit us on the second Christmas day. They are Nazi lovers too. You can have a great time together."

"Don't be angry Jenny. Not everything you see or hear is necessarily true. That probably goes for what I am telling you too."

"I think you are telling me that I shouldn't try to dig too deeply into your activities. You're probably deeper involved than before. That's why I will not go back to Leiden. I can get a job here and stay with my family. It will give both of us time to find out whether we should be together or find other friends."

"It doesn't have to be that black and white. But I have a job to do and I think that you will be happier staying with your mother and father."

They kissed distractedly and walked home arm-in-arm, each wrapped up in thought. They passed the woman with the Pekingese. The dog had found a tire track and strutted happily alongside his stooped mistress.

If Mark had any illusion that Christmas Day would be joyful, it was soon dispelled. The morning began with Hubert's reading of the New Testament's verses of Matthew and Luke that relate to the birth of Jesus. Other than attending church, there were no plans to venture out of the house on this, the most Christian of days.

They partook heartily of the Christmas meal of boiled potatoes and Brussels sprouts. The meat was courtesy of a fat rabbit that Hubert had been feeding since August in a small cage at the back of the garden shed.

The afternoon brought some levity when a board game of Chinese checkers was placed on the living room table and the family engaged in a distinctly uncharitable competition. The players were passionate if not downright aggressive. At one point, when Hubert was close to being eliminated from play, he pounded his fist on the table with such force that the game pieces fell off the board, thereby saving himself from a certain loss. The rest of the family remained silent but seemed to relish Hubert's humiliation. The evening ended in more readings by Hubert followed by an extended prayer. By ten, it was bedtime and another Christmas had passed in the Glory of the Lord.

On the afternoon of Boxing Day or Second Christmas Day as Mother Marty called it, the senior van Weerens announced their arrival by a fierce knocking on the door. "We are here," Thomas van Weeren said loudly as he stepped inside at the same time as his wife Gerda, pushing her aside.

Thomas was a crude, ill-mannered man, in his mid-forties with a pit-bull face, set in a permanent sneer. His bald head bobbled back and forth as he spoke. His suit was cut in a military style but he had left his swastika armband at home. His wife Gerda was a mousy woman, intimidated by her husband. Her face brightened when she saw Mother Marty. They embraced and headed for the kitchen. Jenny and her sister followed.

Hubert led the men folk into the 'fore room', a feature of most Dutch households that is opened only when visitors come to call. Thomas fell back into the armchair stretching his legs displaying his hobnailed half boots and a piece of hairy leg. He looked at Hubert with a questioning half nod towards Mark.

Hubert scraped his throat. "This is Mark; he's a friend of Jenny's from Holland. They have been writing each other for two years and he thought it was about time to show himself."

Thomas' face darkened, "I remember you boy. My son Henk gave you a good licking at the Jamboree, I hear. You are one those Jew lovers that suck the life blood from the working people."

Hubert exhaled in disgust, causing his lips to flutter. "Now Thomas," he said, "Gerda promised that you wouldn't do any politicking today. It's Christmas, man."

Mark slipped into his role as a friend of National Socialism. "I am happy to finally meet you Mr. van Weeren. It is true that Henk and I had our differences, but I have learned a lot since then. I have met the NSB leader in Leiden and what he says makes a lot of sense."

"Yeah? How so?" Thomas was getting comfortable. He nudged the tip of one boot under the heel of the other and extracted his foot halfway. They were obviously too tight.

Hubert sputtered into action. "I didn't know you were into NSB politics, boy. Jenny told me you work for the intelligence people."

"I have been relieved of field duties," Mark said, "Mainly because I am interested in the success of Germany. Only ten years ago, that country was on its knees. Now look where they are. They are manufacturing thousands of planes, the Ruhr area is in full production, and the standard of living is up. Austria has joined them. The amazing Autobahns are a hundred times better than our rutty roads. There is something right about that."

"Right boy and you know why they can do those things?" Thomas said, bending down to get his other foot out of its painful boot. He straightened up, red in the face. "They made the Jews pay the freight and put the commies to work in labour camps."

"Oh don't start again, Thomas." Hubert pleaded.

Mark decided to stay with it. "I hear that you are active in the NSB here in Groningen. Are you?"

"I am a *wachtmeester* – a sergeant major in the NSB. Our field house is not far from here. You should come and see this evening what we are doing." His ugly face gleamed with satisfaction as he had now freed his feet completely and put the boots beside his chair.

Hubert must have caught a whiff of foot odour for he averted his head quickly. "I know the meeting is a big deal for you, Thomas," he said with his nose crinkled up, "but Mark may not want to spend an evening away."

"It's alright Mr. Bos," Mark said quickly, "If you will excuse me after dinner, I'd like to meet these people."

Hubert was clearly displeased and clammed up. Not Thomas though. He held forth on his importance as a district leader. Mark's mind wandered. He knew Jenny would be upset when she heard about his plans for the evening. He was right.

She dragged him outside in the snowy back yard. "Thomas van Weeren is a slob who parades around town in a Nazi get-up." Jenny began. "He doesn't even go out to dig peat any more because he spends all his time playing an NSB fool." Mark stood there in the cold slush dressed in his woollen pullover shivering while Jenny pummelled his chest in frustration. She declared Mark's visit to the meeting was an insult to her and her parents not to mention a betrayal of his principles.

She finally stopped and buried her head in his sweater. "Why are you spoiling our Christmas to see those traitors?" she wailed. Suddenly she stiffened. "I am going with you," she declared. "You came here to see me, and then you get all mysterious, saying you like the NSB. I want to find out what's going on."

"But Jenny..." he protested.

"It's been decided," she said, and it was.

Although pained by not being able to be honest with Jenny and her family, Mark felt good about his invitation to the field house. He needed to report on something. Here was his chance.

Hubert's dinnertime Bible reading was about Judas Iscariot and his betrayal of Jesus to the Romans. There was little doubt that it was a parable on Mark's road to perdition.

The poorly lettered sign on the old gym hall read, "Strength for Peace". It was one of those meaningless Nazi propaganda slogans. The building had once been a communal gymnasium for the schools in the district. Built in 1860, it had exceeded its expected lifespan. The front door swung on hinges that might rust through at any moment. Inside, the building's cracked walls showed dribbles of rust stain. Two sodium lights cast everything in a yellow tinge.

Men were marching four abreast, singing the *Horst Wessel* song – a tribute to a Nazi martyr. With their chins high in the air, they were oblivious to their ramshackle surroundings. Dressed in brown shirts and belts with leather cross straps, their ages varied from 16 to forty-something, with a noticeable gap of the age group conscripted into the Army.

Thomas van Weeren goose-stepped across the worn linoleum floor. He screamed a loud halt to his troop and introduced his visitors to his deputy Derek Hovinga – a lean, ascetic looking man with a deep scar that marred the left side of his face. As Mark shook hands, the man's cold, blue eyes bored into his. For an eerie moment, Mark felt threatened.

Thomas ordered the deputy to resume the drills.

Mark steered the conversation to Thomas' role in the NSB section.

"Are you the head of this district?" he asked.

"Our former mayor is but we have our differences. He views the NSB as a political party, competing for votes. I don't agree. Talking politics will get us nowhere. That's why I am forming troops that can take charge should it become necessary."

"Troops to support the German army if they invade?" Mark pressed.

"Should the German forces come to our assistance we shall act against those who would resist their progress," said Thomas citing the party line.

"You mean the Dutch army?" Jenny asked incredulously.

Mark sensed that she was anxious to leave. When Thomas was momentarily distracted, he whispered, "Please, don't go, I want to know more." She pouted but stayed.

When Thomas came back, Mark asked, "When your men are called into action, will they be armed?"

Thomas was evasive, "We would expect some help in that respect."

"Do you have weapons stored somewhere?" Mark was really pushing now. Thomas was about to say something but thought better of it. "We don't need weapons for what we intend to do. For example, if the Dutch army removes all the traffic signs, our men might man the major intersections to guide our German friends."

"What if civilians obstruct your men, will you shoot them?"

"We will be able to protect ourselves and control the situation."

"So you must have access to some weapons?" Mark probed.

"Enough to make us feel secure."

"If I joined your section, would you give me a gun?" Mark persisted.

"Why not join us and then we'll see," Thomas smirked.

Mark and Jenny were about to depart, when two imposing men stood at the door to the fieldhouse, blocking their exit.

"Mr. Mark Zonder?" The man produced his identification badge. "Sergeant Lubbers of the State Police and this is my colleague Detective Sandbergen. We would like to talk to you."

"What about?" Mark asked in surprise.

"From CID surveillance, it is known that over the last few weeks you have been involved in discussions with various leaders of the NSB. CID regulations prohibit employees consorting with members of the NSB."

Jenny grabbed Mark's arm. "Oh no!"

Thomas jumped into the fray, "Since when is talk between friends a criminal offence?" he shouted. Sergeant Lubbers ignored him.

"I am sorry Mr. Zonder, please come with us to the station."

"Can my girlfriend come with me?" Mark asked.

"I am afraid not." Jenny trembled as Mark was shoved into the back of a paddy wagon. Thomas looked on with a sneer.

The short drive to the headquarters of the State Police passed in silence. Neither of the officers said a word. At the station, he was hustled into the outer office of the Commissioner.

"Ah, Mr. Zonder," the Commissioner boomed as he strode in, in his black uniform with three silver bands on his sleeve. Gustaaf Emmerik was a tall man with a pleasant, florid face "Please join me in my office."

Mark accepted his offer of coffee and listened impatiently as the Commissioner droned on with uninteresting details of his posting in this Northern Province. Mark interrupted his monologue. "May I ask why I was arrested, Sir?"

"My dear Mr. Zonder, you weren't arrested, Sergeant Lubbers asked you to come to the station with him."

"It wasn't very friendly and it left my girlfriend in tears."

"Quite so and I apologize for any rudeness. It's The Hague. They wanted to see you arrested in front of van Weeren. They wanted you to gain credibility with the NSB leaders."

"You were contacted by CID?" Mark asked.

"Well not CID officially but by an influential former colleague."

"You mean van Zandt?"

"Yes, quite so."

The Commissioner, having done his favour for a friend, felt compelled to give his own view of the situation. "I don't know why van Zandt wants credibility from van Weeren's comic goons. Sure, they have weapons such as hunting rifles, old handguns and a supply of pitchforks. A disciplined German army would not use these buffoons to assist them. There must be more to it," he maintained. "When are you going back to The Hague?"

"Less than 12 hours from now."

"Well, go in peace," Emmerik said. They shook hands.

It was close to midnight when Mark returned to the Bos residence. The house was in darkness. He decided against ringing the doorbell. He went around the back of the house and threw snowballs at Jenny's bedroom window. After several splats of slush on the window, the light went on and Jenny came down to open the back door. He stepped into the kitchen and tried to kiss her while she stood shivering in her nightgown. She shied away. "What is going on?" she demanded, "What happened to you?"

"It's all very complicated, I'll tell you later."

Mark turned and saw Hubert standing there, wearing Mother Marty's bathrobe. It barely covered his bony knees. "Young man, Nazi sympathizers are not welcome in this house. You can stay here for the night but I expect you to be out of here first thing in the morning. Neither my daughter nor the rest of her family want to see you again." Jenny was in tears.

Mark turned to her. "I am really sorry for what happened tonight. I hope that someday it will become clear what this is all about."

Hubert snorted derisively and motioned for Jenny to go upstairs and back to bed. Mark barely slept. At dawn, he woke and packed his things. Passing Jenny's bedroom, he thought of waking her, but didn't. The train ride home was dismal.

22

1939
THURSDAY, DECEMBER 31, 8:00 PM
VON BECKE RESIDENCE, JULIANALAAN 45
OEGSTGEEST, NEDERLAND

"Please come," Paula had urged, "Willem would like to see you." It was the only bright spot since returning from his wretched Christmas visit with Jenny's family. The New Year's Eve party at the von Becke villa promised to be both a change of pace and a chance to become closer associated with the higher echelons of the NSB.

When he arrived, he waited a few houses down and out of view to make sure a number of guests would be there before he entered. The large, elegant living room was alive with the chatter of well-dressed friends of the von Beckes.

Alexander enveloped him in a bear hug. "*Welkom*, my friend," he exclaimed in his clipped German accent. Mark kissed Paula's hand. She acknowledged his old-fashioned gesture with a faked girlish giggle. Heineken beer was the beverage of choice for most although the next-door neighbour was working on his third shot of Jenever, a strong, Dutch gin.

A gigantic bowl on a side table held a supply of *oliebollen,* the doughnut type treat without which no Dutch New Year's Eve is complete.

Paula introduced him all around as a friend of the von Becke family. Mark got some polite nods but he felt out of place. Except for Willem, ten years old and going on 25, he was the youngest in the crowd. Willem was a tiny perfect host asking people if he could get them another beer or a glass of wine. From time to time, he passed a tray around with little blocks of Gouda cheese. He had a friendly patter for every guest and even addressed the German Consul and his wife in impeccable German. Paula looked from across the room and smiled appreciatively.

Alexander noticed Mark's discomfort. He took him by the arm and introduced him to one of the guests. "Here is someone who wants to meet you," he said. "This is Anton Kranz, the owner of Leiden's largest textile factory. Anton is a great supporter of the NSB; he is one of the earliest members dating back to 1933. I think his membership number is 30."

"Seventeen actually," Kranz said. He was a short heavyset man with brilliantine-slicked hair combed over his forehead. His starched wing tip collar was so tight that it surely would choke him to death if ever a morsel of food were to lodge in his windpipe. His myopic piggy eyes behind a pince-nez made him lean in closely to anyone talking to him.

"I hear that you have been a big brother to Willem," he said, "How did you meet him?" Mark suspected the man knew the story but wanted to hear it again. He told Kranz about the harassment by a man in an overcoat and his intervention.

"Those kind of incidents are unfortunate," Kranz, said, "They are all based on a misapprehension that our party wants to sell out to Germany." He looked around the room. "Willem," he called out, "Fetch your friend a glass of beer." Mark politely declined with a wave of his hand.

"Nonsense," Kranz said, "It's New Year's Eve." He took a sip of his own beer. "Now," he said, wiping his mouth with a napkin, "We want to see a disciplined, ordered country, free of the anarchic strikes by the Bolsheviks and the public disturbances instigated by the socialists. We believe in law and order so that business can operate in a stable environment."

He leaned in closer so that his nose was only inches away. His eyes were a watery blue. The volume of his voice adjusted in relation to proximity and he went on in a near whisper, "We need a strong police force and strict judges who will order long jail terms. Only those kinds of actions will rein in the communists who want to turn over the means of production to the masses, many of whom never worked a day in their lives." He appeared out of breath after this tirade, drained his glass, and looked around. "Did Willem bring your beer yet?" he asked.

Mark decided to probe deeper into the old man's views. "I think many people are turned off by the hostility expressed toward the Jews," he said.

"That is purely a German obsession. It is true that the banks in Germany are largely controlled by Jews. Hitler blames them for the defeat of Germany in 1918 and stokes the fires of fear that unless control of the financial and cultural assets is in so-called 'pure' German hands the country cannot emerge from the Depression."

"The NSB is not hostile to Jews?"

"Not at the leadership level but there is a very large streak of anti-Semitism in the rank and file."

"May I ask what your role is in the NSB?"

"I am a financier of the Party. Industrialists have a large stake in an orderly society. I leave the political side to Anton Mussert, our Leader."

"Do you think the party will ever get enough votes to form a government?"

"If the people want law and order without petty crime and strikes they will vote for strong leadership," he replied.

Mark wanted to steer the conversation towards the party's possible assistance to Germany.

"If Germany were to attack—" Alexander jumped in. "Germany will never attack this country," he proclaimed, "the Dutch are of the same Aryan blood as the Germans; we are brothers."

Paula who had been listening broke into the conversation. She spoke defiantly, "When the Party says Germany will not attack, they do not preclude the possibility that Germany may come marching in to protect us from an unspecified peril."

Alexander smiled broadly. "You see we have differing views in this household," he said to general laughter.

By now, several guests had pulled up chairs around the large sofa. Mark gave up his seat to a sombre looking man who was introduced as Rost van Tonningen, the head of a national bank. The genial white-haired mayor of the nearby town of Warmond took a seat on the marble ledge of the fireplace – a perch from which he nodded sagely at appropriate intervals but never spoke. Mark stayed within earshot. He hoped to hear about stockpiling or purchasing arms but all these polite folks talked about were political structures. He ventured a question.

"If Germany came to protect us from British aggression," he almost choked on the words, "Would an NSB government be in favour of retaining the House of Orange?" A startled Alexander von Becke responded eagerly.

"Of course it would. The Dutch population would never assent to another form of government. The rule by the House of Orange is too deeply engrained in Dutch social order."

"I'm not so sure," the banker countered, "Queen Wilhelmina is very religious and very conservative and while an NSB government might want her to stay, she might abdicate."

"The Queen is also very pragmatic," Alexander submitted, "In my view she would keep the reins and work toward a realistic compromise."

"How can you reconcile a popular Queen and a single, all-powerful Prime Minister who is in effect a dictator," Anton Kranz argued. "No. The Queen has no place in any NSB government unless the Constitution is amended to take away the limited powers the Monarch now has."

Mark left the discussion and wandered into the fore room, where Paula entertained the women. Politics were largely for men, it seemed. The discussion evolved around the rationing of sugar and leather goods.

After exchanging some pleasantries with the gathered wives, he ambled back to the political talk. The group's fervour had dissipated.

Alexander sensed it and clapped his hands, "Ten minutes to midnight everyone, get ready for the New Year," he announced. "Even though we are under a blackout, we can still have fire and noise in the house. Willem served sparklers and matches. The female entourage entered the living room carrying pots, pans, spoons and anything else that could make noise to ring in the year 1940. Radio Hilversum broadcast the countdown.

Couples embraced and quietly wished each other happiness in the New Year. Men shook hands; women kissed. Paula disengaged herself from the embrace of Willem and Alexander and came over to kiss Mark on the cheek and to whisper a quick thank you. Kissing over and done with, the banging of pots and pans began. Those who didn't have anything to bang waved sparklers around the room.

The racket was short lived and a bit forced. There was a sense that it was obligatory to be jolly, but their hearts were not in it. The guests settled down to coffee and liqueur and finished off the bowl of greasy oliebollen. The party slowly slipped away. One by one, the couples made their goodbyes and set out for home on the darkened, slippery streets.

Paula was cleaning up in the kitchen when Mark came to say thank you and goodbye. Alexander told him not to go yet because he wanted to introduce him to a guest who had just arrived. He was a corpulent man with a face that would not have been out of place in a painting of characters from the Old Testament; a cruel peasant face, redeemed by sharp intelligent eyes.

"I want you to meet Arnold Koopmans; he is one of our leaders. His responsibility is security, especially security of our members who – as you know – are frequently set upon and harassed. Arnold heads a group of young members who will protect our people if they are threatened."

"Are those the *knokploegen,* the 'strong arm bullies' as the papers call them?" Mark smiled as he said it, but Koopmans wasn't smiling.

"You can call them what you like but they defend our right to make a political statement in public."

"Your people have been in some serious brawls; I bet you wish you could provide them with arms," Mark probed.

"We can't do that legally, but we will take up arms if it becomes necessary." Mark was tempted to push harder but Koopmans surprised him by asking about his work at CID. He told of his status as an inventory clerk. Koopmans appeared well informed as to the reasons why. He also seemed to know about the State Police in Groningen inquiring about Mark's NSB connections.

"You could be of some real help to the Party," he began, "You know the inner workings of the CID. If you hear anything that might help advance our cause, you could call me."

"If I hear anything, I will tell Alexander."

"Alexander is our political leader," Koopmans shot back brusquely, "I am the one to be informed of any police moves against us." Alexander nodded his agreement but with some discomfort.

"Arnold keeps us from being victimized by the State," Alexander said. "Our members have many talents and come from all social backgrounds. Many outsiders would be surprised to know that the physical force of our party is housed in Leiden's finest pastry shop." Mark shot a surprised glance at Alexander. "Yes," he explained, "Koopmans Pastry Shop on the Breestraat." Mark knew the prestigious address on Leiden's main street.

It had been an interesting evening. He would have something to report.

23

1940
THURSDAY, JANUARY 21, 2:00 PM
OFFICE OF THE COMMISSIONER FOR RATIONING OF COAL AND ANTHRACITE
THE HAGUE, NEDERLAND

"Talk, my boy," he sighed, "Talk, that's all it is. They are just rehashing the few good things Hitler talks about and trying to convince themselves that it will be a bright future."

Van Zandt had decorated the office since his last visit. Some paintings of bucolic scenes hung on the walls and on a shelf stood two small porcelain vases topped by beautifully decorated lids. He spread out in his chair behind the massive desk and added, "The top guys are debaters; the lowlife are the haters. That is why the bit about the pastry man as the NSB strong man is interesting." He paused to jot a note on a yellow legal pad before him. "But tell me about the boy Willem," he said. The old spymaster seemed more interested in the family life of the von Becke family. "Is the boy happy? van Zandt persisted. "Is it a happy family?"

"I think that Paula is troubled by Alexander's NSB convictions. I sense that she disapproves of the boy's participation in the Jeugdstorm but she goes along with it for Alexander's sake."

"How is the boy taking it?"

"He dislikes the propaganda and the uniforms."

Van Zandt looked down at his desk and said, "That's good; he is resisting. Excellent." Mark did not understand the remark but did not ask.

"They have invited me back. I promised Willem a book of photographs of houses in Amsterdam."

"Come by the house. I have dozens of that type of book and my wife would love to see you. She likes you, you know."

Alice knocked and peeked in to announce that Dirk Vreelink had arrived. Mark looked surprised.

"I have asked Dirk to come by because he has uncovered another bit of information about the NSB," van Zandt said. He motioned for Vreelink to sit down. "Go ahead," van Zandt said, "Tell him what you heard."

"The week before Christmas I had a few beers with an old friend who works for a trucking company. He told me that he delivered a long heavy crate to Koopmans Pastry Shop and had to take it down to the basement. The tip was generous."

Van Zandt got up and paced around the room. He stopped to pick up one of the vases, lifted the lid and peered inside as if to look for guidance. He replaced the lid and sat down. "I want to know what was in that crate."

Mark wanted to know more. "You mean we should break in?"

"I don't profess to know how you should do your job. I want to know what's in the crate without Koopmans knowing."

From the picture window in *The Golden Turk Restaurant*, they could see the pastry shop on the other side of the Breestraat. Koopmans, like most small shop owners, lived above the store. At nine, the sliver of light emanating from behind the heavy blackout curtains of the living room went out. The restaurant closed and they waited outside in the cold for the right time to enter.

The building housing the pastry shop was built in the mid-1800s. Vreelink had studied old surveyors' plats and found that the building had been constructed over top of the basements of the large patrician mansions that long ago lined the Breestraat – there were basements below basements. The plat also showed a tunnel that led to the Lange Brug, the street that ran parallel with the Breestraat.

"Those rich folks must have needed an escape route," Vreelink said as he jimmied the storefront door with his tools. He opened the door and reached up to silence the bell that would have jangled had they walked straight in. Mark had brought his squeeze cat flashlight and led the way through the store and into the bakery. The basement steps led into a dank storage area. Mark shone his flashlight along the rough-bricked walls.

The flashlight flickered across stacks of folded pastry cartons, a dough-mixing device that looked like a miniature cement mixer and stacks of baking trays. Nothing like a crate that might contain weapons.

"Over here," Vreelink whispered as the flashlight found a concrete slab in the floor that looked as if it had been recently pried open. Mark found a small crowbar behind a post and pried the slab up. Vreelink lifted it off and put it aside. A series of wooden steps led into a mouldy smelling enclosure. They stood and listened for a few moments for any footsteps, then gingerly descended into the clammy area.

The flickering light revealed newly built shelving. On the bottom shelf was a crate the size of a coffin.

In nervous haste, they pried away slat after slat until they hit upon what, in the poor light, look like a mummy – a heavy bundle made of oilcloth, tightly wrapped with rope. They cut the ropes, unrolled the cloth and found it filled with many smaller oilcloth-wrapped units. Vreelink unfolded a tall package and produced a brand new Karabiner 98K rifle, the standard rifle of the German Wehrmacht. Two dozen rifles in all, plus many hundreds of rounds of 8 mm ammunition.

Vreelink went deeper into the cellar and found the entrance to the tunnel that led to the street... A flash! An explosion! Darkness.

Mark woke in the early morning. A rush of pain stabbed through his head. The tinnitus in his ears was deafening. A small nightlight showed he was in a bed. He drifted in and out of consciousness. He saw the Crucifix above the medical instruments on the wall. He tried to recall but couldn't. The morning brought some relief as a nun brought him bouillon and dry toast. His hearing improved. He asked the nun what had happened.

"You were practicing Judo at the Army barracks when you hit your head against the wall and lost consciousness," she said while bustling about the room in her cumbersome garb. He tried to remember. The story made no sense. Images of a cellar and a crate played through his mind but no martial arts practice. It wasn't just the nun; his mother also mentioned his fall when she visited him later that morning.

After her visit, he felt deeply tired but couldn't relax. He read Jenny's card that came with flowers. Paula and Willem had left a gift at the reception desk. It was an album of Willem's photographs. The latest entry showed Mark talking to Kranz on New Year's Eve. A photograph taken at a family dinner caught his attention. It showed his parents, grandparents and a distinguished looking gentleman, Frans van Zandt! He quickly leafed through the rest of the photographs and found several other shots taken in the garden and at a birthday party where van Zandt featured prominently. He was confused.

Dirk Vreelink showed up in the early afternoon. "How are you bearing up, scout?" he asked jovially.

"You better tell me what happened," Mark retorted, "The story that I fell during a Judo practice is nonsense. I recall going into that pastry shop, I remember finding the rifles in the cellar and then—"

Vreelink raised his hand to silence him. "Van Zandt's orders are that the cover story must be maintained. CID should not volunteer that we broke into a pastry shop. Moreover van Zandt doesn't want it known that the NSB might be hoarding weapons."

"What really happened?" Mark asked.

"I went into the tunnel while you were groping in the crate. I heard a loud bang and a flash of light came from your direction. When I got back, you were sitting against the wall. Blood was oozing from your nose. You didn't respond," Vreelink explained.

"Was it a booby trap?" Mark asked.

"I don't think so. It was more of a flash-bang thing – a warning, a lot of noise, but no shrapnel."

"I remember pulling at something." It all became clearer to Mark. "So what happened then?" he asked.

"I hoisted you over my shoulder. I dragged you through the tunnel and hauled you up to the street. The police station was only a few blocks away and the cops took you to the St. Elisabeth Hospital."

"What about Koopmans?"

"I don't think he's anxious to report that someone found his shipment of German rifles. I think he's waiting for someone to come to him."

"Will the cops make trouble?"

"Van Zandt will keep them quiet."

It was too much to absorb. His mind drifted. Dirk noted his flagging attention and said goodbye.

He awoke and looked at Willem's photo album and wondered again about van Zandt's appearance in the family photos. He dozed off over the meal that had been left on his side table.

24

1940
MONDAY, JANUARY 29, 8:00 PM
VAN ZANDT RESIDENCE, KIEVIETLAAN 22
WASSENAAR, NEDERLAND

The streetcar from Leiden rumbled its leisurely way toward Wassenaar. With the stops every few hundred metres, it would take half an hour. Whenever van Zandt talked shop at home, it meant the discussion was on an unofficial basis.

Since leaving the hospital, Mark had been kept busy with the job of monitoring agents' reports. Being a general's aide had many boring moments. His disenchantment with the casual ways of the CID had deepened. He often felt his Boy Scout troop had been more focused. England and France now battling in a shadow war with Germany did not appear to instill any sense of impending danger in the population. The old policy of neutrality continued to dull the political acuity.

The papers had not carried any stories on the Koopmans incident.

His mind wandered from that thought to his concerns that Alexander might connect the pastry shop affair with his New Year's Eve visit. To test his welcome, he had visited Willem to return the photo album and been received warmly by Alexander and Paula.

Thinking back to the mysterious presence of van Zandt in the family photo album, Mark had casually asked Willem who the man was. Willem had referred to hims as 'Uncle Frans'. Mark probed deeper to learn that Willem thought of him as a 'pretend uncle' who visited about once a month. He did not know what his parents discussed because he was usually sent to his room shortly after van Zandt's arrival.

The streetcar conductor interrupted his musing and announced his Wassenaar stop. At the van Zandt mansion, the doorbell was answered so quickly that Kirsten must have seen him approaching. She looked very desirable – for an older woman of course, he told himself. She extended both arms in greeting, embraced him and kissed him on the lips.

"You promised me you would come and play tennis, Mark. That was last fall. Now that spring is here I should persuade Frans to give you an afternoon off so we can play." She added a singing lilt to the word 'play' that sounded suggestive. He politely sidestepped the invitation.

"You may wait in the drawing room because van Zandt is busy on the telephone, as always." Kirsten sat down, her skirt exposing her long legs.

"I had the maid brew some real coffee. I don't know where Frans gets it and I don't ask," she smiled. "He also tells me your girlfriend has returned to her family up north so you must have some free time to visit us?" She bent forward and touched his knee.

"Perhaps, yes if Mr. van Zandt needs me."

"Of course he will need you. He often mentions your work with the von Becke family."

"Have you met the von Becke family, Ma'am?"

"I met them at a reception at the Palace. I think they are distant relatives of the Royal Family. Frans takes a very deep interest in that family, probably because Her Majesty wants him to."

One could always sense van Zandt before he actually stepped into a room. Mark rose.

"Hello Zonder. Up and about I see, and none the worse for wear," he boomed. In his grey silk floor-length robe and a maroon ascot, fashionably tied, he looked quite different from his regular garb. However, his attempt to dress like a suave Englishman was negated by his braided gold slippers and red socks. From the knees down, he looked a bit like Ali Baba.

"Sit down. I see Mrs. van Zandt has taken you under her wing." He sat down heavily. Kirsten left discreetly to check on the coffee.

"Important initiatives are in the offing," he said adjusting the ascot as if it was too tight. Mark worked up the courage to interrupt.

"Sir, I would like to ask a question about the von Becke situation."

Van Zandt looked up sharply, stopped struggling with the ascot, and reached for his fountain pen on the side table next to him.

"I would like to ask why I am monitoring the von Becke family when you know them quite well. I saw you in several family photographs."

"I am sure I mentioned that the Palace is interested in the family. Alexander is related to the Queen's husband Prince Hendrik. The Queen is concerned about Alexander's Nazi leanings and wants to make sure Willem is okay."

"Why do you need me to get close to him?"

Van Zandt started to twirl the pen; damage control was in effect.

"It's hard for an older man like me to be close to a young boy and find out how he is bearing up under the Nazi propaganda. That's why I need you to watch Alexander and get to know the boy's outlook on life."

Mark wanted to ask another question but van Zandt changed the subject. He took a writing pad from the table and prepared to scribble notes as he talked.

"The Palace," he began – he always said the Palace when he meant the Queen, "Is concerned that this Cabinet is asleep as far as the Nazi threat is concerned. The population, on the other hand, is realistic and fears both the Germans and the lassitude of its own government. There is a sense that preparations for our country's defence are insufficient. The result is a general resignation that if war comes, we must surrender. The Palace feels that the population must wake up to the reality. This feeling is not shared by the Prime Minister." He paused to scribble a few sentences. He put the pen to his lips as if to ask for silence to let him think.

"Minister Bracken of Defence and I have been asked to alert the population to the threats our nation faces both from within and outside." He must have thought this was a good line for he scribbled again.

He looked at Mark. "Do you know what the Communists mean by *Agitprop*?" he asked. Mark shook his head. He had heard the word used but in an unflattering context.

"It means propaganda by theatre. Proponents stage events, most often fabrications to stimulate the population to support certain actions. The Communists are masters of the art. Hitler also dressed up a group of his soldiers in Polish uniforms who then pretended to attack a German radio station. The press ran with it, the people were whipped into hysteria and supported the invasion of Poland." Van Zandt put the writing tablet on the side table, got up, and paraded around the room in his silly slippers.

"We don't want to fabricate stories but we can illuminate actual events." He stood in front of Mark and wagged his finger in the air. "We must rouse the Dutch population to resistance instead of abject surrender." He looked at his finger and put his hands behind his back. He must have surprised himself with his outburst, Mark thought.

"The Minister of Defence will pound on every infraction by Germany of our neutrality and publicize it. Nothing will be too small. Our job at CID is to highlight the threat from within. It is important that the public knows about the threat posed by the NSB."

"Are they really that much of a threat, Sir?" Mark asked.

"It doesn't matter. The NSB is sympathetic to the Nazis. It is our job to demonstrate that they are enemies of the state." He sat down and began writing again. He only looked up when Kirsten brought a tray with three cups of coffee, milk and sugar and *speculaas* – a spiced cookie for each. She sat down. Van Zandt smiled at her and continued, "The plan is that on the Easter weekend, in 12 cities around the country, we round up all the known leaders of the NSB and put them under arrest for espionage and whatever else we can think of."

"Is there any proof?"

"Of course. We have your weapons cache and I am confident we will find more evidence when we search their homes."

"What do you expect from me, Sir?"

"You know those goons in Groningen, van Weeren and his gang. You will work with the police in the roundup there. You are our liaison."

Kirsten was all aflutter. "Oh, you will see your girlfriend. Oh, to be young again and in love," she crooned. Van Zandt looked annoyed.

25

1940
SATURDAY, APRIL 6, 12:00 NOON
HOTEL DE VILLE, OUDE BOTERINGESTRAAT
GRONINGEN, NEDERLAND

The major railway stations on the route to Groningen were crawling with military activity. Mounds of sandbags barred vehicles from the city streets. Armed soldiers inspected each departing and arriving train. Reality had set in that war was almost inevitable. The feeling that Nederland would be spared from German aggression had given way to a determined defensive mindset. A palpable sense of dread was evident on the drawn faces of travellers.

Mark was pleasantly surprised that Alice had provided a first class ticket. He reminded himself to thank her.

He had read the reports but still did not understand why van Zandt had sent him to Groningen. Van Weeren's unit had made several scouting trips to the German border. Twenty of his marching goons had gone on bicycle tours of many minor border crossings. Some were merely walking paths but others could sustain light traffic. Derek Hovinga, the one with the ice-blue eyes had been photographed marking maps. The report ended with the recommendation that the unit be neutralized in some manner.

In spite of the chaos in rail traffic, his train was only 20 minutes late. He had written a postcard to Jenny to say he was coming to Groningen but he was afraid that Hubert's edict would keep her away. He need not have feared. She ran to him as soon as he stepped out into the sunshine of a beautiful spring day. She wore a gray herringbone skirt with pleats riding on her hip and a heavy pale blue cable-knit sweater. He thought she looked beautiful.

He plunked his baggage down and held out his arms. They kissed passionately, not caring about bystanders most of whom – but not all – showed smiling approval.

"Why are you not in uniform?" an elderly man sneered.

Jenny sprung to his defence the way a lioness might defend her cubs. "Because he does more important work than sticking his nose in other people's business," she retorted sharply. The old man shrugged his shoulders and shuffled off.

"Everybody is a critic," Mark laughed, "Thanks for speaking up. It's wonderful to see you. We didn't part under the best of circumstances."

"My father is still very angry about your political views but my mother tells him he should be more flexible. I told him you were coming here on an assignment but you can't stay at our home."

"That's okay; the office has arranged a room at a place called Hotel de Ville. Perhaps we can walk there." Jenny chatted excitedly about the school and her adventures with the children. It was a welcome relief from the gloominess of war. His mood brightened.

The hotel had stood on the Oude Boteringestraat for 150 years. It served as pub, restaurant and meeting place for the neighbourhood. The entrance hallway offered a choice of taking the stairs to the second floor or entering the swinging half-doors leading to the pub.

It was early Saturday afternoon and the place was busy. Two burly men were playing billiards at the ornate table that formed the Centrepiece of the pub. The clientele consisted of working men gathered around small tables laden with glasses of beer. Most were smoking cigars. Cigar smoking might be for the upper classes in many countries, but in Nederland, every man, from prime minister to peon, would light up a cigar any time, any place.

The owner – sleeves rolled-up, white apron tied around the waist – stood behind the massive bar, skimming foam off a patron's beer. The bar was his bastion. Leaning against it with a foot on the brass footrest was required protocol. The white enamelled nameplate on the wall exclaimed boldly: Albert Hark, Proprietor.

All eyes were on the stranger with the attractive girl. Mark put his suitcase on the floor and placed his fedora on the bar. Mr. Hark eyed Jenny with suspicion.

"We are only allowed to rent rooms to married folks," he snapped in his Gronings accent. Jenny blushed; Mark hid his annoyance. He took off his coat and put it on the bar counter.

"Perhaps you could check the reservations made by my office in The Hague. The name is Zonder, Mark Zonder." The bartender's attitude immediately changed to that of a servile minion.

"Of course" he snivelled. On a board behind him, hotel keys hung from hooks. Each key was weighed down with a chunk of wood, light enough to be carried to the room but too unwieldy to be taken beyond the premises.

"Room number nine," he pronounced loudly, as if the entire pub needed to know. He looked at Jenny.

"The young lady would perhaps like a cup of coffee while you unpack?" he asked, thereby enforcing his personal code of morality.

Mark turned to Jenny. "I have to see the Commissioner of Police in an hour. Perhaps you should go home and we will meet later." This caused a murmur among the habitués as any mention of the police generally did.

All eyes followed as Mark walked Jenny out to the street. After a quick kiss, he re-entered the pub to pick up his bag. He looked sternly around the pub. Eyes either went down or stared intently at some far away object.

He walked to Police headquarters and was quickly ushered into the office of Commissioner Emmerik.

"Mr. Zonder, we meet again," he gushed. "The situation has gotten a bit out of hand. Thomas van Weeren and his troops are getting too brazen in their support of a Greater German Reich. CID has decided that a public demonstration of official disapproval is in order. Hence, we are planning to round up a number of these Brownshirts on Easter Monday when most of them will be at home. I'd prefer to take them on Easter Sunday but the Church would likely object."

Mark voiced his concern, "I am not sure what my role is."

Emmerik smiled at his frankness. "Van Zandt asked CID to assign you to Groningen because you have met some of the NSB leadership here."

"I really only know van Weeren and I have met some of the others. I would like to understand what my role will be during the operation?"

"You observe and later report. This is a CID operation conducted by the State Police. Can't do without the client in attendance, can we?" he chuckled jovially.

"When does it start?

"Report here at 07:30 hours on Monday. You will accompany the raid and witness the activity. The press will be alerted to arrive early in the morning to report as events unfold."

"Will these people be charged with anything?"

"We have charges ready to be laid, ranging from suspected espionage and possession of illegal arms to undermining the security of the nation."

"Can any of it be proven?"

"It doesn't really matter. The idea is to alert the public to the treachery. We have tolerated their disloyalty, now it is time to harden public opinion against them."

He left his contact address with the sergeant on duty and walked out into the gentle spring evening. It was suppertime and soon the city would be enveloped in the total darkness of the blackout. The thought of finding himself at the blunt end of Hubert's disapproval caused him to take a long detour to gather his courage.

It was dark when he approached the house. He bent down to open the gate in the low hedge that surrounded the front yard. He heard the swoosh just before he felt the blow on the back of his head. Someone pulled him up by the collar and jerked him around. His assailant reached deep down and brought up a fist that connected squarely with his chin. His eyes lost focus. He groaned in agony and dimly heard a voice he had heard before.

"You treacherous bastard," the voice told him, as Mark tried to clear the fog from his brain. It was Thomas, he realized. The man holding him from behind suddenly pushed him toward Thomas who buried his knee deeply into Mark's crotch. Mark fell, curled in the fetal position. The pain was excruciating.

"That will teach him that we don't tolerate snitches," the other man said. The voice registered on his fading consciousness. Hovinga!

He tried to stand up but fell back onto the pavement. To lie down was less painful than moving. Crawling the few metres to the gate, he reached over to undo the hasp. He slumped over the gate as it slowly veered open. He dropped onto the flagstones and crawled up the wooden steps. It hurt to bang on the door. He was afraid they might not hear him. Finally, the door opened slightly. Hubert stared into the dark night. He looked down and saw the crumpled mass on the doorstep.

"Marty, Jenny, come."

"Oh my god," Jenny shrieked, "It's Mark. He's dead!"

Mark stirred and lifted his head. "No," he croaked, "Not yet."

Jenny knelt beside him on the stoop and held his head in her arms. "Are you hurt badly?" she asked rocking him gently in her arms. "Mother, get us a blanket," she yelled over her shoulder.

"No, I think I can stand," he groaned. With the help of Hubert, he lifted himself to his feet. Marty threw the blanket around him. With Jenny and Hubert supporting him, he walked inside and lowered himself gingerly into Hubert's favourite chair.

Jenny cleaned the blood off his face while Hubert got him to move his arms, legs and feet to make certain there were no broken bones.

"This boy is tough," Hubert declared, "He got a good thump on the head and there are some cuts but other than that, I think he'll be okay."

"Who did this to you," Jenny asked, "What brought this on? Who even knows you're here?"

"It has to do with my work," he offered vaguely.

Hubert nodded in total agreement. "Trouble seems to follow you, boy." Jenny hushed him. Mark was dimly aware that his head was being bandaged. He realized that he was being led upstairs.

The touch of Jenny's cool hand on his forehead woke him. In spite of the throbbing headache, he managed to wash up, get dressed and negotiate his way down the stairs. Mother Marty rushed to make him some porridge and created a cup of ersatz tea by adding hot water to a brown tablet the size of a guilder coin. Hubert vacated his chair and waved for Mark to sit down. Jenny kept the discussion focused on the well-being of their guest but Hubert was intent on getting to the bottom of things before the family had to leave for church.

"Do you have any idea who beat you, Mark?" The use of his first name was new; up to now, he had been referred to as 'boy'. "At Christmas the

CID had you arrested for cuddling up to that bunch of Nazi lovers. Are they now sending thugs to beat you?" Hubert persisted.

"I think it was Thomas van Weeren and a guy called Hovinga."

"You think the NSB beat you up?" Hubert looked confused, "I thought you and Thomas had become great friends."

"I guess he thinks differently now," Mark closed his eyes. He didn't want to talk about it. He moved slowly over to the living room table and began eating his porridge. Hubert looked aghast. Mark realized he had forgotten to simulate a prayer before starting in on his porridge. He hastily faked a semblance of silence and piety.

"Time for ten o'clock Easter Sunday service," Hubert announced, leaving the two of them alone in the house.

Mark stretched out on the sofa. Jenny tried to follow up on Hubert's inquisition but Mark didn't respond. Jenny persisted, "I have had a long time to think about this. You are not a Nazi sympathizer at all. You faked interest in the NSB. I know I'm right."

"Can we leave the interrogation until I feel a bit better?" Mark pleaded.

Jenny walked over to the sofa. Mark groaned as she lifted both legs in the air, sat down and put them back in her lap. She slowly stroked his legs. First below the knee, then venturing a few strokes higher up. Too high perhaps, because Mark arched his back.

"I am afraid I have a painful knee-print in that area."

When Hubert and Mother Marty came back from church. Hubert got back to the inquisition. "If you were a true NSB supporter, the NSB wouldn't have beaten you up," he said.

"CID wanted me to get information on the strength of the extremists in the NSB. I had to gain their confidence so they would talk to me."

"So you lied to us."

"I was instructed to tell no one of my mission. I am sorry."

"I guess in the defence of one's country one must be able to match wits with those who wish us harm," Hubert pontificated, "In Joshua's trek in the desert, he told an untruth to save the life of a beggar; God did not disapprove."

Mark smiled at Hubert's versatility to adapt to a change in circumstances. His life was ruled by the strictest, Protestant interpretation of the Bible. The Ten Commandments were the lights by which he lived. As long as he could find a precedent in the Scriptures, he could accept change. In Mark's home, religion was something stored on the back shelf, in the unlikely event that you'd need it.

Hubert did not give up. "Why would van Weeren want to punish you? How would he have found out about your masquerade?" Hubert was beginning to enjoy the intrigue.

"Only the people at the State Police knew." Mark suddenly stopped. "I must get to a phone," he said raising himself from the sofa. "I must call." He got dressed as best as he could. Jenny escorted him to the phone booth. Told of the attack and Mark's suspicion of a leak, Commissioner Emmerik sounded quite casual.

"We'll deal with van Weeren tomorrow, and as to a leak, we are ahead of you. We have identified an officer who is informing the NSB of our moves. We have kept him out of the loop on our plans."

Back at the house, they sent him upstairs to rest, while the family conducted the Easter bible readings. Half-awake, he realized that his cover was blown. If van Weeren knew, Alexander and Koopmans would soon know. His clumsy effort to remain close to the von Becke family would have been in vain. He couldn't make the case that it had been worthwhile. Tomorrow he would witness the arrest of few dozen toy-soldiers to show the public that Nederland was prepared to defend itself.

Lying in bed, he recognized he should stop his negative musings. Screw the politics, he thought. Better to think of Jenny. He thought of her soft yielding body, the curve of her breast and that crinkly-eyed smile that promised fun and excitement in equal measure.

Supper was a replay of the Christmas dinner. One of Hubert's fat rabbits had involuntarily supplied the entrée for which Hubert, in his prayer, declared he was truly grateful. The post dinner Bible reading was Luke 15:11-32, the Return of the Prodigal Son. It was evident to all that the parable meant that Mark had made a U-turn on the road to damnation.

After dinner, he declared that he felt well enough to sleep in his hotel room. Bundled in his overcoat with a fedora to cover the bandage, Jenny walked him to the hotel. They kissed goodbye on the street. Neither of them fancied an amorous display for the benefit of the pub's clientele. He walked up the stairs feeling lonely and in pain. His small hotel room felt desolate in its plainness but he could only think of sleep, healing sleep.

26

1940
MONDAY, APRIL 8, 6:00 AM
HOTEL DE VILLE, OUDE BOTERINGESTRAAT
GRONINGEN, NEDERLAND

The sound of the night man placing his newly-shined shoes in front of the door woke him up. It was six o'clock. His head felt better and his limbs moved without having to wince. Instead of washing up in the men's communal washroom, he used the water pitcher and the ceramic bowl to refresh his face and the body parts he could reach without moaning. He dried himself with the thin cloth, utterly useless for its intended purpose.

He made his way down to the pub to find something to eat. The place was eerily empty. The smell of rancid beer and cigar smoke hung in a nauseous haze. Mr. Hark was cleaning behind the bar and offered Mark a half-full pot of chicory coffee. Its only redeeming value was that it cleared his head. The pub's icebox yielded a hunk of smoked ham and dark bread. He ate greedily. He debated with himself whether he should pack the Colt but decided against it; the observer role suited him just fine.

He arrived a half-hour before the raid was to commence. The raiding party was "battle ready," Commissioner Emmerik announced. To Mark it looked more like a version of the *Keystone Kops*, a silent film his mother had taken him to when he turned eight.

He looked around the hall to size up the force. An aging policeman, with a sea-lion moustache and wearing an ill-fitting uniform appeared to be the staging director. With a cellophane-covered map in one hand and a hand-written list in the other, he shouted who was to nab whom.

"Alright men, let's go!" he yelled, herding the stragglers as if removing misbehaving pets from the kitchen. Outside an idling touring bus was trembling on its worn tires. It would serve as the paddy wagon.

A dozen police agents of various ages and sizes gathered around the vehicle. The Commissioner pointed out the four aging 1935 Fords would be used to make the arrests and bring their captives to the bus.

The Commissioner announced he would lead the raid from the sidecar of the station's motorcycle. He donned his leather helmet and slipped the aviator goggles over it just as he seen Errol Flynn do in *Dawn Patrol*.

In a commanding gesture, he invited Mark to take the saddle behind the helmeted rider. With a banzai wave by the Commissioner, the rickety caravan was on its way. On this beautiful Easter Monday morning, the streets were deserted. Tulips and hyacinths – in early spring bloom – graced the carefully tended front gardens of modest homes. The chestnut trees in the park were beginning to show their green luster.

From the sidecar he had grandly named his 'mobile headquarters', Emmerik ordered the Fords to begin the chase. The rickety bus trembled in anticipation. A reporter with his photographer, sent by a tipped-off editor, huddled in the entrance to the Martini Church. A *Pathé* News truck carried a camera on its roof to record the event for the newsreels.

The first Ford arrived surprisingly quickly. The detainees, dressed in pajamas, bathrobes or undershirts looked about the square with a mixture of indignation and sullenness.

"Into the bus with them," the Commissioner yelled. He climbed out of the sidecar and pushed the photographer toward the bus making sure he stayed within range of the camera at all times.

It all went rather quickly. Within an hour, some 40 of the party faithful had been roused from their homes. Thomas van Weeren appeared to be one of the few struggling to resist arrest. Commissioner Emmerik in the sidecar and Mark clutching the bike rider's waist led the wobbly bus through the quiet streets to police headquarters.

The station was a noisy beehive of milling policemen, shouting detainees and objecting lawyers. The sea lion handed Mark an envelope. "This is the stuff we found at Thomas van Weeren's home. He's over there, in the corner." Mark quickly scanned the contents consisting of photographs and maps. He saw Thomas talking to a well-dressed, scholarly looking man with pince-nez embedded in a florid face. Turning the man around, Thomas pointed at Mark yelling, "There he is! That's the prick who started all this."

As Mark approached, Thomas looked at his bandaged head and snarled, "I see somebody beat you up pretty bad."

Mark ignored him and turned to the neatly dressed man who responded aggressively. "I am the legal counsel for Thomas van Weeren and I am here to set him free. He is not guilty of anything; no charges have been laid."

Mark showed the man his identification and explained that the police were acting under instructions from the national intelligence agency.

"Thank you," the pedantic man said, "but that does not give the police the right to haul citizens from their homes."

"There are pending charges, counsellor," Mark retorted waving the envelope in his face. "Police found this envelope in Mr. van Weeren's home. It contains maps of little known border crossings as well as photographs of defence installations."

"That may be so," the lawyer sputtered, his face getting redder by the minute, "But it is not a criminal offense to take pictures, at least not yet."

"Just the same we have sufficient evidence to hold these detainees including your client. They'll be brought in for arraignment first thing in the morning. Charges will likely include espionage and illegal possession of firearms."

Mark asked the sea lion for the use of an office to telephone his superiors. He reached van Zandt rather quickly.

"I hear it all went well. I trust the press people and the movie folks got all the pictures they needed?" van Zandt chortled.

"Yes, reporters are still here gathering quotes. We also have a swarm of lawyers protesting the round-up of their clients."

"Wonderful," van Zandt said. "Our objective was to get publicity, and from what I heard on the radio, we succeeded quite well. The newspapers should be full of stories tomorrow because similar raids were carried out in the big cities in the West. The public at large should be impressed with our vigilance to keep the NSB in check. It will make them feel safer."

Mark wondered what value a PR effort could have when war was threatening, but van Zandt happily added, "You have done well. Take your friend to dinner and see me tomorrow as soon as you are back."

He decided to stop off at the hotel on the way to Jenny's house. He wanted to take the ugly bandage off and replace it with a plaster. After all he couldn't romance a girl looking like he'd come from a street brawl.

The pub was remarkably quiet. The steady clientele would be at home with their families. It was his last evening in Groningen and he intended to ask Hubert if he could take Jenny out for dinner. It might not be that bad, he thought. Hubert's attitude had improved when he found out that he was still an active CID agent.

Jenny greeted him at the door. Hubert sat in his favourite chair looking grumpy. Mark decided on the direct approach.

"Why do you want to take her out to eat?" Hubert said testily, "We have dinner here; why spend money?"

"Oh, Hubert don't be so dull," Mother Marty admonished. "You were young once. I remember once you asked my father if we could go out for something to eat and you were most upset that the old man said no, so let Jenny go and let them have some time together."

Hubert looked at her sternly but then his face dissolved into a smile, "You remember that, do you Marty? Your old man was a lot stricter than I am." He turned to Mark, "Have her back by curfew."

"Thank you, Papa. I must change," Jenny said as she rushed over to kiss him. Hubert pretended to be offended by the display of affection but his smile betrayed him. Mark felt uncomfortable being watched by the parents of the girl he would like to make love to at the earliest opportunity. He was quite sure that Mother Marty could read his mind.

Jenny wore the same outfit she wore when she met him at the station, the gray skirt with the pale blue cable-knit sweater. She carried her white raincoat over her arm. He thought she looked chic. They walked arm in arm. Jenny suggested possible restaurants. He responded coolly for he figured if they were to eat anywhere but the hotel it would be difficult to invite her up to his room. He couldn't just walk into the hotel and march her upstairs; Albert Hark would have a moral fit.

"I saw the menu at the Hotel de Ville and they serve very nice meals," he offered tentatively.

"Well, I was thinking of the hotel myself but I thought you might misinterpret that," she grinned.

"If you think I hoped that you would come up to my room after dinner, you are totally correct. My concern about the hotel is how we can sidetrack Mr. Hark when we make our move to go upstairs."

"Let's not get ahead of ourselves. Let's first find out if they have anything good to eat."

As they walked through the pub's swinging doors, Albert Hark looked at them with greater respect than the first time. He showed them to a small table at the window and was almost obsequious in presenting the menu. "It's the mobilization," he apologized, "There isn't much choice but we must do our bit. Right, Sir?" he asked fawningly.

Mark ignored him and looked at the menu. "What do you suggest?"

"Have the sprouts and pork chops," a woman at the next table chimed in, "It's good."

Jenny smiled at her. "Actually, I think I would like to have a glass of wine and then decide." Mark agreed and ordered a carafe of *vin ordinaire*, the cheap French wine that was still available.

Jenny, no doubt stimulated somewhat by the grape, talked animatedly. After Mr. Hark delivered another carafe they ordered dinner of *patates frites, carbonade* and *compote de pommes* or applesauce. As they enjoyed the meal, he listened to her happy talk. Not surprisingly, his mind was preoccupied with the logistics of getting her upstairs, past the watchful eye of the pub's host. Jenny noticed Mark's silence and suddenly looked at her watch.

"I think it is time to go," she announced.

Mark was startled. "Yes, of course," he said rising and reaching for her coat.

"Not so fast," she whispered. He sat down again. "How do we arrange this?" she said. His mouth was dry with pent-up excitement. He outlined his well-considered plan.

"Let's put our coats on and pretend we are going outside for a walk. I'll go to the bar to settle the bill. That'll divert him. Meanwhile you go out into the hallway but instead of going outside, you turn right and go up the stairs to room nine on the right."

"Okay give me the key under the table," she said. The key; he didn't have the key. It was on the rack behind the bar. You couldn't take that key outside. It had that damn block of wood attached to it.

"Can you go upstairs and wait in the hallway until I get the key?" he suggested. Jenny looked doubtful. "I'll be as fast as I can," he added. They donned their coats and he walked over to bar.

Albert Hark asked expectantly, "Did you enjoy the supper, Sir?"

Mark responded nervously, avoiding eye contact. He turned to Jenny as she pushed through the swinging doors.

Albert looked at her leaving and smiled. "Would you like to charge the dinner to the room, Sir?"

"Yes please and let me have the key to the room."

"If you intend to walk the lady home, Sir, let me suggest that you leave the key here until you return." Hark sported a smile of triumph. Mark felt momentarily stumped.

"No, I'll take it now," he snapped. Hark reached behind the bar and handed him the piece of timber with an exaggerated flourish.

"Have a good night, Sir," Hark said. Mark looked up at him. He thought he detected a flicker of a knowing smile.

Jenny leaned against the door of room nine, looking uncomfortable. "I thought, you'd never come."

"It's okay, no problem." He was nervous opening the door.

Jenny looked around the room. "Not very luxurious is it?"

"It's the best room in the house."

"It's the best room because there is no one here to bother us." She put her arms around him; her lips parted in a smile. It was the easiest thing in the world to kiss her. She kissed him back, nervously at first, then hard. They unclenched for a moment but only long enough to throw their coats onto the floor. His arms reached around her sweater and rubbed her back while they kissed, more hungrily than before. Jenny felt his excitement and pulled away from him a bit. She looked down.

"I remember him from an earlier meeting," she grinned. Her hand slid gently over the bulge.

He reached under the back of her sweater and tried to loosen her bra with his hand but gave up after some feeble attempts.

"You poor thing," she said with mock pity. She took off her sweater, reached behind her back and unfastened her bra with a swift movement, and let it drop to the floor.

He had felt her breasts before but had never had a long glorious look. They were firm, white and round; the brown-rimmed nipples were puckered and stuck out with excitement. She put her arms around his neck and pulled his body toward her. She reached to undo his shirt. He helped but in his excitement he almost ripped the buttons off.

"There," she said as she pushed her breasts against his chest. "That's warm and comfortable."

He gently slipped his fingers inside the back of her skirt and brought them slowly around to the front. He stopped in front of her navel and wriggled his fingers inside the seam. Jenny shivered. "I want this to come down," he said kissing her while tugging at the skirt.

"I want this to come out," she mumbled, stroking the front of his trousers. Without any words spoken, they stepped out of their remaining clothes and kissed, standing up, naked as the day they were born.

The tension became too great. She walked over to the bed. It was exactly how he had imagined it. He sat on the bed beside her. "May I," he asked, motioning that he wanted to lie beside her. She giggled.

"Oh, Mark, you are so polite." He knew it was silly but he didn't know what else to say. "Don't talk," she whispered. When they made love, it was slow and intense. "I have wanted this for so long," she whispered as her breathing became deeper and thrust her body in synch with his powerful strokes. Orgasm roared through her tensed body from her stretched-out toes to her shoulders. Exhausted but entirely at peace they reclined, looked at the ceiling and wondered where all of this might lead.

They left the hotel not caring whether Mr. Hark saw them or not. Mark stowed the huge key in his coat pocket and walked Jenny home in time for curfew. As they sat in the living room, he wondered how Jenny could act so natural after what they had done. He was on cloud nine, enthralled with the wonder of it all. He felt Hubert's eyes boring into his as if to determine if anything untoward had happened but then again, maybe not. If anything, he was more agreeable than before.

As he said his goodbyes to return to the hotel, Jenny stepped outside and promised to walk him to the railway station in the morning.

Hark smiled a wicked grin when Mark returned. He asked to borrow the old-fashioned two-bell alarm clock and slept very soundly.

He woke up reliving the intimate moments of the night before. The wonder of it had not abated. He loved this Jenny Bos. In an hour, he would see her again. He wished that they lived closer together so they could meet more often. There was no conceivable way that he would be transferred to the Northeast.

He decided against the communal washroom again. A dribble of lukewarm water was the only advantage to be gained by competing with the other male hotel guests for space along the three-metre sink. He debated skipping the shave until he realized that upon arriving in The Hague, he had to immediately report to van Zandt.

He was hungry and could even appreciate a cup of chicory coffee. He dressed quickly and went downstairs. To his surprise, the pub was full with early morning workers crowding around the big Philips radio. "What's happening?" he asked a mailman who was blocking his view.

"The Germans have invaded Denmark and Norway. It's happening right now; listen." In sombre tones, the newsreader of the ANP repeated the earlier bulletin.

> *"The German High Command in Berlin has announced that this morning at 4:15 a.m., Forces of the German Reich crossed into the territory of Denmark and Norway. At that moment, the respective German envoys in Denmark and Norway informed the respective governments that Germany wished to protect both countries against Franco-British aggression.*
>
> *The communiqué further added that the action "Was in response to intercepted plans for a French-backed British invasion at Trondheim." Two hours ago, German assault troops landed at the principal Norwegian ports of Kristiansand, Stavanger, Bergen, Narvik and Oslo.*
>
> *The Ministry of Defence in Copenhagen has announced that the Danish Royal family is held captive by German parachute commandos. Denmark is expected to surrender by noon today.*
>
> *The Norwegian government has issued a statement that it will repel the invaders with all forces at its disposal.*
>
> *In The Hague, General Winkelman, Chief of the Armed Forces announced that all Dutch Forces – land, air and sea – have been placed on high alert. Stay tuned for additional bulletins."*

He felt the dull pain of fear deep in his stomach. Suddenly the war was only a two-hour drive from where he stood. Talking about war was easy but the recognition that it was creeping ever closer was bone chilling.

"What do you think?" he asked a burly fireman.

"I think we're next."

"Oh, don't be so nervous, they don't want us. We are neutral," the mailman volunteered.

"The Danes were neutral and see where that got them."

Deep in thought, he packed his suitcase, paid the hotel bill and walked to Jenny's house.

The family had heard the news on the radio. Hubert had listened and gone to work. Mother Marty seemed unconcerned but Jenny was in tears.

"I hear that all forces are on high alert. Will you be affected?"

"I'm sure there will be new assignments." He looked at his watch and added, "We must go. I can't miss the train."

Mother Marty gave him a hug. "You'll come back and see us again, won't you?" Mark nodded and steered Jenny to the door. "Must go now," he said rushing her off.

They arrived 15 minutes early and opted for a final cup of coffee in the First Class waiting room. "They must like you in The Hague to let you travel in style," Jenny teased.

"When all the troubles are over and we are married you will always travel in style, Mrs. Zonder," he held her hand as he spoke.

Jenny choked back a tear. "Marriage?" she asked.

"I mean it Jenny. I would like to ask your father for your hand so we can be officially engaged. The actual marriage will have to wait." Jenny bent her head and kissed his hand.

"When do you think you could come again?"

"I have made it for Christmas and Easter. I'll try to get leave for the *Pinkster* long weekend, the Pentecost, *Whitsunday*? That's only six weeks from now."

The train was ready for boarding. He stood on the lower steps of the carriage and bent way down to kiss her.

"See you in six weeks," he said as the locomotive let out a burst of steam on its first chug-a-chug, trying to get a grip on the tracks. He closed the door and lowered the window. He leaned out and waved. She waved back, her image disappearing in the distance.

27

1940
TUESDAY, APRIL 9, 4:45 PM
OFFICE OF THE COMMISSIONER FOR RATIONING OF COAL AND ANTHRACITE
THE HAGUE, NEDERLAND

"You mean he's happy?" Mark asked incredulously. Alice, her sweater more form fitting than before, received him with a big smile and confirmed that van Zandt was in great form.

"He is in a better mood than he has been for months."

"I wonder why."

"You'll find out," she said busying herself with make-believe work that secretaries tend to perform at such times. "Be sure to knock. You know how quickly his mood can change."

Van Zandt looked up and welcomed his protégé with a big smile. "We have done it my boy. We are looking like pure genius."

"Thank you Sir, I expected a more subdued reception, seeing what's happening in Denmark and Norway."

"That development was good for us," van Zandt seemed oblivious to the war up north. His own war took precedence. "I received a complimentary note from the Prime Minister that our arrest of the NSB extremists just before the invasion was a master stroke that proved that our intelligence service is on the ball." He inspected a fingernail on his right hand and rubbed it against his teeth.

"Does the Prime Minister believe that you had prior knowledge of the invasion?"

"No, of course not, but if that is the public's perception, the Prime Minister is happy to take credit for it. There have been other developments as well," he paused with a smile. ""The Prime Minister noted that it was German special commandos who captured the Royal Family of Denmark. Therefore, I have been reinstated as a Lieutenant General in the Dutch Army. I'll be stationed at the Palace as Military

Advisor in the Queen's Guards. In that capacity, I shall be responsible for the protection of the Royal Family in case war comes upon us."

The nail still bothered him and he rubbed it once more against his teeth. He looked at it again and tried to pull at it. He slid his hand under the desk and continued,

"What does this mean for your responsibility for coal and anthracite?"

"The coal and anthracite business was merely a front. It will continue under the same administrator who ran it all along. Meanwhile, CID remains under Colonel De Bruyne. I shall be in uniform at my new office at the Palace within a few days."

"What does it mean for me?" Mark asked.

"You will be transferred from sergeant in CID to sergeant in the Queen's Guards. You will be housed in the Guard's bivouac at the Palace and you will serve as my aide-de-camp." He looked at his nail again, "Damn nuisance hangnail," he said, shaking his hand as if to fling it off.

Mark didn't know whether the change was good news or trouble. "I expected to deliver my report on the Groningen mission, Sir," he said.

"You can dictate that to Alice and she'll type it up for you. Sergeant Vreelink led the round up in Leiden. His arrests included your pastry baker and, regrettably, Alexander von Becke.

Mark got up to leave. "One more thing," van Zandt said, "Please re-establish contact with Paula and Willem quickly."

"They will be suspicious, Sir."

"Don't worry about that. Now tell Alice your story and get out of here. Report to the Queen's Guards tomorrow morning. Induction, quartermaster, uniforms and whatever."

Mark did not know whether to salute the new general or say goodbye to the Commissioner for Rationing of Coal and Anthracite. Van Zandt did not care; he was busy looking in his briefcase, probably to find a nail file.

The Quartermaster's office reeked of mothballs, leather and sweat. The supply room contained floor-to-ceiling shelves. The private who asked Mark for his size dug into a bin marked 'large' and pulled out a jacket that might be in the range to fit him. He repeated the procedure for the pants, shorts, underwear and kepi. A toilet kit containing shaving brush, razor and comb was thrown his way.

"Go and see the tailor for your alterations. And these you have to sew on your sleeves yourself," the private smirked, tossing a package of sergeant stripes on the counter. "You can collect your rifle, revolver and ammunition at the Armoury," he added.

The tailor was a humourless man with a hangdog expression. He yielded his tape measure and chalk with disinterest. He took Mark's measurements and mumbled through a half dozen pins clenched between his lips that he should check back later.

A booklet on the responsibilities of non-commissioned officers bored him sufficiently to doze off in the sergeants' mess. He woke when he was handed a message to see the Regimental Administration Officer.

Later, when he picked up his altered uniform it didn't look too bad but the kepi was ridiculous. It looked like a khaki soup can with silly black visor attached. There was no way that it could be worn with any dignity. The walk to the railway station led him past the blooming Japanese cherry trees of the Canadian Embassy. The latest gasoline rationing had removed all but a few government cars from the streets. He bought a third-class return ticket to Leiden. The girl at the wicket gave him a broad smile; maybe the kepi wasn't that bad after all.

Fortunately, Paula was at home. She gasped at his appearance.

"Willem, come and see, we have a soldier at the door. He says he is a friend." Willem came running from the living room, "It's Mark, he is a sergeant now," he said and pulled him inside.

"I've come to see how my pal Willem is doing," he explained.

"So nice to see you," Paula said looking at him fondly. "You look so handsome in a uniform." Willem tried on his kepi but it immediately sank down to his nose. Mark explained that he could only stay for a while. After reading about Alexander's arrest over the weekend, he wanted to know how the family was doing, but Paula did not appear overly concerned.

"They took him, Koopmans and some others but the message we got was that he will be home tomorrow at the latest."

"I guess the round up was in response to the fears of an invasion," Mark suggested.

"That's what Alexander thought too." It appeared that the von Beckes had not made the connection between the Koopmans incident and his

New Year's visit. He promised Willem he would be back soon and would try to persuade Brenner Zijlberg to take them sailing on his next visit.

When he arrived at the barracks, he found a message on his cot informing him to report to the Quartermaster's office in the morning.

"You must have some pull around here, Sergeant." The Quartermaster was a cadaverous looking chap with a sadly sagging grey moustache. "We've orders here to fit you with a walking-out uniform of the Queen's Guards. The Quartermaster's depot does not stock any of that fancy gear here so I will issue a purchasing chit for the military dress store downtown. They'll get you all spiffed up." Mark had no idea why he should be issued a second uniform in as many days but he took the purchasing document and did not question it.

He had only seen the unimposing north façade of the Palace. He took a stroll around the grounds and was surprised to find a large, elegant garden. He peered into the hothouse where Queen Wilhelmina grew her prized orchids. A Javanese servant was grooming the tennis court, installed for Princess Juliana when she was a teenager. Over on the left, a large gazebo, encircled by sturdy park benches served as an intimate stage for *al fresco* musical performances.

He felt as if he was intruding on the Queen's personal space, yet no one challenged him. He made a note to raise the issue of security with the General that afternoon.

Lieutenant General Francis van Zandt looked resplendent in his uniform with two rows of colourful decorations on his chest. The two gold stars on each lapel reflected the light of the chandelier above his worktable. The office was an imposing, high-ceilinged room with potted palms in the corner. The walls featured gilded wallpaper, its gaudiness broken by paintings of retired generals of the Queen's Guards. Off to the side stood a meeting table with writing pads for each of its eight seats.

The General sat at his desk. Nothing as plebeian as a desk with drawers, phones or in-and-out baskets; this was a billiard-sized mahogany table with nothing on top and only the general's legs under it. His hat hung from a coat rack in the corner.

"Getting used to the place, are you, Zonder?" he asked.

"Yes, very impressive General."

"Some officers see a problem with your role," van Zandt said. "They have difficulty with a sergeant serving as an aide-de-camp to a General. Tradition has it that it should be a commissioned officer. I have solved the problem by elevating your title from aide-de-camp to 'equerry'. It once had to do with supervising horses for the Queen's household. The nice thing about it is that the position automatically bestows you the rank of First Lieutenant. It also means better pay." Mark was stunned.

"It is an honour, Sir. Thank you for your confidence."

"I am sure I can count on you, but don't get carried away. You are an assistant to a general and not an Assistant-General. Now for the show business aspect; you have to get some fancy officer's duds. The Army says you have to pay for that yourself but I have told the Quartermaster that the Queen's Guards will pick up the tab. You must look the part when we do the dog and pony show for her Majesty and her courtiers."

"I have received the chit for the uniform from the Quartermaster."

"That's the Army for you. If our troops moved as fast as the news of promotions do, we would have Hitler on his knees in a week," he grumbled.

"I took the liberty of looking around the gardens, Sir," Mark ventured. "No one stopped me."

"That will change. The Queen has ordered a complete revamping of security with the proviso that she wants to enjoy the gardens without guns or soldiers. The Guards' job will be to create an armed perimeter to protect the Royals that must remain out of sight to anyone in the garden." Van Zandt waved him away and dropped a stack of documents from his briefcase onto the pristine table. As long as van Zandt continued to wage his paper wars, it might not ever be clean again.

First Lieutenant Mark Zonder, he thought. Two tiny silver stars. It sounded strange and intimidating. He reminded himself to look up what equerry meant.

28

1940
THURSDAY, MAY 9, 5:00 AM
ROYAL PALACE, BARRACKS OF THE QUEEN'S GUARDS
THE HAGUE, NEDERLAND

The lead car, an armoured vehicle of the Marechaussee, had been idling for ten minutes. Its occupants, impatient to get going, were silently cursing the habitual lateness of General van Zandt. Even though he had no idea, Mark told the driver it would be only a few minutes. Four sharpshooters of the Queen's Guards waited in the second car, a Citroën convertible with the top down. Behind them stood the Queen's Cadillac Fleetwood, empty, except for its driver. The car at the tail end was an Army truck that held more Queen's Guards and a Bren gun mounted at the back pointed at any would-be pursuers.

Mark watched van Zandt trotting down the steps, fumbling with his hat and limping towards the big Cadillac. Mark took up his position in the truck's cab and the convoy was on its way. Destination: Soestdijk Palace in the centre of the country, the home of Princess Juliana and her family.

Massive troop movements along the Dutch and Belgian borders raised fears that a German invasion might be imminent. The Queen had ordered that her daughter and family be moved to the Royal Palace in The Hague.

"It is easier to protect the Royal Family when they are all in one place," van Zandt had argued but the Queen feared that such a move might unduly alarm the population. However, given the latest intelligence, the relocation of the Crown Princess was now a necessity.

The convoy, accompanied by six motorcycle outriders, sped through the country roads and arrived at the Palace well before nine o'clock. Mark accompanied the General to the foyer where the palace staff had gathered to say farewell to the Crown Princess and her beloved little girls.

During a break in the action, he went outside and joined the milling group of officers and men of the various security branches involved in the move. The men were stretching their legs and consuming the coffee and sandwiches the kitchen staff had set out on a large table on the lawn.

A Marechaussee captain tugged on his sleeve motioning him to step away. "We have been alerted that NSB extremists have learned of the relocation and that sniper fire might be encountered on the route back."

Mark informed the General who did not take it all that seriously. "Perhaps a demonstration with placards," he suggested, "But I don't anticipate any shooting."

Inside the foyer, the stirring among the assembled staff indicated that the Princess and her family were on their way. Like the Red Sea, the gathering parted to provide a pathway for the family. They were likely lined up in order of rank and seniority.

Both Prince Bernhard and Juliana worked the room with a kind word for all. Princess Beatrix, almost three years old, bounced happily from one servant to another for a kiss, a hug or a gentle pat on her straw blond hair. Princess Irene, just one year old, received more gentle pinches on cheek and chin than any baby should endure, yet she maintained regal decorum by smiling through it all.

Princess Juliana stopped in the Centre of the hall to address the assembly. "Because of the international situation, the Queen has summoned her family to be with her in these fearful days. Prince Bernhard, the children and I wish to thank you so much for your service to our family. We do not look upon this as a departure. It is merely a cautionary step. Please look after our beautiful home. We shall return as soon as possible."

Many of the old retainers cried as the entourage headed out to the waiting cars. After a final wave, the family took their assigned seats.

The Cadillac with its fold-down seats accommodated the family of four and Mieke de Jonge. Beatrix was as chatty as a three year-old can be. She covered her ears as the motor cycle escorts kicked their starters.

The convoy sped out of the Palace grounds. The driver had no knowledge of the route chosen by the motorcycle escort. Two motorcycle officers raced to block the upcoming intersection. Once the procession passed, they rejoined the rear of the motor cycle escort. The two new front riders hustled to block the next intersection. They hop scotched their way through country roads and hit the highway at Utrecht for the last 50 kilometres. If there were any snipers along the way, they would have seen only a blur pass by.

Beatrix was oblivious to the tense situation. She played happily with her doll. Only when they were racing through the streets of The Hague did she show some concern. "I sure hope Grandma is home," she announced to no one in particular.

The Officers' Mess was abuzz with talk of a possible invasion. Many officers who had sincerely believed that the country would remain unscathed now feverishly discussed the pending reality.

"Hey, there is Lieutenant Zonder, the instant wonder," a voice taunted from the back. Mark knew his promotion wasn't popular with the professional soldiers who had worked many years to achieve their rank but then again, he hadn't asked for the position.

The adrenalin was still flowing after the harried trip to Soestdijk and back. He hadn't come to the Mess to eat or drink; it was the nearest place with a pay phone. He asked the long distance operator to connect him to Jenny's kindergarten in Groningen. She would probably still be there for a half hour or so. The headmistress who answered the phone refused to interrupt Jenny's class. Discouraged, he hung up. He made his way to the Palace's command centre to ask the operator to place an urgent call from the Queen's Guards. He hoped that respect for military authority would get through the principal's objection.

In less than a minute Jenny was on the phone. "What's wrong?" she asked nervously.

"Nothing's wrong, I just wanted to hear your voice." He realized that it sounded lame. He wanted to say how much he cared. How lonely he felt without her. He wanted to tell her what he could not tell anyone else. That he was afraid. Afraid of war, of death, and of losing her. Instead, they talked about the weather and daily trivia. His time was up.

"I'll see you soon," he said.

29

1940
FRIDAY, MAY 10, 4:20 AM
BARRACKS OF THE QUEEN'S GUARDS
THE HAGUE, NEDERLAND

"It's war goddamn it," The words were barely audible – drowned out by the deafening hoots of the claxon. He heard footsteps running down the hallway. Yells, screams and commands blended into confusion. He leaped out of his cot and opened the door. Officers were running down the hallway. Grabbing a half-dressed man by the sleeve, he demanded, "What the hell is going on?"

"The Germans are attacking," he yelled. Mark quickly donned his uniform and ran to the assembly area.

"What do we know?" he demanded from a Military Police corporal guarding the entrance.

"Command Centre has issued a high alert. German forces crossed the border about half an hour ago. That's all I know."

Mark hastened to van Zandt's suite where several senior officers had gathered in the outer room. Their discussion bordered on hysteria.

"Quiet," the General yelled, hopping up and down to get his other leg into his pants. "Get your officers together and order the Guards to report in full battle gear at the plaza in front of the barracks."

"Lieutenant Zonder, notify the private secretaries of both the Queen and the Crown Princess to prepare for any emergency." He finally finished buttoning up his trousers and motioned for Colonel Tom Meyers, his second-in-command, to follow him to the Command Centre.

He was still buttoning his tunic when he suddenly turned and barked, "Oh, Zonder, bring back my sidearm and helmet."

He found the helmet under the General's bed. His new Walther P38 hung from a hook behind the toilet door.

The on-duty officer reported Heinkel bombers dropping their lethal loads on bridges across the big rivers to the North Sea. Mark was shocked to hear that barely half an hour after the attack, the city of Groningen had fallen into enemy hands. There were no reports of civilian casualties, nor indications of any treacherous actions by the NSB extremists. Jenny was safe, he hoped.

Van Zandt addressed the men and officers lined up in the parade plaza, Colonel Meyers one step behind on his left.

"Men, our task is to secure the Palace from attack by ground or air. Our primary job is to protect the lives of the Queen and the Royal Family. The German objective will be to isolate and capture the Queen, the Princess and her family." He paused and strutted around the parade ground, chin in the air. "We can be sure that German paratrooper commandos will be deployed. The perimeter around the Palace will be widened to defend against any attack through the City."

He looked on in disbelief when the rumble of approaching aircraft caused a dozen Guards to break rank and head for the trees.

"Hold your formation, GODDAMMIT," Colonel Meyers screamed. "The General is speaking. Get back in line."

Van Zandt stood immobile, his expression stony. The Guards slowly returned to the original formation. Colonel Meyers' face was livid with agitation. "We are at war," he yelled, "Running away from your post is desertion and punishable by execution. Let's have that straight right now," he turned to the General and saluted.

Van Zandt resumed his address without referring to the incident. A squadron of six Heinkel bombers with their peculiar Plexiglas noses roared overhead, the hated swastika clearly visible on the tail. After the initial shock of finding themselves at war, the men were attentive now. Colonel Meyers outlined the defensive plan and one-by-one, detachments marched off to their assigned positions. Suddenly, the thumping sound of bombs exploding a few kilometres away sent shivers through the ranks, but they kept in line. They could not be blamed for their apprehension; neither their fathers nor grandfathers had ever experienced war.

"To judge by the direction of the sound, the airfield at Ypenburg is the target," the Colonel ventured. "That is five kilometres from here. They will try to put our few fighter planes out of action."

As he spoke, another squadron of low flying Heinkels passed overhead and turned southwest. Unexpectedly, the planes banked and disgorged dozens of billowing canopies that drifted down the clear blue morning sky like so many fluffs of a dandelion.

"Paratroopers are landing at Ockenburg airfield, six kilometres south," van Zandt remarked matter-of-factly. "They will come this way. The Army must pin them down at the airfield."

At the Command Centre, adjacent to the Queen's garden, distressing reports poured in. Thousands of paratroopers were landing at the airfield near Valkenburg. The Hague was being encircled. The five Dutch fighter aircraft stationed at Ypenburg had managed to take off before the bombardment and the paratroopers' assault. Two German Heinkels were shot down as they attempted to land at that airfield. They crashed on the runway rendering the strip inoperable for the rest of the day.

At seven o'clock, van Zandt demanded to hear the morning news on the national radio. The announcer sounded calm, "This morning at approximately four o'clock, several hundred aircraft of unknown origin entered Dutch airspace in a westerly direction."

"Unidentified origin" van Zandt burst out. "That'll come as a surprise to the people who are seeing goddamn Germans dropping from the sky. Why is no one telling those dolts what is going on?"

A leather-clad motorcycle dispatch rider, helmet under his arm, handed Colonel Myers a message. "Two German paratroopers, who landed wide of Ypenburg, are held captive in Rijswijk," he read aloud.

"We must know the plan of attack," van Zandt snapped. "Lieutenant Zonder, take a couple of men and bring those bastards in."

Mark hesitated for a second before he approached one of the new Queen's Guard recruits guarding the barracks. "What's your name?"

"Private Schilder, Sir," The lad was a solidly built farm boy with an engaging grin.

"Come with me. We need a car."

An imposing sergeant major, in charge of the motor pool, stood in the centre of the driveway, surrounded by a milling group of officers and NCOs demanding transportation. "Get lost assholes," he yelled with remarkable disregard for military protocol, "I've got nothing. Bugger off."

An old olive-green Ford with Army plates arrived in the compound to unload two walking wounded. As the medics helped the last man from the car, Mark ordered Schilder to get into the back seat and jumped in the passenger seat. The driver was not the least bit intimidated by either war or officers. He put the car in gear and asked, "Where to Boss?" Mark half expected him to set a meter. "Hope it's somewhere peaceful?" he added with a snicker.

"What's your name, soldier," he asked the driver.

"You can call me Koos, boss," he said obviously intending to stick to civilian discourse.

On this beautiful, clear spring day in May, war seemed utterly out of place. The streets were largely devoid of vehicle traffic. People clustered in groups to discuss this new thing: War! There was no panic. Instead, an odd excitement hung in the air. At every corner, they encountered a roadblock, manned by nervous soldiers, many of whom had known less than three months of army life. The military appearance of their vehicle evoked more suspicion than trust. Mark chafed at the persistent demands for identification. He understood the reason but he had a job to do.

Many homeowners were protecting their windows by gluing strips of packing tape to the glass in a grid-like pattern. So far, it was the only useful suggestion Radio Hilversum had managed to broadcast.

"The tape will prevent glass shards from flying around," Koos explained. The sound of an aircraft passing low overhead made him duck and a loud detonation nearby made him simultaneously hit the brakes causing Mark to bang his helmet on the windshield.

"Sorry, boss," he said, with a chuckle.

"You are likely to kill us before we even see a German!" Mark chided.

"Doing my best, boss," Koos said.

The trip to Rijswijk, normally 20 minutes, took twice as long even though they did not encounter any enemy fire. Machinegun reports near Ypenburg indicated that the base had not yet fallen to the enemy.

An infantry lieutenant directed them to a tool shed in the community garden were the prisoners were held. There, amid the rakes and shovels, the two Germans sat on upturned baskets, guarded by a soldier pointing a loaded rifle at the enemy.

The German paratroopers wore their full camouflage battledress including high-laced boots. Their helmets were intertwined with grasses and twigs. Their uniforms, featuring pockets and zippers everywhere, were of far greater quality and utility than the Dutch military garb, some of which pre-dated the war of 1914.

The older of the two captives wore the insignia of *Oberleutnant* – a rank equivalent to Mark's First Lieutenant. The other was a trooper. They rose as Mark entered. The Oberleutnant gave the military Luftwaffe salute, not the Heil Hitler salute. Mark returned the salute and introduced himself. "Lieutenant Zonder, Regiment of the Queen's Guards."

"Oberleutnant Schreiber, Fallschirmjager Division, Deutsche Luftwaffe and this is Gefreiter Teucher," he said with a motion toward the corporal.

"I need to know your objective," Mark said motioning for the German to sit down. The officer smiled. "Herr Lieutenant, I have given you all that is required under the Rules of Warfare of the Geneva Convention. My rank, name, and if you like, I'll recite my serial number."

Mark sighed. "Let us talk," he began, "You attacked our country, unprovoked and without warning. That is also against the Geneva Convention. Therefore, we are even. I need to know the objective of your attack on Ypenburg." Schreiber looked away but did not speak.

The soldier with the rifle spoke, "When we captured him he had a lot of maps and papers in those big pockets," he volunteered. "They are over there on the shelf." He pointed his bayonet at a shelf filled with shears, clippers and other gardening paraphernalia. Mark opened the chamois wrapped parcel. The Oberleutnant appeared anxious.

"Well, look here. Maps marking access routes to the Palace," Mark said.

He glanced through the documents that confirmed van Zandt's assessment that the objective was to encircle The Hague against the North Sea. Six thousand paratroopers were assigned to land at Ypenburg and another 3,000 at Valkenburg airfield. A smaller group that landed at Ockenburg that morning numbered 1,000.

He told the infantry lieutenant that had been standing guard to take the other paratrooper for a walk in the community garden. He decided to take the Oberleutnant back to the Command Centre at the Palace. As they returned to the car with their captive, he put Schilder up front and joined Schreiber in the back keeping the muzzle of the Colt .45 in his ribs.

Koos said, "*Guten morgen. Haben sie eine gute reise gemacht?*" Schreiber, in spite of his predicament had to laugh at the question whether he had a good trip. "*Sehr gut, danke,*" he said playing along.

They raced down the Rijswijkerweg. About 200 metres ahead, Koos spotted a group of camouflaged paratroopers buying milk from the local milkman. Without being told, he turned right, went around the block and joined the main road again.

Around the corner, a bomb crater made the road impassable. Suddenly, a German Junkers, a single-engine fighter plane, swooped lengthwise along the road. It was a pass only, no cannon fire.

"*Er wird zurück kommen*," yelled the Oberleutnant, fearing the plane would return. Seeking cover, Mark hauled Schreiber out of the car and into the ditch. Koos and Schilder dove behind the wall of a nearby house. Moments later the Junkers approached, this time at treetop level. A Dutch roadblock further down unleashed a barrage of machinegun fire on the approaching aircraft. The pilot made an evasive turn and flew away in a westerly direction, unharmed. They waited a minute before continuing.

In the Moermanlaan, a group of curious neighbours surrounded a crashed German fighter plane, its nose stuck deeply in the lawn of an attractive villa. The pilot could not have survived.

Leaving the Palace had been troublesome; getting back was worse. They were challenged at a dozen posts. Each questioner, at every barricade, was determined to have a good look at an actual German officer. Schreiber endured it all with a stoic mien.

The mood in the Command Centre was one of quiet resolve. Its focus was narrow; protect the Royal Family. They needed to know the situation beyond the enclave of the Palace even though their role was purely defensive in nature.

"We are a shield rather than a sword," van Zandt explained to an agitated Jonkheer van Hoogland, the Queen's Private Secretary. The older man was dressed to the nines in grey pinstriped trousers and cut-away jacket. He perspired heavily and was obviously upset that his daily ritual, so formally prescribed, had turned to utter chaos.

"How will these hostilities affect the comfort of her Majesty?" he puffed. He nervously checked his shirt cuffs to see if they were still there.

Van Zandt looked at the man with barely concealed disdain. "The Germans did not give us the courtesy of a program for today," he snarled. "We are improvising as we go along."

The man muttered something about rude people. Van Zandt didn't care. A corporal interrupted the discussion to announce the German captive had arrived.

"Please excuse me I must attend to more pressing matters," he said dismissively, leaving van Hoogland to his distress.

Mark did the introductions while Schilder kept his rifle pointed at Schreiber. "Oberleutnant Schreiber of the 21st Fallschirmjager Division captured near Ypenburg." The German officer clicked his heels and gave the standard military salute. Van Zandt gave him a rather desultory wave. He led Schreiber to his office. Mark and Schilder came along and took their position against the wall on either side of the door.

"Lieutenant Zonder, please report," van Zandt said, sitting down behind the mahogany battleship of a desk.

Mark stepped forward and summarized the captured documents that confirmed the General's assessment that the plan was to encircle The Hague with 14,000 paratroopers landing in three locations. Lieutenant Schreiber listened. He caught most of the words but did not register any outward emotion.

"I can add a little humour if Lieutenant Schreiber is interested," van Zandt said, "After dropping their parachutists, seven German aircraft landed at the airfield of Valkenburg. The pilots didn't know that construction on the runways was not completed. The aircraft are now stuck in the mud. Three other aircraft were forced to land on the beach; they are stuck too."

"It matters not," Lieutenant Schreiber responded, "We come with overwhelming force. The struggle will not be long."

Van Zandt was impatient. "Yes, yes. Thank you for the party line. Your mission is to capture the Royal Family. What reasons you were given for this non-military objective?"

Schreiber spouted the party line, "We come as guardians. Life in the occupied territories must carry on as usual; therefore Germany cannot allow the Royal Families to go into exile."

The General was visibly angry. "We shall do our utmost to ensure that you will not succeed. You should be home with your family within a few weeks." Not even the General believed that, Mark thought but admired his chutzpah.

"Take him to the Palace prison," he snarled, "those walls haven't seen an enemy prisoner for centuries. We will bring him some company as we capture more of his fellow jumping jacks." Schreiber was quiet as he was led through the catacombs of the Palace.

"Don't you think it is ironic that you have arrived at your target before any of your troopers?" Schilder asked.

Schreiber smiled a weak smile. "We are all soldiers. We follow orders."

It was early afternoon. Mark had not eaten anything since the previous evening. The Officers' Mess was deserted except for some administrative types who looked entirely out of place. He went to the unmanned lunch counter and grabbed a couple of slices of the heavy dark bread that the Dutch army never seemed to run out of and a big pot of strawberry jam. That's about all there was, save for some cold pea soup.

He longed to smell the garden and walked outside with his lunch. A battle-ready anti-aircraft battery stood along the orangery and the soldiers' helmets were camouflaged with shrubbery from the garden. The Queen would not likely object. He saw the green grass and the budding trees. It was the kind of day with a hint of summer to come. Some birds flew in disciplined formations, some in ragged mobs; and up high, flew a loner who didn't like discipline. It looked so normal. How could people at this very moment be killing other people, destroying buildings and maiming civilians?

In his mind, he had always seen war as an uninterrupted stream of unrelieved horror. Yet he sat here peacefully, eating bread while the birds chirped in the bright spring sunshine.

The radio was blaring away in the mess hall. In a mechanical voice, the announcer delivered bulletins as they were handed to him. In Zwolle, a bus with 22 schoolchildren was destroyed by a German bomb. There were no survivors. The town of Valkenburg near Leiden was largely destroyed. Many of the villagers hiding in the church were killed by a direct hit.

Tank columns were advancing on the Grebbe Line, the defence installations designed to protect Amsterdam, Rotterdam, Utrecht and The Hague. The Dutch prided themselves on this armed bastion. It was said to equal the Maginot line – impenetrable. In the day's overwhelming events, he had not fully comprehended that the German advance also covered France, Luxembourg and Belgium. Bulletins made clear that German forces had dropped paratroopers on top and behind those legendary defence lines, rendering them ineffective.

It was all so stunningly swift. In the north, the provinces of Groningen and Friesland had fallen into German hands. He wondered if the Bos family watched the enemy's trucks and troops parading through the streets. Would the Germans free the NSB sympathizers immediately?

At two o'clock came the announcement that in the United Kingdom, Winston Churchill had replaced Neville Chamberlain as Prime Minister.

The next bulletin shocked him. The Fourth Regiment Infantry – his father's unit – was involved in heavy fighting at the *Haagse Schouw*, the bridge across the Old Rhine River. The bridge was a crucial span on the highway from The Hague to Amsterdam. If it were to fall into enemy hands, traffic to North Holland would be severely interrupted. He thought of his father leading his raw recruits into action.

More droning aircraft overhead startled the listeners. More nearby explosions. Mark tried to relax as he realized that if the enemy were intent on capturing the Royals alive, they wouldn't bombard the Palace.

A recruit brought a message that Colonel Meyers and Mark were expected in van Zandt's office. The General paced up and down the small cubicle and finally spoke. "The Queen's Guards will secure the inventory of gold reserves in the Bank of Nederland and prepare them for transport to England."

"General, what transport will be made available to achieve that goal?" Colonel Meyers asked.

"By air is too risky. We must use surface transportation. The gold is located in vaults here in The Hague. A detail of our best men must take up a position in the Bank and stay there until the gold is moved out."

Nearby gunfire interrupted the briefing. The colonel rose with gun in hand. The firing stopped. In front of the Palace, a truck carrying provisions had ignored a sentry at the barricade nearest the Palace. As the truck bulldozed the barbed-wire obstacle aside, the solder emptied his rifle – all five army-issued cartridges – at the truck. An itchy-fingered machine gunner behind a wall of sandbags had joined in the excitement and riddled the van with a hail of bullets. The driver, unharmed, stood on the street screaming obscenities. "I don't give a shit about your war," he yelled, "I got work to do." The man's feelings probably echoed the sentiment of many citizens: war was for soldiers and civilians should be left out of it.

As evening fell on this first day of war, it became clear that war also sleeps. Aircraft stopped flying at dusk and as the noises of war abated, both German and Dutch combatants slept anywhere they could put their heads down. Orders at the Queen's Guard were that off-duty military personnel must sleep fully clothed, guns at the ready.

30

1940
SATURDAY, MAY 11, 4:00 AM
BARRACKS OF THE QUEEN'S GUARDS
THE HAGUE, NEDERLAND

Dawn saw thousands more paratroopers descending from the sky. On the parade ground, Colonel Meyers urged his dejected regiment to repel the "treacherous hordes of the East." There was no sense of potential victory, only a raging emotion that the enemy must pay a price for their unprovoked attack. The best news was that the Dutch had recaptured the airfield at Ypenburg.

General van Zandt was in a much less buoyant mood when he summoned Mark to join him in the Command Centre.

"Looking damned depressing, Zonder," he mumbled pointing in the direction of the flag-covered maps. "There is heavy fighting at the Grebbe Line but if their tanks break through, the route to Holland is wide open. Only 70 kilometres to go and they are at the Palace's doorstep." He stood up and made a big show of straightening his uniform jacket as if proper dress would improve the situation.

"What are the orders for the day, Sir?" Mark asked.

Van Zandt sat down again. "Stay close. Do not get bullied by some over-zealous officer who wants a warm body for his defence position. Stay put. That's all." He rose and opened the door that led to the main operations centre; it was an unspoken command to get out.

The Command Centre exuded a strange calm. On a hastily installed plywood wall, overnight reports – hand printed on index cards – were pinned with a fast-dwindling supply of thumbtacks.

A giant wall map of Western Europe showed the German progress in Belgium and France. The German Seventh Army was near Dunkirk, a mere 20 kilometres from the Channel.

On the map, the German blitzkrieg looked stunningly simple. If an opponent builds a massive wall in front of you, go around it. Relying on the Maginot Line had proved to be a bone-headed error. Even a green lieutenant could see that now.

Van Zandt summoned Colonel Meyers and Mark once more. This time he had a spring in his step. He looked purposeful after having attended a conference at the Cabinet Chamber at the Palace.

"We're on the move," he declared, "The Crown Princess and her family will be evacuated. Her Majesty has decided that Princess Juliana and her family will go to England," van Zandt declared.

Meyers was taken aback, "Is the situation that desperate that the family should flee?"

"The Queen has so ordered. Some Cabinet members are concerned that Prince Bernhard might be co-opted to take a leadership role in a defeated Nederland because he was born in Germany. They want the family off to England. I understand that, but as far as the prince being co-opted by the Germans, that is a load of rot. The man is a Dutch officer, defending his country."

"So the party will consist of four Royals," Meyers summarized, "And how many courtiers?"

"Only Jonkvrouw Mieke de Jonge." Mark remembered her from the evacuation of Soestdijk Palace.

Van Zandt looked happy to be in action again. "Colonel Meyers, you have carte blanche to get this thing done. Bring me a detailed plan this afternoon so we can go over it with the Queen's Private Secretary; that is if he has recovered by then."

The first efforts were in vain. The Air Force had no suitable aircraft available. Moreover, the Luftwaffe controlled the skies making air travel hazardous. Sea travel was the only option.

Mark's job was rousing senior naval and army commanders to come to the phone for strong-arming by Colonel Meyers. The telephones rang incessantly. Finally, a call from the Admiralty in London confirmed that the British Royal Navy would send an A-Class destroyer to transport the Princess and her family, provided the Palace would designate the appropriate harbour within the next 30 minutes. Meyers was delighted.

"I doubt that the Rotterdam harbor will be accessible," he said, "Heavy fighting is reported around the Shell refineries. Hoek van Holland is an option..." Another call interrupted the discussion. Meyers listened and slammed the phone down. "Discussion over. The British have chosen IJmuiden, west of Amsterdam as their only acceptable point of embarkation. Keep pursuing the availability of vehicles to get us there."

At the Army Supply Corps, Mark couldn't find an officer in charge. He spoke to a Sergeant who laughed when asked for an armored vehicle for use by the Palace. "You must be joking," he said before hanging up.

In short order, Mark got a primer in obtaining military assets in wartime. He called every vehicle depot, private and public in or near The Hague to no avail.

Stretching his legs, he wandered over to the message board with its index cards. The reports listed defeats, troop withdrawals, surrender and destruction. One positive note caught his attention. The country's gold reserves at the national bank had been successfully transferred to a British Navy vessel in Hoek van Holland. The valuable cargo had been delivered by the Bank's armored trucks.

The Director of the Bank of the Netherlands needed no persuasion to make the armored vans available for the Royal Family. Elated with his success, Mark reported to Colonel Meyers who also had good news. The British Navy had agreed to send the destroyer HMS Codrington to IJmuiden the next morning, Sunday May 12.

The meeting with the Queen's Private Secretary went well, almost too easy. He had no demands and appeared befuddled by the swiftness of developments. Van Zandt presented the plans in a way that suggested that he was the sole author of these elaborate undertakings.

"The Crown Princess and her family in an armoured van?" Jonkheer van Hoogland sighed. He was clearly at a loss to reconcile the dignity of the Palace with a money truck. "I guess we must adjust ourselves. The Crown Princess must go," he said with tears in his eyes as he rose. "Her Majesty will stand alone, the only man in her government."

"Right," van Zandt stated curtly. "Please ensure the evacuation party is ready to travel no later than eight o'clock. The only persons travelling with the family will be Princess Irene's nanny and Mieke de Jonge." His forceful remarks thus far had been delivered off the cuff but now he had to refer hastily to the document that Mark handed him.

"The Crown Princess will travel with Princess Beatrix in one car; Princess Irene will be with her father and her nanny in the other. Personal belongings including part of the Crown jewels will be distributed over both cars." He looked at the Private Secretary long enough to create the impression that he was seeking approval but before the man could utter a syllable van Zandt announced, "Colonel Meyers is in charge of the details."

The Colonel rose to state his requirements but did not realize he was about to face his first obstacle. "I require six motorcycle escorts," he said.

Van Zandt dumped on Meyers. "Colonel, you will not get any escorts. First, you do not want to attract the attention of the Messerschmitt fighters and as a distant second there are no riders available."

"What about the Marechaussee? After all, they are responsible for the safety of the Royals," the Colonel sulked.

"The Marechaussee has named Captain Joost Blinker, a veteran of many years, to command the convoy. They will also supply armed personnel for each vehicle plus one lead vehicle with sufficient fire power."

Meyers was annoyed that his plan had been significantly altered but kept his silence. At least he still commanded the Army component of the mission. However, van Zandt had a different idea about that too.

"Colonel, I commend you on arranging the evacuation so efficiently. Your presence is needed here. Therefore, Lieutenant Zonder will represent the Queen's Guard and will report to the officer in command."

Meyers rose to attention. "A wise decision, General," he said. But by the look in his eyes, Mark could tell he was really thinking how much he would like to kick the man through the windows of the Command Centre and watch to see which way he bounced off the garden's flagstones.

A short while later came the report that the HMS Codrington was steaming toward IJmuiden and would arrive by dawn. Mark co-ordinated places and times with the Palace, the bank and the Queen's Private Secretary. Only the Marechaussee responded haughtily that they had no need to confirm anything because they were in charge.

The sky in the East began to brighten; the first birds chirped. Out in the garden, the flowers anticipated the coming morning. In five more weeks, it would be the longest day of the year. Mark wondered if he would still be alive then. None of his colleagues voiced any fears. They were all gung-ho, or so it seemed. Was it just him or were others feeling the same sense of dread?

War was also waking up to the morning. The Germans had brought in heavy artillery overnight, bulky monsters drawn by Belgian clay horses that lobbed their first shells into the ports and military strongholds. The attack was now directed south, towards the port of Rotterdam and the bridges across the big rivers.

Mark walked over to the boarding area of the Palace. Even though the armoured vehicles were not scheduled to arrive until seven o'clock, he checked his watch every few minutes.

In the Command Centre, the bulletin board was a total mess. Outdated index cards were pinned in a haphazard manner and reports were hanging atilt from their thumbtacks as if their precarious suspension might lessen their alarming messages. He told an exhausted soldier to take down any reports more than 12 hours old and store them somewhere.

He wanted to do something, anything, to take his mind off the most worrisome part of the day: crossing the Old Rhine River where his father's regiment was fighting to retain possession of the bridge. If it were in German hands, a difficult detour through the narrow streets of Leiden would be the only alternative. He checked the latest information on the river crossing. There had been no overnight reports.

The armoured trucks arrived on time, accompanied by a posse of Marechaussee officers and their vehicles. They immediately inspected the trucks that normally carried valuable currencies and gold. This time their live cargo would be even more important. There had been no time to provide much in the way of amenities. Two opposing rows of wrought-iron benches had been welded to the floor. It was not comfortable, but if all went well, the ride would only take an hour.

At precisely eight o'clock, Colonel Meyers and Captain Joost Blinker descended the steps from the Palace's inner court and escorted Juliana, Bernhard and their children to the waiting trucks. A bevy of palace staff came out to say goodbye. Princess Juliana paused to embrace Mieke de Jonge who had lost her place in the evacuation to the Queen's physician.

"Let us stay in touch, Mieke," Juliana said. Mieke sobbed and held her friend in a close embrace. The Princess gently moved away and stooped to enter the truck. Captain Blinker helped her inside. Beatrix entered the van on her own. She wore a little red coat and white ankle socks. She turned around on the truck's running board and waved a happy goodbye to the tearful palace staff. Two officers entered last and flanked Juliana on both sides, loaded Walther P38 pistols in their laps.

Baby Irene's nanny carried her charge into the second van followed by Prince Bernhard, in his full uniform of Lieutenant General of the Army.

Mark joined the driver in the first van and informed him that two twin-tailed G1 Fokker fighter-bombers would provide aerial protection on the trip. The makeup of the motorcade had changed from its original plan. The lead car, preceding the convoy by a few hundred metres, was a civilian sedan with a loudspeaker on the roof blaring instructions to make room for an important convoy. This was done in the hope of minimizing the number of trigger-happy Dutch recruits from firing at the passing parade.

Colonel Meyers nodded his approval and the lead car, tires squealing, sped out of the palace gates followed by the Marechaussee vehicle and then the armoured trucks. The barricades at the north end of the Paleis straat were moved aside to allow the speeding convoy to enter the street unhindered. The control posts at the Mauritskade and the Leidsche Straatweg were already open with soldiers standing at attention in a silent salute. As they turned onto the Rijksweg to Leiden, Mark looked back into the windowless cab and saw Princess Juliana squeezed in her seat between the armed Marechaussee officers. Beatrix sat in the opposite row flanked by the Queen's physician and Captain Blinker. The little Princess looked scared but remained silent. The villas of Wassenaar showed no visible signs of war. The stately mansions looked at peace in the morning sunshine, the gardens awash in flowers and blooming shrubs.

At a heavily guarded intersection at Den Deyl, an infantry sergeant waved a huge yellow flag and brought the motorcade to a stop. He told the driver that sporadic firefights at the Old Rhine Bridge, just four kilometres ahead, made the crossing dangerous.

Captain Blinker and Mark stepped outside. The captain ordered the flagman to contact the units at the bridge to tell them that the convoy was coming through. To Mark he snapped, "Get in, we're going."

Within seconds, the convoy was speeding toward the bridge. Coming from behind, one of the accompanying Fokker aircraft suddenly overtook the convoy at treetop height and zoomed straight upward. Captain Blinker took this as a warning that German attack aircraft might be in the vicinity. They were now less than a kilometre from the bridge.

"Turn right at the next road," Blinker yelled.

"What about the lead cars?" the driver protested.

"Turn right, now!" While the lead cars committed to the bridge crossing, both armoured trucks turned rapidly onto the Rijndijk, a local road that paralleled the river. Barely 20 metres into the turn, the captain spotted a parking area covered by the ample foliage of trees.

"Turn left," he barked. Both trucks raced into a gravel parking area next to a bakery shop. The trucks now faced the Old Rhine River. The sound of sporadic gunfire emanated from different directions. A makeshift bunker made from a pile of sandbags was the only visible defensive position at the foot of the bridge. Captain Blinker got out and walked to the water's edge. Prince Bernhard had been let out of the second vehicle. He stood looking skyward in his immaculate uniform.

The thunderous overhead sound came on so unexpectedly that there was barely time to flinch. Mark and the captain hit the ground and rolled under the truck but Bernhard stood immobile. A Messerschmitt, swastika clearly visible on its tail, roared in from the East. Flying low over the river it spewed a barrage of 20 mm cannon fire into the bridge structure and the sandbagged emplacement. There was no return fire. The German aircraft pulled up at a seemingly impossible angle.

A second roar followed as one of the Fokker fighters followed the German and fired its guns into the climbing aircraft. The German fled, its engine trailing smoke. Mark and Captain Blinker crawled out from underneath the truck. Bernhard smirked and said, "I don't think that Messerschmitt will come back soon." He looked at Blinker. "We should go," he said. They were about to board when a trio of Dutch soldiers came from the back door of the bakery shop, rifles at the ready. The corporal in charge recognized the Prince and executed a smart salute.

"Don't salute officers when in battle, Sergeant. You know the rules," Bernhard admonished gently.

Captain Blinker was all business. "Where are the enemy positions?"

The exhausted sergeant answered, "You must have passed some of them. The main group is across the river, northeast of here. There may be a hundred paratroopers holed up in the cemetery along the highway."

"Get back to the bridge," Blinker said, "Inform the officer in command that the second part of the convoy will be running through and to create a diversion to draw away enemy fire."

The trio turned to leave when Mark shouted, "Who is the officer in command?"

"Major Zonder, Sir."

As he climbed back into the van Mark shouted, "Tell him you saw his son." The sergeant raised his thumb in response.

The trucks backed rapidly out of their green hideaway and careened around the corner toward the bridge. Its tarmac was pocked by hundreds of rounds of aircraft ammo and large metal shards dangled from the upper structure. A mortar had destroyed the north lane leaving only a single way through. A soldier peered out from the sandbagged reinforcement and saluted as the trucks passed. From the cemetery came small arms fire that ricocheted off the heavy steel walls of the vehicle. The bulletproof windshields proved to be as advertised but the impact of the bullets left whitish puffs on the glass.

Mark looked at Princess Juliana; her lips were moving in silent prayer. The Queen's physician had his arm around Beatrix who cried softly against his shoulder. The lead car rejoined them and took its place in front but the sound card had disappeared. Captain Blinker's shoulders sagged with relief.

At the Sikkens Paint factory in Sassenheim they turned north towards Haarlem. Tearing through the main street of Sassenheim, parishioners headed for the morning service stared disapprovingly on the speeding parade. There was a war on, true, but this was Sunday!

In the town of Bloemendaal, 15 kilometres from IJmuiden, a Dutch armoured half-track blocked the main street. A ruddy-faced army captain informed them that at dawn, hundreds of paratroopers had landed around the town of Velsen, blocking the shortest route to the harbour.

Blinker left the truck to talk to the Captain, briefed the Prince and climbed back into the truck. "Let's go," he barked, "The paratroopers appear to be heading to the Noordzee Kanaal to cut off all marine traffic inland." The waterway from the North Sea to Amsterdam was the only access to the city's important harbours.

At Velsen, they came upon a troop of Dutch infantrymen trudging single file along the road. The soldiers waved as the convoy sped past. The road turned westward. The villages and farms were behind them now. Open fields, leading into the dunes left them exposed. Up ahead another platoon of soldiers walked single-file along both sides of the road. Their helmets looked quite distinct. The driver of the lead car realized too late that they were about to pass a column of German paratroopers.

"Make a run for it," Blinker yelled. The convoy sped forward, accelerators to the floorboards. As they passed, an officer in the last vehicle emptied his machine gun at the platoon. The Germans rolled into the ditch alongside the road; they did not know that the 'sloot' is a goo-bottomed body of water covered by a solid green carpet of watercress.

"They are in the green water," the driver announced gleefully.

The human condition is such that during extreme stress, an unexpected silly event can cause extreme hilarity. The Princess laughed loudly and even little Beatrix, initially terrified by the rat-a-tat of the machine gun, looked at the laughing faces and giggled along, not quite sure why.

Dutch Marines guarded the heavily fortified gateway to the navy harbour. The Royal party was expected. The barricades opened on cue; military personnel saluted as the caravan came to a halt. The Navy harbour did not offer amenities for luxury passengers. The Royal party was led into the Navy Officers' Mess.

HMS Codrington lay at anchor, awaiting not only the Royal party, but also a group of 50 or so British citizens fleeing before the Nazi onslaught.

Prince Bernhard thanked Captain Blinker and the assembled Marechaussee personnel and shook hands with Mark and the armoured car drivers. "That was rather uneventful, wasn't it?" he remarked dryly, "I'll see the Princess and the children off to Harwich and I shall be back later tonight. There's a war to be fought."

The Marechaussee detachment was ordered to stay with the Royal family until the Codrington set sail. Captain Blinker turned to Mark. "You are on your own now. You can return the vans to the bank."

Mark ordered one of the drivers to retrace the route through tulip country. To avoid the Rhine Bridge he ordered the other van through Leiden, directing the driver to pass the von Becke house. No one appeared to be home. He wondered how soon Alexander would be freed once the Germans took over. The driver then followed the country roads back to The Hague. Safely enclosed in their cocoon of steel they made the last 15 kilometres without attracting enemy attention.

Upon his return, he found the General in the Command Centre.

"Well done, Zonder," he barked, "Colonel Meyers is drafting plans for tomorrow. Unless the British Army comes to our aid overnight, the Queen has decided to transfer the seat of government to the province of Zeeland." He stared at the ceiling as if he was trying to convince himself. "We cannot retain the entire country. We must fight to delay the inevitable as long as we can. However, know this: our country will only cede its territory in Europe; we will not sign a peace agreement. Our possessions in the Dutch East Indies and the Netherlands Antilles will not be signed away by a mere stroke of the pen. The Kingdom will carry on."

31

1940
SUNDAY, MAY 12, 6:00 PM EDT
GLADSTONE APARTMENTS, FIFTH AVENUE
NEW YORK CITY, USA

It was the promise of summer that had enticed him to cross Fifth Avenue for a walk in Central Park. Ferenc Kolmar found peace in watching the children sail their boats on the pond. He envied the young couples, hand in hand. Oh, to be young and in love!

He had to break into a light sprint to make it home in time for the CBS six o'clock news. Ever since the German attack on the Low Countries, he had not missed a single report by Edward Murrow reporting from London.

He was approaching the 'ripe old age' of 33 as his friends joked. The calendar told him so, but he felt much older. The doorman held the door open as he hurried into the vestibule and headed up the elevator to the apartment. Marcy wasn't home yet. He tuned the radio and plopped down on the couch in his luxuriously appointed living room.

The broadcast shocked him. Murrow, in his deliberate paced voice, announced that Princess Juliana, her husband and children had fled the country that morning and were now staying at Buckingham Palace.

He was aware that the Danish Royal Family had been detained but King Haakon of Norway had evaded capture and was isolated in Trondheim awaiting evacuation by the British. He understood the reasons for the House of Orange to prefer exile. The Germans would exploit Juliana's young family to gain the trust and loyalty of the population.

The passing years had not diminished his emotional connection to the Princess. Does anyone really ever forget one's first love?

His life as a performer and conductor had been an éclat, a brilliant success. If not yet at the pinnacle of his musical career, he was rapidly approaching it. His piano recitals and performances with the New York Symphony were the highlight of the City's social calendar. Admirers swamped him after each performance. Even with so much adoration, he felt unfulfilled. His friends knew that he found his personal life unattractive and boring. Several live-in women friends had shared his bed but they had never managed to engage him, emotionally or intellectually.

After he and the vacuous Margot had parted ways, Marcy Skorczeny a beautiful Hungarian émigré imagined herself to be the mistress of the Kolmar musical empire and had taken over the management of both his career and daily life. While he liked her very much, he secretly detested her cocktail parties where boring people bent his ear, asking about the 'situation' in Europe as though he were any wiser than they were.

Marcy was a fierce Hungarian patriot, mightily troubled by her homeland joining Germany in the conquest of Europe and the persecution of Jews. She was sensitive to the underlying anti-Semitism in New York's upper crust and purposely exploited their guilt by demanding their support for his benefit performances for B'nai Brith.

She was an imaginative lover and never failed to satisfy the physical needs of her brilliant compatriot. Her joyful outlook and efficiency in handling his business affairs had made her indispensable. Perhaps love is not all ecstasy but a sense of trust and feeling secure. He had to admit Marcy gave him peace of mind that might be mistaken for boredom.

He heard the elevator stop in the hall. It was Marcy.

"You look troubled, Ferenc," she always used the Hungarian pronunciation, 'fay-wrench', "What is wrong?"

"Shocking news about the war in the Netherlands. Princess Juliana and her family have fled to London. She and I had a wonderful friendship. I worry about the people and the country who gave me my start."

"You cannot carry the burdens of the world, Ferenc."

"No, but I could do something. America has not joined the war. We can still travel. I would like to do another benefit for the victims of Nazi persecution. Hundreds are arriving daily on British soil. I want to do my bit. I want to perform in Britain and perhaps get an opportunity to visit Princess Juliana and her family."

"England might be invaded next. Don't be foolish. You may get caught up in the German blitzkrieg."

"There is danger in everything Marcy, please see if you can arrange concerts in London."

32

1940
SUNDAY, MAY 13, 4:30 AM
BARRACKS OF THE QUEEN'S GUARDS
THE HAGUE, NEDERLAND

Mark read the overnight reports with dull disbelief. The Grebbe Line had been breached. German tanks, personnel carriers, armoured vehicles and horse-drawn artillery units were pouring into the economic heartland. The Wehrmacht was pushing for the port of Rotterdam.

In the Command Centre, the atmosphere was one of quiet acceptance. All knew the battle was lost. It was just a question of holding on until cabinet decided how to proceed. One rumour was that government leadership would move to a safer location within the country. Among the officers, the whispered choice was to establish a government-in-exile in England.

After swallowing a cup of remarkably good coffee, Mark found Colonel Meyers in the conference room shouting at the Deputy Minister of Defence. He was a kindly man of about 50 with a bird nose and freckles. In spite of being inside, he still wore his navy blue gabardine raincoat and a Fred Astaire hat.

"If you silly-assed pencil pushers at Defence had done your job, we would have the men and means to fight the bastards," Meyers yelled in response to the man's polite question whether the Army would surrender soon. "Instead, you and your political cronies sat on your ass hoping that we would be spared in the rape of Western Europe. Now you want to know how we are making out against this juggernaut with our horses, sabres and broomsticks!"

"I am sure our soldiers are fighting bravely," the man offered weakly.

"You're right," blazed the colonel. "The country is 120 kilometres wide from the border to the North Sea and it has taken an enemy five times our size to get half way in three days. But we have not much more to give. You will probably kiss the ass of your first German occupier tomorrow."

"We may still expect help from the British," he argued.

"They are shitting themselves on the beaches of Dunkirk hoping that some fucking rowboats will come from England to pick them up and take them home. We are alone, Sir, undermanned and underequipped. Tell that to your politicians."

"What are the plans for her Majesty's safety?" the man persisted.

"That woman is a hell of a lot tougher than all you politicos combined. She will make her decision. My guess is that unlike you shitfaces at Defence, she will stay on to fight." The nice man slithered from the room.

"Sorry Lieutenant that you had to hear that," Meyers said. "They are assholes," pronouncing the last three words with great emphasis as if Mark should write this definition down and save it for future reference.

"You don't expect help from Britain?" Mark asked.

"No land forces. They are caught with their pants around their ankles in France. The Royal Navy is protecting our harbours and promises to help evacuate our officials. That's all."

"Are the plans finalized for the relocation to Zeeland?"

"General van Zandt is meeting with the Queen's officials. There will be a cabinet meeting at eight this morning; we'll know more then."

At 08:30, General van Zandt strode into the Command Centre and motioned for the Colonel and Mark to join him in his quarters that looked out on the Queen's rose garden. It seemed too beautiful a day to sit inside and make gloomy plans. Mark notice two gardeners working away, oblivious to the chaos of war. One was pruning the rose stems, the other busied himself digging small holes.

"General Winkelman has concluded that the enemy will overrun the West tomorrow morning or possibly even today," van Zandt said. "He recommends Her Majesty relocate the seat of government."

Talk that the Queen should leave the centuries-old seat of the House of Orange seemed utterly incongruous with the gardeners tending to the roses. Van Zandt followed Mark's glance out the window but continued, "The British government will provide the destroyer Hereward, to sail her Majesty from Hoek-van-Holland to the port of Breskens in the province of Zeeland. The Queen's Private Secretary has confirmed that she will be ready to depart at ten this morning."

The man digging the holes retrieved some potted rose bushes and shook one free of its pot. The pruner leaned over to the younger man and whispered something. Van Zandt glanced into the garden and said to Mark," They have to do the job when the weather is dry."

Colonel Meyers believed this to be relevant to the evacuation. "Is a change in the weather expected?" he asked.

It was van Zandt's turn to be befuddled. "No, not that I've heard."

"Will her Majesty be accompanied by the Cabinet?" The Colonel was anxious to get the discussion back on track.

Van Zandt looked at him and continued, "Prime Minister de Geer and selected members of his cabinet will follow on the HMS Windsor." The man had finished planting the second rosebush. The pruner was not quite satisfied and tamped the earth around the stems.

"Will the newspapers be informed?" Colonel Meyers asked.

Van Zandt looked away from the rose garden. "The press-relations boys have been told to describe this as a relocation of her residence and not give the papers the impression that the Queen is fleeing the country." He dismissed the Colonel and motioned for Mark to stay behind.

"The Queen insists that I should be among the officials who will travel with her. Some of us will bring our spouses." A couple of shells landing nearby momentarily distracted him. "I must ask you, Zonder, to take my car and collect Mrs. van Zandt in Wassenaar. Be quick about it. The Queen's party will leave in an hour and a half." He threw him the keys.

The gardeners had gone; the new bushes were on their own. Grabbing his helmet, he found the Citroën behind the greenhouse gate. Two gold stars on a red license plate provided an easy pass through the barricades.

Civilian traffic was nonexistent. Several military motorcycle couriers raced past in the opposite direction. The Germans had better means of communication: short wave radio. The Dutch Army relied on the telegraph and Morse code. When the enemy cut the wires, couriers had to carry the messages. At least these days the couriers had motorcycles.

The quiet tree-lined streets looked striking against the blue sky of the beautiful Monday morning. A couple of cyclists were riding two abreast, likely on the way to work or seeing relatives. War or no war, people's regular routines were not easily abandoned.

Kirsten stood outside on the red-tiled veranda. She wore a white flowery dress and a beret. "My dear Mark," she exclaimed cheerfully, "You still owe me a tennis match." She hugged him a little longer than appropriate. Turning to the maid and gardener, she said, "I'll be back soon. Don't forget to keep up the garden!"

The back roads into the city were quiet. Milkmen and bakers were making their daily rounds. They were delayed by a crowd of onlookers who were watching an infantry platoon roust a pair of German paratroopers from a park; otherwise the trip to the palace was uneventful.

Kirsten was herded into a salon where she joined other spouses waiting for evacuation. Mark watched the formation of the motorcade. The lead car was a panzerwagen with six officers armed with grenades, rifles and light machine guns.

The Army, eager to be included in this historic event, followed with two open trucks with soldiers seated on the opposing benches, rifles between their legs. Another closed van, presumably filled with baggage, preceded the Queen's limousine. Two limousines carried the dignitaries.

Van Zandt marched out to inspect the line-up. He called out to Mark. "I'll be travelling with Her Majesty; you go in the car with Mrs. van Zandt, the Private Secretary and Palace staff."

"Should I bring my kit and walking-out uniform?"

"Don't bother. The Army has Quartermasters in Zeeland too." As he spoke, Queen Wilhelmina emerged from the palace. She wore an army helmet; her face had a look of fierce determination. She passed Mark within a few feet. He had never seen her up close, certainly not wearing a helmet. Van Zandt helped her into her limousine. Mark took the second limousine. He helped one of the Queen's ladies-in-waiting climb into the rear seat, where she squeezed between the ample girth of the Private Secretary and his spouse.

Kirsten jumped in the front seat next to the driver. Mark was about to suggest her place was behind the glass partition with the official party but he thought better of it and squeezed in next to her.

"Eight people in one car is not very comfortable," Mark apologized to no one in particular. Kirsten merely wriggled against him to make herself comfortable.

The convoy swooped through the streets, passing all roadblocks unhindered. Along the way, rural folks in the hamlets and villages stared in amazement at the speeding convoy. In the town of Poeldijk, the motorcade slowed and took a sharp turn to the right and followed a paved road so narrow it allowed for one-way traffic only.

Tree branches whipped the windshields. Mark's driver mumbled that this had to be a mistake but the caravan drove on. When the landscape changed from agricultural to sandy dunes, the parade stopped. General van Zandt leaped from the Queen's limousine. Kirsten elbowed Mark in the ribs, "Go with him," she urged.

It appeared that the Army's open truck with its armed soldiers was now the lead vehicle. The panzerwagen and its armoury had disappeared. The truck driver explained that in turning a corner in the town of Poeldijk, he had lost sight of the panzerwagen. He carried on until he saw a traffic sign that read Hoek-van-Holland and followed that road.

"That cannot be," the General hissed.

"Yes, Sir. It was a sign with red lettering," the driver stuttered.

"That means it is a bicycle path, idiot," the General exploded, "Find a place to turn around."

A few kilometres farther, the occupants of a greenhouse farm were stunned to see five vehicles and a throng of armed soldiers making a U-turn in their yard and depart in the direction from which they had come. Back in Poeldijk, the panzerwagen waited at the intersection where the convoy had left the main route. No time for recriminations; the detour had cost a valuable 20 minutes.

At 's-Gravenzande, a few kilometres from the harbour, a group of citizens stood around the broken hull of a Dutch Fokker fighter, the cloth of its fuselage torn to shreds by cannon fire. Queen Wilhelmina demanded to speak to the villagers. Van Zandt nixed the idea. Her Majesty was not amused, but obliged.

As the convoy approached the ferry terminal, a Messerschmitt dove out of the clear blue sky and began a strafing run down the pier and toward the British destroyer Hereward. Heavy return fire from the warship caused the intruder to pull up and veer away. The party made its way to the empty terminal building. Suddenly the heavy artillery guns of the nearby fort blasted four shells from its cupola in an easterly direction. The Queen flinched slightly but kept her gaze on van Zandt.

"When can we board, General?" she asked.

"Commander Greenings of the Hereward will come forward when the vessel is ready to be boarded, Ma'am."

"Well then, we shall just wait," she declared, and took a seat on a wooden bench in the waiting room, a small reticule at her feet. Many of the Queen's party, who had expected more comfortable arrangements, hesitated but finally joined her on the plebeian seats.

Mark took a look at the huge warship. He recognized the markings on her funnel *H93*, the same ship he had seen in Rotterdam during the Jamboree. He thought about Jenny. He would return in a few weeks and then they would become engaged.

War or no war, the British will have their pomp and circumstance. Lieutenant Commander Charles Woollven Greenings, in the uniform of His Majesty's Royal British Navy entered the ferry terminal along with an honour party. The group moved smartly toward the Queen who rose from the bench.

"Lieutenant Commander Greenings, Madam. May I have the honour to escort you to His Majesty's Ship, the Hereward?"

"Thank you, Commander." Wilhelmina rose, adjusted her helmet and strode out of the terminal followed by her retinue as if it was just another formal troop inspection.

A small group of sailors lined up along the railing to pipe the Queen aboard. The 60-year-old, gray-haired Queen adjusted her helmet at a jauntier angle for the navy photographer and walked up the gangplank staring straight ahead.

The crew settled everyone quickly. The Queen, her ladies-in-waiting and the Private Secretary gathered in the Captain's cabin. The ladies took the three chairs; the Private Secretary sat on the cot. The rest of the retinue had to share the wardroom with the ships officers. The seas were calm as the destroyer set a westerly course.

Mark stood on deck, near the access to the bridge when an ensign approached, "Radio message for the General, Sir." Mark read the hand written radiogram. It was from General Winkelman.

> *Breskens under heavy Luftwaffe bombardment. Recommend HM destination be changed to Harwich, England. Winkelman"*

A small smile curled the lips of the General. "Ah, Winkelman, true to his devious ways." He went down to face the Queen.

"Absolutely not," she responded, "I am staying with the troops. The men need my support. I am not deserting them in this time of peril."

"No one shall accuse you of that, Majesty," van Zandt said smoothly, "The Hereward has set course for Breskens but the Luftwaffe has destroyed the port. The Royal Navy will not permit Commander Greenings to enter the port. It is force majeure, Majesty; it cannot be helped."

"I detest General Winkelman; I shall not forgive him for making me flee my country." Wilhelmina retreated to her cabin. Van Zandt returned to the bridge.

Greenings looked at him inquiringly. "Did her Majesty assent?"

"She did not like it."

"I don't know what I would have done if she had refused. My orders were very clear from the outset; evacuate Queen Wilhelmina to Harwich. I can only guess who fabricated the Breskens scenario."

HMS Hereward, escorted by two Royal Navy vessels, docked in Harwich in mid-afternoon. The entrance to the harbour was surrounded by artillery posts and machine gun emplacements. The Queen was received with an abbreviated ceremony accorded heads of state and was escorted to the nearby Harwich train station where the Royal Train was waiting; King George VI had seen to that.

Customs and Immigration officials stood by to inspect baggage and passports but a British Brigadier of the King's Guards waved them off.

Outside the Customs Hall, van Zandt led the party aboard the train to London. "You too, Lieutenant Zonder," he commanded.

"Should I not return to Hoek-van-Holland, Sir?"

"You are my aide-de-camp, Lieutenant. I shall remain at her Majesty's side and you report to me."

The General boarded the Queen's compartment while Mark was directed to the flatbed car behind the steam locomotive, where a squad of helmeted soldiers manned two anti-aircraft guns. He would have enjoyed the rural sights of East Anglia on this sunny day if it hadn't been for the foul smoke belching from the locomotive. Initially he assumed that the black streaks on the soldiers' faces were some sort of camouflage paint, but he found that he too was beginning to look like a chimneysweep.

As the train pulled into the Liverpool Street Station, the ceremony began in earnest. A detachment of the Grenadier Guards, in full battle gear, stood at the precise spot where the Royal compartment would stop. The Guards looked a lot fiercer without the red tunics and the Busby hats.

King George VI emerged from of the Royal waiting room at exactly the moment that Queen Wilhelmina arrived at the top of the train's exit. There was no music. King George and Queen Wilhelmina departed for Buckingham Palace through a throng of curious spectators held back by helmeted Bobbies.

As he washed up in the lavatory, Mark realized that only this morning he was driving the beautiful country lanes of Wassenaar. Now he was in wartime England with no money, no passport and no way of getting back.

On the opposite platform, an army officer motioned with his baton. It was the Brigadier of the King's Guards who had so efficiently steered everyone through customs and immigration. He was the archetypical British Officer, stiffly erect, moustache curled up at the corners, baton clenched under his left arm.

"My driver is waiting outside" he said in his clipped Oxford accent, "Brigadier Ennis, King's Guards."

"Lieutenant Mark Zonder, Sir, Queen's Guards of the Netherlands."

"Looks as though we are working for the same dog and pony show; except you are with the Clogs." Mark smiled although the meaning of the British slang pronounced through a stiff upper lip escaped him. He'd have to look up what clogs meant.

"We'll be putting you up for the night in our barracks next to Buckingham Palace. The officers' quarters will have lots of room; most of our lads are fighting on the beaches of France, you know."

The trip through London was thrilling. Old Broadstreet, Threadneedle Street, the names were familiar. On the Victoria embankment along the Thames, he spotted the anti-aircraft balloons hovering over Whitehall. Other than soldiers walking around in battledress, it was the only visible sign of war. At Trafalgar Square, the pigeons were indeed as omnipresent as the travel brochures proclaimed. Travelling down The Mall, the car turned off at the Birdgatewalk where it entered the King's Guard Barracks. Buckingham Palace was a mere 300 metres away. Queen Wilhelmina should be embracing her daughter and granddaughters by now.

The Officers' Mess of the King's Guards was a colourful setting compared to its counterpart in The Hague. Flags, banners attesting to past glories, paintings, uniforms and sabres decorated the walls. Inexplicably, Brigadier Ennis ordered warm beer. It didn't even have a head of foam as Dutch custom demanded. A few fellow officers, excited to know Mark had 'captured' a German officer, wanted to know all about the Blitzkrieg. The beer kept flowing but finally, someone thoughtfully ordered a tray of little sandwiches that quickly disappeared. That evening, amply supplied with toiletries and clean underwear, he found an empty cot. He collapsed.

33

1940
TUESDAY, MAY 14, 09:45 HRS
KING'S GUARDS BARRACKS
LONDON, ENGLAND

There might have been a reveille for the King's Guards; if so, he had been oblivious to it. Being a member of a foreign army had some advantages, Mark realized. Nobody knew or cared where he was or what he did. He slept until nine.

The sign on the door to the Officers' Mess said it would close at 10:00 hours. The corporal at the door noticing his curiosity explained that Cabinet had declared that all of Britain would now be on the 24-hour clock to align with the military usage. "Same as the Jerries, Sir," the corporal explained. "Once you work with it becomes a lot easier."

The Mess still offered kippers and, of course, the English breakfast. He ate greedily, but left the kippers alone. He recalled tasting them once at breakfast and then again at hourly intervals. If the coffee at home left a lot to be desired, what passed for coffee in England tested the boundaries of human tolerance. It should be swilled, instead of drunk. Mark mused that tire-track scrapings had to be the defining ingredient. He quickly found out that complaining about coffee didn't yield any results.

"Tea is what you should drink, Lieutenant," the white-jacketed steward kindly advised, "Coffee's for nobs." Mark reminded himself to add nobs to the 'look-up' list headed by clogs.

After his table was cleared, he was surprised to see General van Zandt enter the mess. Contrary to all convention, the officers present jumped to attention when they spotted the gold stars on the general's tunic.

"At ease, men," he smiled, waving them to sit down.

All eyes followed him as he sat down at Mark's table. The sight of a general sitting down with a mere lieutenant caused a ripple.

"Damned nuisance to be without the convenience of a home," van Zandt sputtered, "Mrs. van Zandt left last night to stay with friends in

Cheam, not too far from London. She'll stay there until I find an apartment in the city." Van Zandt looked around the Mess. "Pretty nice place," he observed. "A lot nicer than The Hague."

The white-jacketed lance corporal came up to the table offering a stencilled menu. "Will you have some tea, Sir?" he asked timidly. He skilfully hid the food stains on his white jacket behind a large serving tray. Van Zandt declined with a look of distaste.

"Foul stuff that tea," he said, "It's a cup of warm milk with enough tea added to discolour it."

Mark was more anxious to get some indication of what was ahead. "Will we return home soon, General?" he asked.

"Not likely. The Queen has called a meeting for 13:00 hours at our Embassy at Hyde Park Gate. You will accompany me. There are no cars so we must take a taxi. Make sure there is one ready for us." He stomped out of the room; some British officers rose but he waved them down before most of them got out of their seat.

With an hour to kill, Mark reached for the *Daily Telegraph*. Naturally, the articles focused on the war in French Flanders where the British Army was fighting with their backs against the sea. The battle in Nederland was not mentioned except that Queen Wilhelmina had fled to England and was now staying at Buckingham Palace. On page 12, a six-line synopsis noted that the Germans were closing in on the main cities along the coast.

BBC radio led with the story that the morale of the Dutch army had plummeted upon learning that the Monarch along with her government had fled to England. The commentator quoted an unnamed highly placed source that Nederland would surrender within hours. Mark realized that he might not be going home for a long while. He set out on the unfamiliar task of getting transportation to the Embassy.

The old commissionaire on duty at the main entrance of the barracks just laughed. "No cabbies at lunch time, Sir. They're all too busy driving generals and politicians to expensive restaurants for long lunches."

"I'm looking to get my General to a Cabinet meeting of the Dutch government."

The old gent cackled, "I suggest you just commandeer a car from the motor pool but don't tell them the general is Dutch."

In his best Welsh accent, he telephoned the motor pool and ordered a car for 12:30 to transport the General to a Cabinet Meeting.

"Name?" the operator asked.

The name van Zandt would raise the issue of spelling and other uncomfortable questions. In his best Welsh accent he said, "Lieutenant General Vaughn Sand, King's Guards." To his surprise, there were no further questions. Van Zandt complimented him on the roomy 1939 Vauxhall Statesman car. "You've learned the system pretty fast. Much better than a cab," he said.

Mark spotted her Majesty as the General slipped into the meeting room. She sat at the head of the table with Prime Minister de Geer seated among his cabinet ministers, a clear indication of the royal will to prevail. The Embassy staff had placed a number of chairs in the hallway and Mark took his place alongside the various assistants. About an hour into the meeting, a military courier, all goggles and leather walked down the hall and knocked on the impressive double doors.

"Message for the Prime Minister," he announced to the assembly.

"I shall take it," he heard the Private Secretary say. The door remained closed for perhaps another five minutes when van Zandt emerged ahead of the others. Faces were ashen. Wilhelmina looked stern. Embassy personnel drifted from their offices and crowded around the General.

"At 13:00 hours today," he announced, "General Winkelman surrendered all Dutch forces in the country. Ninety minutes later over 100 Luftwaffe bombers commenced the indiscriminate destruction of civilian neighbourhoods in Rotterdam. The city is aflame and casualties are estimated to be in the thousands."

The Queen stepped into the hallway. Her face showed fierce determination. The hallway gathering shifted its focus to her.

"We shall carry on the fight against the attackers from our bases in London and the colonies. We mourn and pray for our fellow citizens in Rotterdam undergoing this hell unleashed upon them by our enemy. This betrayal shall not go unpunished. The Kingdom fights on, in the Indies, both East and West. We shall resist the invader at home at every opportunity, any time, anywhere. We shall not submit to the Hun."

34

1940
MONDAY, JUNE 24, 12:00 HRS BRITISH DOUBLE SUMMER TIME (BDST)
CARLTON MANOR, 23 BOURNE STREET
LONDON SW, ENGLAND

Out of breath from climbing six flights of stairs, Mark dropped his heavy kit on the floor and sat on the bed, happy to finally have a place to call home. The first six weeks in London had been chaotic. It seemed that every other day he had been moved to another place. His only routine was his work at the Embassy.

The problem of where Queen Wilhelmina should reside had been solved rather quickly. She had moved into a stately home at 11 Sloane Square, two miles from the Embassy. The British demanded that her security be placed in the hands of Scotland Yard. General van Zandt felt that an important task had been taken away from him; the Queen assuaged his bruised feelings and charged him with creating an organization dedicated exclusively to the liberation of Nederland.

Ask a bureaucratic empire builder to look after a clapboard doghouse and you end up with a luxury zoo complete with an administration office building. Van Zandt had no equal when it came to building empires.

He had obtained the use of Carlton Manor, at 23 Bourne Street – a grand Victorian place – as the site for his newly minted 'Netherlands Defence Institute' (NDI). The harmless sounding entity on the corner of Caroline Terrace had the task of promoting, coordinating and supporting the Resistance movement within Nederland.

Mark had been surprised when van Zandt told him he would be involved in the new project. "You have shown you can navigate the British system; see to it that the job gets done. You report directly to me."

"Where do I begin, General?" he objected, "There is no mail, no radio, no telegraph, no phones – no communication with Nederland at all."

"We are all flying by the seat of our pants, son. Improvise! You were at CID; you know how to get there by bending the rules, breaking them if you must. Start with an outline of how you plan to proceed. I'll get you secretarial help."

That was in the morning. He opened the glass doors to the balcony and looked down on the row of stately homes along Bourne Street.

Downstairs, the brass plaque in the entrance hall read that Sir Henry Coombs of textile fame had built the mansion in 1820 as a home for his family of 12 and offices for his business. The firm of Henan and Ferguson, barristers and solicitors, had recently vacated the building. It would now house the Institute's offices and provide lodgings for the Dutch live-in staff.

Mark had been assigned a room in the garret. The seventh floor was subdivided into four separate suites, originally intended to house the domestic help. Each apartment had a small kitchen and living area with a table and chairs and a quite comfortable bed in a curtained-off nook. The array of pots, pans and crockery included that very symbol of Britishness: a teakettle. The room's heating was quite intriguing. It was a gas hearth that needed to be regularly fed with shillings or it would die. After living in assorted army quarters for the past few weeks, Mark didn't mind any of these minor inconveniences. The fact that the main bathroom was a communal affair for all four suites didn't bother him either.

Van Zandt and Kirsten occupied the big suite on the second floor. Alice Hegt had also been assigned one of the garret suites. Up to now she had lived with friends somewhere in London but he had no idea how she managed to get to England in the first place.

In the corner of his room stood a 1934 Philips radio, the size of a large suitcase. Most of the station buttons didn't work; the ones that did were set to the BBC. The news announcer reported on the just-completed evacuation of the British Expeditionary Force from the beaches at Dunkirk. Originally sent to France to help defend the country, the half-a-million strong army had been pushed onto the shores of the Channel.

For some inexplicable reason, Hitler had stopped his advance on the coast, allowing the British to stage a mass evacuation. It soon became evident that the Royal Navy and the Merchant Marine with 200 ships could not possibly evacuate the encircled forces in time. Churchill had called on all owners of boats along the coast to join in the rescue effort. Seven hundred boats – fishing boats, sailboats, yachts, pleasure craft and garbage scows – ferried soldiers for nine days, ultimately succeeding in bringing 400,000 British soldiers back to England.

Only the British could exalt in such utter defeat, Mark thought. He liked the British people. Their spirit was admirable.

While the British citizenry prepared for the anticipated German invasion, Queen Wilhelmina took charge of running her government in exile. She detested the politicians who had led the country down a path of destruction, 'asleep and with their eyes closed'. She had called a meeting with Prime Minister de Geer and the Cabinet ministers who had fled to England and told them that they derived their power from Parliament and since there was no Parliament, the responsibility of governing fell on the Monarch. She sugar-coated the pill by appointing them to an advisory body whose council she would hear but not necessarily heed.

Without any logistical support in Britain, save for what the Embassy could offer, the effort to install a Dutch Government in exile was improvisation at all levels. The Queen, one of the wealthiest women in the world, personally guaranteed all salaries and expenditures until a financial structure could be established.

His kit bag was still only half opened. The googly eyes of the gas mask peered from under the British tin pot helmet. The General had ordered him to wear a decent uniform to the Embassy meetings. He had arrived in Britain with only his battle dress. The Quartermaster of the King's Guards had kindly supplied him with a British army uniform that looked very much like the Dutch version, except for the markings of rank. Transferring the two tiny stars from the collar of his battle dress to the orange boards of his lapel had restored him to the rank of First Lieutenant in the Dutch Army, except for the hat. The British hat – "bus driver's hat," as van Zandt had sneered – suited him just fine.

On this sunny June day, he decided to walk to the Embassy at Hyde Park Gate, his bus driver's hat at a jaunty angle. Walking north on Sloane Street he noticed that most of the stately homes had been turned into offices to house the myriad of wartime agencies. Turning onto Knightsbridge, he was amazed by the amount of traffic operating in England. He felt upbeat. It was a lovely day; it did not seem like wartime.

In the Embassy's hallway, he ran into Alice. She had her hair done up and wore makeup. He recalled her as a bit dowdy but she looked very attractive. Her well-tailored navy blue jacket over a white blouse didn't hide her prominent bust line.

"Well, hello sailor," she beamed. "How are you? Where have you been? I knew you were in London. I hear we are going to be working together."

"I understand we're also going to be neighbours at Carlton Manor."

"Yes, Mr. van Zandt arranged for me to work with the Institute and I am looking forward to it."

Mark couldn't help but wonder whether there was more to it than a working relationship. He asked her, "How did you get to England?" Alice was about to answer when they were called into the meeting.

Van Zandt had appropriated the Ambassador's meeting room, a comfortable space with oak walls and a beautiful oak conference table. Nonetheless, the General had strewn the table with his documents and an assortment of coloured pencils.

"Ah, the planners have arrived," he brayed, "Sorry we could not meet earlier. I have been busy." He continued to colour various graphs as intently as a pre-schooler would. "Her Majesty deemed it advisable that the Crown Princess and her daughters be relocated to Canada – Ottawa to be exact. The fear of an invasion is on everyone's mind." He broke the tip of the red pencil and stared at the offending stub before putting it down and shoving his graphs to a less cluttered corner of the table.

"Prince Bernhard is flying with them as we speak, but will return to England. He will be our commanding officer. The Queen has promoted him to Brigadier General. It'll be the Institute's task to recruit the manpower, so we need to map out our plans."

Van Zandt produced a stack of note cards and proceeded to move the chairs away from the table. He asked Alice to write in big letters on one card, 'Armed Forces' and on the other, 'Resistance'. He then placed them face-up on the expensive carpet and said, "This is how you build an organization chart." Without consulting any documentation, he outlined the functions of the brigade's recruitment procedures. Alice wrote a card for each of the functions that sprang from his fertile mind and placed them in the correct position on the carpet.

"Throw in whatever you can think of," he encouraged Mark and Alice, "We'll sort it out later."

"Should we not look for officers with more experience in this sort of thing?" Mark asked.

"There aren't any. Our warhorses were trained to fight the war of 1914-1918. They are too ossified to adapt. The Institute has to innovate, improvise, learn on the job and correct mistakes so they will not be made again. You, Lieutenant Zonder, and the people you recruit will have to beg or steal whatever tools you need. Her Majesty is willing to foot the bill, at least for the time being. Everything is scarce here."

The cards below 'Armed Forces' looked like a Christmas tree. Alice sat on the floor and copied the position and title of each card on a yellow pad.

"Now for the Resistance structure," the General chirped happily. Mark thought how ironic it was that here sat a General, on his knees, planning the liberation of his country by placing pieces of cardboard on the floor. Van Zandt seemed to sense his bewilderment.

"Let me tell you, Zonder, what we are doing here is laying the groundwork. Alice will type it out and then we will go at it again. We will impress the hell out of the powers who have no ideas of their own."

After tea in the cafeteria, they went back to planning the Resistance function. The main emphasis, the General explained, would be to recruit potential agents from among enterprising men who fled Nederland and who would be willing to be infiltrated back into the country to help build a Resistance movement. The Special Air Service (SAS), a new branch of the British Army, would do their specialized training.

Apart from staffing, obtaining radio capability was a main priority. "We need to establish contact with the Resistance cells," the General said. He was in his element now.

Mark admired the coolness with which Alice handled the torrent of words and ideas that poured forth. It was well past suppertime when everything had been recorded and filed away.

"One more thing," van Zandt said donning his red-banded general's hat and straightening his uniform. "I know you have a lot of work to do. However, tomorrow I need both of you for other tasks. Alice, you will accompany me to an all-day meeting at the War Ministry. Zonder, you will take my car, collect Mrs. van Zandt in Cheam and bring her to our suite at Carlton Manor. Make sure she gets settled in." As the General left the room, Mark scrambled to his feet to salute but van Zandt waved him off.

Alice crammed the papers in her briefcase and said, "My things should be at Carlton Manor by now, so if you give me a few minutes I'll walk with you." With double summer time in effect, London wouldn't get dark until well after ten o'clock.

At the Knightsbridge underground station, they passed the famous Magpie and Frog, a pub that traced its origins back to the 1600s. "Want to eat something?" Alice asked, "I am famished." Even though the nice weather would encourage outdoor activity, the pub was crowded. The low-beamed ceiling barely allowed enough room to walk erect. Heads down, he found a table in the corner underneath a big print of a greyhound race.

They ordered the Dover sole and scalloped potatoes and a huge glass of warm beer. The publican, noticing the uniform and the tiny silver stars on the lapel awarded him a higher rank as he placed the food on the table. "There General and Miss, eat 'eartily," he said in his cockney accent.

Alice leaned over and rubbed one of the stars. "My first dinner date with a two-star general," she chuckled.

The din of voices made it difficult to have a normal conversation. They ate their meal without speaking.

"So tell me," Mark hollered, wiping his mouth with the serviette, "How did you get to England?"

"It's very simple. When the evacuation of the Queen was certain, the General called the Private Secretary and said 'I need the services of Alice Hegt so see what you can do.' Next thing I knew I was on the British ship Windsor that brought ministers and bureaucrats to Harwich. Until last week, when things started to take shape, I stayed with friends."

"You must be awfully good friends with the General too."

"What do you mean?"

"Nothing, really. It just seems strange that in all this confusion in the evacuation, that he found time to allow his able and competent secretary to come along."

"I think I know what you are implying but since we have to work together, you'd better not suggest impropriety." They finished their meal and walked the rest of the way in silence.

At Carlton Manor, she turned to him and said, "Are you going to help me get settled or are you going to mope all evening?" After climbing the six flights of stairs, she was thrilled with her garret suite. She flung open the doors to the balcony and breathed in the warm summer air.

She took off her jacket and loosened the top two buttons of her blouse. He couldn't help noticing her ample bosom, but quickly turned his eyes away. He wondered why she asked for his help, since all she did was hang up her clothes and stow away her unmentionables. He chatted for a while, said goodnight and went to his room.

35

1940
TUESDAY, JUNE 25, 5:00 PM, EDT
GRAND CENTRAL STATION
NEW YORK CITY, USA

Marcy was waiting for him on the platform of Grand Central Station as the *Dayliner* from Philadelphia pulled in. It was exactly on time. She had asked Sebastian, their grumpy Jamaican driver to wait outside the station while she collected Ferenc who was returning from his performance of Beethoven's Concerto No.4 at the Philadelphia Concert Hall.

This morning's review in the *New York Times* – a novelty because the paper hardly ever reviewed anything that didn't take place in Manhattan – was full of praise. *"Ferenc Kolmar unequalled in interpreting Beethoven's oeuvres,"* the headline read.

A porter carried his baggage to the curb of the 42nd Street exit where Sebastian wheezed and moaned as he stowed the two heavy suitcases in the trunk of the black Cadillac.

Inside the roomy vehicle, Ferenc kissed her and thanked her for meeting him at the station. "I could have found my way home all by myself, you know," he smiled. "I could have taken a Yellow Cab."

Marcy, happy to have him home again, said, "Sebastian needed a break from polishing the car and I love to see the swirl of traffic."

They rode in silence for a few minutes when Marcy spoke, "I decided to abandon our efforts for a benefit concert in London, Ferenc. I know you want to do a benefit for the Jewish émigrés but you have to cross the Atlantic. Air travel is a long way via Portugal and you don't want to risk sea travel with the U-boats. You can play anywhere, people will come."

"You know I want to go to London, why are you changing plans?"

"Well, Ottawa is closer, dear, and it makes a lot more sense now."

"I cannot think of a single reason to go to Ottawa."

"Ferenc, darling, it's the same reason you wanted to go to London. Princess Juliana and her daughters arrived in Ottawa today to sit out the rest of the war in safety." Kolmar was silent for few moments.

"That is great news," he said quietly. "Did Prince Bernhard go with her?"

"The report did mention that he was promoted to General to lead a Dutch Brigade, so I don't think he can do that from Ottawa."

"Ah, I see," he said pensively.

"Oh, Ferenc I thought you'd be more excited. I came to the station to see your face when I told you. I know how grateful you are to the Queen and Juliana for sponsoring your career. We can do this benefit by overnight train travel instead of ten days of *mal-de-mer* on the Atlantic."

"Can you change the concert from London to Ottawa?"

"I've already started, Darling, but you are booked so far in advance, it'll take months."

"It would be good to see Juliana again…" he closed his eyes and let the phrase hang in the air between them.

36

1940
TUESDAY, JUNE 24, 08:30 HRS
CARLTON MANOR, 23 BOURNE STREET
LONDON, ENGLAND

Alice was waiting in the hallway in front of the brass plaque to meet the General. She had forsaken the formal outfit and looked very summery in a light green dress and red sandals.

"The General decided that we should walk to the War Ministry on a nice morning like this," she said, "The driver should bring the car around for you in a moment to get you to Cheam."

Indeed, a shiny Rolls-Royce drew to a gentle stop in front of the building. The driver was a civilian, clad in a gray chauffeur costume and cap. Mark stood at the right front door of the car, waiting for the driver to open it.

"Are you driving, Sir?" the man asked with a smile. He realized that the lieutenant had forgotten about the right hand drive in British vehicles and opened the rear door.

"I would rather ride up front with you, if you don't mind," Mark said.

"That would not be quite proper, Sir," he said in a gentrified worker's accent, "The General insists on privacy for the passengers."

"This isn't a staff car, then."

"No Sir, it is the General's personal vehicle." Mark always supposed that the General was financially well off, but how he could obtain an expensive car for his own use was a mystery. Van Zandt was a strange mixture of pomp, folksiness and often, icy reserve.

The Rolls-Royce had the luscious smell of new leather. A sliding glass partition separated the driver from the passenger compartment. A speaking tube allowed for communication between driver and passengers. More separation could be achieved by drawing the heavy damask curtains on the side windows and the glass partition.

It was Mark's first trip beyond the Centre of London. Like any tourist, his nose was glued to the window as they crossed the Lambeth Bridge towards Cheam, a 40-minute ride away. He eagerly read all signs, streets, stores, billboards, anything. The town of Tooting and its Tooting Road made him smile. They had driven from London in dry weather with the sun shining through a gap of blue sky but now the sky was clouding over and the colour drained from the landscape.

The driver had to ask for directions several times but they finally arrived in Cheam and found Cuddington Park Road. A massive Tudor-style house stood on the edge of a golf course.

As the car pulled into the circular driveway he spotted the tennis courts on the edge of the manicured lawn and saw Kirsten engaged in a relaxed tennis match with an athletic looking man in his forties. They were laughing. She stopped play, waved at the car and yelled that they would soon be finished.

She invited Mark to wait in her upstairs anteroom as she dressed and packed her last items.

"If you don't mind, I'll take a quick shower," she said. He sat gingerly in an upholstered chair, part of the collection of expensive period furniture. The place looked more like a salon than an anteroom. She had left the bedroom door open and he could hear the water running in the shower. The shower stopped and he was startled to see her walk into the room wrapped in a towel.

"You must help me, I have some soap in my eye," she squinted, as she walked toward him. She handed him the tip of the towel and pulled her head back. He gently wiped at her closed eyes. She slowly opened them and smiled.

"You smell nice," he managed to say in a croaking voice.

She dropped the towel and put her arms around him. "You smell nice too, I love the smell of young soldiers," she cooed. She kissed him and he stood transfixed.

"Are you trying to seduce me, Mrs. van Zandt?"

"Yes, I certainly am. I thought that I had made that very obvious when you visited us in Wassenaar." She still had her naked arms wrapped around him. Mark had no choice but to assume that the required protocol governing this situation was to kiss her on the lips. They stood for a while with Mark rubbing her naked back and she slowly insinuating her groin into his. She suddenly disengaged.

"Better not keep van Zandt's driver waiting. I'll get dressed and pack my things and I'll be ready in a few minutes."

Mark had learned early in life that a 'few minutes' could stretch out to half an hour or more when a woman was involved. Kirsten finally appeared dressed as informal and sunny as Alice had been that morning: a flower-print dress, sandals and a huge white hat with a red ribbon.

"If you're wondering where my hosts are, they are away in some dreary little corner in the Midlands. They are hiding away in a goat herder's cottage, safe from the fear of a German invasion."

"Who was the man you were playing tennis with?" he asked.

"We have barely kissed once and you are already jealous," she teased. "Actually, he is the groundskeeper. Tomorrow he will answer the call for re-enlistment and join his former regiment in the Grenadier Guards."

He carried her two small suitcases down to the front door where the driver was engaged in an animated discussion with the groundskeeper. The driver loaded the suitcases in the boot. Kirsten hugged the groundskeeper and kissed him squarely on the lips.

The Rolls had barely pulled out of the driveway when Kirsten closed the curtains all around. "You saw everything on the way here," she said briskly, "There's no point in seeing it all again."

She settled with her back against the door, kicked off her sandals and put her legs in his lap.

"Tomorrow I will be back to my boring routine of the being the General's wife," she said, "Dreadful cocktail parties and receptions – what the diplomats call entertainment. Frans told me that you are also staying at the Carlton Manor so when things get boring I can always count on you. And you can keep that trollop Alice away from my husband."

Mark got the uneasy feeling that he was being dragged into something he didn't want to be part of, yet her wriggling feet in his lap aroused him enormously. He prayed it wouldn't show.

They talked for a while. Kirsten asked about his little girlfriend, what was her name again, Jenny? Where was she now? Did he miss her? He talked about his family, the fear that his father might be a casualty or, if healthy, a prisoner of war.

When the conversation dwindled, they rode in silence but suddenly Kirsten scrambled to get her feet back on the floor and said, "I'm tired, I'd like to rest for a while." She turned and slid down with her head on Mark's shoulder. She was quiet for a spell and then gently stroked his thigh much too close to the bulge in his trousers.

"I see somebody is alert," she said coquettishly. Mark hesitated but finally reached his hand under the top of her summer dress and worked his way into her brassiere. She moaned as he slowly manipulated the nipple. The stroking of his thigh came ever close to the danger point. She managed to turn her head toward him. They kissed. He realized that she wanted him to go farther but he thought of the General and Jenny and his promise. He straightened up causing her to sit up as well.

"To judge by the traffic we are in London now," he said drawing the curtains open. When the car pulled up to Carlton Manor, the driver opened the door for Kirsten. Mark thought he saw a glimpse of disapproval on the man's face but that could have been his guilty conscience. He helped the driver carry the luggage to the apartment on the second floor. It was a huge suite compared to the garret. It had a large living room with a formal dining area, a kitchen equipped with the latest gadgets and a den with two leather easy chairs and a desk covered with books and papers. Kirsten tipped the driver with a pound note.

She pointed to the bedroom door. "You might be interested in seeing what it looks like," she said huskily, unbuttoning his tunic and undoing his tie. He put his arms around her and kissed her while he unbuttoned the back of her summer dress. Conquest was imminent.

37

1940
FRIDAY, SEPTEMBER 13, 10:00 HRS BDST
NETHERLANDS DEFENCE INSTITUTE
LONDON. SW1, ENGLAND

The spectre of a German invasion – so feared in summer – had abated. Hitler's strategy was to bring Britain to her to her knees by declaring war on the population of the big cities, particularly London, through an endless blitzkrieg.

Night after night, hundreds of Luftwaffe aircraft would set cities ablaze with incendiary bombs. In their wake, the Heinkels would drop 500-pound bombs, razing entire neighbourhoods. Instead of surrender, the German attack instilled a spirit of solidarity in the British population.

In the daytime, 80 staff members worked at Carlton Manor, but at night, only the Dutch live-in staff remained. Access to the bomb shelter was eight flights down from the garret suites. Kirsten and Alice had made the shelter more liveable by covering the earthen floor with old carpets and used furniture snatched from the storage rooms at the Embassy.

The Dutch enclave gathered night after night, each uncomfortable in their own way. After their tryst, Mark felt uneasy around Kirsten, especially on evenings when the General joined them. Alice was edgy around Kirsten. Mark hoped there wasn't a relationship between her and the General but he knew Kirsten suspected one and Alice sensed it.

The nightly confinement was brightened when Jos Caspers, a Belgian from Antwerp joined the NDI. The Flemish speak Dutch with a softer accent and he fit in immediately. Jos had applied to join Prince Bernhard's Irene Brigade (named after Juliana's youngest daughter.) He was a lean, dark-haired chap with a ready smile. At age 21, he had learned a lot about communications in the port of Antwerp where he handled all facets of radio traffic. He had left Antwerp on one of the last ships to depart.

Caspers was fast-tracked to the Resistance side. He was assigned a suite in the garret and Mark put him to work building a communication centre on the third floor. He received carte blanche to beg, borrow, steal or even buy whatever he needed. Within weeks, the radio room was established and Jos made contact with a fledgling Resistance cell in Rotterdam.

Mark conducted about ten interviews a day, many lasting more than an hour. The adventurous types – who had escaped Nederland in boats or on land via Spain and Portugal – were recruited to be dropped back into Nederland to bolster the Resistance.

One of these young men was Brenner Zijlberg who had sailed his sloop from Katwijk to King's-Lynn in two-and-a-half days unseen by patrols. He wanted to join the Navy but he too was steered to the Resistance.

One of the more rewarding interviews was the unexpected arrival of Timmerman, his CID instructor who recounted his travels to Sweden and then a ten-day journey on a Liberian ship before he landed at Plymouth.

They discussed the possibility of Timmerman training agents at Sheddington Park near Southend-on-Sea. The base was nominally an air station but was actually run by MI-6 to train agents for infiltration into Europe. Van Zandt had insisted on developing a section exclusively focused on Nederland with language instruction in English and Dutch.

It was eight o'clock when Mark finished his day. Many interviews had been unproductive. The applicants were enthusiastic but were either too old or unfit. Then there were the reckless ones who would get into trouble in no time. He closed the office and checked in with Alice.

"Time to close Alice; the Luftwaffe is on its way. Let's have a drink before the sirens begin to wail," he suggested.

She nodded, cleaned off her desk, locked the office and said, "First I have to freshen up a bit." Together they climbed the stairs to the attic. She paused at the door and said, "If we go to the pub and the alarm sounds we'll be forced to seek shelter in the tube station with a bunch of strangers. I have a bottle of wine. We could have a drink here?"

"I am flattered that you prefer my company to hundreds of hard-working English folks."

"I don't know why you always act so hostile. I would like to relax with my feet up and enjoy a little chat after reading and typing all day."

"Sorry, I was trying to be witty. I accept your generous invitation and will join you after I shed the Queen's uniform." Since the time he had inferred that she had an intimate relationship with van Zandt, Alice had been aloof. He changed into a pair of khaki pants and a woollen pullover.

She received him wearing slippers and dressed in a white T-shirt under a kimono that barely reached her knees. She had let her hair down so that it fell over her shoulders. As she bent down to fetch the bottle, he noticed she was not wearing a bra. She served him a glass of red wine and curled up in the easy chair folding her shapely legs under her body, like a cat.

"Now tell me all about Lieutenant Mark Zonder," she said. He told her about his family, sailing with Brenner Zijlberg and his fears for Jenny.

She took another sip of her wine and lit a cigarette. She bent down to put the lighter on the table. He got another glimpse of those magnificent breasts. She looked up and smiled at him. "I guess it's my turn now."

"We both owe a lot to van Zandt," she began, "I was born in The Hague, I am 27. My mother was a linen maid at the Palace. When I asked who my father was, she always told me that he was a man of means who died before he could marry her. She never told me his name. Uncle Frans used to come by our little apartment and always left an envelope on the mantelpiece. When I left high school and passed my stenographer course, he got me a job at the police station. Wherever he moved in his career, he somehow found me a job not too far away from him.

"You are not telling me that van Zandt is your father?"

"No," she laughed, "I asked him that once but he said no." She got up to pour another round of wine and provided another enticing view.

"We should go out one evening," Mark said, "I hear the Flanagan and Allan show at the Victoria Palace is wonderful. They say it is even funnier when the air raid sounds. The comedians keep on improvising while the crowd looks for the shelter."

"I would like that, minus the fun of the shelter of course." She stood before him, wine bottle in hand. "Would you like to kiss me?" she said matter-of-factly.

He was startled but tried not to show it. "Of course," he said, rising to his feet and placing a little peck on her cheek. She put the bottle down.

"I mean like this," she put her arms around his neck and kissed him.

"Why did you do that?" he asked dumbly.

"To remove the anxiety. This way we get the first kiss out of the way and then we can enjoy the evening."

He contemplated the concept of pre-emptive foreplay when someone knocked at the door.

"Evening, all," Jos Caspers, the radioman pretended not to notice the kimono and the wine glasses. "A bit of business, Lieutenant. A Resistance unit in Nederland gave your name to vouch for his identity. He signed himself out as OZ as in the Wizard of Oz. Do you know this man?"

Mark felt instant excitement. "Did he identify his region?"

"He said Rhineland, *Rijnstsreek* in Dutch."

He turned to Alice, "You must excuse me. I would like to go down and see if we can contact this unit. I think it's Vreelink." Alice cheerfully said she would be expecting both of them back to finish the wine. Jos Caspers gave her a thumbs-up. Mark was not enthusiastic about Jos coming back with him; there was unfinished business to deal with.

Caspers, a born scrounger, had enlisted an operator, a 55-year-old technical representative of Philips Radio Company assigned to England for the past ten years. Bertus Meurs knew the shortwave radio inside out.

Mark asked Meurs, "Can you raise this fellow OZ? I think he might be a friend." His Morse code knowledge was not good enough to understand the words as they clicked around the ether. He still had to see the dots and dashes on paper before he could grasp the message. Jos however, instantly translated the clicks as OZ confirmed his presence.

"Ask him for two words that relate to Zonder and Boy Scout," Mark asked. The telegraph clicked away and the answer came back quickly.

"Jamboree. Jenny," Jos said. He turned to Mark, "Mean anything?"

"It's Vreelink!" he shouted. He enveloped Jos in a bear hug and spun him around. Before he could ask anything more, OZ had signed off and did not respond.

When he went back up to the attic suites, the light under Alice's door was out. "Good thing too," he thought.

38

1940
WEDNESDAY, DECEMBER 31, 20:00 HRS BDWT (GMT-1)
NETHERLANDS EMBASSY, HIGH GATE PARK
LONDON, ENGLAND

Alice looked attractive tonight, Mark thought, with her dark eyes and her hair all done up. When she was relaxed and away from work, she had that breathless way of speaking that made a man think that she'd been waiting anxiously to see him again.

Alice had received an invitation to the Embassy's New Year's Eve party and had insisted that Mark be her escort. When they arrived, the party was in full swing. Garlands of coloured streamers brightened the Embassy's reception hall. A piano trio was playing *Deed I Do*. The old songs made popular by Victor Sylvester like *Me and My Shadow* and *Doing the Lambeth Walk* had many of the elite dancing.

The bar did not offer much variety – warm bitters or Dutch Jenever. That was it. The meagre supply of Heineken beer had gone within the first half hour. No one complained because any amount of alcohol was better than none. The Ambassador must have confiscated the ration coupons from his entire staff.

Alice found them a table in the corner near the piano trio and proceeded immediately to the bar.

Over the last six months, he and Alice had become close co-workers. They met quite often in either Alice's suite or his to discuss the problems of the day. After their first kiss, they studiously avoided sliding into a more intimate relationship. Alice accepted Mark's devotion to the girl he left behind, but no matter how much they tried to avoid it, sexual tension always hung in the air. By accident or design, she added to the apprehension by often dressing in her short kimono.

Even though the nightly air raids continued unabated, they now only fled to the basement shelter when the explosions came close, proving once again that human beings can get used to anything.

On the evenings when they did join the other residents in the bomb shelter, Kirsten would sometimes comment on the limited seating and teased Mark to sit in her lap – something that annoyed Alice even more than it did the General. There had been no repeat of Mark's tryst with Kirsten. His steadfast avoidance of being alone with her had helped.

"You are awfully quiet tonight," said Alice. Before he could answer, a familiar voice broke in.

"Well, hello, look who is here." Kirsten had arrived with the General in tow. Protocol demanded that the van Zandts should join the tables of those with cabinet rank but then Kirsten did not care about protocol.

The General peered around to see whom he might offend by sitting down with his staff members but many of his peers were either at the bar or dancing; one man even danced with his wife.

The General immediately began working the room as if trawling for votes. Kirsten didn't wait long, "Forgive me Alice but I must steal Mark for a dance," she beamed as she dragged him to the floor and began to shimmy to *Tea for Two*. Kirsten drew him close. "Alice does not seem too happy that I took you away, but I hardly ever see you," she said with an edge to her voice. He looked at his shoes, careful not to step on her toes.

"I always look forward to your splendid parties, Kirsten. I enjoy your company and I appreciate the confidence the General has placed in me."

"My god, you sound like one of those mealy-mouthed politicians. Always ready with an answer you can take three different ways."

He returned her to their table where the General chatted with Alice.

"Now it's my turn," Alice said with a stiff smile and whisked Mark back to the dance floor. She held him close as the trio played *Getting Sentimental Over You*. As the dance ended and they walked back to the table she asked, "Is Kirsten looking for more companionship from you?"

"Oh come on, Alice, she was just making us feel comfortable, to show that the General and his wife can be chummy with their staff."

Alice whispered angrily, "She wants to add you to her stable of studs." Mark hushed her and hoped Kirsten hadn't heard.

With a sugar-sweet smile Kirsten leaned over to Mark, "After the midnight festivities are done, Frans and I would like to have you both join us in the suite for a nightcap." Mark looked at Alice and hesitated. Kirsten caught his glance. "Oh do come, there'll be others too."

"Thank you. We'd love to," Mark said, smarting from the kick in the shin under the table.

At the moment of midnight, the trio launched into *Auld Lang Syne*, a custom totally ignored by the Dutch revellers who had no cultural connection to the song. Instead, they celebrated the way they always did. Noise! Traditional firecrackers were out of the question so they beat every plate, pot and pan with whatever utensil they could find.

Kirsten was the first to lay down her noisemaker. After a quick peck on the cheek with her husband, she reached up and kissed Mark while he stood holding a coffee urn in one hand and a cup in the other. Alice took him for a waltz and after a deep, final dip, she kissed him. It was theatrical enough to earn polite applause from the folks at the next table.

When they arrived at the General's suite, the tension had abated. However, since the Underground would stop running at 1:30, guests didn't stay for more than a nightcap.

The General was in an expansive mood. "Ah," he sighed, taking off his shoes and putting his feet on the coffee table, "Just us roomies of Carlton Manor are still here." Kirsten waved at van Zandt to take his feet off the table and move over to let her join him on the sofa. He ignored her muted instruction, but obeyed.

"I'll tell you, both of you have done a great job. I have had many compliments for how you are handling the work."

"I spend most of my time in the radio room, monitoring messages from the Resistance cells," Mark said. "I am trying to learn how our agents are faring after being dropped in Nederland. We haven't been able to confirm that any of them succeeded in contacting Vreelink and his OZ cell. He is supposed to be the focal point."

This seemed to anger him. "Some of the chaps we sent were unprepared. Most of them had far less training than you had at CID. But amateur days are over!" he shouted forcefully, slamming his fist on the table, causing his schnapps glass to fall off the table and break.

Van Zandt didn't seem to notice the mishap. "Have you thought of getting back to the type of work you did for CID?"

Mark was startled, "I'd like to be back in action, Sir."

"In this phase of the occupation, I don't think that the best use of your talent is to drop you behind enemy lines. But, I do think you can offer more than monitoring radio communications. I am going to assign you to create a training course for agents to be placed in occupied Europe."

Alice was silent. Kirsten busied herself picking up the glass shards.

"You mean head up the training, General? With Timmerman?"

"Damn right. You are one of the best agents to come out of his program."

"Alice, make sure you get the papers to me." He rose to indicate that the party was at an end. Kirsten bestowed an airbrush kiss on Alice but hugged Mark tightly and kissed him on the lips again.

They walked up the stairs to the attic together. "I have some wine, if you would like a nightcap." She opened the door to her suite knowing that Mark would follow. "Just pour us a glass while I change," she warbled. She quickly returned in her kimono and slinked into the easy chair.

"If you are transferred to Sheddington Park we won't see much of you," said Alice sipping from her wine. "We'll miss you."

"You have so many other friends here; you'll be too busy to miss me."

"But you are my special friend," she pouted. He decided not to pursue that line of conversation. They talked for a while; he finished his wine, stretched and got up.

"Must go, Alice, it's nearly two." He gave her a friendly peck on the cheek. "Thank you for a wonderful evening. Happy New Year."

She put her arms around him. "Don't you ever feel lonely and want to hold somebody close?"

He bent down and kissed her moist lips: "You mean like this?" They stood in the middle of the small room lost in each other's presence.

She raised an arm around his neck, "This is nice," she murmured seeking his lips again while undoing his tie.

"I have a surprise," she whispered, "I traded my cigarette ration for four eggs. We'll have a great New Year's breakfast."

39

1941
TUESDAY, APRIL 15, 09:00 HRS BDWT
SHEDDINGTON PARK, SOUTHEND ON SEA
ESSEX, ENGLAND

The NDI's training camp at Sheddington Park had been in operation for three months. As the lead officer, Mark had worked 16-hour days to get the small unit in shape to train the Dutch agents who would be landed behind enemy lines. The first five had graduated and were dropped by British naval craft along the shores of the North Sea, most of them heading for The Hague or Amsterdam.

When he had landed in England almost a year ago, Mark hoped that the war might be over by this time, but if anything, the situation had worsened. Hitler had invaded the Balkans and now practically controlled the entire underbelly of Europe, although Greece had not yet capitulated and the fight for Athens was ongoing. Mussolini had recklessly started that war but Hitler had come to his rescue when *Il Duce's* army proved incapable of beating the Greeks.

In Africa, Britain benefitted by Italian incompetence. Montgomery was able to capture Tobruk and portions of Somalia but Hitler again helped the hapless Mussolini by sending General Rommel and his Afrika Corps to take back all British gains. German domination looked assured.

This morning Mark watched the hand-to-hand combat training. He wanted to talk to a newly arrived recruit – a student of Leiden University, Erik Hazelhoff. He was a handsome 24-year-old who had managed to board a Swiss ship in Rotterdam bound for Lisbon and from there had made his way to London. He asked Hazelhoff to join him in the NAAFI cafeteria for a cup of tea. The young man sweated profusely. He had a towel around his neck that he used to wipe his brow.

Mark said, "I read about your roundabout way to get here; quite a journey. What can you tell me about the situation back home?"

"Well, the thumbscrews are tightening," Hazelhoff puffed as he mopped his forehead. "As you know, almost everything is rationed. I showed the list to the debriefing officer this morning." He wiped his hands with the towel and pulled out a folded piece of paper from his pocket and read, "A pound of meat per person per week. No more than five kilograms of potatoes per month. One pair of shoes per year. A maximum of ten cigarettes per week made of vile smelling African tobacco. Milk products, limited to two litres a week for a family of four and that includes butter and cheese. If you want to dine in a restaurant, you must take the coupons for whatever you think you'd like to order. Waiters seem more worried about collecting coupons than tips."

"What about the persecution of Jews. Is it as bad as the reports say?"

"There are many stories of Jews being taken."

"Have you seen this?"

"Friends of our family have disappeared and have not been heard from. Hitler makes no secret of his intentions. Jews are forbidden to attend university. They cannot go to movies or participate in organized sport. The definition of Jew has been expanded so that children with one Jewish parent or grandparent are now designated as Jewish. That hugely increases the number of people living in fear of persecution."

The perspiration was still bothering him and he took a sip of the NAAFI tea but immediately put the cup down with a smirk of distaste. Mark wanted to know more of the man's motivation.

"You risked your life to come to England. None of those problems touched you directly. Your parents are rich; you were close to obtaining your doctorate. Why throw it all away to work for the liberation?"

"I could spout a lot of patriotic bullshit but this Nazi tyranny has to end. There is a depressing acceptance that Germany has won this war; that England alone cannot fight Russia and Germany. The Americans have not given any sign that they will enter the war." Mark offered to get him another cup of tea but Hazelhoff declined politely, too well bred to say the stuff tasted bad.

"There is pessimism among the Dutch who are in England also," Mark said, "Prime Minister de Geer recommended that our government-in-exile enter into a peace agreement with Germany so that Nederland could function as a member state in a Greater German Europe."

"That's why there is a new Prime Minister now, I guess," Hazelhoff laughed.

"The Queen is adamant that the resistance against the enemy must be stepped up."

"I hear the training is cruel and wicked," Hazelhoff quipped.

"Both of those, I hope." Mark laughed. "You have met Sergeant Major Timmerman. He was my instructor at CID. He worked us beyond exhaustion; I hated his guts. However, when the British SAS units looked at what he taught in Nederland, they laughed and said it was amateur stuff. So he took their course, survived it and adapted it for our use."

"Did you take the course yourself?"

"Timmerman argued that I should not be in charge if I refused to take his course. A lot of new subjects have been introduced since 1939. We learned how to drive cars and break into homes but none of the sophisticated things that are done today such as centralized intelligence gathering and threat assessments. We didn't know anything about radiotelegraphy then, but now it has a special focus. A special course deals with how to snatch and hold people."

"Hostages you mean?"

"SAS calls it the involuntary relocation of assets."

"How will agents be inserted behind enemy lines?" Hazelhoff asked, "I assume by parachute?"

"Not necessarily. We dropped some at Katwijk. A Royal Navy submarine gets as close to the coast as possible and then crew members row the agent ashore."

"I assume swimming tests are included?"

Mark laughed, "Yes, that and long distance bicycle riding. What else would you expect in training Dutch agents?"

The whistle blew for the resumption of the unarmed combat session. Hazelhoff got up to leave "I'll give it a good go. Thank you."

Mark watched him leave, convinced that Hazelhoff had what it took. In a way, he was jealous. This man would soon be in action, while he was stuck training others.

40

1941
SATURDAY, APRIL 26, 13:00 HRS CENTRAL EUROPEAN SUMMER TIME (CEST)
REICHSKANZLEREI, UNTER DEN LINDEN
BERLIN, GERMANY

The Reichskanzlerei was aglitter with military brass. The general officers of Oberkommand Wehrmacht, Kriegsmarine, Luftwaffe and SS gathered in the magnificent Paul von Hindenburg Room. They rose, clicked their heels, and raised their right arms in a chorus of *Heil Hitler* as the Fuehrer entered the ornate chamber.

The Reichskanzler was in an ebullient mood.

"*Meine Kameraden*," he exclaimed after the military leaders had taken their places. With a robotic stiff arm, he dramatically turned and pointed to the huge map of Europe on the south wall. Little swastika flags outlined Europe's conquest by the forces of the Third Reich. "I am announcing that tomorrow morning Greece will sign the terms of surrender."

The crowd jumped to its feet, chanting, *Sieg Heil, Sieg Heil*!

"From the borders of Bolshevik Russia to the Atlantic, from the Mediterranean to Norway, Europe is now under German protection. In time, a new Europe will arise. A new Europe, prosperous because of our National Socialist ideals," he shrieked.

"This is no time to glory in our conquests. One major obstacle still stands in the way of our complete victory. The yoke of Bolshevism must be lifted from the back of our Continent. Therefore, I have ordered preparations to begin to eradicate the communist menace. We shall deploy five million glorious German warriors against the Communist curse. It shall be known as Operation Barbarossa."

"We must be ruthless in our conquest. Pity has no place in our elimination of the Jew-run Bolshevik empire. We shall be strong and be victorious. Then our glorious Greater Germany shall stretch from the Urals to the Atlantic." He stared straight ahead with his chin in the air and paused with a maniacal grimace. Raising his arm straight out in his trademark salute he roared, "*Sieg Heil*," turned and strutted towards the exit.

The gold-braided crowd jumped to its collective feet and brayed "*Heil Hitler*" as their messiah paused at the door in a final acknowledgement. Heinrich Himmler scurried in his wake. Hitler's Private Secretary, Martin Bohrman, emerged from a dark recess and whispered that Himmler should follow him to the Fuehrer's private quarters.

Himmler's meetings with Hitler had always been in the Reichskanzler's office, never in the living quarters. The elevator took him down five stories underground to a brightly lit reception area from where he was led into the Fuehrer's living room. Valuable furniture and priceless works of art – 'liberated' from the occupied territories – decorated the surprisingly intimate room. A white-jacketed SS Gefreiter offered him coffee or tea. Himmler, a self-professed ascetic, like his leader, asked for mineral water.

In spite of his exalted position of overseeing all security forces including the secret service, the Gestapo chief feared Hitler's sudden mood swings that could range from jovial to murderous outrage.

"The meeting went quite well, don't you think, Heinrich?" Hitler said as he entered. "Those generals who so opposed my strike at the West now all want to bask in the glory of my success in creating the New Order."

"It was ever so, My Fuehrer," Himmler said.

Hitler moved closer to him and lowered his voice to a conspiratorial whisper. "The problem with the bourgeois military minds is that I can not share the ultimate design of our new Europe with them. They do not grasp our National Socialist ideal of a united Greater Germany of 200 million people. They cannot understand that the *Untermenschen*, the low-lifes, cannot be allowed to poison our heritage. We must keep the focus of the Generals on what they do best – slaying opponents. They are useful but we, my dear Heinrich, must plan beyond our military victory."

"I share your vision, My Fuehrer," said Himmler fawningly.

Hitler responded bitterly, "Regretfully, the world sees us as land-grabbing vandals but the aim of our movement is to create a Greater Germany encompassing all the nations with Aryan blood, Norway, Denmark, the Swedes, the Low Countries, and of course England."

"It will not be easy." Himmler said, "The Nordics, Dutch, and the others have their centuries-old royal ties. They will not easily accept becoming a part of Greater Germany."

"We must not give the impression that these countries will be forced into the German State against their wishes. They must voluntarily join in the Federation, similar to the United States of America. Countries will have specific state powers, but not independence. The states of our Greater Germany must keep their flags and symbols including their Royal Houses," Hitler explained.

"The SS has been working toward that end, my Fuehrer," Himmler said. "The Kings of Denmark and Belgium are co-operating. The Abwehr intelligence assures us that the Duke of Windsor is willing to wear the crown for the United Kingdom."

Hitler rose, paced the floor and shook his fist at Himmler. "But you have failed in Norway and Nederland," he screamed. "Your orders were to capture King Haakon in Oslo and you failed. He fled to England."

"A solution is possible..." Himmler began.

"I committed 14,000 paratroopers to encircle The Hague," Hitler turned red in rage, "Yet you failed to capture Queen Wilhelmina and her family."

"A solution is possible, my Fuehrer," Himmler tried anew, "King Haakon is hiding in England but he is old. His son, Prince Gustaf is a student at Heidelberg University and he is sympathetic to our ideals. We shall use him as a successor for King Haakon in the member state of Norway." Hitler seemed somewhat assuaged.

"Make sure he stays in Germany and keep him under our protection for re-education. But what of our Aryan neighbours, the Dutch?"

"We have Prince Bernhard, of course. He is a German and even has been a Member of our National Socialist Party."

"That will not do," the Fuehrer said, as his face reddened, "He is a German stud, hired to produce heirs for the House of Orange. He will never be accepted as a successor to the Orange Nassau dynasty. He is not of their heritage. We must have a Royal related by blood to the House of Orange. Solve this situation by any means. You have my full authority."

"You mean kidnapping Princess Juliana or the young Princes Beatrix? That is nearly impossible. They are in Canada."

"I am the architect of the New Order. You, as Reichsfuehrer of the SS, will provide me with the tools."

Hitler turned abruptly and left Himmler fretting. Martin Bohrman slinked into the room and showed him to the door.

Back in his office, Himmler phoned Admiral Wilhelm Canaris and explained Hitler's wish. "You head the perfect agency for that sort of thing, Wilhelm," he said, "make it your responsibility."

41

1941
FRIDAY, MAY 2, 19:00 HRS CEST
NSB HEADQUARTERS, LANGE VOORHOUT 14
THE HAGUE, NEDERLAND

One by one, they arrived at the old Page House in The Hague. Some wore the brown uniform of the NSB with the swastika on a red armband; others were dressed in smart business suits. Many centuries ago, the Page House had been home to the noblemen serving at the Court of the House of Orange. Before the German occupation, it was the principal office of the Dutch Admiralty. After the invasion, it was taken over by the NSB.

The party leadership consisted of men drawn from the middle class who were attracted to the professed ideals of National Socialism – hard work, personal responsibility and clarity of purpose. A desire for law and order was their main motivation.

Anton Mussert, the NSB leader was definitely not a Jew-hater, nor was that a feeling shared by the general membership. If any were appalled by the cruel actions towards the Jewish citizens, they rationalized that the 'greater good' required a slight adjustment to one's principles as in the adage 'you can't make an omelette without breaking a few eggs'.

The German occupier considered the NSB 'useful idiots' who would help to appease the Dutch population and promote the State of Nederland within a Greater Germanic Europe.

Alexander von Becke was among the first to arrive. He had walked over from his nearby office. He was now Executive Director of the Office of Reconstruction, the agency in charge of repairing war damage. He had met the two qualifications for the job, an experienced architect and a trusted higher-up in the NSB.

The year of occupation had been good to him. His new position had yielded him a substantial increase in salary and a higher visibility among the new rulers in The Hague.

Willem would turn 12 in a few weeks time. Alexander was happy that the bullying about the Jeugdstorm had stopped. Fear of reprisals had deterred most of the hooligans.

Most of the attendees had now arrived. The meeting room on the main floor was set up theatre-style, with a raised podium for the speaker. A white-aproned matron with a stony expression served coffee at the back of the room. She would point to the saucer on the table where a dime was to be deposited to show appreciation for her services. It had been a long time since a smile had crossed the harridan's charm-deprived face. With each cup she also dispensed ginger cookies as though they were her only earthly possessions and extremely painful to part with.

A corpulent sergeant-at-arms called the meeting to order. Alexander took his place in the front row. Anton Mussert entered the room to raised arms and shouts of *Hou Zee*. His wan face and weak chin contrasted sharply with the tailored martial uniform with beautiful brown leather belting and polished knee-high boots.

The room of regional commanders and dignitaries fell quiet as Anton Mussert proudly relayed his face-to-face discussions with the Fuehrer.

"For all intents and purposes, Continental Europe west of Russia is now under German control," he said. "This is in line with the Fuehrer's plan to create a Greater Germany where former national entities will take their place as proud member states. Once the peace discussions with Britain are finalized, each member state will reinstitute its original form of government. The Royal Houses of Belgium, Denmark and Norway will resume their respective thrones although their roles will be largely ceremonial." He left the lectern to strut around the front of the room. He became more animated and began to use his hands and arms for emphasis; it looked awkward and rehearsed. He could not possibly match his idol in the manipulation of an audience.

"Herr Hitler condemned Wilhelmina for her cowardly act of deserting the country and allowing Crown Princess Juliana and her children to move to Canada." His disdain for the disgrace showed theatrically and he continued, "For a successful transition to the New Order, it is imperative that the House of Orange be re-installed in our country." He took one of the empty chairs in the front row, dragged it to the centre, put his left boot on it, rested his arm on it, and rested his chin in his hand. All this in order to establish a greater intimacy with his listeners.

He continued, "Therefore, the National Library has been charged with researching blood relatives of Orange Nassau that could fill the role of the country's formal Head of State."

Alexander felt a sudden anxiety. His heart pounded. He loosened his tie and looked around; no one seemed to notice his discomfort. The vow, the annuity payment, the opportunity for Willem, the opportunity for Nederland – conflicting thoughts swirled around his mind.

Alexander did not hear the remainder of Mussert's speech. He went through the motions of singing the NSB song and the *Hou Zee* shouts.

The wild-eyed look of her husband told Paula that something was wrong. Alexander was struggling for words. "I'll get you a small Jenever," she offered, "Perhaps that will settle you down."

"Paula," he swallowed a sip of the firewater, "Willem could be King some day."

She looked at him in astonishment. He related that Berlin was seeking a blood relative of the House of Orange to assume the throne.

Paula was aghast. "You would sacrifice our son to become a puppet of the German Reich?"

"It's not a sacrifice; it is an honour that belongs to him. It is destiny!"

"What if he doesn't want it?" she cried out with fear foremost in her mind.

"He doesn't have to agree. He *is* of Royal blood. He understands the philosophy of National Socialism and our ideals for a better world."

"Alexander, so far I have gone along with your view of the world and your involvement with the NSB. I hoped you'd come to see that it is evil. Depraved. Monstrous. And you will not surrender our son to that evil."

"He is not our son; he belongs to the nation," he responded, his face red with anger.

Paula stormed into the hallway and opened the front door. She waved him towards the door and said in a measured voice, "Get out Alexander! Go back to your strutting friends in their ridiculous uniforms. You disgust me and you are a traitor to our son."

He argued but ended up taking the train back to The Hague. He slept on the couch in his office.

42

1941
THURSDAY MAY 15, 14:15 HRS CEST
ABWEHR HEADQUARTERS, TIRPITZUFER 76/78
BERLIN, GERMANY

"I am apprehensive about meeting Admiral Canaris," Anton Mussert said. He looked more like a schoolboy fearing the headmaster's displeasure than the Leader of the NSB. He and Alexander von Becke were in Berlin to meet with Canaris at Abwehr headquarters.

A week ago, when Mussert approached the office of the Fuehrer with the news that he had located a descendant of the House of Orange, he had been referred to the Office of Reichsfuehrer Himmler who in turn steered him to the Abwehr. Now they were to present their case.

Alexander looked at the slight man beside him who cowered in his chair. Mussert was dressed in a dark blue, well-cut civilian suit and bright red tie. His allegiance to Hitler went as far as sporting the same black rectangle moustache. When Alexander told him that his son was actually a scion of the House of Orange, Mussert had been ecstatic. The Fuehrer would be pleased with him, he thought, but then caution overtook him.

"It is a story-book tale, von Becke. The authorities will want proof."

"My wife Paula and I were sworn to secrecy but I felt it was necessary for the future to tell you that Princess Juliana is my son's birth mother."

"Even if it is proven that he is Princess Juliana's son, he is an illegitimate son." Mussert said.

Alexander was prepared for this argument. "I know the constitution prohibits illegitimate children from assuming the throne. However, the new constitution will be substantially different from the current document. Descendants will be declared following bloodlines. This will solidify my son's status as a legitimate heir to the House of Orange, especially since Juliana has two daughters," Alexander said.

To still Mussert's anxiety he reviewed the proof of Willem's birth. Professor Pronk, the Queen's personal physician, now deceased, had left detailed notes in his papers. Alexander also found the address of Mrs. Plein, the nurse who had been present at the birth. She testified that she had handed the baby to the von Beckes. From her personal files, she produced a print of the baby's right foot, taken immediately upon birth.

Mussert stirred himself from his slouch. "Insolent man," he snapped. "Admiral Canaris doesn't appreciate that the Fuehrer and I are of equal rank. We both are leaders, of our respective National Socialist Parties."

"The Admiral has many priorities," Alexander soothed. After a 20-minute wait, the admiral's secretary led the two men into the inner office. Canaris was not there.

The room was in sharp contrast to the seedy outside of the building. A large glass-enclosed bookcase covered the wall opposite the large picture window that looked down on the river Spree. The shelves contained a collection of military memorabilia including models of ships once under the admiral's command. There were medals, diplomas and gifts from the days of his foreign service. The centrepiece was the *Ritterkreuz mit Eichenlaub*, the Knights Cross with Oak Leaves awarded by Hitler for Canaris' services in Spain. The massive mahogany desk in the centre of the room was uncluttered with no paper or other sign of business activity.

Unannounced, Canaris entered the room. Mussert jumped to his feet and rendered an impeccable Heil Hitler salute.

"*Ja, Ja,*" Canaris waved him to sit down while he walked over to Alexander to shake his hand. "Now then, Baron von Becke," Canaris said jovially, ignoring Mussert, "Tell us the story of your son."

Mussert couldn't wait to jump in, "It is all in my report to the Fuehrer, Admiral," he said huffily.

"Thank you, Herr Mussert. I would like to hear the Baron's report first hand." Mussert sank down in his chair, the air taken out of him.

Alexander related in detail the reasons why he and Paula were entrusted with Juliana's son. In support of the story, he referred to the affidavit of the nurse. Canaris smiled enigmatically and said, "The Abwehr, independently, will pursue additional evidence. Is there any suggestion who the father might be?"

"No Sir, the Royal family made sure that the identity of the father would not become known. The only person who knows is General van Zandt but he has fled to England."

"Well then, we shall pursue that also." He opened a drawer in his desk and pulled out a file. He took off his steel-rimmed glasses, retrieved a small cloth from his glasses container and carefully wiped each lens. He held them up to the picture window and, judging them clean, used his right hand to hook one ear awkwardly and then the other one.

"The long-range plan to be put before the Fuehrer is that the boy will study in Germany at the University of Heidelberg. The boy's mother may make her home in Heidelberg to give him parental support. I assume she is in full accord with her son's new role in life?" Canaris asked.

"She will need time to adjust to the idea, I am afraid," Alexander said.

"Make sure that she adjusts," said Canaris looking sternly over his glasses. "Now, the Fuehrer wants to meet the boy as soon as possible. Once our investigation is complete, we shall make further arrangements."

He lifted some papers from the file and searched for the right one. He opened it slowly and studied the contents. "There is a note here from Minister Goebbels. It says you, as the father, must become a role model for the youth of Nederland. For reasons of state and propaganda, you must enlist in the Dutch Waffen SS Brigade. You will be offered an officer's rank." He closed the file and put it back in the drawer.

Alexander had anticipated the change in Willem's education but not his enlistment as a combatant – Paula in Germany and he, an officer of the SS? "When might all this come into effect, Admiral?" he asked.

Mussert felt the need to interject again. "Right away, Comrade von Becke," he said decisively, twitching his clownish moustache.

Canaris shook his head imperceptibly with dismay at the man's awkwardness. He said, "The Abwehr needs time to check the background of this surprising development. Other issues must be decided. For instance, who will act as Regent before Wilhelm can assume the throne?"

"There is a precedent, Admiral." Alexander replied. "Queen Emma was Wilhelmina's Regent until she reached 18 years of age."

Canaris sneered slightly, knowing what von Becke had in mind. He snapped dismissively, "Queen Emma was Wilhelmina's mother. You are Wilhelm's caretaker. Meanwhile, please remember that nothing is decided. The boy will carry on with life as normal at the moment."

Admiral Canaris rose and shook Alexander's hand. Anton Mussert clicked his heels and snapped the Heil Hitler salute.

"*Ja! Ja!*" Canaris waved his hand up and down like a salute but it looked more like a gesture meaning 'relax already'.

43

1941
FRIDAY, MAY 16, 17:00 HRS BDST
VAN ZANDT SUITE, CARLTON MANOR, 23 BOURNE STREET
LONDON SW, ENGLAND

"We should really serve better drinks than that paint remover you call Jenever." Kirsten said. "Our British guests crave London Gin and I always have to disappoint them. In your position it should be easy to get some decent alcoholic drinks."

"It's our patriotic duty to drink the Dutch stuff," van Zandt replied, slouching down in his lazy chair and putting his feet on the coffee table.

"Let me pour you a double then," she teased. "The young Jenever is drinkable but that Old Jenever should either be banned or sent to the Resistance for Molotov cocktails."

Their banter was interrupted by the doorbell. Jos Caspers stood at the door with a message. "Sorry, Sir, a radio message from OZ, rated High Importance. No one else has seen it." Van Zandt accepted it silently.

"Thank you, Sergeant," said van Zandt walking back to his chair.

> *Alexander von Becke has informed Nazi High Command that his son is a child of Princess Juliana. Our inside NSB informant confirms. Subject travelled to Berlin 15/5/41 to meet Canaris. Oz.*

Van Zandt had feared this moment. He knew Hitler would exploit the sudden discovery. The bill for his manipulations was being rendered. That son-of-a bitch, he thought.

"What's the matter?" Kirsten asked as she put his drink on the coffee table. "You look ghastly."

He needed to talk. To unburden himself. All these damn secrets kept inside. "I must go," he declared, "I must speak to Her Majesty."

He went into his den and called Wilhelmina's private secretary. It was a brief discussion. He stepped back into the living room. "Must get back in uniform, I fear," he said, "She's waiting and she won't be happy."

44

1941
SATURDAY, MAY 17, 11:00 AM EDT
STORNOWAY, 541 ACACIA RD
OTTAWA, CANADA

Among the ambassadorial homes on the tree-lined Ottawa avenue, the house didn't stand out. It was relatively new, built in 1914 for a local grocer, A. J. Major and named *Stornoway* after his ancestral home in Scotland.

"I wish that Papa would come home every evening just like Liliana's papa, next door," Beatrix said to her mother.

"Papa is busy with the war, but he comes to see us as often as he can. He will fly across the ocean to see us again next month. Soon we can go back to our home in Soestdijk and then he will be home all the time. You remember Soestdijk , don't you?"

"Yeah..." Beatrix said hesitantly.

The telephone rang in the book-walled study. Nurse Monique Dionne, the children's nanny picked it up. "*C'est pour vous, Madame,*" she announced as she walked into the living room. "*C'est la Reine Wilhelmina, votre Mère.*"

Juliana closed the door, expecting another stern lecture on rearing children in the Dutch tradition. In fact, the little ones were getting along just fine in all three languages.

The connection was raspy but she could hear her mother's commanding voice.

"My dear Juliana, what I am about to tell you is disturbing. The distress of you being with child has come back to haunt us."

"Oh, Maman," Juliana sucked in her breath.

"Your dear, departed Papa recommended one of his German family members and his Dutch wife as parents and they registered the boy as their natural child. To all reports, they have reared the child well, but the father has become immersed in the NSB. This week, he informed Berlin that his son is of Royal blood and should be eligible to ascend the throne."

Juliana let out a gasp. Wilhelmina continued, "The government of Nederland has moved to Britain to save us from having to debase the House of Orange to govern Nederland as Nazi serfs. We shall not let the Huns despoil our proud heritage."

"Maman, am I to understand that the occupiers may use the boy for their political aims?"

"Evidently so, my dear."

"But Maman, the shame," sobbed Juliana. Tears began to form.

"Hush dear. The Kingdom comes before any personal embarrassment. Steps are being taken to prevent this outrage from succeeding."

"What about Bernhard? He will detest me."

"We shall not inform him as yet. If needed, Bernhard will be made to understand what is good for the country, his wife and indeed himself."

"The people will never forgive me," Juliana cried.

"They may never find out, but I would like to think our subjects would understand. Now listen; General van Zandt has a plan to have an agent extract the boy from the country and bring him to England. Once the boy is here, we can decide what's best for all concerned."

"The Germans will exploit my downfall and the whole world will know," Juliana cried loudly.

The door to the study opened and Monique looked in. *"Etes-vous bien, Madame?"* Juliana dabbed her eyes, nodded yes and motioned for the door to be closed.

"Be strong Juliana, have faith and if it is God's will, this too shall pass."

Monique was waiting for her in the living room. "If it is bad news Madame, please tell me what I can do," she had switched to English.

"Nothing, thank you Monique."

"Perhaps I can cheer you up Madame. This morning a special delivery letter came, inviting you to attend a piano concerto at the Orpheus Musical Theatre next week. The invitation is very personal, Madame; it's from the artist himself. Ferenc Kolmar, the famous pianist from New York."

45

1941
SATURDAY, MAY 17, 15:00 HRS BDST
NETHERLANDS EMBASSY, HIGH GATE PARK
LONDON SW1, ENGLAND

The train ride from Southend-on-Sea to Waterloo station had taken over two hours. Mark had read about the effects of the indiscriminate bombing on London yet he was not prepared for the devastation of so many homes in Greater London.

German attacks had now eased. It had been a week since the last massive bombardment. The Blitz had begun a year ago with the bombing of London for 57 consecutive nights. Since then, 21,000 civilians had been killed and more than a million houses were damaged or destroyed.

Mark had a feeling of foreboding about being summoned so urgently to meet with General van Zandt. If it had to do with the Training Centre, a memo or telegram would have sufficed. This had to be more important.

He didn't have to wait long before he was ushered into the big office – a scene of incomparable chaos. Books were piled everywhere. Most of them were decorated with coloured slips of paper indicating pages of research that had never been pursued.

The General seemed ill at ease. His usual bravado was absent.

"A problem has arisen in Nederland and I need you to solve it," In a serious situation van Zandt always came to the point, without preamble.

"You asked me once why my picture appeared in the von Becke family album. In 1929, I persuaded Paula and Alexander to accept a child, born out of wedlock, whose birth mother's identity could not be revealed."

"You mean, young Willem? He is adopted?" Mark was astonished.

Mark noticed the General's discomfort. He fidgeted in his chair. He liked to swing around in the swivel chair in his old office. This wasn't a swivel chair but he kept throwing his weight from side to side as if hoping that it might become one.

"We need to extract Willem from Nederland; bring him to England."

"Along with his parents?"

"The mother, if need be. The father definitely not!"

"If I may ask, General, why? And how?"

"It is a matter of the highest importance for our country. As to how it will be done, that is something we must work out later."

"I don't know if I have the right training, Sir."

"SAS will give you additional training."

"What about timing, Sir. When is this extraction to take place?"

"Your drop is tentatively scheduled for June twentieth, which gives you a month to prepare."

"I need to know why the boy has to be brought to England, Sir. If I am to risk my life I have a right to know why," Mark insisted.

Van Zandt looked pained. "You are right. However, what I tell you is confidential. It could cause serious political upheaval," he paused to consider how best to say it. "Willem is the son of Princess Juliana."

Mark leaned back in his chair and let the air escape through his pursed lips.

Van Zandt continued, "The Germans have recently learned that the boy is of Royal blood and want to use him for propaganda purposes. Her Majesty wants to have the boy beyond Nazi reach. A great responsibility rests on your shoulders."

Mark was silent, absorbing the enormity of his task. "May I ask, Sir, does Princess Juliana know her child will be brought to England?"

"I am not privy to that information but I would think she knows. As you prepare for this mission, you will be asked many questions. It goes without saying that you are not to reveal these details to anyone."

"Understood, Sir."

Mark left the building, confounded, elated and dismayed. His mood changed to disquiet. He knew the dangers. Two agents dropped on the beach at Katwijk were never heard from again. Three agents dropped in North Holland were arrested as they untangled the wires of their chutes.

He longed to see his home. On dark days, he yearned for the safety he felt as a child. The shadows were so different then.

But why him? He was not mentally prepared for action behind enemy lines. He shook the negative thought. Actually, that should be the least of his concerns. He had a month to get ready.

In his daydreaming, he had walked along Knightsbridge without thinking. He debated whether he should stop at the Magpie and Frog. He decided to push on to Carlton Manor where his old room was still unoccupied, or so he was told.

It was after five now. Sloan Street was filled with people going home. He wanted to talk to Alice. He walked up the stairs, briefly wondering if he should stop in to see Kirsten in the General's suite but decided against it. His room was more or less as he left it. It was still spartan. A musty smell, peculiar to long-empty rooms caused him to toss his kit on the bed and knock on Alice's door. There was no immediate response. He sensed she was in but didn't want to be disturbed. He turned but then decided to knock once more. After a wait, the door opened partly. Jos Caspers stood naked with a towel around his hips.

"Hello there Mark," he giggled in embarrassment. "Are you moving back in? Alice is just freshening up a bit. Would you join us later for a drink?" Mark turned without speaking.

He walked back to the Magpie and Frog. The place was filled. He found a chair near the table with the picture of the greyhound race above it. He had sat there with Alice. He ordered a Guinness and the special of the day – bangers and mash.

In the opposite corner, a bevy of office girls was chattering away. One of them ogled him repeatedly. She screwed up enough courage to approach. "Hey, look at this then!" the cute dark-haired girl called out to her girlfriends. "An officer with two silver stars on an orange lapel patch. Can't be a general, he's too young," she slurred slightly. She rubbed her finger across the 'Netherlands' badge at the top of his sleeve. "Oh, you are a Dutchie then. My name is Tracy; you look lonely. Want to talk about it?"

She put her arm around his shoulder and slid onto the chair beside him. She smelled of jasmine and red wine. He liked it. He bought her a fuzzy-looking sherry made in Dumfries, Scotland. He found it difficult to get drunk on weak, warm beer, but he tried. He talked a lot about home and Jenny. Later, when he and Tracy climbed the stairs to his room in the garret, he noticed the light under Alice's door. He didn't knock.

46

1941
MONDAY, MAY 19, 10:15 HRS BDST
CARLTON MANOR, 23 BOURNE STREET
LONDON SW1, ENGLAND

Alice was talking to someone in her office. He waved a non-committal hand as he went by on his way to the tea station. The timing was perfect. Neither he nor Alice needed to say anything. Dora the lovable tea-lady, badly in need of basic dental care, poured him a cup of tea. He nibbled at the scones that had petrified over the weeks.

Just as Mark soaked the last scone in his tea to make it edible, a ramrod-straight Warrant Officer, bearing the insignia of the SAS walked into the reception area and snapped to attention. "Warrant Officer Passmore of the SAS, Sir." He pronounced Sir as Sah! Even after a year of immersion in English, Mark still couldn't understand why the upper-class accents ignored the existence of the letter R. In Leiden, his hometown, people pronounced the letter R as a growl emanating from a four-ton truck. In listening to some of the elite, it had taken him a while to understand that the word *shaz* had nothing to do with Iranian heads of state but rather a form of intermittent precipitation.

"I must interview you Sir, prior to your joining the SAS training unit."

"This soon?"

"Priority One, Sir," he snapped. "Can we find an empty office?"

Mark located a vacant interview room, and for two hours, he endured a brain-draining interrogation in order to be permitted to enter the shady world of SAS. He promised that he had no intention of betraying secrets to a foreign power. That he did not abuse alcohol or take illegal drugs. That he was not a sexual deviant of any kind. That he did not have debts that he could not pay. That he was not experiencing marital problems. Having signed and initialled all the necessary documents, he was told to report to the Embassy that afternoon at 13:00 hours. He checked his watch – time to spare. He decided to walk.

It was one of those rare days when the sun in London shines as bright as at the beach in Aruba. Pedestrians, young and old were out enjoying the beautiful weather. He walked north along Sloan Street, toward Kensington. There was a girl walking towards him along the sidewalk, her hands pushed deeply in the pockets of a black leather coat, a leather bag was over her shoulder. He had seen her somewhere around the Manor, in the pub maybe, or pushing a teacart down the hall. She looked straight ahead – the war stare. No one ever seemed to look at anyone these days, least of all on the sidewalk of a busy street.

When the girl was about five metres in front of him, she appeared to stumble over a grate in the pavement. She fell heavily, spilling the contents of her handbag.

Mark moved quickly and knelt beside her. "Are you all right?" he asked.

"Thank you," the girl said. She sat up and began picking up her things. Passers-by looked, but didn't pay much attention.

"Let me help you," Mark said.

He heard a car accelerate on Sloan Street. He turned around and spotted an old Land Rover speeding towards him. It was then that he felt something hard pressing against the small of his back.

"Get into the car, Lieutenant Zonder," the girl said calmly, "Or I'll put a bullet through your spine." The car skidded to a halt next to the curb. The rear door flew open. Seated in the back were two men wearing balaclavas. One of them jumped out, pushed Mark into the car and then climbed in next to him. The car accelerated rapidly, leaving the girl behind.

He awoke slowly. He had no idea how long it had been since they had thrown him into the car. He opened his eyes and saw nothing but a sack of black cloth over his head. He took stock of his injuries. He was sure that the people who assaulted him were the kind of professionals who could beat a man without leaving a mark. He couldn't breathe through his nose and his skull hurt in a dozen different places. His ribs ached, so even a shallow breath caused shooting pain.

Minutes later the car drew to a stop. The door opened and he felt a gust of welcome wind. Two of the men took hold of his arms and pulled him out. Suddenly he was standing upright. He tried to take a step, but his knees buckled. His captors caught him before he hit the ground. They drew his arms around each of them and carried him into the house. They passed through a series of rooms and hallways, his feet dragging along the floorboard. A moment later, he was placed in a straight-backed chair.

Finally, he heard the door open and close again. A man had entered the room. Mark could hear him breathing and he could smell him – cigarettes, hair tonic, and a breath of woman's smell that reminded him of Alice. The man settled into a chair. He must have been a large man because his chair crackled beneath his weight. "We will remove the hood now, Mark."

He was a man of blunt edges – a broad forehead, heavy cheekbones, and the flattened nose of a boxer. His square chin looked as though it had been shaped by a hatchet. "How are you feeling, lad?" he inquired.

"Where am I? Who are you," Mark said, gingerly touching his cheek.

"Sorry for the rough reception. Call me Ben. For the record, I am a sergeant but we don't use ranks here. We like first names. You told Timmerman that you didn't need the SAS training, but you do. Just to convince you that it is different from what you did before we thought we'd give you a sample. By the way, you are in a no-name place on the border between Herefordshire and Wales."

"So I have to do the stuff again that we taught in Southend-on-Sea?"

"No just the stuff you didn't teach."

"Like kidnapping and intimidation, I suppose."

"Yes, but you will also learn new crafts such as creating false documentation, changing your appearance, living off the land and boating skills. Most importantly, we'll bring you up to date with the changes in your country. It won't do to have you thinking it is the same as you left it. You'd be captured the first day."

"You mean an Englishman will bring me up to date with changes in Nederland?"

"No, we have an agent who just came back. He can tell you a lot."

The door opened and in walked Brenner Zijlberg. "Hello Mark, I'm back," Brenner smiled.

47

1941
FRIDAY, MAY 29, 10:00 HRS EDT
PRINCESS JULIANA'S RESIDENCE, STORNOWAY
OTTAWA, CANADA

"I shall, of course, accept the invitation to attend the concert," she had told Monique, "But I also want to ask Maestro Kolmar if he would perform a private recital for us here at Stornoway. We shall have a limited guest list, instead of an official affair. I would like to invite our neighbour, The Honourable C.D. Howe, Canada's Minister of Supply. And Gunnar Bergstrom the Ambassador of Sweden; he loves Rachmaninoff," Juliana was in her element, "And of course Ambassador Fonseca from Portugal. Let's keep it to 15 couples."

She had asked Monique to arrange a telephone appointment with the virtuoso and was nervous as the phone rang in New York. The initial conversation had been stiff and formal as between strangers. Neither talked of personal things. She was the princess who was pleased to hear from him again. He was the maestro and was delighted she would attend the concert. Juliana had come to the point rather quickly and asked if he would consent to a brief private recital at a soiree for friends at Stornoway the evening before the concert at the Orpheus. He had agreed and offered to play *Morceaux de Fantaisie, Opus 3*.

The elegantly dressed guests were nibbling at hors d'oeuvres and sipping wine when Ferenc Kolmar arrived. Juliana saw him enter, politely excused herself from the guests and went to meet her long-ago beau.

"Mr. Kolmar, how marvelous of you to accept our invitation to perform at this intimate evening." She held out her right hand at a strange angle; he wasn't certain whether he was expected to shake it or kiss it.

"Your Highness, it is my distinct pleasure to perform for you again. It is so wonderful to see you. We have so many things to talk about. Our lives now are so different from when we last met."

"Mr. Kolmar, there isn't much time before we must join our guests. I am afraid I must come right out with it. I must speak to you privately, after your recital, on an urgent matter of great importance."

"Yes, of course. Shall I wait until after the guests have left?"

"If you don't mind, yes. I shall end the evening as quickly as possible without appearing to be rude." She sighed and straightened herself.

"Allow me to introduce you to the guests in the salon," she said. He ignored the protocol of walking three paces behind her and strode by her side to welcoming applause. He went into his practiced routine of making the rounds, charming everyone in the room, chatting, smiling and accepting compliments.

After dinner, he launched into his performance and held everyone spellbound. He graciously acknowledged the applause and after more polite chitchat, the guests departed. While Monique and the caterers cleaned up, Juliana sat down with Ferenc in the study.

"Mr. Kolmar," she began.

"Your Highness," he interrupted, "I hope I am not too brash but, within these walls, might we resume the use of our first names?"

"Given what I am about to tell you that seems appropriate."

"My dear Juliana, after I these years, I wonder: why now?"

"That will be quite clear after I tell you of events that happened after we last met. I will assume the directness of Maman's style of speaking and tell you that our... union... in Katwijk resulted in a pregnancy. On May 29, 1929, I gave birth to a boy; your son."

There was silence for a moment while the information registered. "My God! Why wasn't I told?" he asked in exasperation.

"No one was told, Ferenc. The Queen decided to keep the event from becoming public. The event simply did not occur; all tracks were covered."

"Did that include getting me out of the way by offering me a scholarship at Juilliard?"

"You deserved that opportunity, Ferenc. Do not make it into something squalid," she admonished.

Kolmar considered this in silence. "What about the child?" he asked.

"I was kept from the public with the explanation that I was studying in Batavia. Only medical professionals trusted by Maman were present. I was not allowed to hold the child. It was taken by family members of Papa. They registered the boy as their natural son."

"Does your husband know about this?"

"Bernhard doesn't need to know and if all goes well he may never know. Should it become public knowledge, he will have to accept it. He is not without blame himself with respect to extramarital behavior."

"Where is the boy now," stammered Ferenc, clearly shaken by the revelation. "What is his name?"

"I don't know his name. I was only told that it was a boy. Maman tells me he is healthy and intelligent. The difficulty is that his father is an NSB official and has betrayed his vow not to divulge my identity."

"Why is this all happening now, Juliana," Ferenc asked, his face ashen.

"A confederated Europe under German control requires a member of the House of Orange to be propped up as the Monarch of Nederland."

"What does your government in London think about this?"

"In order to keep the Germans from exploiting the situation, the Queen has ordered that the boy be extracted and taken to England."

Ferenc burst out angrily, "Only to hide him again! The boy's existence will be buried and the House of Orange will remain without stain."

Juliana dabbed a tear away. "Damage to the honour of the Royal Family is not the reason for bringing the boy to England. The Queen wants to deny the Germans a weapon to manipulate the Dutch people."

"Does the father not count in this conspiracy?"

Juliana was in tears. He walked over and held her close. "I'll bring him out Juliana, trust me," he said.

"Wait, Ferenc, agents are in place to bring him to England."

"I will not let the Queen shove me out of the way again. If the boy is to have a new life it will be with his father, not another caretaker."

Ferenc left Juliana in the care of Monique. He wondered if the nanny had overheard.

That night, in the hotel, he dialed Marcy's number in New York intending to tell her of his newfound son. He let the phone ring twice and then, suddenly, feeling incapable of explaining, he hung up.

48

1941
MONDAY, JUNE 1, 16:15 HRS EDT
GLADSTONE APARTMENTS, FIFTH AVENUE
NEW YORK CITY, USA

A whiff of goulash welcomed him when he stepped out of the elevator into their Fifth Avenue apartment. "Is that you, Darling?" Marcy called from the kitchen.

On the seven-hour train ride from Ottawa, he had rehearsed how he would tell her he had a son, but he was still nervous. She came out of the kitchen in a white apron holding a wooden spoon. She kissed him lightly on the lips. "How was the concert? I am so sorry that I could not go but this committee work keeps me busier than ever," she said.

"It was fine. The critics were quite complimentary."

Marcy wiped her hands on her apron and embraced him. "And how about your private recital for the Princess?"

"That went fine also but there was a most unexpected development."

"What was it?" she said, undoing her apron.

"You'd better sit down, Marcy," he said.

She reached for his hand and sat beside him on the sofa. "What's wrong," she asked, suddenly afraid.

"I hope that what I'm about to tell you will not affect our relationship," He began haltingly, "You know that Juliana and I had an affair in 1928."

"Well, yes; I suspected that. That's why you were anxious to do a concert."

He told her about the pregnancy and the boy born and sheltered, and how the Germans were planning to exploit the situation for political ends.

"So what can we do?"

"Thank you for saying 'we' Marcy. The Queen has arranged to bring the boy to England. We cannot let the Royals kidnap him again and hide him. We must stage our own rescue of the boy. Remember that FBI man, Clyde Tolson who helped us when we faced that extortion threat?"

"Yes, I remember, a charming man; a bit feminine, I thought."

"He is now J. Edgar Hoover's Deputy Director. I will ask if he can help."

"The FBI is concerned with domestic crime. They will not be anxious to become involved in an international affair, will they? Roosevelt keeps repeating we are a neutral country."

"That is true. However, FBI agents know the kind of people who walk the thin line between legal and illegal. I'm hoping Clyde will refer us to someone. I have the money to carry it off and if that it is not enough, the Jewish patrons of my music will help, I am sure."

He walked into the library and dialled a number. He talked for a long time; Marcy could not hear the conversation but when he walked back into the room, he had a smile on his face.

"I'm off to Washington D.C. on tomorrow morning's train."

49

1941
MONDAY, JUNE 16, 11:00 HRS CEST
VON BECKE VILLA, JULIANALAAN 45
OEGSTGEEST, NEDERLAND

On the way home from the railway station Alexander looked at his reflection in every storefront window. The uniform of a Hauptsturmfuehrer looked good on him. At a trim 43, the smartly tailored jacket with the SS insignia on his lapels and cap made him look like a veteran Captain of the Waffen SchutzStaffel.

After his meeting with Admiral Canaris, Alexander had immediately volunteered for the Waffen SS Brigade stationed at Scheveningen near The Hague. In the few weeks he had spent there, he had undergone minimal combat training. Instead, he had received intensive instruction in the logistics of running a brigade. His expertise was now in supply management and personnel administration. He had talked to Paula on the telephone frequently but he had yet to tell her that Himmler had directed him to introduce Willem to Adolf Hitler on the 17th of June, that is to say tomorrow. He knew she would object. They had not spoken face-to-face since the day she had ushered him out of the house.

He debated whether he should ring the doorbell or use his key. Paula met him in the hallway as he opened the door.

"You look smart in that uniform and you have lost some weight," she noted. They embraced. She took his bag and urged him to sit down. "Willem is at school but he should be home soon. He missed you terribly. Would you like some coffee? It's ready." She went to the kitchen while he took off his jacket and draped it carefully over the back of a chair.

"I know you don't agree with my actions Paula but I think I am doing the best thing for our son," Alexander said, accepting his cup of coffee and placing it on a side table next to him.

Alexander lifted his coffee cup, took a sip and in a deliberate motion placed it back on the saucer. Paula had her arms crossed in a defensive pose. He began, "If the Fuehrer agrees to Willem's bloodlines, our son will be allowed to enter the pre-schooling for University of Heidelberg next year; you will stay with him during his studies until he graduates."

"You are assuming that Germany will win the war?" Paula challenged.

"Of course. Germany controls Western Europe already."

Paula was in a combative mood. "Aren't you running a bit ahead of yourself? Has Berlin accepted that Willem is who you say he is?"

"They have accepted Juliana as the birth mother but still want to investigate who the natural father is."

"Why should that matter? Besides, Princess Juliana deserves her privacy. It is inconceivable that she would have been intimate with a man unacceptable to society."

"I think you are right and the investigation will bear that out. Which brings me to the reason for my urgent visit today. Himmler has asked that you and I present Willem to the Fuhrer at the Reichskanzlerei."

"When?"

"Tomorrow."

"That is impossible. It is too soon and Willem must attend school," Paula objected.

"Paula, be reasonable," he said urgently. "We cannot defy the wishes of the Reichskanzler. If we fail to attend without good reason it will be considered an insult to the Leader that can have nasty consequences."

"How can we tell Willem about these things?"

"That is why I am here. We should be together when we tell him."

"He thinks we're his natural parents," Paula said angrily. "The fact that he is adopted will come as a shock to him, let alone the fact that he is the son of Princess Juliana!"

"We must tell him this evening," Alexander repeated, "Sooner or later the facts will come out. I am sure it is better that he hears the news from his parents than the newspaper."

"Let's be careful how we approach this," she said.

Alexander noting the softening in Paula's position pressed on. "We can take the night train to Berlin; it doesn't leave until ten o'clock this evening. We'll arrive well rested in Berlin in time for the meeting."

They heard the front door open and Willem burst in. He saw his father and flung himself into his arms. "You are a Hauptsturmfuehrer! Wow, you became an officer right away." He kissed his father "I'm happy you're home! I missed you."

"I missed you too. We have a lot to talk about, Willem." Alexander said.

Later, in the den, Alexander told of meeting Admiral Canaris and that he had been asked to enlist in the Dutch Waffen SS. They talked about Berlin and his visit to the famous Zoo until Paula cut him short.

"Your Father has something important to ask you." Willem looked expectantly at his Dad.

"I did not see the Fuehrer when I was in Berlin," Alexander began haltingly, "But Reichsfuehrer Himmler told me the Fuehrer would like to meet the three of us in Berlin, tomorrow. That is why I came home – to ask if you want to go." Willem turned to Paula.

"The Fuehrer wants to meet us? Say yes Mom, can we go? Please?"

"There is more to the visit than just meeting Herr Hitler. I will let your father explain." Alexander did not speak for what seemed a long time, but then he related the story.

Any fear that Alexander and Paula had about the news coming as a shock to Willem was quickly abated. He was genuinely excited. What child doesn't want to hear that he or she is really the son or daughter of a princess? After the initial news had worn off, he became quiet, letting it all sink in. Finally, he said, "Why did Princess Juliana give me away?"

Paula hugged him. "Because she loved you so much. She wanted the best for you and she believed that your father and I could do better than she could. She was not married, you see and there was no father to help."

"Will she be upset if I become King and she doesn't get to be Queen?"

Paula smiled at him. "Those questions don't need an answer right now. All the Fuehrer wants is to meet with you. If he decides on another way to govern the country our lives will carry on as normal."

"If Princess Juliana had kept me, I would be living in London and be an enemy of Germany. I wouldn't like that!" Willem said.

50

1941
TUESDAY, JUNE 17, 06:00 HRS CEST
POTSDAMERPLATZ RAILWAY STATION
BERLIN, GERMANY

"We are here," Willem shouted with his head hanging out of the open compartment window. As the train chugged to a halt, the massive clock at Berlin's Anhalter Railway station ticked to 6:02 in the morning. Willem and Paula had slept well in a lower berth but Alexander was the one who had climbed into the upper. He hadn't slept well. It was his second nine-hour train ride in two days and the fatigue showed on his face.

The Anhalter terminal was the biggest in the world. As many as 145 trains arrived each day, 80 of them long-distance luxury expresses that came complete with cocktail bars, sleeping compartments and diners. Beneath the arrival hall, baggage porters labouring under steamer trunks led the arriving passengers directly into the plush foyer of the Excelsior Hotel. They would be conveniently close to the fine shops of the Leipzigerstrasze, the embassies, palaces and grand houses, the Tiergarten and the government office of the new German Reich.

On this June morning, it seemed to Alexander that the passengers were more subdued and the ambience less glittering. They walked towards the exit on the Potsdamerplatz. The railway staff smiled at this picture of the ideal Aryan family: a proud father, an officer in the Waffen SS, a strong mother and a bright-eyed youngster in the uniform of the Jeugdstorm.

"*Wohin, bitte?*" an eager porter inquired.

"He is asking where we want to go," Willem bubbled, excited that he could practice his German for the first time in Germany itself.

"Tell him to deliver our baggage to the Albrecht Hotel on the Friedrichstrasze," Alexander said. Turning to Paula he asked, "Shall we walk to the Albrecht? It is only a 20-minute stroll from here. The fresh air will do us good and breakfast will taste even better."

They walked along the Potsdamerstrasze admiring the shops and the tall buildings. Looking into a side street, Alexander noted that a few houses had been reduced to rubble by a Royal Air Force bombing raid. The infrequent attacks caused little strategic damage but as Churchill said, "Keeping four million Berliners awake at night is worth the trouble."

After a solid German breakfast at the Albrecht hotel, they went for a walk along the magnificent Unter-den-Linden, named after the hundreds of stately linden trees that lined the boulevard on both sides.

Willem took photographs at every opportunity. "Make sure you have some film left for this afternoon," Paula admonished.

When they arrived at the Reichskanzlerei, an officer of Hitler's elite bodyguard showed them into a reception area furnished with heritage chairs and settees, most of them pilfered from the royal houses of Europe. Twenty minutes later, he returned to announce that the meeting had been moved from the *Horst Wessel Kammer* to Hitler's private residence.

Willem had expected the living quarters to be on the top floor of the Reichskanzlerei. He was surprised when the elevator descended deep into the bowels of the building.

"Perhaps the Fuehrer is afraid of bombs falling on the building," Willem noted innocently. The grizzled elevator operator allowed a brief smile to cross his face. The elevator doors opened directly into a large carpeted area perfectly lit to evoke the impression of daylight. A voluptuous blond woman in the trim blue Luftwaffe uniform received them. Her long hair was in two plaits and rolled to make 'earphones', a hairstyle virtually unknown outside Germany. She showed them through the massive oak doors with carved eagle heads. Inside the hallway, a guard stood immobile. Behind him, an attractive woman with dark blond hair waited with outstretched hand. "I am Frau Eva Braun, and let me welcome you. The Fuehrer will join us in the library when he is free. May I offer you some sparkling water?"

"Sure!" Willem said loudly as his intimidated parents nodded silently.

A polite knock on the door made them look up. Hitler entered the room with Admiral Canaris. Alexander leapt to his feet and rendered the Heil Hitler salute. The Fuehrer raised his hand like a traffic cop stopping a car. He wore a dark blue suit with a narrow blue tie, a small swastika in the buttonhole of his lapel. It was a surprise to his visitors who had expected to see him in his Nazi uniform. Canaris wore his gold-braided Kriegsmarine uniform with a cluster of colourful ribbons. The Fuehrer's private demeanour was quite the opposite of his public persona. After Canaris introduced the family, Hitler behaved like a charming, well-mannered man who shook Willem's hand while rubbing his other hand through the boy's dark hair.

"Very good to meet you my young man. I am happy to see you wearing the uniform of the Dutch Jeugdstorm. It means you are a child of the new Europe." Next, he bowed to Paula, clicked his heels silently and lightly kissed her hand. "I am delighted to meet you Frau von Becke."

Paula appeared enchanted. "It is so wonderful to meet you my Fuehrer," she said in her accented German, beaming a warm smile.

"And you Hauptsturmfuehrer Baron von Becke, I welcome you as a leader of the Brigade Nederland of our valiant Waffen SS." He waved in the direction of the massive easy chairs situated near a faux picture window that purported to be a picturesque valley in Bavaria.

Hitler launched into a monologue about the aims of a confederation of European States under German protection. "The member states will keep their language, their culture and their history, with their leaders attuned to our ideals. God willing, my young Wilhelm, you could be the symbol of a new Nederland. I certainly hope so." Canaris listened and shifted uncomfortably in his chair.

They chatted for a while until Eva Braun came in to announce that the photographer had arrived. Hitler posed for photographs, one with the family and several of Willem with the Fuehrer's hand on his shoulder.

"Now I would like to have a picture to show my grandfather," said Willem handing his Hasselblad camera to the surprised photographer. He positioned his parents to the left of the Fuehrer and himself on the right. Hitler laughed a peculiar cackle and ruffled the boy's hair once more.

"You are quite the personality," he smiled, "and that is good." Before he turned to the door, he addressed Alexander: "Thank you for meeting on such short notice. We shall meet again in the very near future."

Canaris stood as the Fuehrer left. After the door closed, he sat down again. "Please, finish your water," he urged the von Beckes. The admiral was in an expansive mood and told tales of U-boats in the Battle of Jutland. Willem was spellbound.

When it was time to go Canaris rose and spoke to Alexander. "I was delighted to spend some time with your family," He had a distant look in his eyes. "I remember when my son was Willem's age. He is serving the Fatherland in North Africa. He has been missing in action for six weeks."

Alexander snapped his Nazi salute. The Admiral turned and with mock annoyance, waved him to relax.

51

1941
THURSDAY, JUNE 19, 09:00 HRS BDST
SPECIAL OPERATIONS EXECUTIVE (SOE) BASE
FELIXSTOWE, SUFFOLK, ENGLAND

The train from Ipswich rumbled along the platform of the old Felixstowe Pier railway station and ground to a hissing halt. This early in the morning the station looked deserted except for a farmer with two children and four caged chickens, waiting for the local to Port Frayne. Mark's train was 45 minutes late. His trip from the SAS base in Wales – with an overnight stopover in London and then to Ipswich – had taken the better part of two days. Felixstowe, north of Harwich, was a port on the North Sea that dated back many centuries.

The grey overcast sky did not make for a happy impression of the dilapidated town that was to be the jumping-off point for his insertion into Nederland. The SOE air base was also the base of the Royal Air Force's floatplanes, one of which would bring him home, but behind enemy lines. The attraction of the town didn't matter much; he would be here for only a few days at most.

Brenner Zijlberg was waiting for him at the end of the platform and enveloped him in a bear hug. "Good to see you, Mark. What gives with the moustache? If it gets any bigger you'll look like Stalin."

"All in the line of duty. I was ordered to grow a moustache. You are looking at two weeks' worth of work," he laughed.

"Should I ask why?"

"I need to look more mature," Mark winked.

"To look more like the date on your passport, I suppose?" Mark didn't respond; Brenner picked up his army kit and carried it as they walked together to the station building.

"What have you been doing since I saw you in Wales?" Mark asked.

"Training as a Marconist here at the SOE base. That's what they call an operator using Morse code via short wave radio. I completed my training and I'm waiting for an assignment."

"That's why I am here too."

"I know. I am here to tell you that you are scheduled to meet the Commanding Officer at 12 o'clock. After that long train ride I bet you'd kill for a shower and some clean underwear."

"You know it," Mark laughed.

At the front of the station, they bummed a ride from a military bus headed for the base.

The SOE air base sat on a large peninsula that overlooked the estuary of the rivers Orwell and Stour. It had a small natural harbour and had the distinction of being the only target in England attacked by Italian biplanes in 1940. The RAF had made short shrift of Mussolini's finest and chased them away before they could do any harm.

After dumping his kit in his assigned room, showering and donning fresh skivvies, Mark met the RCAF Squadron Leader, Leonard G.(Pete) Morrissey, a third-generation, Irish-American via Boston. He was a bush pilot in Alaska, flying de Havilland floatplanes, when the war in Europe broke out. He wanted to join the action but America was not at war with anyone. Therefore, he flew to the Yukon and enlisted in the Royal Canadian Air Force in Whitehorse. His skills in flying to remote wilderness lakes in all kinds of weather made him a logical choice to head the flying arm of the SOE. His responsibilities included the insertion of secret agents behind enemy lines, often in lakes or rivers.

Morrissey was a tall man, who walked and talked a bit like Gary Cooper. He had a ready smile and a quick wit. He had never lost his strong Boston accent where 'park' became 'pack' and 'Mark' became 'Mac'.

They met in his sparsely furnished office painted in an industrial green that barely contrasted with the green metal furniture. Morrissey sat behind his desk with his back to the window allowing his visitors a view of the harbour and its marine and air transports at anchor.

"There seems to be some special interest from higher up in your mission, Lieutenant. I am sure you know why, even if I don't. Never mind, SOE is responsible for getting you to your destination with all the stuff you need. We have been told to land you at the Vennemeer, a small lake close to the city of Leiden. Does that agree with your orders?"

"It does, Sir."

"What is the nature of your mission?"

Mark stared at him not responding.

"Quite Correct," Morrissey smiled. "None of my business but I thought I'd see if you're a blabbermouth. I understand that you will not need us to retrieve you?"

"There are no plans for retrieval, unless something goes wrong, Sir."

"It usually does, son, but for now the drill is that you will be issued demobilization papers from the Dutch Army, showing your rank as Sergeant and your real name except you're ten years older. We can't identify you as a Lieutenant because most officers are still held in POW camps. Have no worry about your CID records in The Hague; they were destroyed just before the capitulation."

Morrissey stopped and fished a cigarette from the Lucky Strikes package in his shirt pocket. "Smoke?" he asked waving the package at Mark who held up his hand in a no gesture. "Better than those limey Woodbines," he said lighting the thing and inhaling deeply.

"Now then," he continued. "We have your new *Persoonsbewijs,* your Dutch identity card. We need your photograph and fingerprints today. I also have an identity card for a Pieter-Jan Zonder – a boy who is to pass for your 12-year old son." Mark realized that Morrissey knew a lot more about this mission than he let on. He waved the identity card and said, "You will need the local Resistance people to add a picture. Papers for kids that age don't require fingerprints." He paused to dig into the green metal filing cabinet behind him and brought out more documents.

"Here is your passport and a blank one made out for your son. Then there is a letter from the Vichy government in France – a very nice bit of counterfeiting, if I may say so – attesting to the fact that you're consulting on a harbour project in Bordeaux. That paper will allow you to travel to the Spanish border in style."

"It says here that your French is very good so you can read the letter yourself. It says you can bring your son for a two-month stay during his school holidays." Mark began picking up the documents to put in his army satchel. Morrissey grabbed him by the arm.

"Not so fast, Mark," he admonished, "Your uniform or other army issue will be left behind. You will be issued a used briefcase made in Nederland. Same with shoes, suit, socks, even Dutch underwear. The only items you can bring back to your country are personal things you had when you landed here last year, like your watch." He squeezed out his cigarette in the ashtray and got up.

"Then you're off to the paymaster. He will issue you the new Dutch guilders and Belgian and French francs. After that we will meet with the counterfeiting gang who will give you some rationing coupons for clothing, shoes, meat, bread, milk and cigarettes."

"I don't need cigarettes, I don't smoke."

"In Europe, cigarettes are better than money. Don't squander an asset. I also need to give you an SOE code name. How about Smokey?"

That evening he had dinner in the canteen. The place was half-full with men and women of different nationalities. He had been directed to avoid fraternization with other agents. "The less you know about other operations the better off you are," Morrissey had said.

At the buffet, the English cook proudly presided over his creation. "Steak and kidney pudding - chunks of beef, kidney and peas in gravy wrapped in suet dough and steamed," he proudly proclaimed, as if trying to convince a jury in a culinary contest. Brenner Zijlberg stood behind him and followed him to his table.

"I was told not to mix with other agents," Mark said.

"Obviously that doesn't include me. I was sent to meet up with you, remember? Funny people these Brits," he continued, "they like to mash their food so you can't tell what's in it. Last night we had meat and potato pie. It had mixed chunks of beef with potatoes in gravy, covered with a thick crust. It looked just like this. I am sure it's all the same."

"I went through the dressing-up ceremony today," Mark said. "This is the last day I'll be wearing a uniform. My civilian suit is being altered and tomorrow I'll be a transformed into a harbour consultant with new papers, money and rationing coupons. All set to go back home except I am not allowed to see family or friends."

Brenner liberally sprinkled his food with salt and pepper. "Another thing about English food," he said, "they carefully avoid giving it any taste. You need to spice it up yourself." He chewed his food rapidly but kept talking between bites. "The guys around here who are waiting for their turn are getting a bit scared. Nearly 30 agents have been dropped into Nederland. At least half of them found the enemy waiting for them. The thinking is that they were betrayed by someone in London."

After dinner, they had a beer in the mess. There was no distinction between the civilians and military ranks. We are all in the same boat, Mark thought, or floatplane. He made it an early evening.

52

1941
THURSDAY, JUNE 19, 4:00 PM EDT
GLADSTONE APARTMENTS, FIFTH AVENUE
NEW YORK CITY, USA

"That is quite a steep price, Mr. Galluci." Ferenc Kolmar said, "Many folks have to work for a week to make $25. I am not even talking about your generous expense account on top of that."

Clyde Tolson, Deputy Director of the FBI had recommended Gary Galluci, son of an Italian immigrant, as the man best qualified to bring Ferenc's son to America.

"For 25 bucks a day, few people would take the risk I'm taking, and don't forget my $5,000 bonus when I deliver your son," Galluci said exposing his gold-tooth grin.

They sat in Ferenc's Fifth Avenue apartment study. Even though he was born in Brooklyn, Galluci wore his Italian heritage like a loud tie. His kind smile on a round face was in sharp contrast to his stocky fire-hydrant build. When he laughed – which was quite often – his voice had a grating sound, like a rusty lawnmower.

He had worked on the New Jersey docks as a longshoreman and had become deeply involved in union activities. He was appalled by the mob's corrupting presence in the unions. Many hard-working stiffs had to pay protection money to keep their jobs. When the FBI asked him to infiltrate the mob in order to help convict the mobsters, he had readily agreed.

After his testimony sent half-a-dozen union executives to jail, he could no longer find work on the docks. The FBI retained him as a freelancer for many borderline activities.

At the FBI Training Centre in Quantico, he had become an excellent marksman. His accuracy with a Smith & Wesson .38 Special was legendary. While he had no formal language training, he displayed a remarkable skill getting along in foreign territory.

He slouched in his easy chair as Ferenc looked down at him.

"Do you speak German or French?" he asked.

"I'll get along in any language, don't worry about that," he assured Ferenc, "but I must have a starting point. Can you give me the names of people who can get me started?"

"Well, there was the Chief of Police in The Hague – van Zandt – but he is in England now. Juliana's best friend was Mieke de Jonge. I recall the name of one of her bodyguards – a Marechaussee corporal by the name of De Boer." Gary busily jotted it all down, his pen almost disappearing in his thick hand.

"And you met her in Katwijk, a fishing village near the city of Leiden where she lived in a villa called *Huyze ten Cate*?"

"That is correct."

"Do you recall any of the servants or local people?"

"It's been almost 13 years. I am sorry that I cannot help you there."

"Well at least I have something to go on but it isn't much."

"When can you leave?" Ferenc asked anxiously.

"Tolson has promised me a passport with a special visa. The document should be in my hands by tomorrow. At least I hope so because I am booked on tomorrow night's PanAm Clipper from New York to Foynes, Ireland and then on to Southampton. The day after, I'll fly to Lisbon."

"Why Lisbon?"

"Portugal is neutral and will not give me a hard time with my American passport. There is a train from Lisbon to Madrid and then on to Paris and Amsterdam."

Galluci popped his rigid frame out of the easy chair like a fireplug. "All that I need now is my advance of $1,000. Additional advances should be sent to the Embassy in whatever country I happen to be." Ferenc Kolmar nodded, went into his study and extracted several stacks of bills of various denominations from a wall safe.

"Bring me my son, Mr. Galluci. And please be careful. It is quite possible that his Jewish ancestry is known. If so, it might make your mission much more hazardous. But I trust you. What else can I do?"

Galluci stuck the pen in his inside pocket, extended his ham-sized hand. "I'll do my damndest," he said.

53

1941
THURSDAY, JUNE 19, 16:00 HRS CEST
ABWEHR HEADQUARTERS, TIRPITZUFER 76/78
BERLIN, GERMANY

"*Ja, das ist natürlich wahnsin*, it's crazy." Canaris yelled into the phone. He had just come from a long meeting where Hitler had told the assembled heads of the German Army High Command that he had decided to launch Operation Barbarossa within days. Troops had been massing at the Polish border for weeks. Moscow's objections about the military activity along its borders had been met with explanations that these were only exercises for the pending invasion of Britain.

Canaris vented his frustration on his wife. "The intelligence reports show that the invasion will be a total surprise but an attack on Russia will ultimately be unsuccessful. Napoleon tried it in 1812 and failed," he roared.

"You should be more careful what you say over the phone Wilhelm," said Lotte, his wife of 25 years, "You know better than anyone that there are listeners everywhere."

"I have warned Hitler that our research shows that the biggest enemy will be winter. But for our Fuehrer, research is of no use if it doesn't support his opinion."

"Hush, Willy," Lotte said soothingly.

The buzzer of his intercom sounded. He told Lotte he'd call her back.

"Herr Oberleutnant Kurt Streicher is here."

"Show him in," Canaris snapped.

When Kurt Streicher entered, Admiral Canaris pretended to be writing something important. He only looked up after Streicher snapped a heel-clicking Nazi salute and yelled a loud *Heil Hitler*.

"*Ja! Ja!*" Canaris said, waving a dismissive hand. "Be seated." Without any preliminaries, he came straight to the point. "Oberleutnant Streicher, what have you found out about Baron Alexander von Becke?"

"Admiral Canaris, everything that Hauptsturmfuehrer von Becke has submitted as proof has checked out. However, we have not been able to identify the natural father."

"That is a problem Streicher. The Fuehrer has met with the boy and his family at his private quarters."

Canaris' secretary, a dowdy middle-aged woman, knocked on the door, entered the office and put a bottle of sparkling water, two glasses and a bottle opener on a side table. Canaris nodded his thanks and continued, "Reichsfuehrer Himmler may have been overly anxious to arrange a meeting before the background checks were completed. The puritans in our Party will want to know the man's bloodlines going back several generations." He walked over to the side table, uncapped the bottle and poured himself a glass of water.

He raised his glass and inspected the exploding bubbles as if searching for a deeper meaning. He said, "It is regrettable that under our laws bloodlines trump both talent and achievement. We cannot embarrass the Fuehrer. Double your efforts to find the father." He dismissed the eager Abwehr man with his customary double limp-wristed wave.

Canaris walked over to the window. He sipped his spa water. The Spree River below looked as troubled and dark as his mood.

"The man thinks nothing of ordering the most difficult invasion in the world but he worries about bloodlines," he said to himself.

54

1941
FRIDAY, JUNE 20, 08:00 HRS BDST
SPECIAL OPERATIONS EXECUTIVE (SOE) BASE
FELIXSTOWE, SUFFOLK, ENGLAND

"You will have to strip down to your watch and nothing else, before I give you any of my stuff," the quartermaster sniggered. "Put all your stuff in this bag and we'll save it until you come back."

Mark stood naked in the changing cubicle, waiting for something or somebody to appear. He looked at the Omega watch that his parents had given him for his sixteenth birthday. It was somehow fitting that it was the only object he would be allowed to bring back.

When no one came, he walked over to the counter, where the quartermaster sat, head in hands, elbows leaning on the desk. He was a wiry man with a pointed face and enough hair to show he still had some. His spectacles were of the most utilitarian design. A khaki shirt and heavy boots made up an ensemble that caricaturists would find irresistible.

Mark made his way to the back area where his newly altered brown suit was hanging from a hook in the low ceiling.

"It's all there, lad, from your shoes and socks to your fedora. When you look decent, come out and I will issue you a wallet and a briefcase. The tailor is still working on your raincoat; it should be here soon."

Mark inspected himself in the rusted full-length mirror that must have been the pride of a grandmother a few generations ago. He felt strange in a suit; he had not worn one in more than a year and never a brown one. He put on the fedora at a dashing angle, damned if he didn't look like Walter Pigeon. He checked the inside label: *C&A Brennickmeyer*, it read.

After signing a stack of documents, he was told to report to Squadron Leader Morrissey.

"I got your orders. If the weather holds you will be taking off at 17:00 hours," Morrissey said. "It'll be just before dark when we land on the Vennemeer. The lake is 15 kilometres inland, so we'll be over enemy territory for only a few minutes." Morrissey looked down at the documents before him. "General van Zandt is sending a radioman along. Agent Zijlberg will go with you. He will stay with the Resistance cell in Leiden and keep London informed of your progress."

Morrissey winked and said, "Now for the good news. I fancy taking this mission myself. I am going to fly you boys out in my old Vickers. It's a lovely little floatplane, even better than my old de Havilland up in Alaska. It has room for the pilot, a navigator and one passenger. On the manifest we will list Zijlberg as a navigator and no one will be the wiser."

Mark must have shown misgiving because Morrissey got up, slapped him on the shoulder, and said, "Don't worry; if we ran this war by the rulebook, the Germans would be here in a week."

He had a light lunch. In truth, he could not eat much. His stomach was knotted with tension and even a drink could not relax him or remove the rancid taste of fear from his mouth. He lay down on his cot, trying to sleep, his mind racing. His fear, ever since he served in the CID, was that someone would realize that he was not up to the job. He was ever doubtful of his ability. His carefree attitude was an act. In the past, there had always been somebody to cover for him, to bail him out. Now he was on his own.

The thought of flying a few hundred feet above the waves of the North Sea, with German fighter planes looking for prey, terrified him but the code of macho behaviour would not let him admit it. His briefing officers had assured him that members of the Resistance would be waiting to guide him to a safe house for the evening. What if they were not there?

He woke up with a start at 15:30. He had snoozed a bit anyway. Apart from his Colt .45, he did not have to carry much. The weapon and eight boxes of ammunition fit neatly in his briefcase along with his ID papers as well an illustrated book of harbour building projects.

He walked out of the room, taking a last look and wondering whether he'd ever come back to claim his uniform and other stuff.

The weather was clear; the sea looked calm. In the staging shed Brenner, also dressed in civilian clothes, was adjusting the straps on a waterproof radio that he carried as a bulky rucksack. "This thing is damn heavy," he complained, "If Morrissey dumps us in the middle of the lake, I won't make it to shore."

"Don't put the radio on your back until you're on solid ground, son." Morrissey chuckled. Brenner looked nervous.

The small floatplane was bobbing at anchor. The camouflage paint was offset by the colourful RAF red, white and blue roundels. Morrissey was already at the controls, testing the ailerons.

"Time to board, gentlemen," Morrissey shouted, "Radio man first." Brenner took the radio off his back and stepped onto the pontoon. "Stow the radio behind the back seat," he instructed. "Mark, sit beside me."

Mark stepped onto the pontoon and felt the aircraft leaning over to his side. He took a quick step to balance himself but that made the wobble even worse. After working his way into the narrow seat and belting himself in, he rested his brief case and hat in his lap.

"Sorry, gentlemen, no parachutes, no peanuts and no place to pee," Morrissey alliterated over the noise. He revved the engine and guided the small plane to the back of the harbour. "There's a good wind so we'll get out cleanly," he roared, enjoying the discomfort of his passengers. The plane began its race through the water, and then slowly climbed out of the harbour and over the North Sea. "Next time you see land, you'll be at the target," he yelled over the grinding noise of the engine. They flew at 500 feet above the waves to avoid detection.

Morrissey spotted a convoy of three ships, southward bound. "Ships attract nosy fighter planes, ours or theirs; or both. I'm going to give them a wide berth," he shouted. Mark began to relax. He tried to talk to Brenner but the engine noise made it nearly impossible.

Mark was first to spot the dunes of the Dutch coast yet it took another 15 minutes before they roared, treetop height, across the tulip fields north of Katwijk. Brenner tapped Mark on the shoulder and pointed to the Kagermeer, the lake where his parents operated the marina. Mark nodded. The aircraft turned southeast toward Leiden. He could see a couple of cyclists on a road. The sun was beginning to set behind them.

"Got to make a turn to land this thing into the wind," Morrissey announced. As he completed his approach, the pontoons bounced hard on the surface of the Vennemeer. The sheltered cove, an inlet off the Zijl River, measured less than a kilometre across. It was really a large pond. Several small pleasure craft were moored along the wooden dock. Thick reeds girded the shoreline. Morrissey steered the aircraft toward an empty spot on the dockside. He was all business now.

"Quick, get out," he yelled. Mark worked his way out of the seat, stepped onto the pontoon and jumped onto the dock. Morrissey threw him his fedora and briefcase.

In the back of the plane, Brenner was much slower getting out. He stood with his rear end toward the front of the cabin, trying to pull the radio out from behind the seat.

"Hurry up, for Chris' sake," Morrissey yelled.

The sunset caused a glint from a motor vehicle's windshield coming toward the dock. Mark turned around. The car had the dull brown-green camouflage colour of an army vehicle. He looked at Brenner who was standing on the pontoon with the radio in his hands. He tossed it wildly onto the dock. The vehicle – a German Kübelwagen – roared closer.

The plane rushed away, leaving a spray of water. The Kübelwagen jerked to a stop in the parking lot, spitting gravel all around. The driver jumped out, raised his Schmeisser and fired wildly at the plane. At the far end of the lake, the floatplane slowly lifted off the water toward the sunset, heading for the coast.

Mark quickly crawled along the jetty toward the moored boats. Brenner raised himself from the quay's edge and scrambled to his feet. The German raised his weapon and fired a burst that struck Brenner in the chest. The impact jerked him backwards into the water. The gunner took aim at the radio transmitter and pulverized it.

The Kübelwagen's passenger, a Wehrmacht officer, stepped out, revolver in hand. He walked behind the car in the direction where Mark had crawled aboard a small pleasure craft. Three shots, in rapid succession, came from the direction of the moored boats. The soldier with the Schmeisser fell to the ground. The officer fired in the direction from where the shot had originated. Making no effort to protect himself, he determinedly strode toward the boat where Mark was hiding under a tarp. He did not get there. Two shots made him crumple to the ground.

"Come on Mark," a familiar voice shouted, "Let's go." Dirk Vreelink, ran towards him.

"Thank God, it's you," Mark gasped.

They ran to the spot where Brenner was floating arms wide and face up in the water. "Let's get him out!" Mark pleaded.

"Don't waste time, he's dead," Vreelink sniffed, clearing his nose, "I'll see if there are any papers or instructions with the radio." He was dressed in a white shirt, white trousers and deck shoes.

A tall man of about 40, blond and dressed in a similar fashion joined them. "Meet Voddeman, not his real name; no need to know it," Vreelink said by way of introduction.

Voddeman picked up Mark's fedora and briefcase and escorted him to a small yacht – *Eendracht* – moored near the end of the jetty.

"Is that your boat?" Mark asked.

"Of course not," Vreelink sniffed, "It will serve as our transportation and safe house for the night, perhaps longer."

"Where are we going?"

"It is Friday evening and we are joining the line-up of boaters who have saved enough of their fuel ration to travel a few kilometres. They usually tie up at a nice spot where they can lie in the sun, swim and relax for the weekend and on Sunday evening, they go back again. Looking at you, I don't think you fit in with the boating crowd. There is a white shirt in my bag. I could not find any white pants your size so you'll have to make do."

Dirk turned the boat's starter and pulled away from the dock. Mark sat down in the small cabin. He counted two cots for sleeping and figured that the benches could be pulled out to make room for two more beds. He opened his briefcase and found the Colt; he toyed with it and waved it at no one in particular. "I am supposed to be an experienced agent. I get into a gun battle as soon as I land and my Colt is packed away!"

They'd been sailing for about 20 minutes. It was dark now. Vreelink clicked the running lights on and turned the *Eendracht* into a narrow slough filled with thick green cress and surrounded by tall reeds.

About 50 metres in, he moored at the tiny dock of an abandoned windmill. The sign above the door read 'ANNO 1842'. The mill had worked endlessly to keep the low-lying 'polder' land dry until electric pumps took over in the early 1900s. One had to bend deep down to get through the narrow door. Inside was a cramped living area, a table, a couple of kitchen chairs, a small stove and a bedstead. A miller and his family once lived there. Most uncomfortably so, unless they were midgets, Mark thought.

"Welcome to a weekend on the Zijl River." Vreelink sniffed and ran his hand over his nose and mouth.

55

1941
SATURDAY, JUNE 21, 07:00 HRS CEST
ABOARD THE *EENDRACHT*
NEAR LEIDEN, NEDERLAND

The grinding of the mooring ropes woke him. He could see the sunshine peek through the slits of the canvas drapes. Vreelink was looking at him from the opposite bench. A battery-operated radio softly played some happy morning music.

"Time for some breakfast," he said washing his sandwich away by noisily slurping his coffee, "I've got some bread and jam and something that tastes like warm coffee. No fancy English breakfast here I'm afraid."

Voddeman was in the windmill, cleaning up. After getting dressed in his white shirt and suit pants, Mark made his own sandwich and poured himself some coffee. "Do you have any news about my family?" he asked.

"Your father was a POW for two months, and then he was set free because he signed an oath of 'non-combatant', which means that he wouldn't do anything against the occupying forces."

"My father signed that?"

"The alternative was deportation to a camp in Germany. He wasn't the only officer to buy freedom; out of 2,000, only 60 refused to sign."

"What is he doing now?"

"He figured he couldn't fight the Germans in a prison camp, so he helps the Resistance when he can," Vreelink smiled.

Voddeman came in with more chicory coffee from the windmill and more bread for sandwiches. Mark assured them the British breakfast was not much better these days. Vreelink related how the Resistance had built on what Mark had begun on index cards on the carpet of van Zandt's office at the NDI in London.

"Are you heading the Resistance?" Mark asked.

"Only here in the region around Leiden but we do cooperate with other cells on more complex operations."

"So van Zandt controls the Resistance from London?"

"No, we carry out some requests from London but their role is to provide a helping hand with weapons and supplies. However, you know the old adage, Mark: the less you know the better. So drop the interrogation and let us focus on what you came to do."

"My orders are to take Willem von Becke to London via Spain and Lisbon. I'd like to get on with it as soon as possible."

Vreelink pulled out a hand-drawn map from a ledge under the wheel. "I propose that we continue up the Zijl River and then cut through to Warmond and then Oegstgeest. From there we will be within two blocks of the von Becke house."

"You are in charge of the route, so whatever you say is fine with me," Mark said, "but will the family be home?"

Voddeman jumped in. "Alexander will not be at home. He is training with the Waffen SS near The Hague.

"We can snatch the boy and keep him on the boat. When the heat is off, we can travel on the rivers to Rotterdam where you can catch the direct train to Paris and then on to Bordeaux."

"What if the Germans stop the boat?" Mark wondered.

They generally don't stop pleasure craft and if they do, we all have ID papers. I even have the receipt to prove I am using my diesel fuel ration for the entire summer on this trip." Vreelink explained.

Mark said, "I am worried about whether Willem will cooperate. He knows me and I think he trusts me, but I'm not sure he'll come willingly."

"We will be waiting here," Voddeman offered, "You can wait 'til dark."

"I'll feel more comfortable if I have a look around the house first and then come back tomorrow with definite plans," Mark said. "I feel rushed."

"You're the one who wanted to get on with it," Vreelink smiled.

"Yes, but I have to be gentle with Willem. He has to adjust to the idea."

"That is your part of the program; we are here to help," Vreelink said as he prepared to lock up the windmill.

Fifteen minutes later, they backed out of the slough and turned in the direction of Oegstgeest. It was after noon when they moored along the canal near the Dorpstraat, across from the *Groene Kerkje*, the eight-centuries-old ivied church where the von Beckes were married. The blue tram to Haarlem rumbled across the rickety wooden bridge. The *Eendracht* didn't look out of place. Several other pleasure craft were moored, their owners gazing intently at their bobbers.

Mark disembarked and walked through the main street of the old village towards the new homes in the Julianalaan. He smiled at the irony of the address. There was no war damage in this area. Most of the fighting had taken place around Valkenburg closer to the coast. Almost everything looked the same except the Wehrmacht had replaced the Dutch Army. An open truck with German soldiers, rifles at their feet, passed him.

He walked past the von Becke house. He pulled his hat down to cover his face. He stopped abruptly to avoid bumping into a woman that was walking toward him. It was Paula.

"Mark," she exclaimed happily, "I almost didn't recognize you with that moustache and the hat. We haven't seen you for a long time."

"I have been away," he explained lamely.

"What brings you to the neighbourhood?"

"I had some time and I wondered how Willem and you are doing."

"Please come in for a cup of coffee. Alexander is away and Willem is with his grandparents in Delft."

He had a choice. Staying might get him into trouble. Leaving might deny him an unexpected opportunity. "If it is not too much trouble, yes, thank you," he said.

He sat at the kitchen table while she made coffee. "What have you been doing for the past year?" she asked. He pretended not to hear.

Paula poured the coffee, sat down and pushed the saccharine and the milk powder toward him. She went on to talk about Willem and how he was doing in school and how he spent many weekends with her father and mother in Delft. "He will be back tonight. It's only 20 minutes by train."

Suddenly her sunny attitude changed to sadness. "Alexander has joined the Waffen SS. He is in training and comes home every other weekend." She paused and lost her composure. Tears welled up in her eyes.

"I shouldn't really tell you these things but our life is not easy. Our neighbours are afraid to talk to us. They are scared they might say something bad about Germany because they fear we would turn them over to the Gestapo. It's good to finally talk to somebody who is sympathetic."

He felt he could risk probing a little deeper. "Are you concerned that Willem may become involved with the German establishment and that you might lose him?" Paula looked startled.

"What do you mean? Have you heard something?" Paula's tears began to reappear. The hanky she had been crumpling in her hand now daubed at her eyes. "I wish I could tell you everything," she sobbed. "I am concerned that Willem and I may have to move to Germany."

"Moving to Germany wouldn't be such a bad thing for young Willem would it?" he asked, playing the devil's advocate.

"It will be. I detest the Nazis. I don't want Willem to be part of their awful view of the world. Alexander is the one with the Nazi ideals. I go along because he is my husband, but I don't want to lose my son to them."

"Can't you just say no?" Mark asked.

"The highest level of the German regime is involved; no one can stop them."

"If there was a chance for Willem to go somewhere where the Germans cannot reach him, would you take it?"

"What are you talking about?"

"Frans van Zandt is in London now; I thought he might be able help."

"Are you in touch with him?" she asked in surprise.

"I hear from him now and then," he said evasively. Paula looked at him questioningly.

"You mean going to England? Alexander would never go along with that. He is an officer in the SS."

"I was thinking of Willem."

"I would never let him go alone." She paused a few moments, intrigued by the thought of a solution to her worst fears. "Is that the real reason you are here?"

"Well in a way, the General wanted me to make contact to see if you want to move Willem to a place where he is beyond the Nazi reach."

"He knows what the Germans want with Willem and so do you, isn't that so?" Paula asked. "Is he offering to bring us out to England?"

"I think so, Willem for sure."

"We could never let Willem go alone. Besides, if you knew what is being proposed you'd realize what a great future Willem could have."

"But you despise the Nazi way of life; you said so earlier."

"Alexander would never agree to escape to England. He has sworn an oath to the Fuehrer."

"Paula, perhaps I have said too much. Please forget what we talked about. Better to keep it quiet. I came to get your reaction. I will come back tomorrow to see Willem." Paula did not object and he left quietly.

Vreelink was sitting on top of the cabin, fishing rod in hand, when Mark arrived back at the *Eendracht*. "Catch anything?" Mark yelled from the street.

"Just you, you idiot. Where have you been? C'mon! They are biting today." Vreelink spoke loudly to convince any watchers that this was an ordinary Saturday for friends.

"Where's Voddeman?" he asked.

"He went to contact London that you have arrived but that your Marconist and his radio are inoperative." After a while, when no one was paying any undue attention, they clambered down to sit in the cabin.

"What happened?" Vreelink asked.

"I was either lucky or unlucky. It remains to be seen. I ran into Paula who asked me in for coffee."

"You damn fool," Vreelink exploded.

"I didn't want to refuse. I felt it was an opportunity," Mark said, "Anyway, both Willem and Alexander were away."

"What the hell were you thinking? You are too damn soft for this business. It is a fatal character flaw. You'll get us in trouble. Why in God's name did they send you instead of a tough guy?"

"I asked the same question but van Zandt thought I could relate to a scared young boy."

"Well, so be it, but we are not staying here for the night. We'll go to that little cove where the swimming pool is. I saw some other weekend boaters there. We'll be a lot safer there than here in the middle of the village." He started the engine.

56

1941
SATURDAY, JUNE 21, 09:00 HRS CEST
OFFICES OF THE HAAGSCHE COURANT
THE HAGUE, NEDERLAND

While Mark was talking to Paula, Oberleutnant Kurt Streicher was busy in The Hague. He hadn't changed much since he worked as an undercover agent at the 1937 Boy Scout Jamboree. This time he operated in an official capacity: he had to find the father of Princess Juliana's son.

The Civic Registry showed Wilhelm von Becke was born on May 29, 1929 in Leiden. However, the nurse who had attended the birth had sworn an affidavit that the child was born at the Soestdijk Palace. She also swore that Professor Pronk, the Queen's personal physician had been present – a dead-end because the professor had passed away in 1935.

Streicher believed the daily newspaper's social page might yield more information. The publisher of the *Haagsche Courant*, a founding member of the NSB, had given him the run of the morgue, the place where newspapers keep their archives. He wanted to learn about the social circle of Princess Juliana in the years 1927-28. In the basement of the building, entire scrapbooks were dedicated to the goings-on of the Royal Family. Page after page showed photographs of Queen Wilhelmina at public events but there were few pictures of the Crown Princess Juliana.

He had worked his way through to June of 1927, when he noted a full-page supplement on Princess Juliana's residence in Katwijk. The story focused on holiday living. One picture showed Juliana talking to a dark-haired young man. The caption read that Ferenc Kolmar, who had performed a recital at the Palace, was an up-and-coming pianist studying at the Royal Conservatory.

An article two days later lauded the performance of Ferenc Kolmar at a concert in Katwijk. In an accompanying photograph, Princess Juliana was at his side. He plowed through the rest of 1927 without seeing any more than the occasional reference to Juliana's studies in Leiden.

He looked at his watch. He had been staring at clippings for two hours straight; he needed a break. He went up to the lobby and lit a cigarette. He had done this type of digging before. It was tedious work and often led nowhere. Yet, he sensed that this time he was on the right track.

He went back down and called for the clippings of 1928. He knew that the tryst must have taken place some time in late August, early September. He quickly found several group photographs with Juliana taken at Olympic events. All of them showed Jonkvrouw Mieke de Jonge. Two pictures included the very same Ferenc Kolmar.

Excited now, he asked the librarian to locate a biography of Kolmar.

The facts jumped off the page. In 1928, he was a 20-year-old Hungarian national studying at the Royal Conservatory in The Hague. His father, now deceased, was a Conductor of the Budapest Symphony; his mother was a well-known opera singer and vocal coach. The biography added that as a compromise between his Catholic father and his Jewish mother, Ferenc had been reared without any affiliated religion.

Streicher read the words over and over, not believing what he saw. There was no doubt in his mind. He had found his man and he was a Jew. All he needed now was confirmation – proof that Kolmar and Juliana spent unsupervised time together during the time in question.

The 'Who's Who' of Dutch nobility told him that Jonkvrouw Mieke de Jonge was married to Jonkheer Frederik van Rosmalen and living in Wassenaar, a mere eight kilometres from the newspaper's offices. He went back up to the lobby and called for his driver.

It was close to four o'clock when Streicher's Mercedes pulled up to the whitewashed mansion. He strode to the front door where he rang the bell. An elderly maidservant opened the door. "*Guten Abend,*" he barked, clicking his heels. "*Oberleutnant Streicher für Junkfrau de Jonge, bitte.*" She looked at him with pursed lips as if she suddenly tasted something sour.

"You will have to wait," she said but did not ask him to come inside. Streicher strutted up and down on the stoop, his leather boots polished to a fine sheen, his right glove held in his left gloved hand.

"You may come in. Jonkvrouw de Jonge will see you. In the library, please," the maid guided him.

"Oberleutnant Streicher, Abwehr," he said much too loudly. "Thank you for taking time to speak to me. I merely want to confirm that you were – as my files indicate – a friend of Princess Juliana in 1927-1928."

"Yes, indeed," she smiled, "Princess Juliana resides in Canada now."

"I also want to confirm that in those years you were her Lady-in-Waiting at Katwijk when you both studied at Leiden University."

"I was, as were other friends."

"Indeed, but you were also with her when she was with child at Soestdijk Palace in the spring of 1929."

Mieke looked aghast. "I think this discussion is over, Oberleutnant."

"Allow me to explain, Madame. I know the facts. I am only looking for confirmation. You confirm; I go away. You refuse to cooperate and it becomes an issue. Neither the occupying authorities nor your husband would want that."

"Well then, yes I did attend the Princess at Soestdijk."

"Thank you. Now going back to the period of conception – that would have been in late August – the Princess was quite enamoured of a Mr. Ferenc Kolmar, a classical pianist now living in New York."

"Oberleutnant, your line of inquiry is appalling."

"Again, Madame, I ask only for confirmation. I have several photographs of the Princess, Mr. Kolmar and you taken at that time."

"Yes, they were good friends."

"Did the Princess have any other intimate male friends at that time?"

"Not that I am aware."

"Did the Princess confide that she was pregnant by Mr. Kolmar?"

"Oberleutnant I will not answer that question."

"I take it from your answer that you do not deny it. One more question Madame. Are you aware that Ferenc Kolmar is of Jewish ancestry?"

Mieke de Jonge rose and said sternly, "You must leave now."

Streicher bowed, clicked his heels and said, "Thank you for your time."

He stepped outside, carefully put on his cap and walked toward the Mercedes holding his gloves in his hand.

57

1941
SATURDAY, JUNE 21, 20:00 HRS CEST
VON BECKE VILLA, JULIANALAAN 45
OEGSTGEEST, NEDERLAND

Coming so soon after Hitler's assurance that Willem's future was all but certain, the afternoon discussion with Mark had shocked Paula. Over the years, she had sleepless nights worrying about the future for the boy she had reared from the first hour of his life. In the initial years, she worried that the Palace might take Willem from them but after a decade; she had settled down and considered him her child.

She looked at the clock. Willem should be arriving at the railway station by now. Grandpa usually put him on the train at 19:30 after the regular Meunier Saturday supper of bread and smoked herring.

She wondered if she should tell Willem about Mark and his suggestion of England, but then she recalled how proud he was about meeting the Fuehrer. A 12-year old boy, being told he may be king some day, would not easily abandon that glittering prospect.

Willem arrived, excited by the day's activities. She hugged him and held him tight. "Did you have a good time with Grandpa and Grandma?"

"Grandpa took a photograph and then showed me how you can put anyone's head on the body of another; it is a great trick."

"Did you tell him about your visit to Berlin?"

"Well, no," he said hesitatingly.

"Did you?" she asked again.

"I did not tell him but when we developed my roll of film he saw the picture with the Fuehrer."

"What did he say?"

"After I told him, he walked away. He looked upset and said that he would talk to you."

The telephone rang. "That'll be him now; he will not be happy." Paula said and answered the phone.

"Is this Mrs. von Becke?" a female voice asked.

"Yes."

"Are you married to Baron Alexander von Becke?"

"Yes I am. Who is speaking please?"

"You may not remember me but we saw each other briefly as you picked up a baby boy at Soestdijk Palace in 1929." Paula reached for a chair and sat down. "Does this mean anything to you?" the voice asked.

"Yes," Paula whispered.

"Then perhaps you can confirm what month we met and I can tell you the date so we can both know that we are speaking to the right person."

"It was May," Paula hissed quietly.

"I can tell you it was May 29th which should assure you of my identity. My name is Mieke de Jonge, I am a friend of Princess Juliana and I was at Soestdijk when the boy was handed to you." She paused to collect her next thoughts, "I am calling to let you know that the Abwehr visited my home today to ask for confirmation about Juliana and the birth of the boy."

Paula felt her tension drain away and said, "The Germans are aware that Willem may be the child of Princess Juliana and it makes sense that they should make inquiries."

"I am sorry to have disturbed you," Mieke said, "But what surprised me was that some of the questions pertained to the boy's Jewish heritage."

"What?" Paula screeched in a most unladylike manner.

"Yes, the natural father had a Jewish mother. I see that you did not know that. I am relieved that I may have reached you in time. I thought I should caution you because several of my Jewish acquaintances have been detained. Shamefully, they have not been heard from since."

Suddenly in a rush to end the conversation, Mieke said, "Should you be asked who gave you this information, I prefer not to be further involved, however if you want to speak to me privately, I live in Wassenaar."

Paula put the phone down and ran to the bedroom where she buried her face into the pillows. Willem followed her in. "Is Papa alright?" he asked as he put his arms around her.

"Yes, I am sure he is. I must call him immediately."

58

1941
SUNDAY, JUNE 22, 10:15 HRS CEST
REICHSKANZLEREI, UNTER DEN LINDEN
BERLIN, GERMANY

The buzz of the intercom interrupted the discussion with his visitor. "Reichsfuehrer your next appointment is waiting," Ilse Schulenburg, Himmler's secretary announced.

"Thank you, Frau Schulenburg," Himmler got up and turned to his visitor and apologized, "I am sorry I must attend to an urgent matter. Have no concern, I shall give the matter the attention it deserves," he said, gently steering the man to the door.

After the visitor had left, Ilse entered the office. She was a mature woman with a pleasant smile. Her blond hair was pulled back so severely that it looked as if she was wearing a bathing cap. She had been Himmler's secretary ever since the Nazis had taken power in 1933. Her husband had died in the 1939 attack on Poland, allowing her to be at Himmler's side at all hours of the day or night.

"Thank you for saving me Ilse. The man was asking for more money for '*Winterhelp*', the program to feed the hungry in the occupied countries. We have better things to do, *Nein*?" He moved to the conference corner and beckoned Mrs. Schulenburg to join him. He walked over to the large Telefunken radio in the corner. He tuned it to the *Deutsche Rundfunk*. "I cannot concentrate on my interviews, Ilse. I am anxious to follow the reports of Operation Barbarossa. The *Rundfunk* has been broadcasting from the front since the attack began this morning. When I last tuned in our troops had already progressed 90 kilometres into Russia."

The invasion of the Soviet Union had commenced that morning, June 21, 1941. An army of over 4.5 million men invaded the USSR along a 3,000-kilometre front. Planning for the operation had begun when Hitler decided to postpone the invasion of Britain. The German aim was the rapid conquest of the European part of the Soviet Union right up to the Ural Mountains that separate Europe from Asia. Hitler did not rest easy with the huge Red Army camped next to his Wehrmacht in occupied Poland. He wanted the annihilation of Bolshevism, control of all Europe and for that, he needed Russia's wheat and oil.

Himmler listened with delight as the reporters followed the glorious progress of the heroic Wehrmacht. "We will be in Moscow by September, Ilse; mark my words." He placed his hand on Ilse's knee. She wordlessly switched his hand to his own thigh.

"Our Fuehrer once again proves to be a genius. The Generals opposed him every step of the way, saying it couldn't be done. They kept telling him about Napoleon and how he failed, his troops dying in the snows of Russia. Look at the way it is going today." The telephone rang.

"Yes, he's here," Ilse answered as she picked it up.

"I told you not to let anyone bother me for a while; who is it?"

"Admiral Canaris, Sir, and one of his officers, an Oberleutnant Streicher want to see you. They say it's urgent."

Ilse put the phone down, turned off the radio and discreetly left the office. A moment later, she showed the two officers into Himmler's office.

"What is so important that the Admiral makes a personal visit on such a glorious day for our Fatherland?"

"Something that may embarrass our Leader, Reichsfuehrer." Himmler's head shot up. "Oberleutnant Streicher has returned from Nederland this morning. He has completed his investigation to identify the natural father of Wilhelm von Becke. Since the report has serious implications, I decided to bring it to your attention immediately."

"And?"

"The father is the famous American pianist and conductor Ferenc Kolmar of New York and—"

"A cultural giant is not a problem and we are not at war with America, so?"

"There is a problem, Reichsfuehrer. Ferenc Kolmar is a Jew and under our laws, the boy Wilhelm is a Jew as well." Himmler blanched at the mention of the word Jew.

"Are you sure of this?" he asked, clearly agitated.

"Witnesses confirm that the Princess consorted with Kolmar during the period in question. A corporal of the Marechaussee who was her bodyguard has confirmed the relationship. Additionally the Dutch visa issued to Kolmar in 1927 states his religion as Jewish."

"*Mein Gott im Himmel!*" Himmler exclaimed grasping his head in both hands. "The Fuehrer has posed for a photograph with this boy. He has all but acknowledged him as a genuine aspirant to the throne. If he learns of this he will be outraged; a bad situation for you, Canaris."

"And for you," Canaris said with an icy stare. "The Fuehrer will no doubt remember he directed you to find a scion of the House of Orange." Himmler ignored the Admiral's riposte.

While his visitors looked on, he paced the room in silence, his narrow face pinched in agony. He held his nose while he was thinking, like a man about to jump into deep water. He suddenly spoke. "This is a disaster. The Fuehrer must be spared this embarrassment," he intoned. "The problem must be made to disappear so it cannot come back to haunt us."

Canaris leaned in closely and asked in an emphatic tone, "Do you mean disappear, as in some other occasions that were problematic for you, Heinrich?" Himmler drew away slightly.

"Nothing violent, but accidents do happen and they can be explained to the Fuehrer."

Canaris straightened up. He smiled with a genial conviction that did not reflect his true feeling. "*Jawohl. Herr Reichsfuehrer*," he said with a sly smile. "May I have your order to proceed as directed in writing?"

"You may not. Oberleutnant Streicher will see to my wish."

"At your command, Reichsfuehrer," Streicher snapped to attention.

"The Abwehr is much subtler in this sort of thing than the SS, Admiral," Himmler smiled, "Oberleutnant Streicher will do his duty as ordered." Canaris rose and turned away without comment.

In the hallway, Canaris turned to Streicher, "You heard it: it is his wish. He did not say it was his order. It is important for your future to understand exactly what was said, Oberleutnant." The sneer on Streicher's face showed his eagerness.

Canaris felt immensely tired. "He is just a boy, Streicher," he whispered, "he is 12 years old." Streicher's eyes shone with maniacal determination.

59

1941
SUNDAY, JUNE 22, 11:00 HRS CEST
BARRACKS, WAALSDORPERVLAKTE
SCHEVENINGEN, NEDERLAND

"That's enough for now. Take a 20-minute break," Alexander told his weary recruits at the Waalsdorpervlakte in Scheveningen, a beach resort near The Hague. Since six o'clock this morning, they had carried out attack exercises in the sand dunes. Alexander had barely finished the training course himself when he was ordered to take on the training of the Dutch Brigade of the Waffen SS. He hated the physical aspect of war training. He was a designer, a planner; sports of any kind did not suit him.

He silently cursed the tradition of the Waffen SS that officers should always wear their formal uniforms, save for battle conditions. The midsummer heat was stifling and the sand literally burned the skin of his recruits as they crawled under the half-metre high barbed wire overhang of the obstacle course.

He hadn't slept much and not just because it was the shortest night of the year. The discussion with Paula had distressed him. He finally fell asleep but woke a short while later when the officer on watch shook him to say his wife was on the telephone. Paula had sounded hysterical.

He told her that he would come home as soon as he could get free. The House of Orange would never consort with Jews. Yet it worried him. If it were somehow true, Willem would be in danger. His anti-Semitism clashed with love for Willem. Then again, he assured himself, it couldn't possibly be true.

During a break in exercises, he made his way to the Officers' Mess. The radio was tuned to Radio Hilversum for reports on the invasion of the Soviet Union. A mixture of joy and apprehension prevailed among Dutch volunteers. Joy, that the forces of Germany and its allies were marching against the detested Bolsheviks, and fear that their black-booted preening on the streets of Nederland might soon change to bleeding to death on the steppes of Russia.

Alexander looked at the clock – 11:30 hours. His deputy would report for duty within an hour. He chose a quiet corner. Toby, the rotund mess waiter approached.

"A quick beer, please Toby."

"A messenger from the radio room is looking for you, Sir."

"Over here!" Alexander called. The soldier saluted with the message clutched in his saluting hand.

"A message from Berlin, Sir," he panted, "It's from Admiral Canaris," he breathed, obviously in awe of the exalted status of the sender. "It is in code," he added in a conspiratorial tone.

Alexander opened the sealed envelope. The radioman kept staring at him. "You may go," he snapped. The man departed reluctantly. The envelope held a standard Waffen SS communication form. It read:

"The Book 2-OT 4-23."

The message was unsigned and no response was requested. He checked the address. It was indeed intended for him.

He went to his room to pack. The Book, the Good Book, the Bible, he thought. He checked the drawers of his nightstand and found a bible. The letters OT, in connection with the Bible had to mean Old Testament. That would make it Book 2 of the Old Testament, Exodus. He feverishly leafed through the book. Under 4-23 he read:

"So I said to you, 'Let your son go so that he may serve me but he is a son of David. Behold, I will kill your son, your firstborn."

A message? A warning? Was this related to what Paula had told him? Son of David? A Jew? Kill your son? Fear immobilized him. He stood in the room, Bible in hand, unable to think, powerless to move. He forced himself into action. He grabbed his bag and ran the two blocks to the streetcar stop that would take him to the railway station in The Hague. With any luck, he would be home by one o'clock.

60

1941
SUNDAY, JUNE 22, 05:00 HRS CEST
ABOARD THE *EENDRACHT*, POELMEER LAKE
OEGSTGEEST, NEDERLAND

The shortest night of 1941 had been too long for Mark. The rush of adrenalin had kept him awake most of the night. He listened to waves lapping at the boat and its intermittent tugs on the ropes trying to get away, like a bored child pulling on its mother's arm. It was five in the morning and the sky was becoming brighter.

At six, he got up and raised the portside canvas drape. Four other motorized pleasure craft had sought shelter in the cove. He lit the petroleum cooker to make some chicory coffee. A loaf of bread wrapped in wax paper was stuck deep in the pantry. He sliced off a big chunk and slathered it with strawberry jam.

Vreelink stirred as he smelled the coffee. "Are you a cook too?" he laughed, "Did they teach you that at the SAS training?"

He turned on the radio. The news was stunning. A few hours ago, the Wehrmacht had invaded the territory of its professed ally – the Soviet Union.

"That's good news," Mark enthused. "With that massive force directed at Russia there will be no invasion of England for at least a year – if ever. But also, Britain is no longer standing alone. Russia has become an ally."

"You mean the enemy of my enemy is my friend, is that it?" Vreelink sniffed. The newsreader changed topic and provided an update on the two German military men who were found at the Vennemeer on Friday. One was dead and the other in serious condition at the Army Hospital in Leiden. The announcer quoted an interview with a local farmer who said he heard a low-flying plane in the area at that time. The broadcast ended with a report that Reichskommissar Seyss Inquart had repeated his recent proclamation that for every German soldier murdered, five Dutch nationals would be executed without trial. The "vile enemies of the state" were urged to give themselves up in order to spare innocent lives.

"Yeah, right," Vreelink sniffed, but louder this time, "They will line up some innocent civilians and murder them so that we will cease our resistance. The Dutch are too stubborn for that," he angrily pounded the engine casing in the centre of the cabin. "Mark my words, instead of the Resistance faltering, support will rise."

Silence hung in the air as both men contemplated the ugly consequences of their actions.

Mark spoke first. "They didn't say anything of a suspicious pleasure boat in the area," he said, erasing the image of executions from his mind.

"They wouldn't announce that kind of stuff. What time are you going to the boy's place?"

"I didn't say but Paula would expect me before noon."

"Perhaps she'll have a Gestapo reception committee to welcome you."

"I told you, she doesn't want the kid to become a Nazi pawn."

They ate their meagre breakfast, each man pre-occupied with his own concern. They eased out of the cove and headed west for the spot near the village centre where they had tied up the day before. Their old mooring spot near the bridge was still free. Rows of fishermen sat on folding stools along the canal.

As they prepared to moor, Voddeman sat on the canal wall, his feet dangling above the water, his bicycle on the grass behind him. "I waited an hour," he complained.

"Good," Vreelink said, "Then you can rest up in the boat while we visit the boy and his mother. What did you hear from London?"

"London is aware of Mark's arrival and ordered the mission to proceed as planned," Voddeman reported.

Before the train had even come to a proper stop, Alexander opened the door and rushed out into the Leiden station. He was distraught to the point of panic. From a principled Nazi sympathizer who reluctantly endorsed the dictum that the world must be rid of Jews, he had become the fervent protector of his child. The persecution of Jews was not an abstract concept anymore; it had become a death warrant for Willem.

Paula fell in his arms the minute he entered the house. She heaved through her crying jags and was unable to speak coherently. "Help, Alexander, help. Willem... I am afraid," she sobbed.

"So am I, darling, but all will be well," he soothed, not feeling any comfort himself. Willem stood with a look of terror in the corner, pressed against the wall, his head drawn deeply into his shoulders, his face ashen.

"Willem, your Mother and I must discuss important things, please find something to do." Alexander said.

An animal shriek emanated from the boy's throat. "No Papa, don't leave me. They'll come to get me," he sobbed, his shoulders heaving violently. "Don't you know? Mom tells me I was born a Jew. Why am I a Jew? What went wrong? Hitler said he liked me! What happened?"

Paula hugged him. "We love you and we will protect you. You are our Willem and you will be safe. Let's decide what we are going to do."

They huddled together on the sofa. Paula said, "Mark promised he'd come by today and we can ask him to clarify his hints of an escape," Paula said. "We must realize that the Nazis will never tolerate a Jew in their midst, so any idea of Willem becoming king is out."

"You are right," Alexander sighed, "I should tell you that I received an anonymous warning." He was determined not to spell out his grim conclusion of the cryptic message. While Paula went to the kitchen to make lunch, Alexander addressed Willem's fears.

"You should not be ashamed that your father has Jewish blood, Willem. The Fuehrer is mistaken that certain races are evil and others are good. You are not evil. You are the son of a Princess of Orange. Queen Wilhelmina sent Mark Zonder to tell us she wants you to be safe."

"Do you think the Germans want to kill me?

"They will do nothing to you because we won't let them. We will take you away from here so they cannot find you."

A knock on the back door made them look up. It was Mark. Willem ran to let him in but Mark had already stepped inside.

Willem pulled him into the kitchen where Alexander sat with his hands on top of his head. In the doorway behind him, a man with a weather-beaten face held a Beretta on them.

"I know you," Willem cried, "You tried to kidnap me and you scared me. Are you taking me away?" Willem sobbed and rushed to his mother.

"Sit down, kid," Dirk said waving him off with his Beretta, unmoved by the boy's terror.

In a gentle tone Mark said, "General van Zandt has offered to bring Willem to England to pursue his education there until after the war." He had been rehearsing that line for a while. He looked at von Becke in his Waffen SS uniform and realized the incongruity of the situation.

"You are still in the service of General van Zandt?" Alexander said softly. Mark had expected a dramatic scene, a weeping boy, wailing mother, an outraged father. Instead, von Becke sounded appreciative.

"The General made sure he was never far away from you."

Paula looked aghast, "You have been watching us since before the war?" she asked incredulously.

Mark came to the point. "Paula," Mark said gently, "I am here to bring Willem to England. I will take him by train to Paris, then on to Bordeaux and to Madrid and then Portugal. From there we fly to England."

"We have no alternative," Alexander said, "You probably don't know that the German leadership has learned that Willem is of Jewish ancestry through his natural father. He is at risk of German capture. Therefore my wife and I are anxious to see our son beyond their reach."

Mark was taken aback by this revelation. Extraordinary, how things coming right out of the blue can change everything. Instead of encountering resistance to a forced removal, he faced a husband and wife anxious for their son to be brought to safety.

Alexander took control. "Look," he said to Mark, "You have been sent to take Willem to England. Paula and I agree that this is necessary, but Paula must come along. Willem will be a burden to you if he goes alone. Paula can help make the trip easier."

"We can't handle an extra person," Vreelink objected harshly. Mark looked at him disapprovingly. "I am open to suggestions but the identification papers I have state that Willem is Pieter-Jan Zonder, my 12-year old son. A letter of introduction allows me to travel deep into France close to the Spanish border. How can I explain the presence of Mrs. von Becke?" he asked.

"We can get an ID card that says she is Mrs. Zonder, your wife," Dirk said, trying to be helpful now.

"No," Paula said hastily.

"It could work Paula, think of it," Alexander said. "With false papers, it is only a question of 48 hours at most before you are in England."

"But it must be believable," Paula argued, "I am 41 and Mark is 22. How can we have a 12-year old son?"

"I am 32, according to my papers, Mark countered, "I'll add a little gray to my hair to look older and while we are making false papers anyway, why don't we make Paula ten years younger. She looks young anyway." Paula was oblivious to the compliment and asked, "On a practical note, what can we take with us? We have a houseful of belongings."

"We cannot take any more than what is necessary for a family of three for a few weeks in France," Mark said. "The rest must be left behind."

"What about my camera and all my photographs?" Willem wailed.

"A tourist can have a camera but not several hundred photos," Mark decreed.

"I could give them to Grandpa," Willem volunteered.

"That is a good idea," Alexander said, "We should at least remove our valuable papers and jewellery."

Dirk Vreelink spoke, "If the Nazis are looking for Willem, the first thing they'll do is come to this house. If they don't find him here, they'll conclude he's on the run and they'll check all buses and trains. You can't risk that. I suggest we take the *Eendracht* and head for Rotterdam. The train for Paris stops there. It'll mean a day's delay, but it is safer."

"If you take the Vliet River we can stop by Delft to drop off our belongings at Grandpa's." Willem was getting into the adventure.

"What about travel papers?" Alexander asked, "All three of us have valid passports. They have a visa, stamped for last week's visit to Berlin."

"You were in Berlin last week?" Vreelink asked in surprise.

"Yes, the Fuehrer wanted to meet Willem."

"This is getting more risky by the minute," Vreelink grumbled, "But go and find your ID cards and passports so that we can start making new documents."

"When can they be ready?" Alexander asked.

"Perhaps as early as tomorrow noon," Vreelink said. "Meanwhile Paula and Willem cannot stay here tonight. The Abwehr likes to come in the middle of the night. You, Sir, you stay here and tell any of your Nazi friends who may come calling that Paula and Willem are away on a short holiday or something. They'll be polite to you; they want the boy, not you. Stall them." Alexander's spirits sagged noticeably as he went off to help his wife and son pack their bags.

Paula rummaged through the armoire and held up Willem's Jeugdstorm uniform. "Do you think I should take this?" she asked.

"It might help at some point," Alexander said thoughtfully.

He went into his den to gather the items to go to his father-in-law's for safekeeping. Intellectually he knew that his family was splitting up but emotionally it had not registered until now as he gathered the papers and memorabilia that documented their lives. He sat in the chair knowing it would never be the same. His inclination had been to flee with them – to find a new home. He still had hopes for a new Europe without the maniacs and racist murderers. He had sworn an oath. He would remain at his post.

By four o'clock, they were ready to go when Paula said that it was silly to sit in a boat until it was time to go to bed. Her practical mind took over.

"I expect that you don't have food in that boat for four people. Therefore, we will eat here. Mark, you and your friend should go ahead, take the stuff for Grandpa, and put it on the boat. Willem and I should leave later, carrying little. It wouldn't do to have the neighbours see us leave, loaded down with suitcases."

"Can I go with them?" Willem asked.

"You can help getting dinner ready – our last dinner with Papa, for a little while," Paula said, "for a little while..." she repeated softly.

61

1941
SUNDAY, JUNE 22, 13:00 HRS CEST
VAN ROSMALEN RESIDENCE, KIEVIETLAAN 23
WASSENAAR, NEDERLAND

At the same time that Alexander von Becke was rushing home to discuss the warning by Canaris, a taxi pulled up at the residence of Mieke de Jonge. Gary Galluci gave the driver a new two-and-half guilder bill and told him to wait. The same elderly woman in the French maid costume answered the door. She looked at the burly man with his dark complexion. A foreigner, she thought, but this one looked a lot friendlier than the German on Saturday.

"Is the mistress of the house in then, madam?" he asked with a grin.

"*Bent U een Engelsman?*" she asked in Dutch.

"No I am an American from Brooklyn." The maid looked at him uncomprehendingly.

"*Even wachten alstublieft,*" She shuffled quickly into the house, as if she walked on small stilts. A moment later, Mieke appeared at the door.

"I am Gary Galluci, from the Federal Bureau of Investigation, Ma'am." He flashed an out-of-date security badge.

She was much too taken aback to look closely. "Come in, please?" she offered, opening the door. She led him into a small reception room.

"This is my husband Pieter van Rosmalen," she said as the slender blond man reached out to shake Gary's hand.

"I may as well start right at the beginning, Ma'am," he said with an accent harsher than they had ever heard, "I am making inquiries on behalf of Mr. Ferenc Kolmar, whom you met when you were living with Princess Juliana in Katwijk." If Mieke was surprised to hear the same topic again, she did not show it.

"I recall meeting him, yes."

"I am looking for his son," Galluci stated matter of factly.

"Whatever do you mean? Why are you telling me this?"

"Because Mr. Kolmar believes you may have been present at the birth. Mr. Kolmar further believes that you know where the boy is now."

"I am sorry but I cannot help you." Mieke said resolutely, surprised that she could lie this well.

"Not even when I tell you that Ferenc Kolmar spoke to Princess Juliana in Ottawa a few weeks ago and that he has promised to bring her son to the United States before his Jewish heritage becomes known to the Germans?" He rose to his full height and although he still came up short, he added, "They are likely to kill the lad!"

"No point trying to intimidate us, old boy," van Rosmalen said in cultured but accented English. "Point is: a bloody German was here Saturday with more or less the same question."

Galluci looked surprised, "Did you give him the name Ferenc Kolmar?"

"He knew it, he only asked for confirmation."

"I am after the name of the adoptive parents. My information is that the father is a prominent Nazi sympathizer."

"That is true," said Mieke, jumping back into the conversation. "After the Abwehr man left, I called Mevrouw von Becke to let her know." She told what she knew of the situation and how she had found the von Becke telephone number through friends.

The cabbie told him it would take less than half an hour to get there. He looked at his watch – half past four.

He asked the driver to let him off at the corner. He stood behind a massive chestnut tree and observed the house. It had that 'someone is home' feel to Galluci who had spent hundreds of hours in surveillance. He walked past the house on the opposite side of the street. He stepped into a front garden with a chest-high boxwood hedge and crouched behind it.

Some time later, two men came out of the house carrying two pieces of baggage. He followed them at a discreet distance. At the end of the street, he knew he had been made. The men were experienced operatives.

They stood at the corner waiting for him to catch up. Galluci had no avenue of escape. He had to pass them. They were an odd-looking couple. The older man's face showed the effect of many hours in a boxing ring.

It was the good-looking younger guy with the moustache who said, "*Goejen middag*," Galluci surmised it was a standard greeting, looked at his feet and mumbled something in return. He turned left onto the main thoroughfare. They stayed at the corner until Galluci was out of sight.

"He was definitely tailing us," Vreelink said, "But who the hell could it be? He is not from the Abwehr. They are not that subtle. They just pounce when they want something."

"Perhaps another cell of the Resistance?" Mark suggested.

"Either that or a local policeman keeping an eye on the von Becke house." They continued on their way to the *Eendracht*.

Voddeman, seated on top of the cabin, fishing rod in hand, waved a cheerful welcome. When the suitcases were stowed, Vreelink handed Voddeman the passports and the ID Cards with instructions to try to have them finished before noon the next day. Voddeman left on his bicycle.

On the opposite side of the canal amidst a row of anglers, Galluci sat down on a makeshift stool. He decided that it was useless to trail the cyclist. Besides, the other two were still aboard.

A few minutes later when the younger man left, Galluci hurried across the bridge to follow him; more carefully this time. He observed him returning to the von Becke villa and took his position behind the boxwood hedge; he had to wait a long time before the young man left again, carrying two suitcases.

A few minutes later, a woman came out accompanied by a boy with a camera around his neck. He had found his quarry. Willem and his mother.

He stepped out from behind the hedge to begin pursuit. He sensed movement behind him. He caught a glimpse of an arm and felt a smashing blow to his neck before he slumped to the pavement. Then, nothing.

Vreelink bent over him and rifled through his pockets. An American passport. Gary Galluci, born in America. The possibilities raced through his mind and he hurried after Paula and Willem. Can this get any more complicated, he thought.

62

1941
MONDAY, JUNE 23, 07:00 HRS CEST
ABOARD THE *EENDRACHT*
OEGSTGEEST, NEDERLAND

Paula was stiff from sleeping on the hard bench. Much of the night, she had replayed in her mind the events of the last 48 hours. Willem was sound asleep on the bench across from her. Children adapt so quickly. Before going to sleep, he had been distraught about being a Jew. She told him what Mieke de Jonge had said; that his grandfather in Hungary was a great musician who had married a classical singer who had a very talented son Ferenc, a famous pianist in America. "You can be proud of your cultural heritage," she had impressed upon him.

Mark was making coffee. He had rolled up the canvas curtains and the early sunlight was streaming in. The gentle breeze blowing across the water smelled good. The ever-present fishermen sat on their folding stools staring at their bobbers in the water, ready to pounce at the first nibble.

"Where, is Dirk?" she asked.

"Last night we had a bit of a confrontation with a man staking out your home and Dirk is checking to see if the guy is back today."

"Who could that have been?" she asked anxiously.

"I think he's involved in Willem's situation, but I have no idea how," Mark said. Willem woke up, said good morning and immediately stuck his head overboard peering at a row of ducks floating alongside, bobbing like ships at anchor. He reached out to grab one but the duck family quickly skittered away, wings flailing.

Dirk approached the boat from the street. He responded to Mark's inquiring gesture by shaking his head and pulling up his shoulders and spreading his hands wide, palms out.

"He didn't see him," Mark translated for Paula. Dirk stepped aboard and without speaking, filled his cup with the chicory coffee. He grimaced at the harsh taste.

"We're going to be delayed a bit," he said, turning to Paula. "Voddeman needs new pictures for your ID. Our man will be in at ten this morning. We will sail from here and moor very close to his workshop in Leiden so we can avoid the streets as much as possible."

After cleaning up, Vreelink backed the boat out and headed for Leiden. They entered the Rijnsburgersingel, part of the moat around the old city. Vreelink moored the *Eendracht* at the foot of the landmark windmill *De Valk*.

"Mark will go with you," Vreelink told Paula and Willem. "I'll stay with the boat." The trio had walked perhaps a hundred metres beyond the towering windmill when Mark pulled them into the alcove of one of the houses along the Beestenmarkt, the old cattle market. A special knock was answered by Voddeman who led them into a side room.

"Please sit," he said to Paula, "Our man will be here soon. We need pictures and thumb prints. It'll take a half hour, but you are safe here."

Mark motioned for Voddeman to come with him to the back of the house. On a small patio – enclosed by grimy whitewashed walls – stood a rusted washtub that held a blossoming lilac shrub. The adjacent two-holer outhouse somehow diminished the picturesque image. "I need to get away for a brief spell. Please stay with them 'til I get back," Mark said.

"Where are you going?" Voddeman asked, sounding suspicious. Mark grabbed him gently by the arm and said firmly, "You must stay with them, please. I'll be back."

He knew his orders but he could not resist the lure of his parents' home, less than a kilometre away. He half ran, half walked to the house in which he had grown up. He stood outside, both afraid and elated. He pulled the brass knob on the doorjamb. He heard the familiar clanging of the bell in the hallway. His father looked at him in numb surprise.

"Mother Zonder! Come see!" he shouted as he grabbed Mark's wrists and held him at arm's length.

"I hardly recognized you with that moustache," he said. "You've gotten heavier too." Mother Zonder came running but his father pushed her back into the narrow hallway, "We don't want a spectacle on the street." He moved out of the way to give his wife a chance to embrace her son. She sobbed into his chest and he held her.

"What are you doing here?" she asked through her tears, "We thought you were in England."

"I am Ma, but I am on a mission. I'll be in Nederland only a few hours and then I'm going back."

"Are you in danger?" Mother Zonder wanted to know.

"There is always danger Ma, there is a war on."

"Do you want something to eat?"

"No Ma, I stopped by for a few minutes to tell you I am okay. How are you two doing?"

"Dad was in a POW camp but he is back and walks a lot every day."

"What about Jenny. Do you ever hear anything from Jenny?"

"She came to see us last summer. She asked about you of course, but we didn't know for sure where you were. Then, last Christmas we received a card from her saying she got married."

Mark froze. He wanted to hear she was pining for his return, desperate for the war to end so she could marry him, the prince of her dreams.

"Married?" he asked, hiding his distress, "At Christmas time? Do you know the name of the man?"

"I have the card right here." She rummaged through the drawer of the tea cabinet, found the card and put on her glasses. "Here it is. Van Weeren, Hendrik van Weeren, a man from Groningen."

"No! It can't be. We promised each other that we would marry," Mark cried.

"Perhaps she thought you might not come back," Mother Zonder said.

Mark sat down. He did not speak for several minutes while his mother stood behind him and stroked his back. He straightened up. "I have to go."

He heard her plead for him to stay longer but he did not listen. He hastened back to the little house on the Beestenmarkt. He stopped in the alcove and took a deep breath.

63

1941
MONDAY, JUNE 23, 11:45 HRS CEST
VON BECKE RESIDENCE, JULIANALAAN 45
OEGSTGEEST, NEDERLAND

While Paula and Willem waited at the counterfeiter's workshop, Oberleutnant Kurt Streicher arrived at the von Becke villa a few kilometres away. His driver parked in front of the house. The WH licence plate identified the car as a Wehrmacht vehicle. Streicher told the driver to wait.

Alexander, packing for his return to the barracks, answered the door. The visage of a ramrod, cruel-faced Abwehr officer and the green Wehrmacht Mercedes confirmed his fears. The man clicked his heels and rendered a *Heil Hitler* salute.

"Hauptsturmfuehrer von Becke?" he said haughtily, "Oberleutnant Streicher, Abwehr, Berlin."

"I was just packing to return to my base; I am in a hurry. What do you want?" Alexander asked, faking a convincing imperious manner.

"May I come in?"

"No you may not. I will be leaving in a few minutes."

"Let me come to the point then, Hauptsturmfuehrer," Streicher said tartly, "I have orders from Reichsfuehrer Himmler to take your son Wilhelm von Becke to Berlin for further meetings with those in charge of his future."

"Let me point out Oberleutnant that I am in charge of my son's future, at least until he is 18."

"I have orders, Hauptsturmfuehrer."

"Your orders are of no effect," Alexander said in a shrill voice. "My wife and son are on summer holidays, away from the city."

"Where, may I ask?"

"You may not ask; it is none of your business."

"Reichsfuehrer Himmler will not be pleased. He gave direct orders."

"I need not tell you that I outrank you, Oberleutnant. If anyone in Berlin has orders for me they should send someone of higher rank, now please let me be about my business."

Streicher appeared to be uncomfortable with the turn of events. "Very well, I shall return with written orders for your son's appearance in Berlin. As early as this afternoon, perhaps. Meanwhile, unless you have arranged for a car, may I offer you transportation to your barracks? Scheveningen isn't it?"

"You may," Alexander said. "Wait in the car until I am ready." When Alexander came out of the house, Streicher opened the car's rear door with an exaggerated flourish. Alexander settled in the back seat while Streicher sat with the driver. They passed the 30-minute drive in silence. Streicher again hustled to open the car door with faked obeisance. Alexander ignored him.

Back in the offices of the Abwehr at Mauritslaan 35 in The Hague, Streicher summoned his Dutch deputy. Piet Prinsen was an opportunistic long-time member of the NSB whose ten-year service as a policeman in The Hague had ended when he was convicted of taking bribes from petty criminals. His stooped bearing made him look servile yet his darting eyes flicked around the room like a cobra hunting for prey. A sleazy smile did not enhance his acne-scarred face.

"I have an assignment for you," Streicher said, handing Prinsen part of the von Becke file. "You must find the wife and son of Hauptsturmfuehrer von Becke. Do not contact them. Remain undetected and report to me immediately when you locate them."

"Where do I start?" Prinsen said with a grovelling desire to please.

"You have the file. Check the boy's friends, neighbours, family, aunts, uncles or grandparents, whatever. Go!"

64

1941
MONDAY, JUNE 23, 12:30 HRS CEST
ABOARD THE *EENDRACHT*, RIJNSBURGERSINGEL
LEIDEN, NEDERLAND

"It's about time; I was getting nervous," Dirk snapped impatiently. Mark assured him all was well as he helped Paula and Willem aboard.

Paula sounded more energetic than before. "It was interesting to see those new identity papers produced right in front of you." She happily waved her new passport and persoonsbewijs. "I am a lot younger now with a new husband." Dirk seemed more anxious than impressed.

Mark handed Dirk an envelope "Here's a gift for you. Voddeman gave me a batch of new ration coupons for diesel fuel and groceries. Hot off the press, and looking genuine." Dirk accepted them but did not look happy.

"It's all taking too long," he grumbled, backing the boat out. "We'll take the canals through the city to the Vliet River. That'll take us to Delft," Vreelink announced. None of them noticed the burly man across the canal pretending to fix the chain on his bicycle.

The *Eendracht* turned in to the Old Rhine River that wends its way through the city's shopping area. German soldiers were among the shoppers browsing the store windows. Willem took pictures.

Once outside the city they cruised through the low-lying polders, passing the ubiquitous windmills and untold numbers of grazing cows. Paula stretched out in the only chair. Barelegged, she caught the summer sun's rays. The radio announcer rhapsodized over the rapid progress of the German troops through the Ukraine and told of cheering populations as they were liberated by the German heroes.

"The Germans are winning aren't they?" Willem asked. No one answered. After the conclusion of the news program, a burst of pompous music introduced an announcement by Reichskommissar Seyss Inquart that five citizens, arrested at random, had been summarily executed in retaliation for the killing of a German officer at the Vennemeer. Vreelink listened without showing any outward sign of remorse.

The river, now straight as a ruler, looked more like a man-made canal. The road on either side saw a lot of bicycle traffic – men in business suits and women carrying children on the handlebars and the back of their bicycles. It made for a relaxing journey, perhaps too relaxing, for no one noticed Galluci among the cyclists, keeping pace with the *Eendracht*.

They made the locks at Stompwijk just before the sluice doors closed. The attendant shouted that it would take 20 minutes to complete the change in water levels. Vreelink tied the boat up against the sluice wall.

On top of both sides of the lock's walls, German dog patrols inspected every vessel. It took an agonizing ten minutes before it was the *Eendracht's* turn. A helmeted soldier unleashed his German shepherd and ordered it to jump aboard. Willem shrieked with glee as the dog began sniffing everywhere. He spoke to the smiling guard in German.

"*Was sucht er?* What is he looking for?" The fatherly looking man said the dogs were trained to find radios, weapons and any kind of explosives.

"You speak very good German," the guard complimented him.

"I learned at school," Willem said scratching the dog's neck. The guard's smile changed when the dog scratched frantically at the trapdoor to the bilge pump, where the guns were stored in a secret compartment. Vreelink stealthily moved the playing radio closer to the dog.

"He probably smells the radio?" Willem suggested innocently. "Where do you come from in Germany," he asked keeping up the patter.

"Wiesbaden, do you know where that is?"

Before Willem could answer, the guard on the opposite side of the lock wall called and showed five fingers. "*Fünf minuten*," he yelled, pointing out that two boats remained to be inspected.

"Have you ever been to Wiesbaden?" the guard asked after putting the dog back on the leash.

"No, but I'd like to visit," Willem said.

The soldier nodded and lifted his index finger to his helmet in salute. "*Danke schön*," he said politely.

No one spoke for a while.

"That was both stupid and well done," Vreelink began, "This happened to work out just fine Willem, but from now on, you don't do anything or say anything without being specifically told."

Paula reached out and hugged her boy, "You did well," she assured him.

After leaving the lock, the *Eendracht* putt-putted into the Schie River, resuming its leisurely pace. By mid-afternoon, they reached the outskirts of Delft. Dirk steered the boat in the direction of the Oostpoort, the most easterly city gate which was a historic remnant from the days Delft was a walled city.

The brick structure was built in the 1600s and still looked as if it could repel an invader. Vreelink used the iron rings embedded in the brick embankment to tie up the boat and helped Paula and Willem to step onto the grassy slope. Vreelink watched the newly documented Mr. and Mrs. Zonder and son Jan-Pieter head for Grandpa Harry's house.

"Be back no later than six," he ordered, "I'm off to the Marina to refuel."

As she approached her parent's home, Paula worried about how they would react to the move to England. While Willem was officially registered as her child, she had told her parents immediately that the boy was not hers and had sworn them to secrecy. She never revealed the name of the birth mother, saying it was a condition of the adoption. Willem ran far ahead as they turned into the Hopstraat. The man who had followed their boat on his bicycle now followed them on foot.

Grandpa Harry was surprised to see his grandson. He stepped out on the sidewalk and saw Paula approaching with Mark.

"Is that the NSB guy I met at your house?" he asked Willem.

"His name is Mark and he is not with the NSB." Before he could ask more Paula arrived and hugged her father.

"Come in. Come in, all of you," he puttered. He called out for Grandma to make tea. Paula settled everyone down.

"Willem and I have a lot to tell," she began. "We are going away for a while." Paula led them through the developments of the last couple of days. She had to clarify things once or twice before her parents understood that the Nazis wanted their grandson because he was Jewish and Mark would get them to England where they would stay until the war was over.

"What route are you taking? When?" her mother sobbed.

"It is better that you don't know, mother. The Abwehr may come and ask questions. They know everything that I have told you except where we are going."

"What about Alexander?" Harry asked.

"He has gone back to his post. He will say that we are on holiday."

"Will he betray you? After all he is a Nazi." Harry did not forgive easily.

"No he loves Willem. He will do anything to protect him."

"Yeah, sure," Harry said with the air of a distrusting father-in-law. "What is in the case you are leaving here?" he asked.

"Our papers, photographs and a strong box with gold and silver coins. We cannot travel with that much money. If we are caught, they will just take it. We will come back for it when all this is over."

They finished their tea. There was nothing more to discuss. Mark broke the silence, "We should be going. We still have more travel today."

Grandma embraced her daughter, her face streaming with tears.

"Be careful Paula, and come back to us," she sobbed. Grandpa Harry held his grandson close, rubbing his hair and bending down to kiss it. Mark stood and watched the emotional scene with a sense of inadequacy. He must not fail. They were his charges now.

"We have to go," he urged.

He checked the street before he let Paula and Willem step out of the house. He waved them outside. They did not look back as Grandma and Grandpa stood at the door. Piet Prinsen watched from behind the display window of the greengrocer's and followed them at a safe distance.

At the Oostpoort, the trio boarded a boat moored there. Prinsen hid behind a hedge and took out his note pad. He never anticipated the judo chop on his neck. He slid silently to the ground, note pad in hand.

Gary Galluci dragged him farther behind the hedge. The man was breathing and very much alive. He searched the man's pockets and found a wallet containing an impressive identity card with a swastika-stamped photograph. Prinsen, a Dutch citizen, was an agent of the Abwehr! Galluci took both the Abwehr pass and the Dutch persoonsbewijs and left the man where he was. He'd wake up soon enough.

Galluci smiled. During the afternoon, the *Eendracht* had become the *Waterman* with a new license number. The boat backed away from the mooring and headed toward Schiedam. Galluci mounted his bicycle.

Vreelink looked solemn, "The owner of the marina told me that access to the Rotterdam harbour is out of the question. The Kriegsmarine E-boats will fire at anything that attempts to sail into the big harbour."

"So what now?" Paula asked.

"We'll end the boat trip at Schiedam. From there you'll have to make your way by foot to the Central Station of Rotterdam," Vreelink said.

"The train for Paris leaves at 1:40 in the afternoon and we are only 45 minutes sailing time from Schiedam." Mark added, "The walk to the station is not far. I am more concerned that if we leave now, we'll be there by early evening and we'd have to hang around until noon tomorrow."

"It would be best if we stay overnight along the river," Vreelink said. "Jaap Smit, a corporal in my old unit runs a farm at De Zweth; he will let us tie up in his boathouse. We will be off the river and out of sight."

"I hope your friend will let us use his bath," Paula said.

"Not only that, his wife will probably cook us a decent supper," Vreelink promised.

When they approached the farm, the boathouse was indeed open. Jaap Smit had tied up his own boat along the river to make room for the visitors. When the boathouse doors closed behind the *Waterman*, the two comrades-in-arms embraced and patted each other's back. Jaap's wife Elsie greeted everyone with open arms. She was a strong, red-cheeked woman with an attitude that brooked no nonsense.

The brick farmhouse looked very much like some of the better villas in the city. The living room had a broad picture window that looked out on the Schie River while an equally large window at the other end looked out on a well-kept garden where fat ducks played in an enclosed pond.

"We are keeping those ducks for our own dinner table and special occasions," Elsie explained, "Tonight is one of those occasions."

"You mean we're going to eat one of those ducks out there?" Willem asked dubiously. Paula assured him the duck had been cooking since well before they got here. The dinner was splendid. Paula and Willem helped with the dishes. Even though it was still light at nine o'clock, Vreelink suggested that after such a strenuous day, they should retire early.

Elsie explained the sleeping arrangements. Paula would sleep in the spare bedroom, Willem and Mark in the hayloft. Vreelink insisted on sleeping on the boat. He had work to do.

65

1941
TUESDAY, JUNE 24, 08:30 CEST
ABWEHR AMT DER NIEDERLANDEN, MAURITSLAAN 35
THE HAGUE, NEDERLAND

Streicher's office was a no-frills, gunmetal grey cubbyhole in a patrician house that served as Abwehr headquarters. Piet Prinsen sat across from Streicher's desk, wearing a horse-collar to keep his neck in alignment.

Streicher said, "I appreciate you calling me from the hospital last night in spite of your injuries. Do you know who attacked you?"

"I observed an unidentified man with the woman and her son as they boarded a pleasure craft. I was writing down the boat's name and licence number when I was rushed from behind. I woke up in the ambulance on the way to the hospital and found that my Abwehr ID and persoonsbewijs were missing."

Streicher busied himself making notes and looked up. "To recap: One person you recognized as Paula von Becke and the other as her son Wilhelm. The third person was unknown to you but appeared to be in charge. Your description says it was a blond man, in his late twenties, 185 centimetres tall, with a bushy moustache."

"He is a professional. He checked every doorway and looked in store windows for reflections. I'm quite certain he did not notice me."

"Perhaps not," Streicher said dryly, "but somebody did. You followed the party to the Oostpoort where they boarded a pleasure craft called *Waterman* with a license number ZH 1641."

"That is correct."

"That may be correct Herr Prinsen, but there is neither a licence number like that nor a listing of a pleasure craft by that name."

"I am sorry, but that's what my notes show."

"After you were released from the hospital you visited the Meuniers."

"Yes, about 22:00 hours. They were going to bed. At first they did not want to tell me anything but after some persuasion, they told me that Paula and Willem were going to England."

"Did the parents know the escape route?"

"No, they did not but they did say that the man who was with them was in charge and looked like a government agent."

"A British agent?"

"They said he spoke perfect Dutch and they had seen him before but didn't know his name."

"The man may be a member of one of the amateur resistance groups playing the hero," Streicher said. "The Reichsfuehrer has ordered me to bring the boy to Berlin without resorting to violence, but if foreign agents are involved that would change the situation."

"What are my orders for today, Herr Oberleutnant?" Prinsen asked.

"They appear to be traveling in a southerly direction therefore I would assume their destination is Portugal."

"What do you expect from me, Herr Oberleutnant?" Prinsen repeated, looking for clear instructions.

"If they are going south then the only route is by train. Rotterdam and Roosendaal are the only Dutch stops on the D-train to Paris. You will check the passengers destined for Paris at these stations. I will coordinate the military police and alert the border police in Roosendaal. I have a hunch they may travel to Rotterdam by boat. I will also ask the police to check the Schie River to Rotterdam."

Prinsen got up with a painful expression. "With permission Herr Oberleutnant I will eat breakfast before I set out."

"No breakfast. You must leave immediately. If you spot your target, demand the complete assistance of both civil and military police. All three persons must be apprehended. Call me as soon you have a lead."

66

1941
TUESDAY, JUNE 24, 08:30 HRS CEST
THE SMIT FARM, DE ZWETH,
NEAR SCHIEDAM, NEDERLAND

"We should leave no later than ten o'clock," Vreelink said while Mark finished breakfast at the Smit farm. "I should bring the boat back to Leiden before the owner begins to panic."

Paula enjoyed breakfast with the view of the river. Cyclists passed and several small barges laden with produce made their way to the vegetable auction in Schiedam. To Paula it looked so peaceful. People were going about their daily routines while she was experiencing the greatest upheaval in her life.

Time passed quickly; after cleaning up and thanking the Smits profusely for their hospitality, they were underway.

"We'll part company at the railway bridge that leads to the station," Vreelink said, "I'll let you off at the foot of the bridge. From there it is only a kilometre along the tracks to the passenger terminal."

Paula and Willem were ready to go. Mark was ready, except for his revolver. He lifted the hatch to the bilge pump and retrieved the Colt .45.

"Give that to me," Dirk commanded. "You can't take that cannon. I'll trade you my Beretta." Mark took the smaller gun, stuck it in the belt behind his back, and pulled his jacket over it. Vreelink looked annoyed. "Take the holster, cowboy and hide it under the leg of your trousers."

Paula took her spot in the lone deckchair and enjoyed the scenery. It was a warm sunny day – an unusual occurrence in Holland. It was Willem who spotted the DKW motorcycle that drew alongside the *Waterman*. It was an SS Feldgendarmerie in a helmet and green leather raincoat with a Schmeisser slung across his chest. A shiny SS Field Police gorget hung on a chain around his neck which meant that he was on official duty. The anonymous figure with the goggles raised a gloved hand indicating for the *Waterman* to lay by.

"He must have a message for us," Willem said. Vreelink looked grim but kept going. The SS man revved the motor bike to gain some distance on the *Waterman* to position himself to fire his weapon. He was no more than ten metres ahead of the *Waterman* when Mark grabbed the Colt – still lying on the engine casing – and fired three shots at the racing motorcycle. The front tire ripped apart, shredding the rubber. The rider lost control and plunged into the river with the motorcycle. As they sailed by, they noted the heavy leather coat made it difficult for the man to climb out of the water. Vreelink increased the boat's speed to the maximum.

"There will be more of them soon," Vreelink breathed rapidly, "But we are not far from the bridge." Willem clung to Paula in fear. The tension aboard was palpable. The shoreline changed.

They were entering the river's working sector. Industrial buildings and warehouses lined the banks. The railway bridge loomed in the distance. Looking back, Mark spotted a Kübelwagen coming up behind them on the towpath on the opposite bank from where the Grüne Polizei officer had hit the water. Dirk quickly turned left into one of the commercial harbour inlets. He steered the boat in between two moored *rijnaken*, the low-slung boats that ply the Rhine to the German Ruhr area. They were now out of sight to anyone on the towpath. The skipper of the neighbouring *rijnaak*, alerted by his yapping little dog, came out to see what the fuss was all about. Vreelink waved at him.

"I was going to drop my friends close to Central Station but I've got something wrong with the propeller, so I'll just drop them here."

"You are close enough here anyway," the skipper said. "You can just follow the road and you'll end up in the shunting yard of the railroad. But you've got to watch out for trains." Vreelink waved in thanks.

"They'll be looking for this boat now. I'll abandon it somewhere in the reeds," Vreelink added quietly.

Mark thanked him and wrapped him in a bear hug.

Paula was next in line. "Thanks Dirk. You are a brave man, risking your life for us." She kissed his cheek. Vreelink looked embarrassed. Mark heaved the baggage onto the dock and pulled Willem and Paula ashore.

Loosening the *Waterman* from its tether, Vreelink looked up at Mark. "Say hello to the General. Tell him I want a promotion when this is over."

As Dirk backed the boat away, he watched them walk between the bales, crates and containers. It was an area that had been bombed mercilessly the previous year and they had to make their way around broken cranes and mud-filled craters. The narrow road to the railway embankment was as close as promised.

They walked along the ditch below the dike to stay out of sight of the sentries and trod through the vegetable gardens planted along the railway line by enterprising citizens. Half a kilometre further, they could hear the noise of the shunting yard. Railway cars sorted into trains, clanged into each other and the steam locomotives hissed their disapproving sounds.

They clambered up on the railway dike and walked along the tracks. The arched roof of the Rotterdam Central Station loomed ahead. Two passenger train tracks leading into the station split into eight parallel tracks each carrying a variety of flatbeds, coal cars and at least a half dozen cattle cars with cows bleating through the slats.

The sound of yapping dogs came from behind one of the assembled freight trains. Suddenly a yardman in a denim shirt and railway cap stepped from behind a freight car.

"Are you on the run?" he asked.

"A Jewish boy," Mark used the three words knowing it would either bring sympathetic help or result in betrayal.

"The dogs are trained to look for free riders. Get in here quick," the man urged. He opened the sliding door of a freight car. Mark hopped in quickly and helped Paula up while the yardman hoisted Willem into the car and rapidly slammed the door shut behind them. It was pitch black. They stumbled into a wall of jute sacks filled with potatoes. They sat down on the floor using the spuds as a backrest.

"I'll let you know when it is safe," he said softly through the closed door. The dogs came ever closer and then stopped outside their car. They heard laughter. The yardman must have said something funny for the voices trailed away. A sudden bang on the door startled them. "We're going to move, I'm going with you, don't be afraid," a voice said.

With a jolt, the car shot forward as the locomotive propelled it towards a line of freight cars. The car floated down the shunting hill, slowly coming to a bouncy halt at the end of another car. The door slid open.

"You are almost at the terminal. Keep going straight," the yardman said hurriedly. "God be with you," the man yelled after them.

67

1941
TUESDAY, JUNE 24, 11:30 HRS CEST
RAILWAY STATION
ROTTERDAM, NEDERLAND

The station's size suggested permanence while its austere design and girder construction gave it anonymity – a vast parking lot for trains made from a construction kit. Coming through the dirty glass roof, the daylight looked green, dusty and mysterious. Trains arrived; trains departed. A young woman wanted to know the time and an ugly couple walked past arguing about something. Sparrows came gliding down from girders on the roof, encouraged by a bearded man on the bench nearby who spread breadcrumbs.

"I am going to buy the tickets; follow me at a safe distance," Mark said. "If I am stopped by anyone, don't stay to watch, go to the first class lounge and wait for me." He scanned the crowd. Everything appeared normal.

At the *Internationale Dienst* wicket, the agent was surprised to serve a passenger who wanted to cross borders at such short notice. His sparse hair was black, his eyes red from tiredness. He had a lopsided moustache because of the way he kept tugging at one end of it. He nervously scanned the official letter authorizing Mr. Zonder to travel to Bordeaux for business. He called his supervisor. After noting all the particulars on the letter and checking passports and ID cards, the supervisor initialled the permit to issue tickets. Mark was relieved. He motioned for Paula and Willem to follow him to the First Class waiting room.

Piet Prinsen arrived at the international ticket counter, flashed his Abwehr ID and demanded to speak to the supervisor. "I need to see the details of all passengers who booked tickets to Paris."

"That won't take long, sir, there not many." the officious manager said.

"Look for families of three or four people," Prinsen said, tapping his feet nervously. Leafing through the carbon copies, the man lifted one group ticket. "Just one Sir, Mr. and Mrs. Zonder and their son Pieter-Jan."

Prinsen smiled. "How old is the boy?"

"Oh, I think, 13, maybe 14."

Prinsen asked to use the office telephone. It took time before he reached Streicher. "Prinsen here, Oberleutnant. I have found them. As you suspected they are booked on the 13:40 train to Paris. The names used are Mr. and Mrs. Mark Zonder and the boy travels as Pieter-Jan Zonder."

"Get help. Find them and arrest them," Streicher commanded. "If you cannot apprehend all three, the boy is your priority."

Prinsen hung up with a smug smile. Streicher alerted the border post in Roosendaal. Zonder, he thought, Zonder, the name sounded familiar.

From his seat in the First Class Lounge, Mark could see the big clock on the platform. It ticked over to 1:25 pm, 15 minutes to departure. The waiter, his shiny tuxedo somewhat frayed at the edges, served coffee and cookies and a glass of *Ranja* for Willem. Paula reminded Willem again that his name was Pieter-Jan Zonder.

The ambience in the old-world style waiting room was soothing. Chicory coffee tastes awful, but its aroma is pleasant. It made the place feel homey. Mark's eyes darted around the room and checked the passers-by. Two soldiers, rifles across the shoulders, followed a stooped man as he scanned the crowd.

At half past one, Paula wanted to go out on the platform to await the arrival of the train. Mark held her back.

"All eyes will be focused on the train when it is pulling in. Then we move," he whispered.

When the train destined for Paris rolled to a stop, Mark grabbed the suitcases and headed for the first door of the first class section. "Get in now. Quick," he hissed.

Prinsen stood on the platform, watching. The clock ticked to 1:39. The stationmaster raised his baton indicating the train was permitted to depart. Prinsen delayed his boarding a few seconds too long. He jumped aboard the last car – a third class compartment. Unfortunately for him, it provided no access to the rest of the train.

In First Class, Mark led the way through the aisle avoiding the glances of those seated in their compartments. Compartment A14 was at the back of the first car. Their assigned compartment consisted of opposing benches, each offering three upholstered seats. Idyllic photographs of pre-war skiing holidays in Switzerland were mounted on the shiny mahogany walls. Mark hoisted the suitcases into the overhead baggage rack. Willem and Paula took the window seats.

A middle-aged couple knocked and slid the glass door open. A bossy looking woman cast an envious glance at Paula's window seat. The man mumbled something in Dutch. To judge by their accent, they were Belgians. The newcomers were still busily stowing their baggage when the door slid open again. A German officer of ample girth took off his leather coat and hung it on a hook near the door. His uniform bore the insignia of Hauptmann, a Captain. He was a tall man with gray hair and a folksy smile. Mark judged him to be in his late fifties. The officer looked at his train ticket and pointed at Willem.

"*Sie sind in meinem Sitz, junger Mann,*" he said showing Willem his seat assignment on the ticket.

"*Entschuldigen Sie mich,*" Willem apologized in perfect German. Paula reacted quickly.

"It's okay Pieter-Jan, you take my seat. You like the window," she said.

The train shocked into motion and started its steam-puffing exit from the station. As it cleared the protective shell of the Central Station, the engineer's whistle shrieked.

The captain smiled kindly at Willem and said, "*Deine Deutsche Sprache ist sehr gut,*" complimenting him on his German. Willem told him he was Dutch and learned four languages in school. The officer was in the mood for a chat and the two of them carried on a conversation about the differences of attending school in their respective countries. The Captain introduced himself as Otto von Malwitz and confided that he had a grandson just about the same age as Willem.

"What is your name, young man," Willem looked at his mother who widened her eyes, urging caution.

"Pieter-Jan," he said after a pause. The Hauptmann did not notice the hesitation. Willem talked about his photography hobby and the pictures he had taken. Mark stirred uncomfortably when he asked the boy where he was going.

"We are going to Bordeaux," Mark interjected.

"So you must change stations in Paris then?" von Malwitz asked.

"Yes, we are changing from the Gare du Nord to the Gare de Lyon to catch the train to Bordeaux tomorrow morning."

"So tonight you are staying in Paris?" Afraid that booking a hotel in advance might give his pursuers a clue, Mark had made no reservations. He quickly improvised and said, "Hotel Bellevue, on rue Agincourt."

"I don't think I know it," the Captain mused. Mark didn't either. He instinctively had thought of the hotel Bellevue on the Steenstraat not far from his parent's home and Agincourt was a name he had seen on a railway poster.

"Where are you going, Hauptmann?" Willem asked.

"I am going to Paris also," he said, "I have a four-day leave and I am going to have dinner with my son who is stationed outside Fontainebleau, not far from Paris."

"You are going all the way to Paris to have dinner?" Willem asked in awe.

"I hope to have more than dinner. My son will get some time off so we can have good talks. His regiment will be assigned to the Eastern Front at some point. I just want to see him before he goes." Neither Mark nor Paula responded. To discourage further questions they stared straight ahead.

"If I may ask, why are you going to Bordeaux?" von Malwitz asked politely.

"I am consulting on a harbour project for the Kriegsmarine," Mark said, hoping to be able to claim the need for secrecy to close down any further questioning.

"Ah so!" he exclaimed with apparent satisfaction. With that, he put his cap over his eyes, stretched his legs and closed his eyes.

The sign for the Oudenbosch station flitted by and von Malwitz woke.

"Just five more minutes to the border at Roosendaal," he announced, "I have taken this trip before. They will order the passengers out of their compartments for passport inspection. Then you will stand in a long line before you are allowed to enter the train again. It is a nuisance for everyone and the long wait is a bore. He rose. Mark helped him to get his leather coat. Bowing courtly to Paula he said, "My dear Lady, may I offer you and your husband and of course young Pieter-Jan the convenience of the German Officers Lounge in Roosendaal." Paula turned to Mark who quickly nodded his approval.

"That is very generous of you Herr Hauptmann," she said.

"It is my pleasure. The advantage is that the passport control comes to us instead of us having to stand in line."

When the train hissed to a halt, Mark reached for the baggage to allow Paula and Willem to follow the captain through the milling crowd. He noticed two *Grüne Polizei* selecting couples with children for inspection inside the building. He sidestepped into the officer's lounge where von Malwitz was signing in his guests.

"Please write your names, birthdates, passport numbers and nationality here. It'll make the lounge manager happy and the inspection will be that much easier."

Various officers sat around tables drinking beer, chatting amicably. Some were accompanied by spouses or in a few cases attractive female acquaintances. Mark noted only one other child, a girl of five or six. The lounge was an oasis of calm compared to the crowd outside. Officers came and went without military salutes. Von Malwitz made his way through the maze of tables and found a spot at the back.

He clapped his hands together in subdued glee.

"Let's sit down and have a beer. They serve good old *Münchener* beer here. The real stuff. And you, Pieter-Jan, shall have chocolate ice cream."

Von Malwitz dominated the conversation with stories about the Bavarian town of Eikenhof, just outside Munich. He was a supply officer in Amsterdam, he revealed, but in civilian life, he had an accounting practice. Mark kept an eye on the door. A Belgian and Dutch railway conductor came in to check railway tickets, followed by a German sergeant with the word *Grenzpolizei* on his tunic cuff.

Von Malwitz handed over his tickets, passport and papers and was quickly cleared. The train tickets were punched and approved by the Belgian railway conductor. The Border Police sergeant turned to Mark with the sign-in sheet in hand. He held the passport pages to the light and felt the imprinted seal on the photographs.

"I am sure everything is in order," von Malwitz said good-naturedly. The sergeant looked up with a withering glance. If it weren't for the Captain's higher rank, he might have told von Malwitz to shut up. He read the letter authorizing the trip to Bordeaux and asked Mark for credentials that would certify he was indeed a qualified consultant.

"I do not carry my degree with me," Mark said in as confident a voice as he could muster. "It hangs on the wall of my office."

"Exactly!" von Malwitz snapped, "Mine too!"

He spoke to the sergeant in a Bavarian *gemütliche*, warm tone. "You don't think the Kriegsmarine would hire an incompetent do you?" The sergeant was not convinced but he was pressed for time to clear the rest of the officers in the lounge. The man hesitated but with an icy glare at the captain, he stamped their passports for entry into Belgium.

A Luftwaffe Gefreiter in a white jacket announced that the officers and guests could return now to their respective compartments. Crossing the platform, Mark noted that the border police were merely observing the officers' party; no more checking.

He whispered to Paula, "I think we are safe. They don't know we are on this train."

They walked past the telephone booth where a stooped man stood talking to Oberleutnant Streicher in The Hague.

"I had the Grüne Polizei question every family with children on that platform," Prinsen told him. "They did not find Zonder, nor the boy and his mother but I am sure they are on the train."

"Follow them, Prinsen," Streicher ordered. If they got off the train where you are, they will try to cross into Belgium on foot. I'll have the Border Police on alert."

"Do you wish me to travel to Paris?"

"Belgium is first, Prinsen. I will also alert the Moeskroen Grenzpolizei at the French/Belgian border. If you have not managed to apprehend the boy by then you must close in on them at Paris."

"Oberleutnant, I will have that boy before the day is out."

"I wish I could share your confidence, Prinsen." Streicher said sharply.

Prinsen hung up and hurried to the train. He failed to see the Italian-looking man seated on a bench seemingly engrossed in his newspaper. Only when Prinsen was aboard did Gary Galluci put down his paper and climb aboard the second-class section.

68

1941
WEDNESDAY, JUNE 25, 17:00 HRS BDST
NETHERLANDS DEFENCE INSTITUTE
LONDON SW1, ENGLAND

Van Zandt admired himself in the mirror as he put the finishing touches on his formal dinner attire. The doorbell rang and he was surprised to find Jos Caspers with a message in hand.

"Sorry to interrupt, Sir, it's an urgent message from OZ."

"About time I'd say. Haven't heard a word from those brigands in the last few days," van Zandt grumbled. He tore open the sealed message.

> "Agent object and mother on 24 June Paris train. Identity compromised. Need French assist for transfer to Gare de Lyon. OZ

Damnit, the operation was compromised so early. The Queen would not forgive a failure. He lifted the telephone and dialled the number of the Legation of the Free French. He did not care for his French counterpart, an imperious upstart by the name of Charles de Gaulle.

As far as de Gaulle was concerned, the honour of the flag had been despoiled and he had therefore resurrected the Cross of Lorraine as the symbol of the Free French Forces. Joan of Arc had been the last French warrior to carry the Cross into battle. Churchill, who detested de Gaulle, privately said that the heaviest cross he had to bear was the Cross of Lorraine. Van Zandt had a better relationship with de Gaulle's adjutant, Colonel Jean-Marc Verviers.

After a few minutes, Verviers came to the phone. Van Zandt explained the urgency of the situation. The colonel sounded doubtful. "The Resistance is not always reliable... There is not much time..."

"You can save my neck, mon ami," van Zandt pleaded. "I need you." Verviers promised he would do everything possible. "I'm counting on it, Colonel," van Zandt said.

69

1941
WEDNESDAY, JUNE 25, 17:30 HRS CEST
ABOARD D-TRAIN 147
ROOSENDAAL, NEDERLAND

The Roosendaal stationmaster cried his last 'All Aboard' and raised his handheld baton to signal that the train was cleared to enter Belgium. The engineer gave a blast on the whistle as the locomotive hissed and spun its wheels before slipping into motion.

As he departed the lounge, von Malwitz took a box lunch of sandwiches that he generously offered to his fellow passengers. A chalice of poison would have been more attractive to the Belgian couple who turned away with upheld hands to ward it off. Willem reached for the cheese sandwich and chewed heartily. Paula and Mark accepted gratefully.

An hour later, when the train pulled into Brussels for a five-minute stop, the Belgian couple collected their bags and left without a word. Von Malwitz suggested to Mark that they should stay aboard instead of walking around the platform.

Unexpectedly, the compartment door slid open and a Kriegsmarine officer stepped in. His insignia indicated that he was an *Oberleutnant zur See*, a ranking that put him a level below von Malwitz. He put his luggage on the bench, tucked his white Navy cap under his left arm and clicked his heels in salute. Von Malwitz remained seated and nodded in response.

Protocol demanded that the senior offer would initiate discussion if so inclined. Von Malwitz introduced himself. The Navy lieutenant – Wortmann – was a tall man, athletically built, with a smile that automatically unfolded whenever he squinted at something, which was quite often. The two of them engaged in anecdotes about life in the Armed Forces. Mark noted that neither of them appeared to be avid Nazis but rather businessmen torn from their daily lives to serve in Hitler's legions.

Willem had gone to sleep and Paula leaned on Mark's shoulder with her eyes closed. Von Malwitz interrupted his talk with the lieutenant and spoke to Mark. "Lieutenant Wortmann here is stationed at the harbour at

Cherbourg, the U boat base. If your mission is not top secret, my colleague would be interested in your consultancy in Bordeaux."

Mark's stomach muscles tightened. Fortunately, his training had included a brief outline of the fake Bordeaux project. "Yes, of course," he stalled, "What is your function in Cherbourg, Herr Leutnant?"

"I am the maintenance engineer for the *Unterseeboot* section. My unit's task is to keep the submarines battle-ready."

"Did you do this kind of work in civilian life?"

"Of course, I was a supervisor in the shipyards at Kiel, on the Baltic." Mark didn't say any more in the hope the discussion would die. It did not.

"What is the nature of your consultancy in Bordeaux, if I may ask," Wortmann asked politely. "There is no military harbour on the Garonne River, is there?"

"Not yet, but at the south-western tip to the entrance of Garonne is a cove near Le-Verdon-sur-Mer which is being considered for a base for the E-Boats. My particular expertise has to do with the effects of waves on man-made structures," Mark said, parroting his briefing book.

Wortmann turned to von Malwitz, "The Hollanders have built a country from the sea, no wonder they are good at it," he said, smiling congenially.

Thankfully, the discussion ended and the officers retreated within their own thoughts. The train clacked along rapidly, passing barely-lit villages adhering to the blackout. As the train slowed down to enter Moeskroen, at the border with France, Willem woke and looked out the window.

"Look, the street signs are all in Dutch. I thought they spoke French in the south of Belgium."

Paula said, "As soon as we pass the French border everything will be in French."

The train hissed to a halt but all doors remained closed.

Two Feldwebels came into the compartment and demanded passports and papers. Mark noticed a civilian looking over the officers' shoulders through the open door. He did not appear interested in the German officers but stared directly at Paula and Willem. Mark thought he had seen the stooped pasty-faced man before. Why was a civilian looking over the shoulders of a policeman?

The Grenzpolizei quickly finished scanning the documents of the German officers and turned their attention to Mark who handed him the letter authorizing travel to Bordeaux for him and his family.

The senior of the two men asked, "To connect to Bordeaux you must change to another station and your train will not leave until tomorrow morning. Where will you and your family stay this evening?"

"We have booked a room in the hotel Bellevue on rue Agincourt," Mark said hoping none of the officials would be familiar with Paris.

"It is late and the Metro will have stopped running, therefore you will need to take a taxi," he said helpfully, while turning back to nod at the civilian in the raincoat. Mark looked at the pasty-faced man again briefly but the younger Feldwebel demanded an inspection of the suitcases. He rummaged through the contents in a manner that suggested he didn't expect to find anything. The border police and the civilian left.

The French railway crew replaced the Belgian locomotive with the SNCF – French railway version. At last, the train departed.

Willem read the sign on the platform that the next stop was Rijssel and yet another sign that said Lille.

"That is just the language wars again, my friend," von Malwitz said. "The Dutch speakers in Belgium call it Rijssel and the French call it Lille. General de Gaulle is from Lille. He'll never admit that his name is Dutch." He chuckled inwardly as if he had just told himself a good joke.

Willem and Paula were sound asleep while they passed Lille and Compiègne. Mark kept an eye on Wortmann while von Malwitz appeared to snooze with his army cap pulled over his face.

The train passed the outer suburbs of Paris. Mark got his briefcase and took out all his French francs stowed them in various pockets. Wortmann too, was dozing by now.

The train slowed down and finally hissed to a stop under the massive roof of the Gare du Nord. The two officers woke up with a start.

"Time to go gentlemen; we enjoyed your company," Mark said, shaking hands with both men. Von Malwitz kissed Paula's hand while Wortmann just smiled. The captain ruffled Willem's hair and said, *"Gute Reise Pieter-Jan."*

Mark hauled the suitcases out onto the platform and was immediately accosted by an aggressive porter who piled their baggage on his cart.

"We don't need that," Mark protested but not wanting to look awkward in front of the German officers, he agreed. The porter made his way rapidly through the crowd of passengers and headed for the exit. Paula and Willem could barely keep up.

A uniformed cab driver joined him in the arrival hall. "Monsieur Zonder, Monsieur Zonder," he whispered looking down on the suitcases.

Surprised by this unexpected reception, Mark acknowledged, "Oui." He turned to pay the porter who put up both his hands in a defensive stance and shook an emphatic no.

"Suivez moi s'il vous plait," the cabby demanded. Mark was wary but decided to go along.

His taxi idled in front of the main exit in a no-parking zone. The porter stowed the baggage on the back seat and the cabby motioned for Paula and Willem to squeeze in. Mark kept the briefcase with him in the front.

The cab driver turned to look at Mark and his back seat passengers. *"Je m'appelle André. Resistance! Vous comprenez?"* Mark felt relieved.

André looked in the rear mirror and steered the cab into light traffic on the rue de Dunkerque. Had he paid less attention to the traffic and more to the car parked behind him, he would have seen the Citroën sedan with the German Army license plate. The driver was a big man in one of those heavy brown leather overcoats with plenty of straps and buttons. The tight fit made him look as if he was about to explode out of it.

Prinsen joined him in the front seat. A third man opened the door to the back seat, jumped in and slammed the door. He was a lanky character wearing a floppy, wide-brimmed, artist's hat – something like a Musketeer, but without the plume. He nearly knocked his hat off as he settled in the back seat. "Follow the taxi," he yelled in German.

André's cab was 50 metres ahead, waiting for a traffic light. The Abwehr car raced after them. Inside the cab, Mark had a feeling that they were being followed. He turned to look back just as André turned into the rue de Saint-Quentin in the direction of the Gare de Lyon. The Citroën was coming up fast behind them.

"Turn left into the next street," Mark yelled. André did not understand. Mark was frantic. He pointed behind him. The Resistance man looked in the mirror and saw the pursuit car. "*A gauche*," Mark yelled, pointing wildly to the side street on the left. At the last possible moment, André careened into the deserted rue de Valenciennes.

The Citroën raced up beside them, the driver motioning to pull over to the curb. André ignored him and drove on. The powerful Citroën pulled ahead and cut in front of the taxi. The cab ran onto the sidewalk and came to a halt against a low concrete pillar. Remarkably, the engine kept running. The leather-clad driver of the Citroën raced to André's side, opened the door, grabbed him by the collar and conked him on the head with the grip of his Luger. André slouched forward, his head dropping onto the steering wheel.

The Abwehr with the artistic hat held a gun on Mark as he struggled to get out of the passenger seat. Prinsen joined in and dragged Paula and Willem out of the back seat and held them at bay with his gun.

Another taxi roared up behind them. For a man shaped like a fire hydrant, Gary Galluci was agile. He was out in the street before the Germans realized he was there. He aimed his .38 Special and shot the leather giant. The man fell back, grasping his chest. His gun clattered to the pavement.

The musketeer, startled by the unexpected gunshot, turned and shot at Galluci who crawled toward the two cars. He missed. The gangly German now focused exclusively on the approaching Galluci. Mark, half out of the front seat, whipped out his Beretta from its leg holster and shot the man from behind. The German grabbed his shoulder and stumbled to the ground, his fancy hat dropping to the pavement.

Prinsen held Paula – with Willem clutched against her – as a shield against the approaching Galluci. Prinsen recognized the classic standoff. He knew that Galluci would not shoot him as long as Paula and the boy were in front of him. Willem was wide-eyed in terror.

Mark stepped quickly behind Prinsen and pushed the barrel of the Beretta in his neck. "You harm the woman or the boy and you are dead," he hissed, "Drop your gun."

Prinsen did as he was told and took his arm away from Paula.

Behind Mark, the musketeer struggled up from the pavement and aimed his Luger at Mark. Before he could pull the trigger, Galluci fired three shots. The German was knocked backwards on top of his hat, his arms spread wide. There were more shots. Paula screamed. She was lying on the pavement, her hand clutched to her abdomen, her dress stained red. Willem was on top of her howling: "Mommy, Mommy."

Gary Galluci picked Willem up around the waist. He carried the screaming boy, legs flailing, to the Citroen and deposited him on the front seat. "Sit here. We have to look after your mother. I'll be back."

Mark sat on the pavement, his arm around Paula's shoulder.

"Where's Willem?" she wailed.

Gary Galluci ran over. "Willem is safe," he assured her.

Mark looked up at him. "Who the hell are you? And why have you been following us?"

"Later. First let's get her to a hospital."

André had slowly regained consciousness. "If Madame goes to a regular hospital she will be questioned by the Germans," he told Mark in French. "Let the Resistance take care of the lady; we have our doctors. Are you coming with us Monsieur Zonder?"

"No, he is not," Gary barked. "We have to get the boy away from here." He helped lift Paula into André's taxi. Paula held Mark's hand.

"You take care of Willem," she wept softly, "Tell him I'll be alright and I will be with him as soon as I can." She was quiet for a moment. "Go," she suddenly urged, "Before they get Willem." She sank into nothingness.

André assured them he would take care of everything. He backed the taxi off the sidewalk and began to drive away.

Mark yelled for him to stop. "The suitcases!" he yelled. André got out of the car, opened the back door, threw the baggage on the sidewalk and sped away. Mark retrieved them.

He looked after the speeding cab as it turned the corner to the rue de Saint-Quentin. With dread, he realized, "He's got my briefcase with all my documents," he yelled, "Oh Shit!"

"We could take the German car," Gary said in an excited voice, "But the Abwehr would catch up with us right away. Leave the car. We have to get away from here. We'll take the back lanes."

Prinsen, still on the pavement, pleaded for help in a whimpering voice.

"Your friends will be here soon enough, you bastard," Mark said with disgust. He lifted the suitcases from the street, gave one to Galluci, took the other one himself and reached for Willem's hand.

"Your mother is on the way to the hospital and we must leave," he said running down the street, dragging Willem along. "Back to the Gare du Nord. Best place to hide!" Mark yelled.

"Okay, but stay close to the buildings," Galluci panted. "If you see anyone coming toward you, duck into an alcove."

They ran toward the avenue du Magenta and entered a garbage-strewn back lane. It was pitch black and smelled of urine. Something stirred along the left wall. They heard a plaintive voice. "It's a man, sleeping," Willem sobbed through his crying jag. The drunk tried to raise himself but fell back with a sigh on his cardboard mattress.

At the end of the lane, they heard the donkey-call sirens of the French police racing toward the macabre scene they had left behind. Galluci turned into the rue de Saint-Quentin, which at least had some dim lights. "Don't run now, just walk," Gary half-yelled, half-whispered. "Don't draw attention to yourself." They crossed the wide intersection of rue La Fayette. "Turn into the boulevard de Denain. I can see the lights of the Gare du Nord from here." He sidestepped into an alcove of a luggage store pulling Willem and Mark into the dark secluded area, well hidden from the street.

"We've got to find a place to spend the night," Gary said, catching his breath. More police cars sped past, lights flashing and sirens braying. "It's only a hundred yards to the freight entrance." They walked quickly. About to cross the rue de Dunkerque, Mark noticed a Parisian cop standing on the corner idly swinging his baton against his leg.

Mark turned Willem toward him and put his hands on Willem's shoulders. He smiled and looked him in the face. "You are a boy going to the station with your father. Please act like it. You can do it." Willem straightened up and reached for Mark's hand. Mark's training taught him that the direct approach aroused the least suspicion. He looked straight at the cop, "*Bon soir,*" he smiled.

The flic lifted his baton and touched the brim of his kepi. "*Et bon nuit m'sieur et bon voyage.*" He thinks we are early for the first train, Mark thought. They hurried after Gary who approached the entrance of the *dépôt de fret*.

"Over here," Gary waved.

The freight hall was busy with men hauling and weighing boxes. No one paid any attention to two men and a boy walking through. Gary led the way to a shipping door at the back of the hall and opened it wide enough to squeeze through. They stepped onto Platform 14 of the cavernous departure hall. On a side track, the morning train to Amiens was being cleaned. Other than the far-off hissing of a locomotive, there was no sound. The dimly lit platforms were deserted. Inside the nearby train, a cleaner bent down. It was the only movement.

"Let's go to the passenger lounges at Platform 6. I noticed them when we arrived," Gary whispered. Even though spoken in a low voice, his words echoed through the immense enclosure.

They found the first class lounge. It was dark; the door was locked.

"Wait here," Gary ordered. He went around the back of the building and in less than a minute, he opened the front door to let Mark and Willem in. "The first train leaves at 6:10 so we should be safe here until five o'clock," he said.

They sat down in the comfortable lounge chairs.

Mark said to Willem "We'd better check our suitcases. The big one contains the stuff for your mother and you. We may have to throw some stuff away." He undid the belts around the rattan suitcase.

"Just a single dress, shoes and underwear for your Mom. Looks like most of it is for you." He held up the small bundle. Your camera is in here and your pictures. And guess what... your Jeugdstorm uniform. I wonder why she brought it."

"She thought it might help if we were arrested," Willem said.

Meanwhile, Gary had foraged through the kitchen. He brought out half a coffee cake and a plate of croissants.

"This should do us for a while and there is more if we want," he said. Willem asked for something to drink.

"No problem, son," he grinned and came back with a pitcher full of orangeade and some paper cups. "It's not real orange juice but it'll be okay." Willem was already digging hungrily into the cake.

"So," Mark said devouring his second croissant. "You seem to know who I am; but who are you? And what are you doing here?"

Gary explained his background and how he had been contracted by Ferenc Kolmar to bring his son to America. "Willem's father is an important man in New York with friends in the FBI. He is prepared to do what it takes to get his son to America."

"You know my real father?" Willem gasped.

"Yes, lad, he only heard a few weeks ago that he had a son so he asked me to find you even though he doesn't know your name yet."

"And he wants me to come to America to live with him?" Willem said, looking ashen. "I want to be with my father and mother," he blubbered.

"The Queen would like you to join her family," Mark told him gently.

"That's not fair," Willem bawled, "I want my Mom." His body rocked with grief again. Mark put his arms around his shoulders and hugged him.

"It'll all turn out well, Willem," he soothed, "Trust me."

He felt no such assurance nor did he feel right about what was being done to this bright boy. The Royal Family wanted him out of Nederland for political reasons, not for the love of the child. Kolmar on the other hand, had the instincts of a father. Yet, Mark was duty-bound to bring Willem to England. He held Willem close and continued to rock him gently.

Gary spoke first. "Mark, I know we are competing in a way," he said, "But let's work together to get Willem out of reach of German hands. You were going to Bordeaux and through Spain to neutral Lisbon, but you can't. The Abwehr knows your plans. The Resistance has your papers."

"I still have my French francs and my Beretta," Mark protested.

"Let's get to England and let others decide how to solve the problem."

"What about my mother?" Willem sniffled, "When she gets better, will she come to get me?" Mark hugged Willem a little closer.

"You know Uncle Frans, Willem. He will tell the Resistance to bring you mother to England as soon as possible," he said, but didn't believe it.

"Will she come to America if Mr. Galluci takes me there?"

"Mr. Kolmar is a very rich man and he will do everything to make you happy," Gary assured him.

"So what about a plan?" Mark asked.

Gary reached for the train schedule in the dispenser on the buffet counter. "We should take a later train to Bordeaux than planned," he said.

"You can bet that they will check that first train very thoroughly. We will stand a better chance taking the second. Don't worry about the money; I'll pay for the tickets." Mark agreed it was the only viable plan.

Willem had curled up in the chair and fallen asleep. Mark covered him with a tablecloth. Gary looked on with a smile.

"Let's grab some sleep ourselves." He dug in his wallet and left enough American dollars near the cash register to treat all first class passengers to free coffee and croissants for the rest of the morning.

70

1941
THURSDAY, JUNE 26, 05:30 HRS CEST
GARE DU NORD
PARIS, FRANCE

Mark woke to the noise of trains rumbling to their designated platforms. It was nearly 5:30. The lounge manager would soon be making an appearance. He shook the two sleeping bodies. "Time to get out," he whispered.

They washed at a bar sink that reeked of stale beer and walked outside. On Platform 2, dozens of early passengers already waited for trains.

"We'll wait here until a couple of trains arrive at the same time and then we will join the passengers trooping to the exit," Gary said. An hour passed before a sufficient parade of passengers headed for the exit.

"I'll lead the way," Gary offered, "They don't know me, so you just follow." Mark was nervous. Up to last night, almost nothing had gone as planned. It had been a week since he left England. He was supposed to be at the Spanish border by now. Now, without documents, he had to rely on a man whom he had barely met. He stared after the determined Galluci who headed for the exit. Every inch of him spelled 'foreigner', so it was no surprise when two Feldwebels in full gear approached Gary and stopped him. Mark grabbed Willem's hand and stood still, causing the passengers behind him to bump into him. He moved out of the way of traffic.

"Stay," he ordered Willem, "Sit on the bench." He sidled over to the edge of the platform to get a better look. He saw Gary gesturing to the military police. One of the German officers turned him around, pressed a gun into his back, and marched him off to an office in the arrival hall.

Mark returned to the bench and plopped down beside Willem. His heart was beating. All was lost. They were on their own now with no papers, no plan and no contacts. He felt deeply fearful. It would be only a matter of time before the Abwehr bloodhounds were onto them. He had a horrifying vision of his future. Under the Geneva Convention, he was considered a spy. He might be executed.

Willem seemed to sense his despair.

"Are we still going to Bordeaux?" he asked.

"The Abwehr will be checking the trains going south. Even if we get to Bordeaux, we still need papers to get into Spain."

"Can we get new papers?" Willem asked.

"Not without going back to Nederland. And to do that we'd have to cross two borders without identification. It's not very likely to work."

"Do we have to go by train?" The lad asked innocently.

"You are right. Some things are in our favour. The French police are not looking for us. They might arrest us for not having papers but they would not harm us. Let's concentrate on avoiding the Germans."

Willem looked around the cavernous train station. "With so many people around, it should be easy to hide," he said optimistically, "We should go back to get new passports and may be new names. I don't like Zonder," he giggled. Mark hugged his shoulder and laughed with him. "I will need a new name too," he said. They sat watching the hundreds of passengers stream by. Mark stood up. "We should plan a route."

He told Willem to watch the baggage while he walked over to the news kiosk on the adjoining platform. He returned with a railway timetable and a road map of northern France.

"Willem, look at this map," he said excitedly. "If we can get to Dunkirque, we are very close to the Belgian border and look how little the distance is from there to Nederland."

"So we are going to Flanders?" Willem asked.

"Let's do it." Mark checked the arrivals and departures. The train for Dunkirque would leave from Platform 1B. Lugging their belongings, they worked their way to the far end. They did not see Galluci at the door to the arrival hall scanning the crowd, nor did Gary see them.

When they approached the ticket booth. Willem reached up, put his hands on the counter, and smiled at the agent. The man focused on the boy and handed over the train tickets and change without a second glance.

"That was good," Mark praised, "You kept him from getting a good look at me." Willem allowed a satisfied grin to cross his face.

They boarded the train at the last minute. By the time they had found their seat, the train was chugging out of the massive station. It clanged and shrieked its way through the switches of the main yard, bouncing its passengers around. The benches, facing each other, were upholstered to eliminate the worst of the train's shocks. Their buttocks did not concur.

The Dunkirque passengers were farm people, carrying their belongings in bundles wrapped with sturdy string. A buxom farmwife of immense girth straddled much more of the bench than the purchase of a single ticket entitled her to. The red kerchief over her hair was knotted under her chin. A blue cotton tent dress, spotted with minute samples of various meals, covered her black woollen stockings. Her only accessory was a silver cross. It hung from a thick silver chain and rested on her abundant abdomen. She had a gap-toothed smile that caused Willem to grin back.

Mark studied the ticket. They would have to change trains twice, once in Arras and then again in St. Omer. With eleven scheduled stops along the way, it would be close to five o'clock before they'd arrive at Dunkirque. The train chugged along as the dilapidated buildings in the centre of Paris gave way to suburban streets and finally the greenery of rural France.

Irregular-shaped farm plots clustered around tiny villages with narrow streets. Each town featured a Catholic Church, seemingly large enough to house the local population five times over. The forested areas were few in number but invariably surrounded a palatial mansion. At the station stop in Compiègne, Willem said, "Didn't we go through Compiègne last night?" Mark put his fingers to his lips, shaking his head.

"*Ah mijn Manneke, gij klapt Vlaams,*" the fat lady beamed in her broad vernacular – a mix of Dutch and French. As far as Mark could decode the heavy accent, she was French but spoke Dutch. She said she lived in Coudekerke just outside Dunkirque and explained that the official language of the northwestern part of the country was French but at home, her family spoke Dutch with a Flemish accent. She had never learned the Dutch language formally and could neither write nor read it.

Of course, she wanted to know where her fellow passengers were going. Mark's inclination was to misdirect the woman but since she was also going to Dunkirque, he told her they were going to Dunkirque and then on to Ostend. "Why Ostend?" she wanted to know. Mark adapted the Bordeaux story that he had a job consulting on the Ostend harbour.

"*Gij werkt voor de Boche, dan?*" she puffed with a disdainful look. Mark assured her quickly that he didn't work for the Germans; only a company that repaired harbour works. This seemed to lessen her disgust. She dug into her big valise, pulled out knitting needles the size of drumsticks and engrossed herself in knitting a coarse shape that might eventually grow into a garment. Willem looked at her inquiringly. She made a motion of pulling something over her head.

"It's a sweater," he translated.

In Compiègne, they managed to extricate themselves from her presence and headed to the lounge to spend the ten-minute stopover. Willem recited his German history lesson about the Fuehrer's visit to Compiègne a year ago. Neither of them felt the need to look at Hitler's historic railway car. They filled up on apples and croissants once more. Mark ordered a cup of acorn coffee. After one sip, he knew it would be his last sip ever. He threw the bitter liquid onto the tracks.

Back on the train, the knitter leaned over to Mark and said, "*Vous ne m'avez pas dit votre nom.*"

"Zonder," he said. He pronounced it Sondaire. "Mark Sondaire et Jean-Pierre," he added, pointing at Willem who rolled his eyes.

"Belges?" she pushed a little more. Mark hesitated to tell her his nationality and asked for her name.

"Madame van Ockeren," she volunteered. "My husband and I have a farm in Coudekerke, very close to Belgium."

The flood of further inquiries was stemmed by the appearance of a greying train conductor in a wrinkled, dandruff-laden SNCF uniform that must have been new in the Great War. His thin gold watch chain swayed back and forth as he bent down to study the tickets in exquisite detail. He expressed his approval by punching a hole in them.

Arras had a much greater military presence. It was here that the route to French Flanders split away from the track to Amsterdam and turned northwest towards the Channel. A special military train for Kriegsmarine and Wehrmacht personnel stood ready to depart for Calais.

"They are ordinary soldiers. They are not looking for us," Mark whispered to Willem. "Besides, no one knows who we are."

Madame van Ockeren gestured for Willem to stretch out on the empty space beside her. He folded up like a cat in a basket and slept. He slept through the stops in Lens and Hazebrouck. It was after four o'clock when they changed in St. Omer for the last leg to Dunkirque.

71

1941
FRIDAY, JUNE 27, 18:00 HRS CEST
RAILWAY STATION
KOWATICE, POLAND

Hauptsturmfuehrer Alexander von Becke got up from his uncomfortable seat and stretched his arms high over his head to unbend his cramped body. The 140-car train of flatcars – loaded with Panzer tanks and 88mm anti-tank guns – stood hissing at the platform of the grim, rubble-strewn railway station of Kowatice. From his seat atop one of the tanks, Alexander could see most of the town lying in ruins. The streets were no more than paths bulldozed through the debris of what once was the cultural centre of an ancient city.

It had been a week since he had kissed Paula and Willem goodbye. So much had happened. The day after Oberleutnant Streicher had driven him to the barracks, orders had come for his Waffen SS Brigade to stand ready for "further training" in Russia. Streicher and his inquisition were forgotten as Alexander became absorbed in the logistics of the move.

They had travelled for three days under spartan conditions. The men slept under tents and tarpaulins on the flatcars to stay near their equipment. The officers were crammed into an obsolete paint-peeled second-class compartment with springs poking through the upholstered seats. The only relief came at the station stops when they could get out and walk. Army kitchens, set up at the platforms, served good tasting, German food. However, since entering battered Poland, both the food and the landscape had become depressing.

Apart from the hardship of army travel by rail, the absence of a timetable was disorienting. They might be in Kowatice for ten minutes or ten hours, no one seemed to know. The idleness allowed his mind to imagine the experiences of Paula and Willem as they travelled south. Accounting for some missed connections or delays, they should be well across the Spanish border, free from the German hunt. They might even be in Lisbon by now, he calculated.

He climbed off the Panzer and joined the throng of military personnel pacing the platform. A civilian train stood ready to depart for Warsaw. The ill-clad, dejected passengers did not glance at the invading tank soldiers dressed in their black uniforms with the *Totenkopf,* the skull marking on their Panzer division caps.

At a decrepit-looking news booth with a pile of Polish-only newspapers, a single scenic postcard was for sale. It depicted the huge Sancta Teresa Basilica, now lying in ruins. "*Grüssen aus Kowatice, Poland,*" it read. He gave the dishevelled vendor ten times what the card was worth, which did not even evoke a hint of a smile. He sat down on a broken bench and wrote an innocent message to Paula and Willem. He addressed it to his home in Oegstgeest in the gleeful hope Streicher would monitor the mail and try to decode it. He deposited the card in the SS *Postfach,* the special mailbox for SS Troops; no stamp required.

72

1941
THURSDAY, JUNE 26. 17:10 HRS CEST
RAILWAY STATION
DUNKIRQUE, FRANCE

The salty breeze off the Channel greeted them as the train pulled into the Dunkirque station. Mark helped Madame van Ockeren down the steps of the railway car. She was out of breath from the sudden exercise. With her free hand, she grasped Willem's arm. *"Gij zijn 'Ollanders, Nee?"* Mark nodded that, yes, they were Dutch.

"Alors," she said with satisfaction, "I think you are trying to get back to the Low Countries, but you have no papers?" She looked straight into Mark's eyes. Mark was surprised at her astuteness.

"What makes you say that, Madame?" he said feigning surprise.

"I saw how afraid Jean-Pierre was when he saw the German soldiers in Arras and how you watched him. So I am asking you, do you need help?"

"We need a hotel for the evening, Madame," Mark said.

She made an exaggerated show of frustration. "Last year's battle at Dunkirque left only two hotels standing and the *Boches* get first choice. You need passports and identification. Do you have those?"

Mark decided to gamble. "We lost our papers in Paris and we are trying to get back to our country."

"Why such a long way around?" she asked.

She didn't wait for the answer as she hobbled away toward a man approaching from the other end of the platform. She took him by the arm and pulled him toward the new arrivals.

"This man and his son are Dutch travelers. They need our help, Jean-Luc," she explained. She told him what she knew.

Jean-Luc shook his head. "No, Annette, no," he said with pursed lips.

Madame Van Ockeren ignored his response. "Your no-good nephew in Bergues can help us. Let him do some good for once. He can get them into Belgium." Mark's instinct told him these were good people.

Jean-Luc was a taciturn man of about 55, thin as a proverbial rail with a sunburned face and eyes that twinkled. In spite of the man's accommodating mien, Mark could tell that he would have no difficulty stifling Annette and taking control should the need arise. He was dressed in the style of the region: corduroy pants, heavy high-top shoes, blue denim shirt, red neckerchief and a cloth cap.

"They're staying at *de Beyaard* tonight and that's that!" she asserted. Jean-Luc smiled, shook hands with Willem and Mark, picked up his wife's bundle, signalled for Mark to take his baggage and headed towards the exit. The station was crawling with Kriegsmarines of all ranks. Jean-Luc did not give them a glance. Outside, he led them to a horse and cart tethered to an iron ring in the wall of the partly destroyed railway station.

"Are we riding in this cart?" Willem asked eagerly. Jean-Luc bent down, swept Willem up and placed him on a side bench at the back of the cart. He hauled his wife's bundle in the back and motioned for Mark to join Willem. He helped his wife to her seat, undid the tether, climbed aboard, pulled on the reins, clucked his tongue and set out for Coudekerke.

Jean-Luc van Ockeren spoke very little as the cart made its way past destroyed farmhouses and burnt hulks of British military transports.

It was close to suppertime when they arrived at the van Ockerens' 200-year-old homestead. The weather-beaten sign above the doorway read *de Beyaard*. "It is the name of a famous church in Ghent. It has a church bell that alerts people to impending danger," Jean-Luc explained.

Mark had to stoop to enter a small, whitewashed inner courtyard with a row of potted geraniums along the walls, all in full bloom.

He opened the door at the end of the courtyard and again Mark had to stoop to avoid bumping his head. The living room was quite dark. A multi-frame window with greenish hand-blown glass provided a sombre light, aided by a small window on the sidewall. Shelves of crockery and copper pots of various sizes graced the kitchen's white and blue-tiled wall. A woodstove held a steaming pot with a wooden ladle.

"Annette, I made thick potato soup," Jean-Luc announced as Madame van Ockeren washed up. She hauled out a set of wheel-sized soup plates and ladled out four big helpings of the steaming puree.

Jean-Luc straightened up and addressed the beautifully carved Catholic cross on the wall. He made a long prayer in his Flemish dialect but switched to French when he asked for blessings on the strangers who had come into his care and promised to look after them.

Within a split second of the 'Amen', Willem dug into the soup. Annette beamed with approval. After their meal, she summoned Willem to help clear the table, while Jean-Luc sank into his rough-hewn easy chair that made up in sturdiness for what it lacked in comfort. He reached into a drawer and found a packet of pipe tobacco. He took his time tearing the wrapper open and sniffing at the contents. "Why are you running from the *Boches*?" he asked looking directly at Mark.

"We have no papers," Mark answered.

Jean-Luc took his time to light up. He sucked in short rapid breaths that made the tobacco flare. He held the matchbox over the bowl of his pipe to increase the draft. Mark suspected that he deliberately let it go between puffs, to give him something to do while thinking.

"Many people lose their papers but that doesn't make them afraid of the Germans," he finally said, letting out his first puff. Mark decided he needed this man's help and opened up a bit.

"The boy is Jewish. The Germans know about him and his family. His name is really Willem. I am a friend of the family and I was helping the boy out of the country though Spain. We lost our papers and now we need to get back to Nederland to get new documents and try again."

Jean-Luc considered this for a while. At least five slow puffs.

"Do you have money?" he asked.

"I have French francs and I need to exchange some for Belgian francs."

"Not at the bank, you don't; not without a passport."

Jean-Luc motioned for him to sit beside him. "My nephew Florien lives in Bergues, about 15 kilometres from here. It was a tourist attraction before the war but the British used it as a defensive position last year and now most of it is destroyed. Florien had a good café but there is no tourist traffic any more so to make a living he exports French cognac to Belgium."

"Exports, officially?" Mark asked for clarification.

"Of course not. He carries cases of the stuff across by himself. He often complains that he doesn't know what to do with the Belgian francs he has. So you could exchange your French francs with him."

"Do you think he would take Willem and me across?"

"We'll ask. I'll go with you tomorrow. We'll take the *calèche*, our church-going rig. We'll be there mid-morning."

73

1941
FRIDAY, JUNE 27, 06:00 HRS CEST
HOEVE DE BEYAARD
COUDEKERKE, FRANCE

The persistent crowing of the damned rooster slowly penetrated his brain. The last thing he remembered was sinking deep into a fragrant pile of hay under the thatched roof of the haystack. He lay dazed for a moment and reached for Willem beside him. He panicked. The boy wasn't there but then he heard the laughter. He crawled on his stomach to the edge of the haystack and looked down. Willem was gathering eggs with Annette. He put his feet over the hay, felt for the rickety ladder, and lowered himself to the outer courtyard.

"Look at all the eggs," Willem cried. Mark marvelled at the ability of his young charge to find joy in the moment. He put his arm around Willem's shoulder. Willem returned his hug by squeezing deeper into his arms.

Annette summoned them to breakfast. Homemade bread, eggs, bacon, fruit – no rationing here. Jean-Luc was amused to see Willem eat everything put before him. Annette packed a big lunch "for the road," she said, bustling about. "I am going with you," she declared, "I haven't been to Bergues since Easter."

A little after seven they set out in the surrey. The bright blue sky promised a warm summer day. The black leather roof was folded back. Annette sat across from Willem and Mark, chattering away and pointing out the many ruined homesteads while citing family relationships. Everyone they passed seemed to know the van Ockerens.

The sturdy mare clip-clopped to a steady rhythm and by half past eight they entered the southwest gate of Bergues. The sagging ruins of St. Winnoc's abbey dominated the centre of the old town.

"The enemy did that," Jean-Luc chuckled, "The Normans in 882."

He stopped in an alley just wide enough to allow for the brass oil lamps on either side of the surrey to squeeze through. Annette climbed out and stepped directly into Florien's doorway, followed by Willem and Mark. Jean-Luc drove to the city stables to board the horse and the vehicle.

Inside the house, Annette finished her explanation for the unexpected visit. Charlotte, Florien's wife busied herself making coffee. Real coffee, too. Florien sat on the sofa cogitating on Annette's scheme.

"I can't smuggle them across," he said as he raised his left shoulder and pursed his lips in a way that was very French. He was a tall man of about 35. His hair had a wave that ran from the back of his head to the front, like an incoming wave at the beach. His eyes were straight, yet gave the impression that they were focused on two different points in the distance. His nose attested to painful experiences in bar fights.

"It's one thing to smuggle alcohol, but smuggling people is something else. If I got caught they'd put me away for a long time," he objected.

"Bah, Flo, it isn't smuggling when you bring a boy home to his country," Annette rationalized. Florien pinched the space between his eyes and held it there, to show he was thinking.

"I want 1,000 francs," he said.

"Ah Flo," Annette protested, "That's 50 times more than I paid for a train ticket from Paris to Dunkirque."

Jean-Luc touched Florien on the shoulder and motioned for him to follow him into the courtyard. Charlotte served coffee and fresh croissants, still warm from the oven. When they returned, Florien looked subdued.

Jean-Luc spoke first. "The good son of my blessed departed brother Gérard," he pontificated, looking upward and crossing himself theatrically, "Will exchange 200 French francs into Belgian Francs and 200 French francs into Dutch guilders." Florien looked away. "He will do so at the official rate," Jean-Luc continued, "And at the border Monsieur Sondaire will pay Florien 300 francs."

Florien looked distinctly unhappy. Mark rose and offered his hand. Flo shook but averted his eyes. Mark calculated that the transaction would leave him with few French francs but the Belgian and Dutch money should last until they met up with Vreelink again.

"*Alors,*" Flo scraped his throat, "Early this afternoon I will lead you to the bus stop in the centre of town where you and the boy will take the bus to Hondschoote. I will board later but you will not look at or speak to me. With all the stops, it'll take more than an hour but you will be closer to the border. When you get off the bus, go to *L'Eglise des Pays Bas*, the Church where Pater Nils preaches. I will find you there."

After a sumptuous lunch where Willem outdid himself, they were ready to go. Annette cried and hugged Willem.

"You write me when you are safe, *mon petit gar*," she sobbed, "And you take care of him," she admonished Mark with a stern look.

Trailing Florien from a distance, they lugged their bags through the ancient town. Happy in the summer heat, children of Willem's age played in the fountain in the centre of town. Not a care in the world, Mark thought. That is how it ought to be for Willem.

The rickety green bus with its small windows squealed to a stop. Its hiccupping motor made it shudder intermittently. A half-dozen bundle-carrying passengers – mainly rural folk returning home after shopping – took their time getting aboard. After Mark and Willem had settled, Florien arrived and took a seat in front.

The conductor got up from his seat behind the driver. He opened the metal ticket book he carried on a chain around his neck and began asking passengers for their fare. The rate apparently depended on the distance travelled as he tore out differently coloured tickets from his inventory.

"*Hondschoote, deux,*" Mark said when the conductor reached them. The gaunt-looking man glanced up at the baggage in the overhead rack as if to say you pronounce it well but you are a foreigner.

The trip through well-tended farmland was pleasant. The bus stopped at empty crossroads along the way, discharging or boarding passengers without any indication where they came from or where they were going.

Hondschoote was a town of perhaps 8,000 people. At least a dozen catholic churches were within a one-kilometre radius of the largest one, *St. Vaats*, which dominated the central square. *l'Eglise Des Pays Bas* was on the northern outskirts of town. It was a white clapboard structure of modest design. Mark found Pater Nils bent over in the vegetable patch of the humble priory.

Pater Nils looked at the newcomer over his small, iron-rimmed glasses. "*Kan ik U bijstaan...*" he began in his Flemish dialect but brightened when he recognized the man who came up behind them.

"*Goeden dag, Flo,*" he smiled. "Come into the House of God."

In spite of the summer heat, the wooden church was remarkably cool. It smelled of fragrant wood. Florien explained the plight of his companions. Mark heard the word *Jood* several times. Pater Nils nodded then smiled at Willem and blessed him with a wave of the hand.

"Are you taking the *route secrète*, then?" he asked Florien, who nodded and ran his hand through his hair which caused the wave to roll back in.

"When do you think is best?"

"Six o'clock is usually when the dog patrol takes a break for supper."

Mark was surprised. "Is there no border post?" he asked.

"Not really son," Pater Nils said, "There never has been. There's only a path, no road. You never know when the patrols come by. Not only do we have the French and Belgian police but the Germans run patrols too."

Pater Nils invited them into the priory where his kind, grey-haired housekeeper served them coffee.

It was after five when Mark asked if they could eat the food Annette had prepared for their supper. "We don't know when our next meal will be," he apologized. Willem declined. Florien decided to partake of his aunt's offering. Pater Nils picked a piece of chicken and chewed contently.

"Time to go," Flo announced as he wiped his fingers on his corduroy pants and sucked the last bit of food from between his teeth.

From the garden shed, he retrieved a large wheelbarrow and wheeled it into the church and down the aisle. He stopped next to the altar, lifted the purple cloth and bent down to retrieve two 6-bottle cases of Hennessy Cognac. "The very best," he smiled as he hoisted the cases into the wheelbarrow. He went back outside, took a bunch of straw from the goat's stable, and covered the cases as best as he could. Willem, seated on a wobbly wooden chair looked on with evident aversion.

"Are you alright?" Mark asked.

"I think I ate too much," he said. He did look a bit out of sorts.

"We must go," Florien said and instructed them to keep at least 50 metres behind. "We'll go up the rise through the forest. I'll meet my client in the clearing. That is the border. You pay me there, you go down the hill and you will see Houtem, a village in Belgium. It's less than an hour's walk."

74

1941
FRIDAY JUNE 27, 18:00 HRS CEST
HONDSCHOOTE, FRANCE

The path was barely wide enough for two men to pass. Willem followed Florien's wheelbarrow with Mark close behind as they weaved their way through the trees. Willem was straggling. Mark took his bag to lighten the load. After half an hour, they reached the clearing. Willem lay down on the soft moss and looked ill.

Florien, anxiously waiting for his client, stomped around the clearing. He stopped at the edge of the trees. Mark heard a guttural sound and turned to see a man clamp an arm around Florien's neck while he pressed a knife against his back. The attacker yelled something unintelligible about money or supplies. He seemed less concerned with the presence of Mark and Willem. Another man, dressed completely in black stood behind him with a Walther P38 in hand.

The gunman approached Mark to pat him down for any weapons. Mark raised his arms indicating he was willing to be searched. As the man came in close, Mark smashed his forearms on both sides of the man's neck and kneed him in the groin. The man sank to the ground holding his crotch. His gun dropped to the soft earth. Mark swooped up the gun and motioned for the man with the knife to let go of Florien.

Willem had crawled into the treed area and was lying on his stomach, away from the altercation. He had dragged the suitcases with him. The knifer did not intend to let Florien go. It was a standoff.

A trampling noise from the forest betrayed the arrival of another man. A figure jumped from the forest but assessed the situation incorrectly. The man rushed at Mark who promptly shot him in the thigh. He fell next to his friend with the knackered testicles. Both moaned in unison.

Mark continued to aim the Walther P38 at the knifer who had retreated after seeing his comrades succumb. Mark put his left arm around

Florien's shoulder and placed the gun in his hand. "You take care of them," he said. He then turned to Willem who sat at the edge of the tree line.

"Mark, I am sick," Willem wailed. His trousers were wet. The boy had soiled himself. He stank.

"No time to be sick," Mark soothed, "I'll take the baggage. Let's go." He dragged Willem by the hand down the path towards Belgium.

He heard voices and the yappy barks of dogs. He caught a glimpse of a uniform. The French customs patrol! He could hear them crashing across the dead leaves.

"Come on!" he urged.

"I am so tired," Willem gasped.

"Don't think about being tired. Think about being alive. And run!"

Suddenly they were at the edge of a drop-off. At least 5 metres down. In the distance, through the trees, he thought he could see flat land.

"We've got to get down there; we can't go back," Mark gasped looking down the embankment. "They'll catch us if we do."

They made it down the hill faster than expected. Half falling, half running they plunged the last few metres to level dry ground.

The police had just reached the brink of the cliff. They looked with lazy satisfaction at the boy and the man running through the underbrush. It wasn't their problem anymore.

A few hundred metres inside Belgium, in a small copse of birch trees and surrounded by waist-high shrubs, they found a small stream that was fed from the hill they had just descended. Mark looked around. No one had followed them. Willem was exhausted. In the rush down the hill, he had vomited all over his shirt. His eyes barely focused.

Mark laid him down on the grassy slope by the stream. He took off Willem's socks, shoes, shirt and pants. His knees and arms were badly scratched from the descent down the hill. He used Willem's shirt to wipe the vomit and excrement. In the suitcase, he found Paula's underwear and used it as a towel. Her dress was pressed into service as a blanket. He rinsed out the fouled clothing in the stream and squeezed them as dry as he could. After hanging the washing on the branches of the shrubbery, he lay down beside Willem, holding him close, warming him with his body.

After an hour, Willem's breathing became more regular. Mark spotted a war-damaged farmhouse about half a kilometre away. During the time they had rested along the stream, no traffic had passed by.

Dusk settled but no lights showed in the ruined shell. It could make a shelter for the night. Willem made moaning noises as Mark woke him. He took the money belt and the Beretta and left everything else behind. He carried Willem piggyback to the ruins. A part of the roof hung over what once was a room. He found remnants of a bale of hay near the disintegrated barn and made a bed. He put Willem down and covered him with hay on top of Paula's dress.

"I'll be back soon." He kissed Willem's burning cheek. As the sun crept down the horizon he ran back to retrieve the belongings and the wet washing. When he got back, Willem had fallen asleep. He crawled up close to keep him warm.

The sun poured through the broken roof of the deserted homestead. The rest had been good for both of them. There had been no rain and Willem slept in the warm sunshine. Today the blue sky promised a warm summer day again. Time to move on. Willem had been sick a few more times and each time Mark had washed the fouled clothing in the creek. He squeezed the excess water out and hung them from a nail on a dangling joist. They were clammy but would dry in the sun. Somehow, today didn't feel like Sunday. The clip-clop of a buggy and horse in the distance must have been a family heading for early mass.

He decided to let Willem sleep some more. There was still some food in Annette's luncheon packet. Seated, with his back to the ruins he enjoyed the morning sun.

Willem stirred and asked for water. He looked a lot better. Mark discovered an old well with a broken bucket. Tying his shoe to the well rope, he collected enough water to slake Willem's initial thirst. He tasted the water. It still smelled of leather and tasted like rusted iron but it was not polluted. He let Willem sip.

After two more visits to the well, he offered Willem a piece of sausage but the boy turned his head in disgust and laid down to sleep some more. Ten minutes later, he sat up and retched again. The boy needed medicine.

Mark remembered that his mother always kept a supply of *Norit*, a charcoal-based pill that settled upset stomachs. The chances of a store being open on Sunday in Catholic Belgium were slim. He could jog the four kilometres to Houtem to see what he could find and then run back –

but he didn't dare leave Willem that long. If he carried both bags, Willem might be able to walk to town. Willem said he felt a little better.

They set out along the dirt road. Willem bravely stumbled along for half an hour but he suddenly sat down by the side of the road and said he could go no farther. Mark sat and watched as Willem laid down on the grassy berm and promptly fell asleep.

A farmer's cart carrying a young family approached. The man reined in his horse and looked at Willem lying down in the grass.

"My boy is sick," Mark said, "We need medicine." The farmer's wife stepped off the cart, rushed over to Willem and helped him sit up.

"There is a druggist in Houtem but the store won't be open until tomorrow morning," the man said as his wife helped Willem onto the cart.

"We are going to church," she said to Mark. "You can put your suitcases on the cart but you will have to walk behind. You can rest up in the park in the centre of town. It's a warm day."

The man appeared anxious to reclaim his leadership role. "Where are you headed?" he asked.

"We are on the road to Brugge."

"There is only one bus from Houtem to Brugge on Sunday. It goes at four o'clock. Leaves right across from the park too," he said. Mark trotted behind the cart relieved that Willem was resting and he did not have to carry the bags.

The town of Houtem had suffered little war damage, just a few bullet pockmarks in bricks and window sashes. The park, a lovely small oasis in the centre of town, was empty. Its focal point was a huge gazebo where the village band performed on summer evenings. It faced the large fountain where sculptures of dolphins and mermaids burbled sparkling water into a white-bottomed pool. A change cabin for the kids stood against a cluster of mature pine trees.

Mark thanked the family for the ride while Willem stretched out on a sun-dappled park bench.

"Willem, listen," he said bending over, "You must stay here with our baggage while I look for a drugstore. It's Sunday and the stores are closed. I am going to get charcoal tablets for you. I'll be back as soon as I can."

Stores ringed the park and the adjoining plaza. He found the apothecary; it was a sizeable store for a small town.

After mass ended, the town came alive. Buggies, calèches and other horse-drawn transportation lined up in front of the church as so many limousines at a diplomatic function. He stood at the drugstore and waited for a few pedestrians to pass. He tested the door handle. It was locked.

Going around the back, he discovered the store was attached to a home. He climbed the wooden steps to the back door. Closed. He used his Swiss Army knife to pry the door latch away from its casing. It gave easily.

He stepped inside and walked into the living area. Jesus stared out from a huge oil portrait over the dining room table and looked at him accusingly. Walking through the neat kitchen, he entered a hallway and found a narrow set of stairs leading to the store. He heard women's voices. He stopped in his tracks. The voices came from outside. Churchgoers passing by! He walked down the steps on tippy-toes. He found a display of home remedies under a glass-topped counter including the familiar white and blue Norit dispenser. He plunked a 20 Belgian franc note next to the cash register. An overpayment to be sure, but then it was special Sunday service. He retraced his steps and spotted a road map for Vlaanderen; he took it. He closed the back door behind him, certain that his entry would not be noticed until the next morning.

Back in the park, Willem was sitting upright on the bench. His feet rested firmly on the suitcases. He looked better, Mark thought. Willem made a face when he chewed a couple of the black pills and then was led to the fountain to wash it down.

After the noon meal, the good citizens of Houtem came out to enjoy the park. There were no German soldiers in sight. The local police man strolled by with his family in tow but the man was so engrossed in admonishing his daughter that he paid no attention to the strangers.

By three o'clock Willem revived. He was hungry, he complained. He had his eye on the ice cream vendor at the edge of the park. The vendor came past, jingling an old doorbell suspended from the cart handle. Mark noted it was Italian ice. As a kid, he had hated Italian ice because – as he complained to his mother – it was just coloured water. He bought a 25-centime cone for Willem and a small one for himself. He remembered his childhood well; it tasted like coloured water.

The bus pulled up a few minutes before four. Mark paid for two tickets to Brugge Markt, the central market square. Willem became more animated as the trip progressed.

It was a little after 5:30 when they arrived at the central square of Brugge. The centuries-old homes looked like the houses in Amsterdam. People of all ages crowded the outdoor terraces, enjoying a late afternoon in the sunshine. Among them were many German soldiers. No guns, no tanks, no goose-stepping.

Willem was asked once again to preside over the baggage while Mark went to look for a place for the night. In the Korte Zilverstraat, he found the Eyck Hotel. The pub was filled with German officers and their escorts. His immediate reaction was to step back but instead he walked over to the bar. The ample-bellied owner, wearing a bow tie and a white wrap-around apron all the way down to his shoes, looked at him inquiringly.

"I would like a room for the night for me and my son," he said.

"*Ah 'Ollander, ey?*" the man said, recognizing the Dutch accent, "Well, a few of these gentlemen may require a room later," he said with a lascivious nod in the direction of his clientele.

"Over here," he said directing him toward a badly lit corner alcove where a small desk pushed against the wall served as the check-in counter. "I can spare a room on the third floor," he said rummaging through a pile of forms. "I'll need both your passports and persoonsbewijzen."

Mark grabbed a wad of Belgian francs in his pocket and waited for the man to look up. He plunked two 100-franc bills on the desk, at least twice as much as the room would cost. "Those are the only papers I have," he said making a downtrodden face.

The owner looked at him sympathetically. Mark leaned back and nodded in the direction of the Germans in the bar. "I see," the man smiled, "If you're out of here by eight o'clock in the morning, it's okay."

"Can we eat something here tonight?" Mark asked.

"You have nerve, don't you?" he laughed. "Sure, but all I have is fried eggs and *patates frites*." Mark could smell and taste it already. He collected the key, walked outside to get Willem and the suitcases and entered the bar. Willem stopped, alarmed by the many German uniforms.

"They don't know about us," Mark whispered softly, "Keep going."

Later that night they went down to the bar for their eggs and French fries. The German crowd had pulled their tables together. The long rows of arms upon shoulders swayed to the songs of the Bavarian beer halls, "*In München steht ein hofbräuhaus, Eins, zwei saufa.*"

They slept in a real bed that night. Tomorrow they would be back in Nederland.

75

1941
MONDAY, JUNE 30, 10:15 HRS CEST
REICHSKANZLEREI, UNTER DEN LINDEN
BERLIN, GERMANY

"I need your advice in a matter of extreme delicacy," Himmler said, pacing up and down his spacious office. He rested his right arm on the marble fireplace mantel. Sturmbannfuehrer Schellenberg was among the few people from whom Himmler would accept advice. They had worked together in the Nazi party since 1932 and Schellenberg often brought a sober second thought to some of Himmler's more impetuous schemes.

The Reichsfuehrer described the Fuehrer's desire to re-constitute a monarchy in the occupied territories that would subsequently become member states in a Greater Germany. He told Schellenberg, "The plans for the Nordic countries and Belgium are well advanced but Nederland is the problem. Queen Wilhelmina and her daughter will never acquiesce."

Schellenberg wondered what new royal intrigues might be in the wind. Eight months ago, he had been sent to Portugal to meet with the Duke of Windsor to persuade him to reassume the Crown in a new Great Britain in the Nazi Empire. The mission had been a partial success. The Duke had not agreed but neither had he closed the door. He was bitter about his abdication over marrying the divorced commoner Wallis Simpson who was now his wife. Schellenberg had remained in contact with the Duke.

Himmler described the Abwehr's efforts in finding the natural son of Princess Juliana. "The Fuehrer has met this young chap and was quite taken with him. He deemed the boy to be an excellent prospect to represent the House of Orange as a future King."

"But that is excellent Herr Reichsfuehrer." Schellenberg said, "The situation in Nederland is farther advanced than my efforts with England."

"I believed that to be the case also, until upon further investigation, the Abwehr found that the boy's natural father is Jewish, which makes him totally unacceptable. I have ordered that the boy must be made to disappear." Schellenberg moved closer to Himmler's desk.

"You mean killed, Herr Reichsfuehrer?" his interest was piqued.

"That is a rather crude way of expressing it. However, a British agent has kidnapped the boy and is trying to take him to England via Spain. The boy and the agent were sighted in Paris but have not been seen since. If the boy reaches England, Churchill will certainly exploit our embarrassment for political purposes. But if they are still somewhere on the Continent, we must find them."

Schellenberg took a moment to compose his thoughts. "Forgive me, Reichsfuehrer, but I think the boy's 'disappearance' will have unwanted consequences. In history, the murder of a royal heir has always had severe repercussions. None of them ever produced the desired outcome."

He leaned in closer to Himmler and lowered his voice to a conspiratorial level. "With respect, Herr Reichsfuehrer, the imagined embarrassment for the Fuehrer is more your discomfiture than his. I suggest that you merely inform our Leader that your thorough investigation has discovered the young man's Jewish ancestry and that you will find the boy and sequester him."

"Your suggestion ignores the fact that the Dutch government in exile in London might expose the captivity of the boy."

"Again with respect, Reichsfuehrer, neither the Dutch government nor Queen Wilhelmina are likely to show public concern over an illegitimate heir they have done their best to hide for more than a decade."

Himmler rose. "I appreciate your view as always. I am turning the case over to you. Put the boy under the protection of The Reich and then we shall reconsider our position."

Schellenberg returned to his office and told his secretary to call Oberleutnant Kurt Streicher of the Abwehr in The Hague.

Streicher answered the call within minutes. Schellenberg was terse.

"Your orders are to take the boy into custody and bring him immediately to me in Berlin. He is not to be harmed in any way. Do you understand? Any harm to the boy will have grave consequences for you."

"With respect Sturmbannfuehrer," Streicher said, "The boy has not been seen for five days."

"Find him and bring him to me in Berlin," Schellenberg yelled and slammed down the phone.

76

1941
MONDAY, JUNE 30, 06:30 HRS CEST
HOTEL VAN EYCK, MARKT 31
BRUGGE, BELGIUM

Early sunbeams bored their way through the slats of the venetian blinds. Willem woke first. He punched the shapeless form under the sheets next to him.

"Come on Mark, let's get something to eat." Mark groaned and luxuriated in the softness of the bed. Within minutes, Willem had run the bath and was splashing about when there was a knock on the door. Mark, still dressed in his underwear opened the door as far as the security chain would allow. A skinny man dressed in a white coverall and white shoes smiled at him.

"Milkman!" he announced cheerfully.

"We don't need any milk," Mark said trying to shut the door. The man's shoe was wedged in between the door and the jamb.

"You may need me," the man said jovially. "Meneer van Eyck, the owner wanted me to make sure you left on time." He looked innocent enough. "Do you need any help?" he asked.

Mark undid the latch and offered the man the only chair while he dressed. Except for his white cap, the man looked like a tennis official. He was about 35, of average height. His bulging eyes and lopsided smile gave him a look of constant amazement. A little black hairy presence under his nose suggested that a moustache was either growing or dying there.

"Meneer van Eyck thought you might not have the right papers. He said you had your son with you, so he didn't think that you were a criminal, yet you were trying to avoid German inspection. Is that so?"

Mark decided to gamble. "We could use help in getting back to Nederland because, it is true; we have no papers." Mark gave him the rehearsed story of being robbed in Paris on the way to Bordeaux.

"Meneer van Eyck thinks it is more likely that you are in deeper trouble than that." Mark decided he might as well tell more. He wasn't likely to get very far without help from the local people.

"I can tell you that the boy is wanted by the Abwehr. We must get back to Nederland so we can get new papers and get him away from them."

"Are you from the Resistance then?" he asked in genuine awe.

Mark thought about the answer. "Yes, you could say that," he confessed. This seemed to spark the milkman to even greater enthusiasm.

"My friends and I are part of the *Weerstand* - the Belgian Resistance. We monitor marine traffic en route to Antwerp. The estuary runs through Nederland, and we operate very closely with a Dutch marine group in Vlaanderen. If you want to cross the border, I can call on them. They operate a cell in Sluis just a few kilometres north of the Belgian border. Once you are there, they can help you further."

Willem listened and put in an urgent request, "Can we eat first?"

"Later," Mark said curtly. He knew that if something was too good to be true, it usually was too good to be true, yet something made him trust this bubbly man.

"My milk route is from Brugge to Koolkerke, where I live and from there it is only a 15-minute ride to St-Anna-ter-Muiden on the Dutch side"

"What shall we call you?" he asked.

"My nom-de-guerre is Potras."

"Do you have a truck, Potras?" Mark asked.

"I have my milk tricycle," he said. When he saw Mark's smirk, he added hastily, "It's motorized."

The commercial tricycle, an everyday sight in the Low Countries, was essentially a load platform on two wheels, propelled like a bicycle. However, this rig had a small gasoline motor. The platform held two huge gleaming copper kettles.

"They hold 30 litres of milk each," Potras explained. "I park on the street and housewives bring their pots; I fill them. I normally carry four kettles," he added, "So I have room for both of you today."

Mark and Willem, squeezed between the milk kettles as Potras wheeled them through the outskirts of Brugge onto the Brugsche Steenweg. Willem was thrilled to be in the open air. He waved at pedestrians and the few passing motor vehicles. At first, Mark had admonished Willem for waving at people, but he was now convinced it made their presence more credible.

In the village of Koolkerke, Potras stopped in front of a small stone home along the cobblestone highway. The rusted enamel nameplate dangling from the doorjamb read *Kouwenhoven*.

"My mother's place," Potras said, seemingly unaware he had betrayed his own code name. "I live here. Come on in."

"Ah Philippe, back so early," the rosy-cheeked matron exclaimed, "Who are your friends?"

"These people need a ride to the border, but the little manneke is hungry. He hasn't eaten yet."

"Neither has the tall one," Mark added hastily. Mevrouw Kouwenhoven quickly cut four heavy slabs of bread from a freshly baked loaf and slathered butter on them with a practiced hand.

"I only have smoked ham," she said apologetically while she stuffed big chunks between two slices of bread. The ham made the sandwich lumpy. She solved the problem by slamming her open hand down on it.

"Off you go," she said handing each a mega sandwich, "Philippe will give you milk." Expressing his thanks, Mark bent down and kissed her red work-roughened hand.

"Oh you charming devil," she tittered with a wide smile.

Philippe Kouwenhoven, a.k.a. Potras hit the road and bounced over the cobblestones at the top speed of 25 kilometres per hour. After a 30-minute drive, they had reached the border zone.

Philippe suddenly steered his vehicle to the left and rode onto a poorly maintained gravel path. Mark felt like his brain rattled around in his skull. Philippe stopped and pointed north toward the village, 500 metres away.

"Follow this mud track and tell the folks at the café that Potras sent you." With that, he lifted their baggage off the strange conveyance and shook hands.

"I must get back to my customers," he said, "God be with you." He turned his tricycle and bucked his way back to the highway.

77

1941
MONDAY, JUNE 30, 12:00 HRS CEST
KOOLKERKE, BELGIUM

The village looked like something out of a film-noire. The cobblestone main street was wide enough for two lanes of cars, but there was no traffic. It was getting warm. A mangy dog had scavenged enough food and now slept in the centre of the road. Every house was shuttered tight, looking gray and dusty in the bright midday light that allowed only a narrow sliver of shadow.

They walked down the silent street. The dog, its left ear missing, awoke and crawled into the shade of a tractor. It growled dutifully at them as they passed, then sank back into sleep. Above the window, faintly discernible in the aged woodwork, Mark saw the word 'Café'.

Three men in uniform with the insignia of the Belgian border control occupied the corner table. They had napkins tucked into their collars and were putting forkfuls of cheese into their mouths and pouring gulps of red wine into their throats. They continued to eat. They were the only people in the room, except for a muscular man seated at the back of the room. His feet were propped up on the chair while he placed the cards of his patience game. They watched him peel each card loose from the pack, stare at it intently and place it face-up on the marble tabletop.

"Sorry to interrupt but I was asked to say that Pot—" The card player looked up held his index finger to his lips and nodded toward the diners.

"Come with me," he said and led them on a path next to the tractor. The dog was still asleep.

"There is a house at the end of this path. It is in Nederland."

"Are there no controls?"

"They are eating. Good thing you came at lunchtime. Go and be good." Mark turned to thank the man but he was already heading back to his card game. The dog got up and sniffed at his pant leg. He shooed the animal away.

It was hard to determine where they crossed the border. Viewed from the wooded area, the house looked deserted. Mark told Willem to stay behind the tree in the back yard while he looked around.

He crouched down close to the wall to avoid being spotted from the windows. He made his way to the gravel street in front. An old Ford T was parked in the driveway next door. It bore a licence plate with the letter Z for Zeeland. He was back in Nederland!

The house looked like any other in the dusty street. It was made of brick and looked like a drawing by a first-grade student. A door with a window on each side of the house, a chimney on the A-frame roof and a potted geranium in each window. The only thing missing was a plume of smoke coming from the chimney.

When he returned, Willem was not alone. A burly man with a three-day growth of beard stood behind him, his hairy arm across the boy's chest. Another, equally intimidating character stood by, holding their baggage. His face was memorable. An angry scar ran down from the corner of his mouth to his neck.

"Who are you?" the bearded one asked.

Mark observed the men carefully. "Potras said to tell you he brought us here and that you would help us get back to Holland,"

"Why would we do that?"

"Because we lost our papers and we need to get new documents."

"Why don't you go to the town hall here and get temporary papers?" Rather than argue, Mark thought it best to gain their understanding.

"The boy is Jewish and I was on my way to take him to Spain when we were robbed in Paris. So we came back to get new papers." The story seemed to have some effect on the ruffians.

"Well, come on inside and we'll talk about it," Scarface said. He released Willem and showed Mark into the front room.

"You two wait here," Beard snapped as he left the room and locked it behind him. It was a barren room. Cheap Cezanne prints of fruit in various positions on plates and bowls served as wall decorations. The floor was made of plain planking, painted smooth in an ugly frog-green. A big doily dominated a small table. An empty vase stood in the centre. A woman's hand was obviously missing.

Four kitchen chairs stood in disorganized positions around the table. A half-eaten pear was being visited by a horde of persistent flies. On the mantle, an ancient wind-up clock tick-tocked the silence away.

They sat but didn't speak. The ticking made the wait seem longer. Finally, a key turned in the lock. Scarface burst in and lunged at Mark.

"You Nazi-loving prick," he yelled as he knocked Mark onto the floor. "Trying to trick us so you could turn us in to the Gestapo."

"You've got it all wrong," Mark said struggling to his feet. Willem made himself small by burrowing into the corner, his eyes filled with fright.

"Wrong?" Beard sneered, "Look what we found in your suitcase," he yelled, waving Willem's Jeugdstorm uniform. "A poor Jewish boy with a Nazi uniform in his suitcase! You want us to believe that."

"It can be explained," Mark said.

"Yeah? How do you explain this?" he asked, holding up a picture of Willem with the Fuehrer. The unexpected turn of events hit Mark in the gut. He did not know such a picture was among Willem's cache of photographs. He did not answer. This looked bad.

"Tie them up and put them in the shed," Beard told Scarface. "We'll ask the captain what to do with them."

Scarface grabbed Mark's shoulder. He was just about to say something but the words never quite exited his mouth. Instead, he yelped, as Mark kicked him in the shin. The man bent forward holding his leg. While he bent over, Mark delivered an upper cut to his chin. Scarface took a few baby steps backwards toppled on his back right in front of Willem who, in dread, tried to shrink himself even tighter into the corner.

Beard launched himself wildly at Mark who sidestepped him and clamped a forearm around the man's neck as he passed. Mark ran forward and rammed Beard's head into the wall.

"Some fancy moves you got there," an older voice said. A man dressed in the uniform of the merchant marine stood in the doorway, a gun in his hand. "What's going on here?"

"Potras helped me get this lad into Nederland," he said pointing at Willem. "He directed me to these gangsters who have taken it into their head that I am a Nazi."

"Let's sit down and discuss this," the mariner said putting his white uniform cap next to the fly-bitten pear. "My name is Captain Simon Vorders of the Dutch ferry system. I sail the route from Breskens to Vlissingen. Your story intrigues me. Tell me more."

"First tie him up," Beard yelled from the floor, still clutching his head. "We found a picture of the boy with Hitler and a Jeugdstorm uniform."

"I don't think there is a need for that. There are the two of you, then there is me and the gun makes four. I don't think even this gentleman, who seems to be an expert in hand-to-hand combat, wants to defy those odds." Willem still stood frozen in the corner.

"It's okay lad," the Captain said, "Why don't you go into the kitchen and see what there is to eat or drink." Willem was anxious to leave the room. Mark could hear him fumble in the kitchen. Scarface and Beard got up and went outside to repair themselves or nurse their egos.

"Now, let's have the story," Vorders said, resting the gun before him on the table. Mark told his tale again of smuggling Willem out via Bordeaux and the subsequent tribulations that landed them in Nederland again.

"That doesn't explain the Jeugdstorm uniform and the picture."

"Willem's father is a member of the NSB," Mark said. "The boy was selected to meet the Fuehrer as representative of the Jeugdstorm. A picture was taken; the boy kept it as a souvenir. A few weeks ago, his parents learned that the boy – who is adopted – is Jewish. I was asked to get the boy out to England. That's it."

"And who asked you to do this?" the Captain asked.

"The Resistance in Amsterdam," Mark lied, figuring that since Amsterdam was the largest city it would be the most difficult to find anybody. Mark tried to re-direct the conversation. "But now let me ask you something. Are you part of the Resistance in Zeeland?" Vorders looked annoyed.

"For a stranger who has a Jeugdstorm uniform and a picture with the Fuehrer that is quite an impertinent question."

"Well, are you? I am asking because if you are in radio contact with London you could find out that I am legitimate."

"Let me tell you something. I am an old navy man and I recognize professional training when I see it. Have you been sent by London?"

Mark shuffled uneasily in his chair. He smiled at the captain and bent down as if he was pulling up a drooping sock. He quickly retracted the Beretta and pointed it straight at Vorders.

"You are right," Mark said standing up. "You can verify my status by radio. I have not much in the way of documentation to prove it except this Beretta. The Abwehr is pursuing us. I need your help to get back to Amsterdam to get new papers. You may not trust me but if I was a Gestapo man, I can assure you that you'd be dead by now." Scarface and Beard who had overheard the discussion broke into the room but the Captain waved them off.

"You are persuasive, when you wave that gun, son. I kind of believe you," Vorders said calmly. "What do you need?"

"Get us on the ferry and radio your contact in London saying that Smokey has arrived and is going to Oz."

"If London asks for verification is there anything you can give us?"

"Two names: Alice and Caspers."

Captain Vorders, Mark and Willem left the house without a goodbye to the bullies. The captain chatted away as they headed for the bus stop in the old town of Sluis. He explained that this part of Nederland had no road connection to the rest of the country except through Belgium. There was no railway. The only exit was by ferry to Vlissingen's railway terminal.

The bus arrived at the Breskens terminal an hour before the ferry's departure time. The weather was turning. A miserable drizzle hung over the Scheldt estuary. Everything looked bleak. The Captain headed for the radio hut at the foot of the pier.

Inside the terminal, Mark scanned the crowd for any surveillance. He waited at least five minutes before he felt safe enough to buy the tickets. He didn't particularly like the look of the ticket clerk. The man had been eying him constantly. He was a wan-looking young man with black hair upon which he had used a generous amount of hair cream. He was writing something in a ledger and did not look up when Mark approached him.

"Two one-way tickets to Amsterdam please. Third class."

"Lovely, I am so jealous; I love Amsterdam," the greaser lisped in an effeminate singsong voice. Mark handed over the money and took the tickets but as he turned and left, he felt the man's eyes follow him.

The waiting room was drafty but Mark's mood improved when the Captain returned from the radio hut with his thumbs up. He had confirmation from London. "We received confirmation right away."

The ferry began boarding the waiting vehicles. Mark carefully scanned each one as it drove up the ramp. Two German freight trucks did not cause any undue alarm. The crews were ordinary ranks.

In spite of his trusting demeanour, Captain Vorders stuck close to them during the boring, mist-enshrouded crossing, walked with them to the railway platform and stayed until the two o'clock train for Amsterdam was ready to board.

"I don't know your name and if you told me, I wouldn't believe it," Vorders said, "But I hope you will be successful in protecting the lad. When you are back in London, tell them there are hundreds of men like me who are willing to resist the Germans anyway we can, but we need help. We need a national organization that will connect the many little groups that are operating now without any direction." The pale blue eyes in his weather-beaten face bore deeply into Mark's. "I hope I didn't misplace my trust in you," he said.

He lifted Willem on the train, heaved the baggage in the overhead rack and shook Mark's hand. He stood on the platform as the train pulled out. Willem waved at him until he disappeared from view.

They changed trains in Roosendaal. Willem pointed to the First Class lounge where they had spent time with the kindly Wehrmacht captain. It had only been a week but it seemed like a lifetime.

The stop in Rotterdam reminded Mark of the Boy Scout trip and his encounter with Kurt Streicher, the spy. Jenny had been there. Jenny! Now that he was back in Nederland, everything would remind him of Jenny.

He had never said so aloud, but he still loved her. Her positive outlook on life, her laughter, her assertiveness, her warmth; he missed her. Many nights he had wanted to talk to her, to hear her perspective, to reinforce his courage. He wished he could ask her why she hadn't waited for him but he knew the answer. He was gone and she wanted to live her life. Now she was married and gone forever.

"Are you crying?" Willem asked.

"I'm not crying. I am thinking of where we will stay tonight."

"My mother looks like that when she is going to cry."

"Never mind. Get your stuff together. We'll be getting off in Leiden."

"But you bought tickets for Amsterdam."

"That was for the Captain's benefit. It's better that he doesn't know where we are going."

It was close to seven when they walked out of the Leiden station. Mark felt confident that the Abwehr had no idea that he was back. He decided to pass by his home on the Morssingel and took the shortcut through Haverzaklaan, the workman's neighbourhood.

Many residents sat on kitchen chairs in front of their tiny homes, inspecting the passers-by and enjoying a bit of sunshine after a rainy day. Some nodded at the young man and his son. At the corner of the Spoorstraat, about 50 metres from his home, he told Willem to stay and watch a group of girls playing hopscotch.

Willem made a lip and assumed a disinterested pose, leaning against a lamppost. Behind the fence of his home, he saw laundry hanging on the line. It was Monday, washday. Someone had to be home because it was time to take it off the line. He walked back and called for Willem. He carefully lifted the hinge of the gate and crept up to the window. His mother sat reading a magazine. He softly ticked on the window with a fingernail. She looked up. He could see her gasp. She ran to the back door. She wanted to speak but he motioned for her to be quiet. He hustled Willem inside and brought the suitcases in.

"Mark," she gasped, "You are back." She embraced him. "I didn't expect to see you until the war is over," she whispered. "Where have you been?"

He took Willem by the hand. "Mother this is Willem von Becke. He is a Leidener and we were on our way to England because he will be safer there. Things went wrong and we would like to stay here for the evening." Mother Zonder nodded without comprehending. "We were in Paris when we lost our travel documents and we had to come back to get new papers."

Still not quite understanding she said, "Welcome Willem. I think you would like the room of Mark's sister Jo. She is away on holidays." She looked at Mark who nodded his agreement. "And how did you like Paris?" she asked Willem.

"I did not see it. It was night, some people were killed, and my mother was hurt badly. She is in the hospital."

She looked shocked and asked Mark, "Is that true?" He spread his hands outward in a gesture that spoke of regret and admission.

Willem put his hand on her elbow and said in his most worldly voice, "Mark and Gary got us out of there. It's okay."

Mother Zonder, who firmly believed that food brought solace in times of distress, said, "You boys must be starving. I'll fix sandwiches."

Mark followed her into the kitchen. "Where's Dad?" he asked.

"He's in Amersfoort, at a centre for officers released from prisoner-of-war camps. He is doing administrative work as a volunteer. He will be back in two weeks. Go sit with Willem," she said as she took the bread from the large breadbox.

Willem was looking at the pictures on the mantelpiece. "Is that you?" he asked, pointing to a picture of a boy flanked by two girls.

"Yes that's me and my sisters, when I was ten."

"Is that you and your sisters too?" he asked pointing at a picture of Mark with his arm around Jenny.

"That was taken in 1939 at Sinterklaas evening. The girl is Jenny. She was my girlfriend but she is married to someone else now."

"What happened?"

"The war happened. That's what."

"Don't you like her anymore?"

"C'mon let's see if we can help my mother."

After Willem had helped her set the table, Mother Zonder served sandwiches of cheese and jam. As a special treat, she had concocted a tasty dessert from macaroni and powdered milk and sweetened by saccharine.

"Our rations for fresh milk and sugar are gone for the week," Mother Zonder said. "Your father had to take his rations with him, leaving us with little. Luckily I had some powdered milk left."

"I like it," Willem declared.

Mother Zonder told stories of Mark's youth, how he went fishing in the canal and fell in only to be saved by a neighbour; Willem loved it.

When Willem grew tired, Mark showed him to his room. Willem was quiet as Mark readied the bed.

"Can I see my house tomorrow?" he asked suddenly.

Mark was taken aback. "No, no that's not possible, Willem."

"But Papa might be home and he would want to see me."

"I don't think your father will be there, but the Abwehr might be there waiting and watching for you and me."

"Can we stay here then, until the war is over? Your mother likes me and then I can go and see my friends from school some time."

"Oh, Willem, you know that is not possible." Mark put his arms around Willem and held him close. "I'll look after you but we cannot stay in Nederland."

After he came downstairs, his mother talked about family and life under occupation. She avoided any questions about his mission. She was an officer's wife after all.

"You haven't asked about Jenny," she probed gently.

"Well what about Jenny?" he said curtly. "She married Henk van Weeren from Groningen; end of the story."

"She writes often and she calls from time to time and talks about her daughter who is almost six months old."

Mark put his head in his hands to hide his emotions. "A baby? Why didn't you tell me that last week, when I was here?"

"You left before we had a chance to tell you. Last week she called again. I couldn't tell her you were here of course but I did say we thought that you were in England and doing well."

"What did she say?"

"She was thrilled that you were safe. She wanted to come and see me to hear more. I discouraged her of course. I can tell you, that girl has not forgotten you." A sudden elation came over him. She still cared for him. His mother sensed his brightening mood and squeezed his arm. "Perhaps you'll get a chance to talk to her," she ventured.

"I'll be here only as long as it takes to get new passports and identity cards and then we are off again."

It was nine o'clock. He kissed his mother and said goodnight. His bedroom walls were still decorated with pictures of his favourite soccer team. His swimming medal hung from the same nail he had pounded in the wall when he was 12, the same age as Willem was now. He suddenly realized how young Willem was and how much the boy still had to endure. He slept in the bed of his childhood. He felt utterly safe for the first time in a long while.

78

1941
TUESDAY, JULY 1, 09:15 HRS CEST
ZONDER RESIDENCE, MORSSINGEL 25
LEIDEN, NEDERLAND

Mark sat down for the meagre breakfast of bread and a single slice of cheese. Mother Zonder told him about a comedian on the radio who had invented 'shuffle cheese' sandwiches. "You simply move the cheese ahead of your teeth as you eat the bread. When the bread is gone you have a slice for the next sandwich." He laughed but remained lost in thought.

"Should you call Jenny?" his mother asked, "I have her number."

"I am on a mission, Mother. I shouldn't even be here, let alone contacting the home of a Waffen SS official." Mother Zonder looked distinctly unhappy. Willem – still moping because Mark had insisted that he stay under cover with Mother Zonder at home – played with his breakfast of a slice of bread and homemade blackberry jam.

Before leaving the house, Mark made sure it wasn't being watched. The walk to the house on the Beestenmarkt took only five minutes. A week ago, he had picked up documents for Willem and Paula at the same place. He rang the doorbell. No one answered. *The Duke,* the nearby pub, was filled with early coffee-klatchers. He took a spot at the window that allowed a good view of anyone approaching the house.

An hour later, after he had swallowed three cups of awful chicory coffee, he saw Voddeman turn the corner. Mark quickly exited the pub and snuck up behind him, just as Voddeman reached for his keys.

"We were expecting you," Voddeman said, without surprise, "Come in!"

"How could you expect me when no one knows I'm back?"

"Your ferry captain did get through to London. They concluded that your only choice was to come back here and get new papers. That's why I was out finding more security paper for Pliny. We still have your negatives and Willem's, but we must wait for the right paper to come in. The documents won't be available until tomorrow afternoon, at the earliest."

The house that looked so tiny from the street was built in the 1700s. In the fashion of those days, it was about five times deeper than it was wide. A long hallway extended for the entire length of the house with five rooms off to the side and a small patio at the back.

A sudden noise in the hallway startled them. Mark ducked into a side room and reached for the Beretta. He relaxed when Dirk Vreelink entered through the patio door. They solemnly shook hands and Mark – in a few sentences – brought him up to date about his return from Paris.

"I hear you ran into the Abwehr there."

"We did and Paula was seriously injured. We left two Germans and one Dutch Abwehr guy behind. They were in bad shape."

"First, good news," Vreelink said, "A message from London that Paula is being taken care of by the Resistance and is expected to recover fully."

"Willem will be thrilled. He needs some good news," Mark said.

Vreelink opened the door to his workroom. It was a spartan office with an old roll-top desk with cubbyholes fitted against the back panel. Mark's Colt .45 sat on top of the desk. Vreelink put the gun into one of the largest cubbyholes, rolled the top down and locked it.

"Now," he said turning to face Mark, "You said 'we' when you mentioned Paris. When we heard the story, we wondered how you fought off three bad guys. Who helped you?"

"An American, Gary Galluci. He's an FBI 'off the books' guy. He saved our ass in Paris. You remember, we met him in front of the von Becke home. It turns out that he was sent by Willem's natural father, a wealthy musician in New York."

"Where is he now?"

"The last we saw of him was when he was arrested by the Germans at the Gare du Nord in Paris."

"I hope they locked him up. You don't need competition. The job is difficult enough."

"He wants to get Willem to New York. My job is to get him to England. We agreed to cooperate and let the powers in London sort it out."

"We do not need outsiders to get involved in this," Vreelink admonished. "Another thing," he continued, "Choosing your mother's home as a safe house was stupid. When the Abwehr realizes that you are in the country, that's the first place they'll go." He shook his head in dismay. "I have people looking for a different location for tonight."

Voddeman who had gone to the pub for more coffee brought sandwiches with ham for lunch. Mark unwrapped the package containing thick slabs of coarse-wheat bread and tough ham; it tasted wonderful.

"How many ration coupons did that cost you?" Mark asked.

"Don't worry, Pliny does a great job of counterfeiting," Voddeman said proudly, "We have enough coupons to last us a while."

Over lunch, Vreelink attacked his sandwiches with gusto and explained that at least a dozen escapees – he called them 'England-farers' – had used the route to Switzerland but every run had encountered problems. Crossing the Alps from Annecy to Chamonix proved too demanding for people inexperienced in mountain travel and the route through Germany to Basel in Switzerland was too heavily policed.

"Sweden is the route you should consider," Vreelink said. "Ships still sail from Delfzijl to Stockholm in the northeast. Allard Oosterhuis, a Resistance leader, owns two commercial freighters. He could help." He finished his sandwich and picked bits of food from between his teeth with the writing end of a pencil. He looked around and didn't know what to do with it. He finally wiped it on his pants.

"We could take the train to Groningen," Mark said, warming up to the idea of a new route. "It takes less than five hours and then it is only 25 kilometres to the Delfzijl harbour."

"Yeah, well let's see what we can get done today."

At the end of the hallway, a glass covered atrium that once was an orangery now served as a studio-cum-print shop. A cumbersome Philips shortwave radio transmitter filled a shelf on one wall, well within reach of someone seated at the huge layout table where papers, inks, photographs and a row of rubber stamps were spread in random disorder.

"Pliny works here," Vreelink said, referring to the round-backed gnome who stood cutting sheets of paper in precise measurements.

"Pliny was serving a long prison term for counterfeiting guilders when the Resistance liberated him from the penitentiary," Dirk said by way of introduction, "He is still on the run from the law but now plies his trade in the battle with Germany."

Pliny, showing a row of really bad teeth, took a polite little bow and stuck out his hand in greeting. If he wore a pointed red hat and let his beard grow longer, he would fit right in with Snow White's entourage.

They left Pliny at the layout table doing his magic. Mark's checklist for resuming travel consisted of clothing, money, ration coupons, travel bags, new identities, names, birthdates and places.

Voddeman met them in the hallway, "The Oosterhuis cell reports that the freighter *Cascade* will sail for Stockholm on Sunday the sixth of July, three days from now and her sister ship *Libelle* a week later on the thirteenth. They confirm that the Dutch Consulate in Stockholm will assist with documentation for Britain."

"Can we make Sunday's sailing?" Mark asked.

"Overly optimistic," Vreelink sniffed, "But we can try." He checked his watch, "I've got work to do, son. Go to your home. It's almost five o'clock, but be careful. You never know who might spot you. I'll talk to you later."

Mark was euphoric as he made his way back home. Paula was alive and recovering. Willem would be ecstatic. London seemed so much nearer now. No more Nazi-policed borders to cross. Mindful of Dirk's warning, he took the back route through the Haverzaklaan and waited for several minutes at the back of the house to watch for surveillance.

He quietly opened the back gate, walked on the tiled path through the small garden and stepped into the kitchen. Shit! He stumbled over a baby carriage parked in the hall. Voices came from the living room; a couple of baby chortles and a woman's voice. He hesitated for a moment but then opened the door to the living room. Mother Zonder, seated in his father's easy chair, was talking to Jenny who sat on the sofa, trying to help the baby stand up in her lap.

"Jenny?" he said, his voice choking, "What are you doing here?"

His mother got up to take the baby from Jenny who rushed over to embrace him. She pulled his head down and kissed him warmly on the lips. Mark stood motionless. He felt a surge of resentment. This was the woman who said she'd wait and then spurned him. Here she stood professing her love for him. He gently pushed her away.

"Good to see you, Jenny. Why the visit? Did you come all the way from Groningen?" he said in a conversational tone.

"Yes. Mother Zonder phoned me this morning that you were here for a few days. I took the eleven o'clock train and your mother met me at the station with the neighbour's baby carriage." Mark didn't answer.

"Where's Willem?" he asked.

"He's fine. He's in your room reading your books," Mother Zonder said.

"I have to talk to him, excuse me." Jenny looked crestfallen at the cool reception. He ran up to his old room.

"Great news, Willem," he said hugging the boy. "Guess what? I met Dirk Vreelink, you remember him. He has heard via London that your mother is in a hospital and is doing just fine."

"Will she come to England?" he asked anxiously.

"She has to heal before she can travel. By that time, we'll be in London. We are getting our new travel documents tomorrow and we are not going back to Paris but we will go to Sweden and from there to England."

Willem looked dubious. So much had gone wrong that the boy could not be blamed for being pessimistic.

"The lady with the baby – is that Jenny?" he asked. "She looks like that picture."

"She is my old girlfriend from before the war. She came to say hello."

"Better go and see her. See made a long trip to see you," he said earnestly. Mark went downstairs where a tearful but determined Jenny held out her daughter toward Mark.

"I want you to meet Anneke," she said, choking back a tear. The baby introduced herself by blowing a massive bubble. Mark acknowledged her by an unenthusiastic tickle under the chin. He knew he was being rude and softened his attitude.

"She looks a lot like you, Jenny," he smiled wanly, "Mom told me you married Henk van Weeren."

"Yes, I did."

"A belated congratulations. I hear he was released from prison and is now in the Waffen SS. Did you tell him you were going to meet a British agent?" he said in an unkind voice. Jenny handed Anneke back to his mother and sat on the sofa, dabbing her eyes with a hanky. He couldn't help himself and continued, "Did you tell him I was here?"

"Of course not. I wrote him a note that Mother Zonder had fallen ill and that she was all alone. I said I was going to visit for a few days."

Mark felt the bile of resentment rising in him. "Why come now? Especially since you didn't wait for me to come back from the war. You promised. Remember?" he said in an accusatory tone.

Mother Zonder had had enough. "Come here," she commanded Mark and handed him the gurgling baby. "Don't be so dumb."

"I don't want to..." he stuttered, fighting back his anger. Mark raised the girl under her arms and held her aloft. In spite of her precarious position, she took a gentle kick at his chest. He looked at Jenny who stood with tears in her eyes.

Mother Zonder said, "Can't you count? Anneke is six months old."

"What do you mean...?" he said hesitantly.

"She is yours," Jenny wept.

"You mean... in Groningen?" He looked drained of colour.

"What about Henk, does he know?" he asked.

"I was six months pregnant when I married him, so he knows for certain it isn't his."

"So why did he marry you?"

"My father could not accept that his daughter would bear a child with neither a father nor marriage in prospect. You have met my father. My mother understood, but my father could not bear the shame in the eyes of his church community. He and Thomas, Henk's father, arranged the marriage. I had no choice. I had no support. You were in England. You might never return. The baby needed a father."

"Why did Henk agree?"

"You know he pursued me since high school days. An arranged marriage suited him fine."

"Does he know I am the father?"

"I have never told him and he does not seem to want to know but he knows of course that you were in Groningen that Easter weekend." Mark gazed at Anneke who was now nestled in his arms. He leaned over and kissed her forehead and fat rosy cheeks.

"This is amazing," he managed to croak, "She is mine?" Mother Zonder took Anneke from him. Jenny rushed back into his arms.

"Oh Mark," she wept silently. He caressed her hair wondering what to say or do next.

Willem clattered down the wooden stairs.

"What's all the noise about?" he asked inopportunely as only a 12-year old can.

"I have just found out that Anneke is my daughter," Mark said with a note of wonder in his voice.

"Is she staying in Nederland or is she going with us?" he asked. Like Paula, he immediately went for the practical.

"Oh Willem, let him get over the shock before you ask such things," Mother Zonder said. "Ever since Mark came in everybody has been standing up. Let's all sit down. I'll make some sandwiches with lettuce. There is nothing else."

"So you will be going to England again soon," she concluded.

"Starting tomorrow evening, I hope."

Jenny looked distraught. "I guess you must go. I don't know what I was thinking. I guess I hoped we could start anew."

"Jenny, you have a husband to go back to and a home."

"Not much of a home. We live with my parents and there is constant friction between Papa and Henk. Papa hates his SS uniform. The neighbours have ostracized us," she wept. "I am so unhappy. I want to be with you."

The telephone interrupted her lament. It was a man's voice asking for Jenny. From the many 'yes' and 'no' answers he couldn't guess what was being said until she shrieked, "A foreign spy?" He jumped up and motioned for Jenny to stop. She quickly said goodbye and hung up.

"Was that Henk?" Mark asked in a shrill voice that frightened her. He grabbed her wrist. "Did you tell him I was here?" he demanded, shaking her wrist.

"I didn't deny it, if that's what you mean." He let go of her wrist.

"Damn," he hissed. "He'll report to the Nazis and they'll will be knocking on this door very soon. Willem and I have to get out of here. We have to find a safe house."

Mother Zonder forgot about the food. "You could go to my sister Geraldine," she said, "She's a widow and lives in a big house on the corner of the Morsweg and the Old Rhine. It's not far from here."

He ran upstairs with Willem to pack their bags. Jenny stomped up the stairs after him, asserting, "I am coming with you."

Ten minutes later, after a hasty goodbye, the four of them left. Willem pushed the baby carriage and Mark and Jenny walked arm-in-arm behind him as any married couple would. As they turned from the Morssingel onto the Morsweg, Vreelink stepped out from behind a hedge at the military hospital.

"What are you doing Mark? I told you I'd find you a safe house and now you're on the run." He turned to Jenny. "And who might you be?" he asked, but on closer inspection he added, "I know you. We met at the Jamboree. Jenny!"

"I am and I am here with my daughter." Jenny said.

Mark rushed his words. "Look, going back to 1937, I've got another name that you will remember: Henk van Weeren."

"What about that Nazi prick?"

"He's Jenny's husband. He is in the Waffen SS and has found out that I am in Leiden and that his wife is with me."

"Jesus," Vreelink paused, curled his lips and inhaled deeply through his teeth. "Turn around and go back to where you came from. Go past your home. At the end of the Morssingel at the corner of the Steenstraat is the former businessmen's club *Amecitia*. It was a classy place but it has been turned into a German officer's mess."

"Why go there?"

"Roelof Smit, a good friend is the manager there. He lives in the basement suite. His wife is on holidays. He'll stay with his brother and you can have the suite for tonight and tomorrow if you need it."

"You mean our safe house is full of German officers?" Mark asked.

"Can you think of anything safer? The Abwehr will never look for you there. Access is by a separate entrance along the side of the building. No need to use the front door."

"Dirk, I am afraid that the Abwehr will soon be at my mother's door. Jenny can't be found there. She will be staying with me until we know what is going on." Dirk thought of arguing but decided against it.

"Let's go," he said.

79

1941
TUESDAY, JULY 1, 19:00 HRS CEST
ABWEHR OFFICE, MAURITSLAAN 35
THE HAGUE, NEDERLAND

Streicher played nervously with a paper clip that he had taken from a tin on his secretary's desk. He had repeatedly stretched the paperclip out, then tried to bend it back into its original shape. It finally snapped. Other than the guard outside in the sentry house, Oberleutnant Kurt Streicher and a young subaltern were the only military men in this converted diplomat's home built in the late nineteenth century.

He got up to get another paper clip when he heard a car pull up below the open window. He looked down from his second floor vantage point and saw Sturmbannfuehrer Schellenberg in his camouflaged Mercedes convertible. In spite of the warm weather, Walter Schellenberg wore the shiny green-leather Army overcoat that reached halfway below the knees. He returned the guard's salute. A few minutes later, he entered Streicher's office without the courtesy of knocking. Schellenberg hardly ever bothered with niceties. He took Streicher's salute and sat in his chair, forcing Streicher to sit as a supplicant at his own desk. The way he touched his fingertips together in a rapid succession betrayed an underlying nervousness.

"I feel it necessary to impress upon you, Herr Oberleutnant that our task of locating Willem von Becke is of the greatest importance. As I told you yesterday from Berlin, no harm is to come to the boy. He will be sequestered in Germany and receive his education there. The Reichsfuehrer considers it unacceptable that you have failed to apprehend this boy."

"We have learned quite a lot Sturmbannfuehrer. The London agent sent to take the boy to England is Mark Zonder. When I perused his file, I realized that we met in 1937. At that time, he caught the eye of the President of the Scout movement, General Frans van Zandt, now the head of Dutch intelligence in London. The General is close to Queen

Wilhelmina and is leading the push to bring the boy out to England." A knock at the door interrupted his train of thought.

"What is it?" Streicher demanded. A young lieutenant peered in.

"A telephone call for the Oberleutnant, Sir." Streicher waved him off.

"We will not be interrupted," he snarled.

Schellenberg picked up the conversation where he left off. "What are your plans for finding the boy?"

"I will continue the search. There are good reasons to believe that Zonder was involved in the killing of a Wehrmacht soldier and wounding an officer when he landed near Leiden on the twenty-second of June."

"That is irrelevant. Even if he was found not guilty of that, he still would be shot as a foreign spy," said Schellenberg cutting him short. "Where are Zonder and the boy at this moment?"

"Our agents lost them in Paris and we do not know their route after that." The lieutenant knocked at the door again saying the caller sounded urgent. "Excuse me Sturmbannfuehrer, I should take this call." He picked up the phone at his corner credenza and listened intently. He made notes as his caller spoke. He finally spoke. "You must travel to The Hague in the morning and report here as soon as possible." He looked triumphant as he put down the telephone.

"We have located them, Sturmbannfuehrer. Zonder and the boy are in Leiden."

"Who called you?"

"A Dutch Waffen SS sergeant, Scharfuehrer van Weeren. He reported from Groningen that Zonder is at the house of his parents in Leiden. I will take action immediately."

"I would remind you of the rules that you must act in harmony with local authorities."

"I know Sturmbannfuehrer. Van Weeren will be here in the morning."

"That may be too late."

"I will act now, Herr Sturmbannfuehrer; the house will be under observation as soon as possible."

80

1941
TUESDAY, JULY 1, 20:00 HRS CEST
GERMAN OFFICERS' MESS, AMECITIA, STEENSTRAAT
LEIDEN, NEDERLAND

Steenstraat looked as busy as any other summer evening. Hundreds of men and women including German soldiers paraded up and down in a never-ending mating ritual. The sidewalk café of Heck's restaurant was overflowing. From inside the eatery, the music of a quartet playing schmaltzy waltzes wafted onto the street.

Mark and Jenny felt as if all eyes were upon them as they passed the *Amecitia* building. Most of the German officers seated on the outdoor terrace were in their late forties or early fifties. The young ones, in fighting trim, were off conquering Russia or fighting in North Africa.

Willem led the little Zonder parade, pushing the baby carriage ahead of the arm-in-arm couple. To get to the side entrance of the safe house, they had to pass right in front of the terrace. Their hope for a quick, unnoticed entry to the building was dashed when the wheels of the pram got stuck in the loose gravel. Willem couldn't budge it. Mark picked it up in its entirety and carried it through the side door. A balding officer, catching the last rays of the day, raised an appreciative thumb and caught Mark's eye.

The suite had all the amenities they needed. There was a small window looking out on the canal, about two feet above the water level. A bevy of white swans made their home close to the kitchen window.

Dirk had arranged for a bottle of milk and a supply of leftovers from the dinner service. As they ate their dinner, they heard singing in the officer's club above.

Willem declared he was tired and appropriated the spare bedroom for himself. Anneke was sleeping in her pram. Mark and Jenny were alone for the first time. Neither of them spoke until Mark finally broached the difficult subject. "What is next, Jenny? You came to show me Anneke, our child. You will go back to your husband. I will go back to England. Where is the happy ending?"

"I have a different ending in mind," Jenny said snuggling in his arms, "Anneke, Willem, you and I go to England. Willem will be safe and we will come back to Nederland when the war is over."

"That is not possible, Jenny. To begin with, you are married."

"But I don't love him. I don't want to be with him."

"Secondly, taking you and Anneke to England is impossible. We would need papers for you and the baby and—"

"You could get papers that say that we are married and have a 12-year old son and a baby daughter."

"I have a mission to complete. I am soldier. I must not complicate my duty by getting involved in personal issues," Mark said, undeterred.

"I know my way around Delfzijl. I speak the dialect. I can be an asset."

"We may have to leave tomorrow. Can you just leave your husband, your parents, and your siblings?"

"I'll see them again in better days," she said with a note of finality. Jenny leaned over and kissed him. "I want to start a new life. Let's do it!"

Anneke began to stir and loudly demanded a feeding. Mark watched in wonder as Jenny lifted her sweater, undid her bra and allowed the little girl to suckle. He had never seen this part of life. He stared as Anneke sated herself. As the feeding ended, Jenny threw a towel over his shoulder.

"Now hold her against your chest and pat her back until she burps," she commanded. He felt the warmth of the child's body against his. This small bundle of humanity was his? A sudden belch surprised him.

Jenny dug deep into her carpetbag and proceeded to clean the baby and put on a new diaper. "You'll have to learn this," she laughed.

Afterward they went to bed. They held each other and slept in a peaceful embrace.

It was well past noon when Vreelink rapped his coded knock on the door; He looked distraught.

"Mark, the Abwehr searched your parents' home this morning. They took your mother to the police station."

"Oh, no," Jenny moaned, "It's all my fault."

"A friend at the police station told me that she gave the address of your aunt Geraldine. They found nothing, of course. They probably hope that you will show up to spring her loose."

"There is no way I can get my mother out," Mark said, the air taken out of him. Vreelink put his arm around Mark's shoulder.

"The city police won't harm her. My informant thinks she'll be set free by this evening. Don't worry, she'll be fine." After the unexpected show of empathy, he became all business again.

"I think you should forget about going to Groningen by train. They will be checking all passengers for the next few days. I am working on another route. We will know this afternoon." Mark looked disconsolate. Jenny took the opportunity to raise the issue of her participation.

"Mark and I talked last night. I cannot go back to my marriage with Henk van Weeren. He will have a blot on his record for having a wife who left him for a British agent. I only married him to give my girl a father and my parents an opportunity to hold their heads high."

Vreelink listened impassively. "So?"

"Anneke and I are going with Mark to England."

"That's insane," Vreelink exploded. "That would endanger the mission and Mark could be charged with dereliction of duty."

"I think it might help the mission because the Abwehr will not be looking for a married couple with two children," she countered.

"Crazy," Vreelink sniffed but he didn't argue anymore. He brooded for a long while. "I see where things might get tough for you but that should not interfere with Mark's duty." He was quiet and no one responded as they absorbed the message.

Dirk finally spoke again, "We have photographs for Willem and Mark but we have no pictures of you or your daughter," he finally said.

"We don't need pictures for Anneke; she can travel on my passport."

"I don't like it," Vreelink said, "It spells trouble."

Mark, recovering from the news of his mother's arrest, said, "I'd feel safer if Jenny and Anneke could travel with us. It looks more natural for a family with children to travel than a man and a boy."

Vreelink shrugged his shoulders and said he would have to check with his Resistance group to see if the new identities could be provided in time.

"I don't know why I should help with this crazy scheme, but it must make sense to you. I'll be back before five." He slammed the door behind him, signalling his disgruntlement.

True to his word, he was back in the suite by 4:30.

"Good news," he beamed, "Your transportation to Groningen has been arranged. You can leave tomorrow morning. Passports and documentation can be ready later this evening but we need a photograph of Jenny for the new passport with her daughter. She needs to go by Pliny's place."

"I'll take her," Mark offered, "It's practically around the corner from here. We'll bring Anneke in the baby carriage. It's a beautiful day and she needs a little fresh air." Jenny grinned. He sounded like a father.

Vreelink, hesitated, "Okay, but Willem stays here with me."

The terrace was busy for lunch but none of the uniformed men seemed to be interested in passers-by.

They pulled the doorbell at the little house on the Beestenmarkt but to no avail. It was only after Mark used Vreelink's coded knock that Pliny ventured to open the door partway and hustled them into his atelier. He had prepared the basics for three identity kits.

"Have you decided on the names and birthdates?" he asked.

"There should be as many facts as possible," Mark said. "My name is on every Abwehr list as a suspect, but Jenny's last name, Bos, should be new to them. Just use our actual birthdays but make both our years of birth 1911, which would mean that we had Willem when we were 18."

"That'll work," Pliny said and asked for the details on Anneke. He wrote it all down in his beautiful calligraphic writing. "I'll work through the night. Vreelink should have it at your departure."

It was late afternoon when they stepped out into the sunshine. Jenny was the first to notice the Kübelwagen blocking the road. She instantly wheeled the pram around to return to Pliny's.

"No, we can't," Mark hissed, "We can't give his place away." They turned toward the Lammermarkt that ran in the opposite direction of their safe house. Another Kübelwagen stood astride the narrow street. A helmeted Feldwebel with a Schmeisser across his chest stared them down and motioned for them to join line-up of people.

Jenny whispered. "The Germans are checking everyone." A black detention vehicle stood ready, its doors wide open.

The line moved slowly. Jenny was the first to hand over her identity card. The Dutch policeman asked her what she was doing so far from Groningen. She said she had come to visit her friend who was ailing.

"What is your friend's name?" he asked.

"Zonder," she stuttered after a delay that was just a bit too long.

"Address?" he demanded.

"Morssingel 25," she said with a terrified look at Mark. The policeman turned to the Feldwebel and muttered something in German. The German demanded to see Mark's identity.

"I forgot my papers at home," Mark said firmly, "My lady friend came to see my mother and I took her for a brief walk with the baby. I can go and get my papers; it is only a few minutes from here."

The German turned and beckoned one of the Wehrmacht privates loitering about the detention vehicle. "Hold these people," he told them.

The soldier wheeled the pram to the vehicle and helped Jenny inside. He handed Anneke to her. Mark climbed in behind her. "It shouldn't be too long," the German soldier smiled. He was about their age and tried to be helpful. "I'll leave the door open, otherwise it gets too hot," he said.

Mark held Jenny's hand. "Sorry I dragged you into this," he apologized.

"I asked for it and we'll get out of this," she said with a defiant look. He admired her nerve. That's what had attracted him when they first met.

After ten minutes, the young soldier announced apologetically that he had to take them to the *kazerne*. "I think he means the Morspoort barracks, my father's former post," Mark whispered. The smiling soldier climbed inside with them while the driver locked the door from the outside. The bars on the windows blocked out much of the view; they did not see Gary Galluci standing in line to have his papers checked.

A few minutes later, Mark felt the cobblestones of the Morsstraat and anticipated the left turn into the barracks. The guard at the gate lifted the barrier without much of an inspection.

"I-know-this-place-inside-out-we-will-get-out-of-this," Mark said gluing his words together so that the Germans could not decipher his Dutch. "They'll put us next to the guard house. It's not bad."

As if on cue, the doors opened and the driver helped Jenny and Anneke out of the vehicle. Two Wehrmacht corporals stood guard in front of the holding cell. They were plump and had apple-cheeked faces so typical of rural Germany. In their mid-forties, they were not in the best of physical shape. However, they were very polite as they led their captives into the holding room.

The place was stark. A single upholstered chair stood near the door. Four army-green folding chairs surrounded an ancient oaken table. A picture of a stern-faced Fuehrer stared accusingly down from the wall.

Corporal Plump took the upholstered seat. After he had closed the door, Corporal Apple Cheeks took up a position on the other side. Plump looked apologetic and offered to exchange Jenny's metal chair for his comfortable seat. She smiled and sat down with Anneke in her lap. Mark nodded his appreciation for the gesture.

Hob-nailed boots clattered down the stone-tiled hallway. The door swung open and Oberleutnant Kurt Streicher entered. In a theatrical flourish, he addressed his audience. "Lieutenant Mark Zonder, you are my prisoner." He made a show of bowing to the detainees and motioned for van Weeren to come in. He extended his arm in an effeminate gesture, pointed at Jenny and said, "Madame van Weeren? Your husband."

Henk grabbed Jenny by the arm. He picked the baby up and hustled Jenny out of the room. At the door, Jenny turned and managed a tearful look at Mark before the door slammed shut.

Streicher stood and looked at Mark. He put his officer's cap upside down on the table and folded his leather gloves inside.

"Fate has arranged that we should meet again," Streicher said pompously. "Lieutenant Zonder or should I say Agent Zonder of the MI-6, the Abwehr has been looking for you. You have kidnapped a boy, Wilhelm von Becke, who is under the protection of the German Reich, an offense that – by itself alone – calls for summary execution. As an agent of a foreign power, you are deemed to be a spy, warranting the same ultimate punishment. Moreover, you stand accused of abetting in the murder of Gefreiter Anton Binsberger at the Vennemeer on June 22 of this year." He paced around the small room and looked at the ceiling before he sharply turned on his heels to face Mark.

"It is a pity that we can execute you only once for these crimes. However at this moment, my superiors deem your crimes to be less important than gaining custody of Wilhelm von Becke." He sat with his face inches away from Mark. "Where is Wilhelm von Becke? I would advise you to answer promptly. You are well aware that we have means of making you answer the question."

81

1941
WEDNESDAY, JULY 2, 19:30 HRS CEST
THE POTTERY FACTORY, RIJNKADE 7
LEIDEN, NEDERLAND

Vreelink's informant on the Leiden police force had told him within minutes of Mark and Jenny's arrest. Dirk had quickly packed their belongings and hustled Willem onto the blue streetcar in front of the German Officers' Mess.

Cobus Lammens, a gentle, soft-spoken man in his early fifties owned the pottery factory that churned out thousands of flowerpots every day. He had been part of Vreelink's Resistance cell since the day the Germans overran the country. When Vreelink mentioned that they needed to hide a boy from the Abwehr, Lammens immediately offered the use of his home.

The factory stood along the north arm of the Old Rhine River. The location was ideal because it allowed the suppliers of clay to moor and unload right in front of the factory's door.

One ship or another was always moored along the street. Once every two weeks, a vessel would arrive laden with peat to stoke the kilns. Dug from the fens in Groningen, the dried bricks were piled high on top of the deck. Those ships, on their return north, would carry loads of pots for the Northern markets. The skippers were obliged to Cobus for a big part of their livelihood and were always quick to do any favours.

After Vreelink told him that a boy and his father needed transport to Groningen, Cobus had approached the skipper of the peat boat moored in front. "The skipper is willing to take them. Will they be ready tomorrow?"

Vreelink sounded frustrated. "We are planning to spring him loose tonight. Our action group will meet in the next few hours to plan it out."

"Is Kat coming? He's good for that kind of stuff." Cobus said. Kat was a partner in the Leiden Fireworks factory. He had expanded his skill in creating fireworks displays to include a more violent use of gunpowder. His specialty was cracking safes where ration coupons were stored.

"Yes. Kat will be here and I asked Utan to join us. The idea is to spring Mark and bring him here tonight."

"I wish I could go with you," Cobus said but he didn't mean it. Cobus was good at arranging transportation and finding safe houses but he didn't like the rough stuff. Utan, on the other hand, was like his namesake, Orangutan. He was a fearless hunk of a man, who loved a fight.

It was nearly ten. Darkness was setting in. The *Zeevaartschool*, the Navy Training Centre across the river from the Morspoort barracks looked quiet. The Kriegsmarine had taken over the facility. Navy recruits were required to row a lifeboat down the river to the North Sea locks and back again, a difficult 18-kilometre row, at top speed.

Vreelink, Kat, Voddeman and Utan gained quick access to the lightly guarded facility and silently made their way to the jetty where the lifeboats were moored. Kat and Utan took one boat while Vreelink followed in the second boat with Voddeman as his mate.

In utter darkness, they rowed to the Morspoort gate. Voddeman and Kat remained with their boats.

Vreelink had been stationed at the barracks for years and was familiar with the gate and the ancient entrance to the garrison. In a tiny alcove in the inside wall of the ancient Morspoort gate was a heavy door that looked as if it hadn't been opened in centuries. Vreelink threw his weight against it and simultaneously twisted the big iron ring that served as a door handle. With his other hand, he jammed a screwdriver into the hole of the ancient lock. The door screeched open. Vreelink motioned for Utan to follow him up to the gate tower.

Vreelink struggled to navigate the narrow brick steps, built in the 1600s. Utan was right behind him. The steps took them to the floor above the holding room where they heard Mark talking to his German captors about the wherabouts of Willem.

Vreelink and Utan worked their way to the airshaft that supplied the windowless holding room. They looked through a slit between the inlet and the ceiling and could see an officer and a corporal.

Vreelink soundlessly loosened the screws of the ventilation screen. "I'll take the officer. You go for the guard," he signalled. He sat up, pulled his knees up against his chest, kicked the screen out and dropped to the floor.

With a blood-curdling yell, Vreelink launched himself across the table at Streicher. The impact toppled the German backward in his chair. Vreelink held him in a chokehold. Mark reacted at once and leapt at the corporal. He collided with Utan who had landed behind Vreelink.

"He's mine," Utan shouted, "Help Vreelink." He tossed him the ether-soaked hanky. Mark caught it and held the soaked cloth over Streicher's nose. The German sagged. Vreelink let him drop to the floor.

"Over here," Utan yelled. He held Corporal Plump around the neck. The man looked panic-stricken as Mark gave him a few nosefuls. He too sank softly to the floor. Corporal Apple Cheeks outside, hearing the noise, unlocked the door, only to also receive a strong whiff of the ether.

"We can't leave them like this," Vreelink said. "They'll wake up in minutes." He took off Streicher's tunic and put it over his head, pouring a healthy dose of ether over it. Plump and Apple Cheeks were next.

"Let's go," Vreelink urged. Outside, they crouched, single file, through the old sluice – a brick ditch, one metre deep – that led from the kitchen to the canal. In less sanitary times, it had served as a channel to dispose of kitchen waste. Voddeman and Kat were anxiously waiting for their return.

Vreelink issued commands, "Voddeman, you take Utan and bring the boat back where we found it. Mark and Kat, you come with me."

Vreelink and Kat took the oars. Mark sat in the stern. The curfew, the total blackout and a merciful moon hiding behind threatening rainclouds aided the escape.

It was close to eleven when they dropped Mark at the Pottery Factory. Dirk and Kat hastened to return the boat to the naval school before it was found missing. Inside the Lammens house, Willem was sound asleep. Mark went to his bedside and patted the boy on the back.

"Good night Willem,' he said. Willem half raised himself.

"Oh, you're back; good," he said and promptly fell asleep again.

Mark was sound asleep when he felt a weight drop on him. Arms clasped around his neck. He was jolted awake, his heart raced. "You are back," Willem shouted, "I dreamed it but it is really true. What happened? Where's Jenny?"

Mark tried to shake himself alert and explained that Jenny had met up with her husband and was probably on her way back to Groningen. Willem thought about this for a moment and then wrote off this loss like so many of the other blows he had encountered in the last two weeks.

Mark marvelled at the boy's ability to adapt. Eventually these traumas would come back to haunt the young man, he feared. He was still in shock himself, having come so close to facing execution.

"Have you seen the peat ship outside?" Willem asked. "It's called the *Estelle*. Last night she was stacked three metres high with peat bricks. It looked like a house. They are almost finished unloading now."

Yellie Lammens, Cobus' wife called from downstairs that Dirk Vreelink had arrived and was waiting.

"You saved my life again," Mark said as he clasped his arm around Dirk's shoulders. Vreelink looked embarrassed.

"The guys were very good," he said. "We got out without any damage."

"Have you heard anything about Jenny?"

"Our man at the Leiden police says van Weeren is taking her back to Groningen today. The good news is that your mother is back at home on the condition that if you contact her, she must call the police immediately. Your father is coming home this weekend so that'll be a relief."

They were interrupted by a knock on the door. The skipper of the peat boat, a tall, lean man with a bronzed face introduced himself as Alphonse "call me Fons" Bouma. He looked to be in his late forties. His body spoke of heavy work in the open air. He said he lived in the small town of Veendam, about 25 kilometres southwest of Groningen. His words had the clipped Germanic inflection, common to the folks in the northeast.

"The *Estelle* has unloaded her peat," he said, "And we are stowing a shipment of pottery for the return. Estelle, my missus that is, not the ship, she always sails with me. Since you'll be travelling with us she has decided to stay with her sister until I come back ten days from now." He turned to leave. "The *Estelle* is ready to go when you are. I'll be aboard, if you need me. Your laddie is already aboard inspecting his bunk. He's anxious to go."

"I won't keep him long," Vreelink said, dismissing the skipper. He handed Mark a parcel wrapped in waxed butcher paper. "Here are the passports for Mr. and Mrs. Bos and their two children. Willem has a separate passport and Anneke is written in her mother's papers." Mark accepted them silently.

Vreelink produced a short list of contacts in Groningen. "Learn the names and addresses and destroy the note," he ordered. "We don't want it to fall into German hands." He reached out and held Mark by the elbows. "Allard Oosterhuis in Delfzijl is willing to accept you on one of his ships to Stockholm. He can be found through the café *de Witte Zwaan*."

Mark took some time to memorize the list of names and handed it back to Vreelink. "I think I've got it. You can take it back," Mark said.

They thanked the Lammens family, crossed the road and stood before the *Estelle*. "Be safe my friend," Vreelink said. "Tell van Zandt to keep supporting us. It may look impossible now but some day we will be rid of the Nazi bastards." Mark watched him mount his bicycle and disappear around the corner.

Fons Bouma stood on deck and welcomed him to the wheelhouse that stood on top of the deck. "First things first," Fons said. "With Estelle gone you are my deckhand and cook. I hope you are a quick learner. I am the fourth generation of peat boat skippers so I am pretty good at it." He waved towards the bow in a dramatic fashion as though he was introducing the ship to a large audience, "She is 30 metres long, four metres wide. Peat boats have a stubby bow with a rounded hull to give us as much load space as possible."

He continued his lecture, "Before diesel engines, skippers couldn't put up sails in these canals, so they used bargepoles to move out of the city. It was only on the rivers and lakes that the main sail was used. Today we use diesel engines to get us out of the city but because of the fuel rationing, we still use the sails in open water. We can get a pretty good speed up when we cross the IJsselmeer." Fons paused to undo the mooring ropes.

Mark tried to stem the flood of information. "Can you show us where we will sleep?"

Fons lifted the hatch below the wheelhouse. A set of steps led into the living area. "Go ahead," he said to Mark, "The boy is already there."

The cabin looked more modern than Mark expected. A tiny table dominated the centre. There were no walls as such, just walnut doors all around that opened into cupboards and closets, large and small. The sleeping accommodations were pullout benches with drawers underneath for clothing and bedding.

"Willem will sleep in one of those large drawers," Fons said. A tall grandfather clock stood in the corner. "It can't keep correct time because of the motion of the ship, but it was owned by Estelle's mother," Fons explained. Two small 'Delft blue' vases, propped up against falling over, decorated the mantelpiece. A glass case containing crockery was lined with bunched pieces of cloth to protect it against sudden shock. A poster of Queen Wilhelmina was fastened to a door with thumbtacks. He pointed in the direction of small peat-burning stove on top of which sat a large cast-iron frying pan. "That's your home for the next three days, maybe four," Fons said, looking pleased.

"I mean the ship of course, not the frying pan," he cackled.

"What route we will be taking?" Willem asked.

"Let's get out of the city first. I'll show you later."

Fons heard footsteps on the deck. He headed quickly for the steps leading to the wheelhouse but stopped when he saw a burly man looking down into the cabin. "I want to talk to Mark," he said in a Brooklyn drawl.

"For heavens sake, Gary, what are you doing here?" Mark said stepping up behind Fons.

"I came to persuade you to let me take Willem to Spain and then to America. Kolmar is determined to give him a new life."

Fons felt compelled to jump into the fray. "Now tell me why you would want to take this boy away from his father?" he asked.

"That man is not his father," Gary said, raising his voice. "He is an agent sent from London to kidnap the boy."

"Is that true?" Fons said looking at Mark. "Vreelink told me the lad was half Jewish and his father was trying to get him to England."

"That's true but I am not his father. Gary's employer in America is. I have been sent from London on behalf of the mother. She wants him safe in England. It's a dispute between parents."

Gary came down the steps and filled the small cabin. "I am an American citizen. Germany is not at war with the United States. I can travel in Europe without any problems. This guy can't do that. He's a fugitive, for Chris' sake."

Mark was upset with the intrusion just when things were looking up. "I am acting on behalf of the mother and you have no papers for Willem. You cannot get him out of the country any easier than I can."

"I came to convince you that Willem would be better off going with me," Gary said in a reasonable tone.

"But I don't want to go to America with you," Willem screamed.

Fons looked from one speaker to the other as if watching a tennis match. "It seems the boy doesn't want to go with you," he said to Gary.

"His father wants him," Gary said, that would win the argument.

Fons was not ready to concede. "So who is this mother that she is able to send someone from London to get him during wartime?"

"I cannot tell you that," Mark said, "but I can tell you who sent me." He pointed to the picture of Queen Wilhelmina pinned to the door.

"Really?" Fons said his face showing disbelief. "The Queen?"

"She's my grandma," Willem cried. The boy's sudden revelation shocked Fons into action.

"You get out of here," he yelled. With both big hands, he pushed Gary in the chest causing the stocky man to stumble back onto the set of steps.

Mark grabbed Gary's arm. "Listen to me you jerk. I'll have the boy in England within days, so get out of our way and let's go to England where the officials can settle the dispute."

Gary was furious now. "You have screwed this up from day one," he yelled, "You will screw it up again." That was about all he could yell because he sank to his knees as Fons hit him on the head with the frying pan. The American slumped to the floor.

"Why did you do that?" Mark shrieked.

"I've got no time to argue," Fons bellowed, "I have a Jewish boy whose grandmother is the Queen. An agent from London who escaped from a Nazi jail last night. I don't need an American to delay me from getting the hell out of here."

"He's out cold but he'll wake up soon enough. Let's get him out of here," Mark said.

Gary was heavier than he looked. They had some difficulty hauling him up the stairs and across the street. Yellie Lammens was too stunned to object to them laying Gary out on the sofa in her living room.

"Who is he?" she asked.

"He's from New York," Fons said, leaving Yellie to ponder this non-sequitur.

Fons ordered Mark to loosen the mooring ropes from the rings embedded in the pavement. He jumped aboard, stepped into the wheelhouse and cranked up the diesel engine.

"You go below," he instructed Mark, "Keep the boy company while I get through the city. Don't show your face until we are well out of town."

82

1941
THURSDAY, JULY 3, 10:00 HRS CEST
ABOARD THE ESTELLE, OLD RHINE RIVER
NEAR LEIDEN, NEDERLAND

"You can come on deck now," he yelled below. Mark sat on Mrs. Bouma's rattan chair while Willem sat on the deck hatch.

"We are doing about 15 kilometres an hour. Once we hit the lake, we'll hoist the main sail and we'll let the wind do the work. And you can tell me what your cloak and dagger story is all about."

"Fair enough," Mark said and gave a recap of Willem's situation and his mission to bring the boy to England.

"Let me show you our route," Fons said and hauled out a map inserted between sheets of mica.

"First we go to Amsterdam, then along the west coast of the Zuiderzee to Volendam, then north to Enkhuizen from where we will sail cross the IJsselmeer to Lemmer in Friesland. We should be there tomorrow night. We will follow the lakes and canals up to Groningen on day three."

Willem was entrusted with the responsibility of paying the bridge keepers' tolls. At every bridge, the bridgeman extended a wooden shoe from a fishing pole. Willem would grab the wooden shoe and deposit the required nickel. Most of the elderly bridgemen knew Fons from his years of travelling the peat circuit. Tradition demanded a short comment on the weather. "Nice day," was Willem's line for the day. "It may change, though," was the answer, suitable for all occasions.

They entered the canal ringing the Haarlemmermeer polder, dug a hundred years before. Willem was delighted to see the houses along the canal were lower than the boat.

"If that dike breaks they'll all drown," he marvelled. He looked apprehensive when they sailed past Schiphol airport where several rows of German aircraft stood in neatly arranged rows.

"There were a lot more planes here when they were planning to invade England," Fons shouted over the putt-putt of *Estelle's* engine, "Most of them are in Russia now."

A little after noon, they entered the Amstel River that led to Amsterdam. Hamlets and villages gave way to suburbs and city streets. Passing freight boats were no novelty and no one paid any attention to the *Estelle* when she chugged into the River IJ, which connects Amsterdam's harbour with the North Sea on one end and the IJsselmeer on the other.

Fons played the role of tourist guide. "Because the water level in the IJsselmeer is lower than the North Sea we have to go through the *Oranjesluizen*, the huge locks named after the Royal Family. The Germans may change that name," he grinned.

"There are three locks side by side. One is for pleasure craft, the other two are reserved for commercial vessels. It'll take some time to get through the locks – enough time for the police to check all ships coming through, so you better get your stuff in order in case they come aboard for inspection." Looking at Willem's stricken face, he added, "Just act normal and everything will be alright."

They were fifth in line to enter the lock. Mark kept a steady eye on the half-dozen Feldwebels patrolling on the walls separating the locks.

Fons kept a careful watch on the high jinks in the line-up of pleasure craft. Two rowboats, propelled by outboard motors, were drawing a lot of attention. Playful crews of German servicemen – obviously on leave – repeatedly rammed into each other, much to the annoyance of some of their boat mates who were attempting to fish. The holidayers appeared to be excessively stimulated by alcohol. The participants, a mixture of army and navy personnel, had a great time pretending to be pirates intent on sinking their adversary. When an unexpected jolt hit his rowboat, one of the inebriated participants promptly fell overboard amid uproarious laughter. The Feldwebels looked on disapprovingly but were unable to act until the culprits were inside the locks.

The *Estelle* waited to be admitted to the commercial locks. The 20-minute procedure of opening and closing the locks provided ample time for inspection. Fons was getting nervous. His livelihood if not his life was at stake. Willem looked grim and on the verge of nausea. The sluice doors opened and the *Estelle* slid into her place along the wall.

"Get your papers out," Fons hissed as a tall officer boarded the ship. Fons immediately offered his large leather wallet containing his permits, licenses and identification.

"*Nein*," the German waved him off, "*Nach unten.*" He wanted to go below. Fons showed him into the wheelhouse and allowed the German to climb down the ladder to inspect the cabin.

A loud explosion outside jolted the German to return to the deck quickly. The deafening sound had alerted the entire detachment of soldiers on the locks. The holidaying fishermen continued whooping it up, scooping scores of asphyxiated fish into their nets.

"What happened?" Willem asked.

"The idiots exploded a hand grenade in the water which sucked the oxygen out. The fish are literally drowning," Fons explained. "That's a murderous way to fish."

The Feldwebels focused their attention on their drunken compatriots and the dead fish. They hauled both species onto the quay. When the sluice gates opened, the *Estelle* was the first in line to exit. Fons looked for the tall German who had inspected the cabin and held up his wallet. He waved for the *Estelle* to proceed.

Mark looked around. The lock for the recreational watercraft was not going to open for a while. Willem rushed over and attempted to embrace both of his shipmates. The three of them did a little celebratory dance. Not too wild of course – the Germans were still close.

Once outside on the open water Fons, in a mock ceremony, pronounced Willem the skipper and told him to hold the big rudder and keep the compass in the NNW position toward the looming island of Marken.

Mark was ordered to raise the mainsail. The staysail was a lot easier to do. The southerly winds played with the sails for a moment until they billowed. Fons cut the diesel and the boat began its glide across the wide expanse of water. Fons felt like reminiscing.

"When I sailed the Zuiderzee years ago, this was all salt water. When the *Afsluitdijk,* the closing dike was built in 1933, the water began to diminish in salt content. They say that around 1960 this will all be farmland with new cities and towns."

Willem enjoyed the day, sailing on the open water with the wind at their back. He prowled up and down the deck in Fons' yellow oilcloth coat, several sizes too big, delightedly inhaling the brackish spray thrown up by the hull. Even an intercept by the Kriegsmarine didn't bother him when he realized they just wanted to see the cargo. He even talked to the lieutenant in German telling him this was his first visit ever to Friesland. The officer smiled benignly and quickly ended the inspection.

They pulled into the fishing harbour of Volendam, the town that served as a backdrop for the 1865 children's novel *Hans Brinker and the Silver Skates*. Fons locked the wheelhouse and led them to the restaurant *de Spaander* at the end of the pier. The townsfolk were dressed in their traditional clothing and wore wooden shoes. Inside the ancient restaurant, they found a table and Fons kept the conversation going.

"When I was Willem's age my grandfather allowed me to sail with him to Holland. It was my first trip and he treated me to a dinner here at *de Spaander*. The place is so old that the planks on the floor are hollowed out by the footsteps from centuries of sailors and fishermen."

Mark had many ration coupons. They ate heartily – bread and smoked eel followed by platefuls of fried potatoes and steamed endive. Mother Zonder would have approved. When in a crisis, eat!

"Give me one of your phony ration coupons," Fons said. "And I'll get a fresh-baked loaf of Friesian bread at the bakery down the street." Fons was back in minutes with the bread still warm.

Mark made coffee, real coffee after he had spotted a grocer and redeemed coupons for a small packet. Fons wanted to make it last longer by mixing it with chicory but Mark said no, "We'll make the real stuff." The weather was promising and Fons decided that breakfast would be served on deck. The wonderful smell of coffee, fresh bread and drying hay in the field made for a perfect start to the day.

"We have three more small lakes to sail through before we get to the province of Groningen. If all goes well I expect to drop you off in central Groningen by seven this evening."

The first few hours of sailing through pastureland were pleasant but the weather slowly changed. Featureless grey clouds stretched across the flat countryside as far as the horizon with only a distant church spire bringing the occasional relief. The vanes of the windmills, secured against the wind, looked like empty crucifixes on the horizon.

"I wouldn't be surprised if we get some rain," Fons said.

The strong gusts from the southwest pushed the *Estelle* faster towards her destination. Alongside the canal, teenagers were pedaling, head down, into the wind. "They're used to it," declared Fons, "It's their only transportation to school and back."

A small enamelled sign along the grassy bank announced that they were entering the province of Groningen. The provincial waterways crews had kindly installed posts to mark the 24 kilometres to Groningen City.

The rain started. Fons closed the windshield of the wheelhouse and retrieved the yellow slicker from Willem who – against his wishes – was banished below to start packing the suitcases.

With 10 kilometres to go, near the hamlet of Vierverlaten, a car, facing the canal in the direction of the *Estelle*, flashed its headlights.

"Mark," Fons called, "Have a look." In the distance, they could make out the figure of a man in a blue raincoat, wearing a grey fedora. He stood in the streaming rain beside his car waving an orange piece of cloth.

Mark considered the risk in stopping for a stranger. "Do you feel safe in pulling along the canal wall here?"

"Why not?" Fons answered and slowly eased the *Estelle* alongside the wharf of a cement factory. The man got in his car and drove toward the *Estelle*. The figure stepping into the rain looked familiar but Mark couldn't place it until the older man doffed his hat. He recognized Gustaaf Emmerik the Commissioner of the Groningen police force. Mark stepped on the deck to talk to him in the slashing rain.

"Zonder," the greying policeman said, putting his wet fedora back on, "Please join me in the car. I have important information." Mark looked at the '37 Ford and decided that with Fons watching, there was safety in numbers. No one else appeared to be around.

Fons nodded his encouragement. Mark jumped onto the wharf and got in the car. Both men were soaked to the skin.

"Mark listen to me. I am not the commissioner of police anymore. I have been demoted to Lieutenant in charge of nothing. For some time I have been part of the Resistance. My cell was alerted by Vreelink that you were on the *Estelle* travelling to Groningen. We have been doing shifts to intercept you.

Mark was relieved to be dealing with a known contact. "You found me."

"Well then, let me tell you that a group of Abwehr types, including Henk van Weeren are blocking all exits from the Groningen harbour into town. We are certain they are looking for you and your young charge. You need a safe house for the night. Both of you should come with me. Now."

Mark went back aboard where Willem was waiting with the suitcases. After a hasty farewell, and a promise to be in touch once they were safe, they ran to the idling Ford. Inside, the gracious policeman formally introduced himself to young Willem who leaned forward over the seat to shake his hand solemnly.

"Young man, we will have a safe home for you tonight so you can have a good sleep," he said solicitously. On the way into the city, he related how most police forces in the country were gradually being Nazified. "If you can believe it, that scoundrel Henk van Weeren is now the liaison between the city police and the German authorities."

"So I heard," Mark said without further explanation. Save for the propaganda posters and the swastika flags, the city of Groningen looked very much like the last time he had seen it. Emmerik visibly relaxed when he pulled up to a newly built church that looked like a massive hull of a ship. The rain had stopped but the wind was still strong.

"You will be staying at the Manse of the Oosterkerk. It's in a residential neighbourhood, and far enough from the centre of town to be secure and yet close enough should you have any business there." He got out of the car, one hand holding his hat, the other holding the door open for Willem.

"Dominee Ackerman has been here since the church was built 12 years ago," Emmerik said as a tall, greying man in a sombre black suit opened the front door to greet his visitors.

"Welcome to the House of God," boomed the preacher so loudly that Mark looked around furtively to see if any passers-by had overheard.

"A special welcome to you, my young friend," he said bending down to ruffle Willem's mop of dark hair. "Let me show you to your room where you can freshen up and then come down for some supper. It's after seven, you must be hungry."

The bedroom looked out on the Roosensteinlaan. Mark figured it would be a few hours before darkness set in.

Dominee Feike Ackerman was a widower. His wife had passed away some years ago and he had ever since relied on Hilda, his housekeeper – a gentle grey-haired woman – to keep him free to tend to his congregation.

"Hilda has been with us ever since my wife and I moved into this church in 1929," the reverend said as they sat down for supper. Miss Hilda smiled as she ladled platefuls of thick pea soup with big hunks of smoked sausage. The dominee did not have to worry about food rationing, Mark thought as he mentally added up the numbers of coupons required for the feast. Willem finished his plate before the others were even half done. Hilda proudly ladled him some more.

After dinner, the reverend excused himself to work with a youth group, leaving Mark and Willem to relax in the cozy living room. The nine o'clock radio news was a collection of boasts announcing the joyful liberation of the Russian people who had slaved for so long under the Bolshevik yoke. According to the reporter, hordes of Russian maidens pelted the liberators with flowers as they paraded on tanks through the ruined streets. Mark sneered and turned the radio off.

Willem yawned and Mark shooed him off to bed. Dominee Ackerman returned from his duties to come and chat with his guest. Mark excused himself saying that he had to make a visit in connection with the next leg of his journey.

"You mean you are going out now?" the reverend said in astonishment. "There is a curfew at ten, you know."

"I know, Dominee, but I must find a contact."

"Shall I go with you my son? It might be easier for you," the reverend offered. "Moreover, I know the town."

"Okay Dominee. But if I am stopped by the German police, you must get away from me as fast as you can to look after Willem."

They walked across the Bloemsingel bridge and headed toward Jenny's.

"What are you looking for?" the minister asked.

"The house where my daughter and her mother live."

"Ah, I see," Ackerman said, not really seeing.

"It is complicated, Dominee, but you see Willem and I want to flee to Sweden and I want to take my girlfriend and my daughter with me."

"Ah, a girlfriend, yes of course," the reverend sighed, comprehending even less, "And you want to bring her to the Manse, I presume."

"No, I want to see if I could speak with her."

"Naturally," Ackerman mumbled to himself.

By the time they found the house, it was dark; the blackout was complete. They watched the house from across the street. Through a small slit in the curtain, they could see that a light was on in the living room.

"Aren't you going to ring the doorbell?" Ackerman asked.

"First I want to see if her husband is home. If he is, I'll have to come back tomorrow." The good reverend understood less and less.

"I could ring the bell and pretend I am on church business," he offered getting into the spirit of things. The situation appeared to be both sinful and dangerous but he was thrilled to find himself in such a covert intrigue.

"I will take a peek through the curtains first, to see if she's home." Mark crossed the street and quietly opened the garden gate and worked his way through the plants to peer into the living room. The roar of a motorcycle made him duck.

The rider stopped his DKW motorcycle and parked directly in front of the house. It was Henk van Weeren in his black uniform. He noticed the gate was open. He looked around and saw an elderly man shuffle down the street. As promised, the dominee was not going to hang around. Henk paused and waited for a while, shrugged his head and walked to the front door. Mark shrunk behind the bushes as van Weeren passed within a metre of him. He used his keys to open the door, mumbled something as he entered and closed the door.

Mark slinked away without looking inside the room.

83

1941
SUNDAY, JULY 6, 08:15 HRS CEST
MANSE OF THE OOSTERKERK
GRONINGEN, NEDERLAND

"Thank you Miss Hilda," Mark said, wiping his mouth with his napkin. He got up from his chair while slurping his last sips of coffee. "The breakfast was wonderful. I haven't had so much food at one time since I left England." Hilda asked if he wanted more.

"No thank you, I am so full I feel like sleeping it off," he laughed as he helped her carry the dishes to the kitchen. "I have to go out this morning," he told her. "When Willem wakes up he will be upset that I have gone out without him. Please assure him that I will be back before eleven."

"I'll let him bake some pancakes for himself. The way that boy ate last night, that should keep him busy until then," Hilda smiled.

He knew the dominee would not approve of his activities on a Sunday but then again the old boy had been quite excited when they came back after the missed opportunity to speak to Jenny. "A British agent and a Waffen SS sergeant on a motor cycle, I felt I was part of a spy thriller," he had tittered to Hilda while having his nightcap of Bols Jenever.

This morning, Groningen looked like a town deserted. Sunday might not be the most opportune time to speak to Jenny alone but the lack of time called for action. The *Cascade* would sail for Sweden tonight.

He watched the house from a distance and noticed that Van Weeren's motor cycle stood where he had parked it the night before. Hubert and Martina Bos were likely to be the first to leave the house. The church service was at ten, he remembered.

He guessed wrong. It was a little after nine when van Weeren, in his Nazi finery, stepped out of the house. After a few angry kicks, the DKW started and Henk roared down the street.

Mark was not sure whether he should speak to Jenny in the presence of her parents or wait until he could talk to her alone, face-to-face. Then again, she might want to join her parents in going to church. He hoped not. It would be awkward to discuss their problems on the sidewalk.

At 20 minutes to ten Martina and Hubert, clutching their psalm books, left for church. Afraid to wake Anneke, he knocked on the door rather than pulling on the polished brass knob that would cause the bell to sound throughout the house.

Jenny looked both frightened and elated when she saw Mark on the doorstep. She looked around for Willem. "Are you alone?"

"Willem is safe," he said, "We must talk." Jenny leaned out of the doorway and scanned both ends of the street before asking him to step into the vestibule.

The words came out haltingly, "Anneke is asleep and I'm scared." She remained standing in the hallway next to the big barometer that perpetually predicted rain.

"I saw Henk leave a while ago," Mark offered. Jenny, trembling, led him inside. She motioned for him to sit in Hubert's chair.

"That man Streicher wants to capture Willem but Henk is obsessed with finding you. He says he wants to kill you," she said daubing her eyes with a hanky.

"How did he know we were coming to Groningen?" he asked. She sat down on the arm of Hubert's chair and slid into his lap.

"He told me you had escaped. He was very angry. He threatened to hurt the baby and me," she wept softly.

"Where did Henk go this morning?"

"To the railway station. He will join Streicher and an Abwehr group. They will check all travellers. Henk suspects you are in the city and that you will try to get to Delfzijl at some point."

Mark took her chin in his hands and looked into her eyes, "Did you tell him you are coming to England with me?"

"No, I didn't, but he knew it somehow."

"By coming here, I am risking my mission, Jenny. I am asking, do you still want to come to England with me?"

"I know, I know, you are asking me that," she said, furiously kneading her hanky with both hands, "I am afraid."

"You were so sure in Leiden. What has changed?"

"My parents are here. I feel guilty about leaving Henk. I don't know what England will be like."

"You'll be with me, Jenny."

"But will you be there or will you be risking your life somewhere else on some stupid mission?"

"I am asking again, will you and Anneke come with me?"

Jenny slumped onto the sofa. "I can't leave my parents. It is so final."

"The war will be over at some point, Jenny."

"Yes, but with the Germans in charge. They are almost finished with Russia and it'll be England next and then we will be considered traitors who ran away from our country."

"America will not stand by and let England be absorbed into the German Reich. They will join the war soon. It's just a matter of time."

"I don't know. What about Anneke. What is best for her?"

"Jenny, there is not a lot of time. We must board the ship to Sweden tonight. Resistance people are driving us to the railway station for the three o'clock train. I will ask the driver to wait here, on the corner of the street. If you are not there, I'll know the answer."

"I won't go without telling my parents," Jenny said.

"Please don't do that. They might contact the police to stop you. That would put Willem and me in danger. If you do come, bring Anneke of course, but carry no more than what you would for a visit to the park."

"I don't know," she cried.

"I know it's a big decision," Mark said. He held her by the wrists and looked deeply into her eyes, "If we want to live a new life, we have to take risks." He got up and got ready to leave. "War has put us in this situation, Jenny. I have to go now. Quarter to three on the corner. I expect to see you there with Anneke." He kissed her lightly on the lips and left.

At the manse, Gustaaf Emmerik was enjoying a cup of the reverend's excellent coffee. He was talking to Willem. As soon as Mark stepped into the living room, Hilda headed for the kitchen and came back with his coffee. There was a silver coffee pot and a cup and saucer with gilt rims on the tray. She poured the coffee, passed the sugar and a big 'Delft blue' plate of thick slices of *Groninger Koek*, a cake made of rye and syrup. The dominee was still in church, she explained, but would join them soon.

"Did you talk to Jenny?" Willem wanted to know. He stood by Mark's chair, searching his face.

"What makes you think I talked to Jenny?"

"Why else would you go out? You have been thinking about her all the time. I could tell," he said with an earnest look.

"She will go with us to England. I still have the papers for the four of us as a family."

"What's this?" Emmerik nearly choked on his coffee.

"My girlfriend and my daughter are going with us," Mark said.

"I don't think that's a good idea," Emmerik said putting his coffee cup back on the table. He missed the coaster Hilda had provided. She hurried over with a damp cloth, removed the brown ring and demonstratively put the cup back in its proper place. "Jenny Bos? Hubert's daughter?"

"Yes," Mark said, "I can't leave her with the bastard she married."

"Who's he?" Emmerik asked

"Henk van Weeren."

"Oh my dear God," Emmerik exploded, "Am I to understand that you are taking on a crazed Nazi husband as well as the Abwehr?"

"I realize the difficulty. If you wish to reconsider your offer to drive us to the railway station, I'll understand. It might be dangerous. Jenny told me Streicher and his men are checking the train station."

Emmerik pulled out the watch from his vest pocket and clicked the lid open to check the time he already knew. The gesture was a stalling device to allow him to consider his response.

"We must forget about train travel from here. We can avoid checkpoints at the station by driving to Appingedam, the first stop along the line. You can catch the train from there to Delfzijl." He fumbled trying to put the watch back in his pocket while looking at the ceiling as if he were receiving instructions from an extra terrestrial source. He got up from his chair and pulled out maps and papers from his battered briefcase.

Miss Hilda, who had stood guard at the end of the room, rapidly cleared the table of her precious heirloom coffee service. Emmerik showed Mark the arrangements for Delfzijl and the map of the embarkation site.

"Your contact will be looking for you at the platform in Delfzijl," he concluded. Mark reminded him of the changed itinerary.

"I told Jenny we'd meet her on the corner at a quarter to three."

"None of our plans include a woman and a baby. You can easily bring her to Delfzijl but you will have to arrange her passage to Sweden by yourself." He sat down again and looked in vain for his coffee cup. Hilda's antennae picked up the vibration and hurried to the kitchen to retrieve it.

"Allard Oosterhuis is the main man there. He owns two freighters. The *Cascade* sails tonight with a Swedish crew. Dutch crews are not allowed for fear they'll not return."

"The Swedes have no desire to escape to occupied Nederland, I guess," Mark quipped. Emmerik ignored the attempt at levity. He busied himself putting milk in his fresh cup of coffee. Hilda beamed from her corner.

"Have some cake too," she urged. Emmerik nodded and relishing his first sip, said, "Oosterhuis frequents the *Café de Witte Zwaan*, the White Swan. Your contact at the station will take you there. The ship's scheduled departure time is around eleven o'clock at night. Daytime departures are not allowed because Emden – the German harbour, 15 kilometres across the water – is an active U-boat base." He took a hearty bite of the cake and chomped away in silence.

The Ford had stood idling at the corner of Jenny's street for at least ten minutes when Emmerik suggested that they move on. Jenny wasn't coming. "We can't stay. Someone will report us."

"Let's wait a bit longer," Mark requested.

"As things stand now, we will have to outrun the train; it leaves five minutes from now. We either go now or abort your mission." Emmerik did not wait for a response. He put the Ford in gear and drove away.

84

1941
SUNDAY, JULY 6, 14:55 HRS CEST
RAILWAY STATION
APPINGEDAM, NEDERLAND

The Appingedam station, a whistle stop along the route from Groningen to Delfzijl, served a town of some 2,500 souls. With seven minutes to spare, they pulled up to the bleak and neglected station. A puddle of rain stood at the corner of the entrance. Its old brickwork and enamel signs were stained with rust dribbles.

Mark helped Willem carry the suitcases into the terminal. "You stay here," he told the boy, "While I thank Lieutenant Emmerik for his help."

"I feel badly that Jenny and the baby didn't join you," Emmerik said. Mark acknowledged the sympathetic remark with a wan smile.

Emmerik stepped into the Ford and drove forward, intending to make a U-turn at the end of the drive. As he turned, a DKW raced towards the station. Emmerik honked the horn. Mark spotted the man as he dismounted. It was van Weeren. He ran toward the side of the terminal building and turned the corner. Van Weeren ran after him, Luger in hand.

Blinded by passion, van Weeren recklessly turned the corner without looking and was body-checked in the gut by Mark who had crouched down and pounced. Van Weeren flew backwards as if hit by a bullet. His Luger clattered to the cracked pavement. Mark lunged and straddled Henk, clasping his hands around his throat. Henk struggled to regain the upper hand but his efforts weakened as Mark dug his left fist deep into the artery supplying oxygen to the brain. The sleeper-hold he had practiced so many times in training effectively rendered van Weeren hors-de-combat.

He had been taught to show no mercy to those who would harm him but he could not kill this man. Jenny would never forgive him. He looked around. The only witness was Emmerik, standing by his idling Ford.

Mark dragged the uniformed figure to the door of the freight shed. He smashed the old-fashioned padlock with the butt of Henk's Luger. The place smelled of oil and rust. He found a pile of jute sacks and fashioned a couple of them into bindings to tie van Weeren's ankles and wrists.

It was Sunday. No one would likely check the shed until the following day. At the very least, they had time to catch the train. He stuffed Henk's Luger in the back of his own waistband and ambled over to the station.

He found Willem sitting on the bench reading Saturday's newspaper. "What took you so long?" he asked.

"Ah, I talked to Emmerik and thanked him."

"You look sweaty," Willem observed.

The train pulled into the station exactly on time. They took seats next to the exit and were first off when they arrived in Delfzijl. The platform looked deserted. This was indeed the end of the line: it was as far into the northeast of Nederland as one could go. The smell of oil and salty air assailed their nostrils. The harbour was close by; the tips of masts showed above the rooftops of the nearby buildings. A teenaged girl in a plaid skirt and pigtails sashayed toward them.

"I am Famke," she said in her Groningen accent. "You are looking for *de Witte Zwaan*. I'll show you the way," she added. "We must be careful. The Abwehr arrived this afternoon and are checking all travellers at the harbour. They are looking for you." She guided them behind a clutch of freight cars onto the street. She looked serious and well beyond her years.

"I will walk ahead with your son, talking as brother and sister, out for a walk. You will follow with the suitcases, but at a distance." In spite of the tension he felt, Mark was calmed by her confidence.

De Witte Zwaan was less than a five-minute walk away. Inside, the place looked similar to many such establishments. The huge billiard table dominated the right side of the room, the side of the drinkers. The walls were covered with photographs of the local soccer team.

The dining area was a bit classier. The tables, covered with white starched tablecloths, were laid out with crockery and silverware, ready and waiting for diners.

Few patrons were present this early Sunday evening in Netherlands Reformed Church country. Two men were playing billiards. Only the clicking of the balls gave any indication of the game's progress. An elderly man was reading the café's courtesy newspaper, its spine clamped in a wooden vice. Reading it was easy, taking it home impossible.

The massive bar held a display of shiny copper spigots fed from the kegs below. The nameplate on the wall read, Tjeerd Houtstra, Proprietor.

Tjeerd himself presided over the bar and greeted his guests. Apron in hand, he led Mark to a table decorated with Amstel beer coasters.

"What will you and the lad have?" he asked, pulling on his black bow tie while he kept an eye on the billiard table. "No beer on Sunday," he added quickly. Mark asked for coffee and a *Ranja* for Willem.

One of the billiard players, a well-dressed man, quit playing and placed his cue forcefully in the rack. In his early forties, the man had dark hair streaked with gray. His intelligent eyes scanned the café before he headed straight for Mark's table. He introduced himself as Allard Oosterhuis. He asked Mark and Willem to follow him to the back room, a bright space with a picture window looking out onto a well-tended garden. They barely sat down when Tjeerd, the proprietor entered.

"This room is for weddings," Tjeerd winked as he trundled in with a tray laden with glasses of beer for his special guests. "The dominee never visits here on Sunday," he grinned. Famke came in and asked Willem to play with her in the garden. The boy blushed but seemed elated.

Allard spread a hand-drawn map across the table. "Let's go over the plans. The harbour sits at the end of a small peninsula that constitutes the international zone. A four-metre high, electric fence closes it off from the town. The site gets lit up like a soccer field when an alert is called." He took a sip of his beer as he looked at Mark who studied the map intently.

"The incoming cargo is stored on the east side, the outbound freight on the west. The two sides are separated by a fenced-in walkway. That's where the passengers and crews walk through to board the vessel."

"How will Willem and I get aboard?"

"Half of our cargo will be sugar beets. They are shipped in wooden bins of two-by-four metres and two metres deep. Each truck carries six bins. The last truckload will be delivered to the export side very close to sailing time. The Germans know the trucks will be late because we notified them that one of the loaders broke down and is being repaired."

He paused for another sip of beer and asked for a plate of *bitterballen*, a deep fried treat. Tjeerd hustled to the kitchen with the empty glasses.

"Now, young Willem and you will be hidden in one of the bins, among the beets. The truck will take that load into the international zone, where you will wait until you hear the ship's horn signalling *all aboard*."

Oosterhuis continued, "At the far western side of the zone, you will find a dinghy tied up to the quay. You will row it to the starboard side of the *Cascade* so no one can spot you from shore. The crew will help you aboard and hide you until the ship is in international waters."

"What about money? How do you get paid?"

"Your fare was paid in American dollars into our Stockholm account by a London Bank; no need to be—" Oosterhuis stopped talking as they heard voices coming from the restaurant. He grabbed the papers off the table and stuffed them quickly in a drawer containing spoons and forks.

Tjeerd was at the door. "Someone knows you're here," he managed to say before he was shoved aside. Gary Galluci had arrived at a most inopportune time.

Gary ignored Mark and addressed Oosterhuis. "I want to book passage on your ship to Stockholm," he declared.

"And who might you be?"

"My name is Gary Galluci. I am an American investigator," he pulled out his phony security badge. "I am here to make sure that the boy Willem gets to Sweden safely." He threw his passport and a stack of hundred dollar bills on the table. Oosterhuis cast an inquiring look at Mark who briefly explained the circumstances, leaving out the part about the Royals.

"So you both have the same objective?" Oosterhuis said.

"Until we get to England, then it becomes a political battle," Mark said.

"An American will add some intrigue for the passengers," Oosterhuis concluded.

Galluci demanded to know the plans to get Willem through the passport and customs inspection. Oosterhuis brought out his map and explained the sugar beet arrangements.

"How did you find us?" Mark asked Galluci.

"Easy. The peat boat was going to Groningen. The only commercial harbour is Delfzijl. With some dollars in hand, some kind people told me that *de Witte Zwaan* is where the action is. Voila!"

Mark sat quietly sipping his beer, contemplating the change in circumstances. Gary, on the other hand, was ingratiating himself with Allard Oosterhuis by eating *bitterballen* and regaling him with boisterous tales of his exploits in America. It was nearly seven o'clock when Tjeerd came into the room and whispered something in Allard's ear.

"Are you sure?" Oosterhuis said in astonishment. He rose and looked at Mark. "Emmerik is here. He brought your daughter and her mother?"

Mark jumped from his chair. "Where?" he blurted out.

Tjeerd brought Jenny in the room with Anneke. She handed the baby to a beaming Emmerik and embraced Mark. Tjeerd smiled, Allard smiled and the American stood and clapped his hands in delight.

Famke and Willem, hearing the commotion, came back into the room. Famke quickly took Anneke from the inept Emmerik and rocked her in her arms. Willem looked anxious. More than Jenny and Anneke, the reappearance of Gary Galluci frightened him.

Mark said, "You came to say goodbye. Thank you."

Jenny held him at arms length and looked him in the eye. "We're not here to say goodbye, Mark. Anneke and I are going with you."

"Lieutenant Emmerik came to our house and spoke to my parents. He told us how brave you were and that you had risked the mission and your life to get me. My father decided that Anneke should be with her natural father and that it was God's will. The Lieutenant knew where to find you."

"Weren't you afraid of Henk?" he asked turning to Jenny.

"No, Emmerik told me Henk was busy in Appingedam." Mark looked at Emmerik who shrugged his shoulders in a what-can-I-say manner.

Allard Oosterhuis knocked loudly on the table. "Things seem to be happening very quickly here," he said irritably. "Now, we have expanded the family from two to four members. We cannot accommodate the woman and child without having the proper papers."

"I have the passports and ID cards," Mark said quickly. "We are the Bos family with two children." He dug into his inside coat pocket and threw the passports on the table.

Oosterhuis leafed through them but didn't really concentrate. "I cannot ask the Captain to take on more risk," he said softly. "He is very well paid but he will expect to be compensated."

Tjeerd, captivated by developments, added his voice. "Captain Hoaglund is in the bar with several crew members. Shall we ask him to join us?" Oosterhuis agreed.

Per Hoaglund, 51, a brooding giant with a big head of dark stringy hair, definitely did not fit the image of a typical Nordic male. His dark eyes were a little too close to the squashed nose. His head looked as if it had been bowled along the ground until the protuberances broke off, and then put back onto his shoulders and neck.

"I have a cook on our muster, but she did not join us in Stockholm. Our steward had to do the cooking. For the right price, I could bring the woman aboard as our cook. And it wouldn't be the first time that a female crew member brought her child on board with her."

"You mentioned price," Mark reminded him.

"There are expenses, you know," Hoaglund began, his hangdog look becoming sadder by the minute. "I have to get the crew papers certified by the authorities. They know it is illegal work but they want to be paid. Then come the ship's officers whose loyalty must be rewarded and then—"

Galluci could not stand it any longer. "Quit quibbling! How much?"

"Ten thousand American dollars," Hoaglund said with a painful facial twitch as if he had to pay instead of receive.

"I don't have that kind of money," Mark said, his face ashen.

"I'll pay for it, including the fare," Gary said loudly pounding his fist on the table. He took the money out of his back pocket; a large wad, secured with a rubber band, which belatedly explained his disconcerting habit of always tapping his behind.

"I don't want cash; the Germans would take it if they searched me. I want it deposited into my account in Stockholm."

"I can look after that. You can pay me," Oosterhuis volunteered. "I have business dealings with his bank every day."

"Done!" Gary shouted.

Mark looked on in surprise. "What do you want in return?" he asked.

"I want to get the boy to London. Once we are there, you will be an agent of the Crown and I'll be an American interloper. In short, I need you. You can pay Mr. Kolmar back if you want to. It's his money," he said in a feisty voice to hide his satisfaction with saving the day.

Hoaglund eyed the money on the table and urged Oosterhuis and Gary to settle the finances. Emmerik, on the other hand, appeared nervous to see so much cash and announced he was returning to the city.

Mark reached out for his hand. "I don't know how to thank you. You risked your life bringing Jenny here."

"I was young myself once," he said wistfully.

85

1941
SUNDAY, JULY 6, 21:00 HRS CEST
CAFÉ DE WITTE ZWAAN
DELFZIJL, NEDERLAND

With more than an hour remaining before dusk, Jenny suggested they sit outside in the garden. Tjeerd's wife had done a lovely job creating a curved flowerbed of white iceberg roses mixed with the red and pink variety. Along the edge stood white, pink and red dwarf impatiens matching the colours of the roses. Two containers featured red ivy geraniums. The overall effect was very colourful. A pond with a miniature fountain gurgled in the background creating a serenity that was simple and beautiful at the same time.

The group sat in silence waiting for the action to unfold. Squinting into the rays of the setting sun, Mark felt more nervous than at any time since his landing, two long weeks ago. The worst was almost behind them. Sweden would bring its own problems but without the Nazi threat.

He looked at the make-believe family listed in the false passports. Jenny hooked her arm into his and squeezed it. Willem hauled Anneke onto his lap and played peek-a-boo with the chortling child.

Oosterhuis interrupted the reverie. "Time for you and the lad to head for the trucks," he announced, "Four trucks will stop briefly behind the *van Gend en Loos* warehouse before they drive toward the international zone. Climb aboard. It's Sunday. No one will spot you."

"I'll take your bags," Gary said as he stomped back into the room, "I'll put them aboard," he said with a wink.

Jenny looked strong and determined as Mark kissed Anneke who was blowing bubbles and cooing. "See you soon," she said as she gave him a perfunctory kiss. Oosterhuis tugged at his sleeve urging him to go.

The international zone loomed as a hellishly lit stage ringed by utter darkness. "The rest of Europe is in total blackout and this place is like a magnet for the RAF," Mark observed.

"It is only that bright when ships dock or depart and then only for a few hours," Oosterhuis said. "The RAF is too busy to come looking for neutral merchant ships. If they were to come this way at all, they'd rather attack Emden, across the water where the U-boats are."

Famke led them on the short walk to the warehouse and then ran back to the Café. Willem gnashed his teeth as they waited. They heard the sound of heavy vehicles before they saw them. Four Mercedes trucks, their tires spinning chunks of clay onto the pavement, rumbled to a halt. Each carried six bins of beets.

The driver of the lead truck climbed out of the cab and urged them to climb aboard. He pointed to the third bin from the rear that appeared only half filled. Mark had imagined the bins to have solid walls but the sideboards were spaced five centimetres apart. At least they would be able to see a bit and they would not suffocate. They laid face down on the beets. The smell of the clayey soil was overpowering. The driver built up a wall of single beets next to them and placed a couple of jute bags on their backs. He covered them with a number of smaller beets from another bin.

Willem complained softly that the weight was too heavy. Mark reached for his hand and held it.

"We'll get used to it," he whispered, "Be strong." The entire process had only taken a few minutes. The trucks rumbled on toward the gates of the export section. The slits on the side allowed Mark a limited line of vision. He could see the gate in the tall fence opening. A uniformed man spoke to the lead driver. "They must have told you that we had trouble with the loader in the field?"

"Yes, but you better hurry. This is the last load. Most of the shipment is already on board."

"How's the inspection?"

"It's been light today. The Germans are looking for people instead of contraband."

Mark suddenly realized they were only in a holding area. Another electric fence stood between them and the international zone. A Dutch customs inspector, along with a German soldier carrying a bayoneted rifle ordered the driver out of the cab. Mark's pulse was racing. Fortunately, Willem could not see the men.

The truck driver looked on as the Dutch inspector hopped onto the truck and helped his German cohort, who was struggling with his rifle, to climb aboard. The soldier drew his rifle into the attack mode preparing to stab deeply into the bins.

The driver reacted quickly, *"Beschädigen sie die ware nicht!"* he shouted – a warning not to damage the merchandise. The German looked apologetic. The inspector moved over to the bin where Mark and Willem were hidden, lifted up several beets held them up high, and then, in a theatrical fashion put them back to show the soldier how it should be done. He pointed to the next bin for the German to copy him. The man did some perfunctory lifting but his heart wasn't in it. The inspector gestured him off the truck pointing to the next vehicle in line. After a few assuring slaps on the side of Mark's bin he jumped off the truck too.

Minutes later, the gates to the international zone opened and the trucks rumbled through. Through the slit, Mark could see the cranes on the quay hauling the beet bins on board.

A couple of stevedores pulling a manually operated davit approached his truck and began the laborious process of lifting the first bin off the truck into the loading area. It was an eerie sensation when their bin was lifted and carried through the air, only to be plunked down hard onto the pavement. The trucks pulled away.

Mark could see passengers pass through the fenced walkway toward the ship. Streicher along with a group of gimlet-eyed Abwehr men were checking the identity papers of every traveller. Gary Galluci got double attention but got through. Germans were loathe to offend Americans, Mark realized.

From a distance, he heard riotous singing. A dozen or more *Cascade* crew, many apparently inebriated to the point of falling down, snaked through the passenger funnel.

A chorus of *hup-fal-de-ral*, a Swedish travelling song rang through the cool summer evening. All wore black woollen caps and swirled together like a swarm of bees. The singing got louder as the throng approached Streicher's checkpoint. The Abwehr men reached for their weapons.

Captain Hoaglund, imposing in his gold-braided uniform with white cap, brought up the rear; his right arm around a crewmember unable to walk on his own. Mark recognized the posture. It was Jenny. Anneke must have been among the swirling multitude, probably yelling her head off, but he could neither see nor hear her.

The cluster of men advanced on Streicher's group manifestly intent on rolling through without being hindered. The Abwehr men struggled with the front-runners, trying in vain to stem the tide. Hoaglund extricated himself from the centre and dragged Jenny to the front holding passports in the air, using his uniform and intimidating persona to walk past the struggling Abwehr men. Streicher, absorbed by the drama in front of him, did not notice.

Mark was fascinated by the spectacle. "They're through, they're aboard," he whispered to Willem who whimpered in response.

The cranes were stowing crates at a rapid rate. Their bin would soon be lifted and deposited in the hold with other bins stacked on top of them.

He had been told to wait for the ship's horn to blare the all-aboard signal. It might come too late. He rose, chucked the beets from his back and freed Willem. They sat up, blinking in light shining from the waters edge. Mark sniffed the air with relish, as a submariner might savour the breeze after a long spell under water.

A dog yelped loudly in the holding area. The gate to the international zone creaked open and a military figure in an SS uniform entered with a German shepherd, frantically pulling on the restraint held by his master. Mark recognized van Weeren who was still some 50 metres away.

"Quick, Willem," he whispered as he leapt from the top of the bin and then caught the boy as he jumped.

He stopped briefly to pull the Beretta from its ankle holster. Van Weeren's Luger in the back of his waistband did not need checking. It had pressed into his spine for the entire truck ride. With a gun in either hand, he prodded Willem toward the northwestern corner of the zone.

In this far corner, the lights were less intense, just ambient light from the centre. Van Weeren was gaining on them. He was shouting in German.

"*Sie sind hier. Ich habe sie gefunden,*" he screamed at his German friends, alerting them that he had found his prey. Van Weeren's frantic shriek had a visible effect on Streicher. He bolted through the fenced-off aisle, yelling for someone to open the gate to the international zone.

Impatient, Streicher clawed at the fence with both hands and immediately bent over in pain as the high voltage tore through his body. He knelt on the ground in a praying position. An Abwehr man raised him to his feet. He stumbled a few steps before settling into a slow wobbly trot.

Mark looked back and realized that van Weeren and the dog on a long leash were gaining on them.

"Run to the far corner Willem! And wait in the dinghy," he yelled. He suddenly stopped. The dog leapt at Mark; a bullet from the Beretta caught him in mid-air. The animal slumped to the pavement yelping in pain. Van Weeren, still ten metres behind looked toward the Abwehr at the gate.

"*Sie haben meine ehefrau gefangen genommen*," he yelled, hoping they would understand that his wife was held captive.

Mark was walking backwards to keep van Weeren within the range of the Beretta when he stumbled across something and fell backwards onto the pavement. Van Weeren seized his chance and aimed his gun. Mark didn't hesitate and pulled the trigger. Van Weeren flew backward from the impact and landed on his back.

The gate to the international zone was now open and a group of soldiers ran toward the sound of the gunfire. Two soldiers stopped to attend the wounded van Weeren. Mark sprinted to the corner where Willem stood, fists clenched to his mouth and a look of terror on his face.

"No dinghy," he managed to choke through his convulsion of tears. It was dark in this deserted corner of the dock. No dinghy.

In the distance, they could see the lights of the *Cascade* lying at anchor. Less than 200 metres away, Mark figured. He considered letting Willem be captured. Life in Germany would be preferable to dying in this bleak corner of the country. He could leave Willem alone and swim for safety. If he surrendered, Willem would live; he would not.

The boy appeared to regain his composure. "The ship is so close. I could swim that far," he said. "We can swim behind it and climb aboard away from the lights."

The water was calm on the leeside of the protective dike. "It will take at least ten minutes to get there," Mark said, stripping down to his shorts. "Do you think you can make it?"

Willem did not answer but took off his shirt, kicked away his shoes and waded into the salt water. "It's not as cold as it looks," he said.

The posse of soldiers slowed down now that they were also in near darkness. Mark and Willem were at least 50 metres into the water when one of the Germans yelled that he could see something move. A volley of gunfire erupted but bobbing heads in the water, in the dark, make for a poor target.

"*Nicht schiessen*," Streicher yelled, realizing that it might be Willem in the water. Gunfire stopped as the group headed back to the gate of the international zone that had let them in. It closed again.

"*Sie müssen ein boot finden*," Streicher yelled after them hoping they could find a boat somewhere.

Meanwhile, the swimmers had shortened the distance to the *Cascade*. The film of motor oil floating on the surface blackened their faces. Willem gagged on the stinking mix of diesel fuel, creosote and salt water. The lights of the *Cascade* seemed farther away than ever.

"I have a cramp," Willem cried quietly and began treading water, "My leg is stiff. I can't swim."

"Hang on to my back by the shoulders. I'll just pull you along." With Willem slowing him down it flashed through his mind that that they might not make it. The shore was closer than the ship. Perhaps his pursuers had left the international zone. Maybe he should swim for shore.

He suddenly remembered his life saving classes where he had been taught to lie on his back, clamp his hands around the drowning person's ears and do the frog kick. The switch made the swim more manageable but he had to look back frequently to see if he was still on course. He had indeed gained some distance. He decided to keep going.

Worry overcame him. What if they believed they had been captured, drowned or shot? Would Hoaglund sail without them? He forced himself to kick more strongly. Willem was silent. He checked. Willem's nose and mouth were above water but his eyes were closed.

He heard a voice, not from the shore but from across the water. "Ahoy! Ahoy," he heard. A white apparition floated atop the waves. It crossed his path in the direction of the shore.

"Ahoy," he yelled back into the darkness. The white silhouette slowly turned. He could see oars splashing in the water. The voice roared again.

"Mark, put your hand up you dumb bastard, so I can see you," Gary Galluci yelled.

"I am holding Willem."

"Okay; keep talking so we can find you."

A lifeboat emerged from the darkness. It came closer. He could read the name on the stern, *Cascade*. Gary and a seaman wearing a black toque were pulling the oars. Hands reached out. Willem was pulled aboard. Mark followed. Willem sat shivering, his chin cupped in his hand. The seaman took off his black sweater and threw it at the boy.

Mark worked himself into one of the life vests for warmth, not safety.

The rowers took a wide berth away from the shore but arrived behind the *Cascade* without being spotted. Willem, pushed by Mark, was the first up the rope ladder. A strong arm lifted him onto the deck. With remarkable speed and efficiency, the ship's davit hauled the lifeboat up to its regular place along the deck. The rope ladder was pulled up seconds after Gary set foot on the deck.

The first mate hurried them along a gangway. "The Germans are on board and checking everyone and everything," he said. He led them down a steel stairway to the boiler room. Two stokers, feeding the gaping fire hole, paid no attention as the first mate lifted a hidden hatch above the coalbunker. "Quick, in here," he said as he clasped both open hands together as a step to boost Willem into the narrow space.

Mark hoisted himself into the hiding place. A mattress and bottles of water indicated this place was a semi-permanent place to stow illegal guests. The hatch shut down with a bang. It was very warm in the confined space, a welcome treat for those wearing only wet underwear.

They heard hobnailed boots clanging down the steel stairway. Loud commands in German meant the inspection was heading their way. Captain Hoaglund's explanation that this was the boiler room received only grunting replies. The sound of a locker being opened and shut was followed by the sound of a metal object scraping pieces of coal apart.

"*Es ist heisz hier drinnen.*" Streicher said, complaining it was hot. After some unintelligible mumblings, the clattering on the stairs meant the searchers had gone away.

Mark's tension eased. He wondered how Jenny had fared. Hoaglund's crew appeared experienced in stowing contraband and people. In a few days, they would be in neutral Stockholm. He held a shivering Willem in his arms, gently soothing him that it would soon be over.

A bell rang in the boiler room. Steam was released. Engines rumbled. The *Cascade* was moving. The ship's horn blasted a farewell. The hatch was lifted. "On the way to Sweden. You are free," Gary Galluci yelled as he lifted Willem from his hiding place.

"Are Jenny and the baby okay? Mark asked.

"Sound asleep, both of them."

Monday, July 7, 1941. Mark looked at his watch: 01.15 Hrs.

86

1941
THURSDAY, JULY 31, 16:00 HRS BDST
CROYDON AIRFIELD
CROYDON, ENGLAND

Croydon Airfield's arrival hall was severely damaged. Tarpaulins covered a gaping hole in the ceiling and puddles from a recent rain were randomly distributed across the heaving floor tiles. In 1939, the airfield became one of the major bases for the defence of London. German bombs had razed many of the administration buildings, runways too, but these had been rapidly repaired.

From time to time, civilian aircraft originating in unoccupied Europe were permitted to land. Today, British Air Command was expecting flight 413 of the Swedish ABA Airlines. For its six-hour flight, the aircraft carried 14 passengers, including eight England-farers who were Resistance people from the occupied territories.

The arrival hall was deserted save for an aging commissionaire and a military officer. Roelof Blansjaar, a captain in the Dutch armed forces paced up and down wearing a British tin helmet. He was a small, bronzed, brown-eyed man of 40 or so with an angry red scar on his cheek. His K.N.I.L shoulder patch indicated that he was an officer of the Royal Dutch Army of the East Indies, the standing army of what is now Indonesia.

Captain Blansjaar had been an Army liaison officer on the Dutch Navy destroyer *De Ruyter* when, in May of 1940, the vessel had been ordered from the Strait of Malacca to join the fleet in the North Sea. Unable to return to his base in Batavia, he had been named to succeed Lieutenant Zonder as operations officer of the NDI, reporting to General van Zandt.

Blansjaar had waited more than an hour when, at last, the aircraft with its yellow cross on royal blue requested permission to land. As it approached the runway, it looked like a tube wrapped in a Swedish flag, identification meant to discourage warring parties from shooting it down.

Blansjaar's instructions were to escort Lieutenant Mark Zonder and Willem von Becke to Carlton Manor for a debriefing.

The Customs procedure took longer than expected and Blansjaar ventured into the inspection area. Lieutenant Zonder, in civilian clothes and holding Willem's hand, had passed the inspection and was talking to a stocky Italian-looking man.

"Lieutenant Zonder?" Blansjaar smiled and extended his hand, "Captain Blansjaar, your replacement at NDI." Mark was surprised. He had always assumed that he would return to his old post and that this mission was a singular affair, asked of him only because of his familiarity with the terrain and the principals involved. Up to now, he had not thought about his London posting but realized that it might be lost.

"And you must be Willem," Blansjaar said shaking the boy's hand. Willem instinctively pulled close against Mark as if to seek his protection.

"My orders are to accompany you and Master von Becke to Carlton Manor where the General will personally receive you," Blansjaar smiled.

"My fiancée and her daughter are still waiting for Customs and Immigration, so we will have to wait."

"I am afraid that we are already more than an hour behind schedule and we should leave." Blansjaar insisted.

"I'm not on any schedule. I'll wait until my family is allowed to enter the country," Mark said with greater anger than he intended to show.

Gary Galluci looked at him in surprise. He introduced himself to Captain Blansjaar. "I am Gary Galluci, American citizen; I arrived with Mark from Sweden." Blansjaar bowed slightly and shook his hand.

"Are you working for the American government?" Blansjaar asked.

"In a way," Mark intervened, "He is working with the FBI on behalf of Willem's father."

"We should really be going," Blansjaar urged again.

Gary resolved the impasse, "Mark and Willem, you go with the Captain and I'll take Jenny and Anneke to the hotel."

"Where are you staying?" Blansjaar asked.

"We are all booked at the Savoy," Gary said. If the Captain was surprised at the choice of the priciest and most exclusive hotel in London, he did not show it. He took Willem by the hand and marched him to the parking area. Mark followed reluctantly.

As they walked towards his car, Blansjaar said, "As a military officer you are entitled to a helmet and gasmask, however neither the driver nor I thought of bringing them." Mark assured him it was okay.

With some satisfaction, he noted that his replacement was not entrusted with van Zandt's Rolls Royce. He and Willem squeezed into the back seat of a 1936 Morris. Willem was amazed at the damage to the city of Croydon. Streets had been made passable by shovelling the loose bricks and debris off to the side as if cleared after a blizzard. People lived in makeshift homes fashioned from partly destroyed buildings and sheltered by anything that would serve as a roof. Tattered tarpaulins and sheets of corrugated tin were among the most popular materials. "There is a lot more damage here than at home," Willem said.

"England stands alone against Germany," Blansjaar said, conveniently forgetting the Red Army's struggle in Russia. He changed the topic and leaned over his shoulder to address Mark. "How was your stay in Sweden?"

"Well it was quite a change. Not having to be afraid of being nabbed by the Nazis was a great relief," Mark said, wriggling his body in the tiny back seat. "Our stay at the Grand Hotel in Stockholm was magnificent."

"That is where Queen Wilhelmina stayed on her visit in 1938," said Blansjaar. "The Embassy must have a big budget for England-farers."

"No, they offered a single room for Willem and me in a dilapidated hotel but nothing for my fiancé and our baby. However, Gary Galluci was magnanimous and put us up at the Grand Hotel and paid the bills." Blansjaar was surprised again but did not pursue the money question.

Carlton Manor looked unchanged. To Mark it seemed a lifetime since he had last seen it but it had been barely six weeks.

Holding Willem by the hand, he was greeted joyfully by the staff on the first floor. Alice caught up to him as he was about to climb the stairs to the van Zandt suite. She kissed him on both cheeks. "I am so happy to see you back safely," she whispered softly.

"I am happy too," he said. "You know about Jenny?" he asked holding the door open with one hand and Willem by the other.

"Yes and I am happy for you."

"You know she is here in London and we have a baby?" he asked again.

"Yes, and we are all delighted," she cooed, "Frans is waiting for you in his office. He said he'd rather talk to you here than at the Embassy."

Van Zandt must have overheard the discussion because he appeared at the top of the stairs that led to his apartment.

"Come on up, Zonder, don't let the ladies make you keep Willem from me," he smiled. The boy trod up the stairs with leaden feet.

"Hello my friend, so good to see you again," van Zandt exclaimed, enveloping Willem in a bear hug, "You must tell me about your travels." Willem was subdued, worried what the next change in his life would be. Van Zandt settled them in his small den.

"You must be tired, after such a long trip," he began, "so I should start with the good news. I have a long letter from your mother for you Willem. It was brought to us by the Free French." Willem jumped up with delight.

"Is she still in France?" he asked. "Is she better?"

"Her injuries have healed and she is living in the countryside with a French family. We shall try to bring her to London soon." Willem had magically changed from a petrified boy to a jubilant young man.

"Come with me to our suite so you can read it to your heart's content. I'm sure Mrs. van Zandt will find you something to eat. You must be starved." He led Willem down the hall, pointedly excluding Mark.

Alice who had followed them up the stairs noticed Mark's exclusion and invited him to come down and wait in her office. She was excited to learn about his experiences and listened raptly as he outlined his travels to France and back. When he was called to the General's suite, van Zandt's joviality had dissipated.

He sat behind his desk in his formal General's pose. There was a fly buzzing around his head. He waved it away with a rather regal gesture.

"Now, Zonder, You are to be congratulated on completing your mission in bringing Willem von Becke to England. You showed bravery and endurance. Those are excellent qualities in a soldier, but you were reckless." Mark watched the fly crawl up the window behind him. He felt that bad news was coming, but somehow he did not fear it.

"You were ordered not to have any contact with friends or family while in Europe, van Zandt said, "You endangered the mission by contravening orders and contacting your parents. Bringing your fiancée and her daughter with you is a blot on your record. Your actions are unbecoming of an officer in Her Majesty's Armed Forces. You stand reprimanded." Mark felt strangely content. He noticed that the fly alighted on a page on the folder before van Zandt and walked insolently across the heading.

"As of now, you are no longer attached to the Netherlands Defence Institute and you will be seconded to the Army's Irene Brigade and demoted to your previous rank of Sergeant." The General looked ill at ease but he continued, "Because you are a single man you will receive neither extra pay for maintaining a family nor reimbursement for any expenses involved in bringing your fiancée and her daughter with you."

Mark heard the words but they did not affect him. Instead, he saw the General's hand shoot forward with surprising speed. His fingers flicked and closed tightly, but when he opened his fingers, there was no fly.

Mark tried to absorb what was being said. He had not expected a hero's welcome but certainly hadn't anticipated this severe dressing down. He wanted to end the conversation.

Van Zandt wiped his hand on his trouser leg just as if the remains of the fly and had been upon it and continued, "Willem will be placed with Lord Prescott of Coulter and his family. Lady Prescott is a Professor of History at Oxford College. They live at the Coulter Manor nearby. Willem will be tutored at home. He will have limited contact with people of his own age for a while lest he betray his connection with Princess Juliana – something that would embarrass the Queen."

He made another unsuccessful grab at the fly and waved angrily as it flew away. "The young man will be brought up in proper British Society and eased into the social life when he fully understands his status in life."

Mark responded harshly. "The status of a bastard, who must never meet his mother nor speak of her, even though he knows who she is."

"Precisely so, and do not interrupt your superiors," van Zandt said quietly. He touched his head very delicately almost as if smoothing his hair. He must have thought the fly had settled upon his head but in fact, it was trampling across his desk.

"It appears that you have developed a certain attachment to the boy but you have no say in the matter. Therefore you will travel with young Willem to Oxford and introduce him to his foster parents."

"What about Paula and Alexander, Sir? You said you would bring Paula von Becke to England."

"One must keep the boy happy!" van Zandt said sarcastically. He had obviously no intention of doing anything for Paula. "Alexander von Becke is an SS Officer. He'll be lucky to escape a war tribunal." Van Zandt picked up the file indicating his intention to end the conversation. The fly went into a holding pattern around his cranium.

"Your last task in this mission will be to introduce Willem to Lord Prescott. My driver will take you to Oxford on Saturday morning." He rose and towered over Mark. "A court martial for your dereliction of duty is under review. That's all, Sergeant." Mark snapped a salute.

Before he left, he could not restrain himself. "Thank you Sir. Now that you ask, my fiancée and daughter are doing well." He expected a blistering response but van Zandt looked old and tired. With his head held high, Mark stepped out of the office. The fly came with him.

When he entered the General's suite to collect Willem, Kirsten pecked him demurely on the cheek, noting his distress. "I hear you did well in Europe. Willem told me all about your dangerous situations. Don't let the military minds grind you down, Mark. I have watched it happen too often. The Army is a soul-destroying machine. Frans has had to suffer many outrages himself. Take it and start again."

He smiled wanly, thanked her for entertaining Willem, and walked with him down the stairs.

Alice was waiting for him along with Jos Caspers. "Hey big guy," Jos said to Willem, "I am the chief radio operator here. Would you like to come up and see our radio room where we get our messages from Europe? You will have to watch from behind the glass but it is interesting." Willem looked at Mark who nodded his okay.

Alice led him into her office and closed the door. She sighed, folded her hands together and intertwined her slim fingers. "I am doing something I swore I wouldn't do," she said. "I can't stop thinking about Willem. Caring parents raised him and now his life is torn apart. His so-called ignoble birth is hidden by a 'fixer' to protect other people's shame and the boy has to pay the price."

"You mean van Zandt? What brought on this sudden concern?"

"I have been a lifetime captive in van Zandt's cage. I am another one of his Royal fixes. My natural father was Prince Hendrik, the Queen's husband. Time is too short to tell you more. Perhaps some other time. All I want to say now is that if there is a chance for Willem to live a free life then you must give it to him."

Mark leaned over and kissed her on the cheek. "I understand," he said. He went downstairs and tore a reluctant Willem away from the lights, buttons and sounds common to any radio room. They took the Sloan Square tube station to make their way to the posh Savoy Hotel.

87

1941
FRIDAY, AUGUST 1, 11:00 HRS BDST
SAVOY HOTEL, STRAND
LONDON SW, ENGLAND

The elegant foyer exuded a gentle ambience, the unhurried pace of the well-to-do. The rubble-strewn streets of wartime London seemed a world away. In spite of the problems and shortages of war, the hotel was its gracious self. The sweet synthetic scent of polish in the air attested to a lot of manual work. The aging elevators, crafted of brass and iron, lurched upwards. The wire cages with their wheezing sounds and abrupt stops persuaded many a fearful traveller to use the stairs for the duration of their visit. There was even a man in a black waistcoat and a green baize apron to carry Mark's kit bag.

The concierge in evening attire greeted the young father and his son with some reserve. The name of Zonder in combination with Galluci brought an immediate change in attitude. The man hustled to the check-in area and busied himself collecting papers and keys from a special tray.

"No need to check in Lieutenant Zonder, Mr. Galluci has taken care of everything. Let me show you to your rooms. Mrs. Zonder and your daughter have already settled in. Master William has a room next to yours. Please follow me."

Mark thought briefly of correcting two small items. He wasn't a lieutenant anymore and the only Mrs. Zonder he knew was his mother. He thought better of it as he walked through the hallway with its gilded cornices and exquisite furniture in elegant seating areas.

The concierge mistook his glance of admiration. "Yes, you are right sir. Most of the chairs and tables are splendid imitations. The real items are stored elsewhere, of course." After some silence to let the need for this subterfuge sink in, he added, "Bombs and war, you know."

He opened the door to Willem's room. The boy ran in and was immediately enthralled with the view of the river. "That's the Thames, Mark," he exclaimed. With the door open, Mark left him there to inspect his own room. The room was obviously in use. Clothes were hanging from a chair back; a bassinette stood by the luxurious double bed. The concierge smiled and said, "The message posted with me said that if Mrs. Zonder was not in her room she, along with Mr. Galluci would be visiting the suite of our celebrated guest Mr. Ferenc Kolmar, the American pianist. Let me show you; it's on this floor."

Willem overhearing the last part of the conversation stepped outside his room, his bubble of enthusiasm entirely deflated.

"My real father is here?" he asked anxiously.

Mark put his arms around his shoulder. "It's been a day of surprises, hasn't it Willem? Let's go and face it."

The concierge led them to a hallway with a single set of double doors. He pushed the doorbell that yielded a gentle sound. Gary Galluci opened the door, looked back into the room and announced, "They are here!"

Marcy Skorczeny was the first to rush forward.

"You are Willem and you are a beautiful boy," she said clasping his head in her hands. "You have your father's eyes." She turned and bumped into Ferenc Kolmar who stood directly behind her.

"Look Ferenc, your son!" Marcy trilled. Both Willem and Ferenc stood motionless. Mark sensed the unease of both the father and the son and gently pushed Willem forward. Ferenc still didn't move. Imperceptibly, he shivered as if to waken himself from a reverie. He stuck out his hand.

"I am so happy to finally meet you, Willem," he said striving to keep his voice under control.

Willem shook his hand, looked at his feet and mumbled, "Yes Sir."

Marcy broke the impasse and grabbed Mark by the hand. "And of course you are Lieutenant Zonder who brought our boy home. Jenny has told us all about it. Please join us."

She ushered them all into the immense living room of the Royal Suite. A Bösendorfer concert grand piano dominated the room. Mark quickly counted a dozen settees, banquettes and sofas. Bouquets of flowers stood about the room. The place could accommodate 50 or more partygoers and still not look crowded.

Jenny sat in an alcove near the window with a splendid view of the Thames. Anneke was wobbling happily on her lap. Mark went over to kiss her.

"We have been so well looked after by Mr. Kolmar and Marcy and of course Gary. Everything is just wonderful," Jenny said.

Mark banished the disturbing meeting with van Zandt from his mind as Marcy made everyone comfortable by taking the lead in conversation.

"As soon as Gary let us know that you were in Sweden, I made arrangements for Ferenc and me to come to London. It took a long time, but here we are," she chirped.

Mark broached the subject of parents. "Willem received a wonderful letter from his mother today. She is in France and doing well. Her injuries have healed. Willem, why don't you read her letter to us?"

Ferenc looked startled when Mark said 'Willem's mother' but listened with deep emotion as Willem haltingly read Paula's letter telling of her longing to see him, her hopes of a happy life for her boy and her expectation that he would do his best under all circumstances. Through the Resistance, she had learned that his father, Alexander was now fighting in Russia and she prayed that soon they would all be able to meet again. By the time Willem ended his recitation with her prayer of hoping to see him once more, Ferenc sobbed. He put his arms around his son's shoulder and held him close but Willem, buoyed by the letter, chattered happily, "Uncle Frans said that he would bring my mother to England very soon."

All eyes turned toward Mark. "I think the General said he would do his best to bring her to England soon, but it will not be easy."

"Oh, he can do it. He can do anything he wants," Willem bragged. Mark managed a wry laugh and asked if Willem would mind unpacking his bags in his room because he had something to discuss with Mr. Kolmar. He could not bring himself to say 'your father', but Willem happily obliged.

"I like the Thames and all the traffic," he quipped as he left.

They took their seats in the alcove where Jenny sat with Anneke. Marcy opened the discussion.

"Ferenc would like to take Willem to New York. There is no war. There is no rationing and we would be able to give him everything he deserves in terms of education, the arts, not to mention financial security." Mark thought it best to put the issue in stark perspective.

"The Queen has directed General van Zandt that he must entrust Willem to the foster care of Lord and Lady Coulter in Oxford. His education and financial security is guaranteed. He will receive private tutoring until the Queen, or perhaps van Zandt, decides that Willem is ready to circulate in England's social circles."

Gary had been silent throughout, leaving his employers to do the talking. "You mean there will be no meeting with his natural mother and grandmother. The Royals just want to hide him?" he asked in an angry voice. "Is that what they asked you to risk your life for? To get him away from the Germans and hide him?"

"I am a soldier," Mark said, "I followed my orders."

"All these decisions about Willem's future do not take into account what's best for him," Marcy said. "If his natural mother rejects him, the father is obliged to take on the responsibility."

She walked over to the buffet table and took a sip of her glass of orange juice. It had stood there since breakfast. She took her seat with the glass still in her hand. "Willem has never known any other parents than Paula and Alexander. They love him and made him into the fine young man he is. The war will be over some day and then they will look for Willem. So any arrangement is tentative, at best."

Ferenc finally spoke, "I think Marcy is right. Parents or guardians have only temporary custody of children. They become adults. In six years' time, Willem will be 18. We do not know how long this war will last or how it will turn out. America may enter the war and then it may be over quickly but if England carries on alone..." his voice trailed off.

Mark was discouraged by the sombre analysis. "One thing is clear. Van Zandt has directed me to take Willem to his new home in Oxford."

Gary rose and raised his index finger in the air.

"There may be a solution that will please almost everyone."

88

1941
FRIDAY, AUGUST 2, 11:30 HRS BDST
THE CANTERBURY ROOM, SAVOY HOTEL, STRAND
LONDON SW, ENGLAND

"Thank you, members of the Press and Radio for responding to the short notice of our Press Conference. An unexpected opportunity has arisen for the many admirers of our special guest today, Ferenc Kolmar."

The speaker was Nigel Cuthbert, President of the London Music Society. He had received a late call from Marcy Skorczeny that the maestro was in London and had agreed to perform with the London Philharmonic Orchestra at the Royal Albert Hall as a benefit performance for the victims of the Blitz. Mr. Cuthbert, dressed in an ill-fitting morning coat was nervous. The attendees at his press conferences were usually limited to the music critics of *the Times* and the *Daily Telegraph* and a few stringers. This time the media had been advised that the famed musician would be present and make a special announcement of a personal nature. He surveyed the many heads staring at him and carried on with his usual spiel promoting the Society. Finally he came to the point.

Standing at the back of the hall, Mark saw Kolmar walk to the lectern and put on his reading glasses. The handsome maestro attired in a sporty navy blue blazer and grey slacks read from a prepared script how pleased he was to be able to perform in London in aid of the bombing victims. He reached for the water glass, took a big gulp, and looked up towards the light as if he had a difficult pill to swallow.

"Many of you may wonder," he read, "Why I would risk crossing the Atlantic for a benefit concert. I am, of course thrilled to perform for my London audience, but it was not the sole reason for our journey. In fact, I have come to meet my son whom I have never met." He paused briefly for the shuffling of feet and murmuring to cease. He took another gulp of water, but in his haste, some drips remained on his chin that he tried to ignore as they slowly dribbled down.

"In Europe, many years ago, I fell in love with a beautiful woman, who conceived a child just before I left for the Juilliard School of Music in New York. She did not want to burden my budding career with a child and did not tell me of her condition. She married a man who currently serves with the German Army in Russia and who helped raise the boy as his own." The dribble on his chin was now running down his neck and he paused to pull the hanky from his breast pocket to wipe it off. He stuck the used cloth in his jacket pocket and continued, "A few months ago, she was severely injured in an accident in Paris rendering her unable to care properly for her son. After more than a dozen years, she established contact and informed me of the son I never knew I had. My life partner and manager Marcy Skorczeny urged me to bring my son out of occupied Europe. Twelve-year old Willem arrived in London a few days ago. I would like you to meet my son, Willem von Becke."

Leaning against a marble post in the back of the hall, Mark watched as Willem walked in from a side door, hand in hand with Marcy.

"Willem will live with us in New York where Marcy and I will provide him with a new life of learning, love and affection. Marcy will apply her many talents to try and free Paula von Becke, Willem's mother, so she may join us in New York. I know you may have many questions but for obvious reasons not all can be revealed at this time. Willem will not be available for questions but Mr. Gary Galluci who facilitated Willem's escape from the Continent is ready to answer your questions. Thank you." Kolmar quickly followed Marcy and Willem into the side room that was immediately barred by two burly men.

A bevy of scribes surrounded Gary's bulky frame as they probed him for more details. Mark smiled knowing how verbose Gary would be without giving any meaningful information.

Mark took the elevator to his suite where Jenny and Anneke sat on the floor engaging in an intensive game of making a rubber piglet squeak. The Savoy would be their home until the real estate agent, hired by Marcy, could relocate them to a comfortable cottage outside London. In addition to the free lodging, Ferenc had arranged for a substantial monthly payment to make up for the lost pay of Mark's demotion and the denial of married benefits.

"How did it go?" Jenny asked as she lifted Anneke into the high chair.

"I'll tell you all about it, but first let's order lunch from room service. I have to meet with van Zandt later this afternoon."

Over lunch, he told her of the late night discussion that led to the story fed to the press.

"Won't they find out?" Jenny asked as she struggled with a slice of melon from the fruit plate that threatened to slide into her lap.

"There is enough truth in the statement. They can trace the birth registry in Leiden that will confirm that Paula is his mother and that Alexander serves with the Waffen SS."

Later that afternoon, he took the Underground to Carlton Manor to report the unilateral actions of the Kolmar entourage. Having lost his position and facing a possible court martial, he was only mildly apprehensive of the fury that van Zandt could unleash on him. He found the General in his den, the afternoon edition of *the Times* opened on his desk. He looked up and acknowledged Mark's salute.

"I see that my orders to deliver Willem to Oxford have encountered a problem," he said suppressing a smile. Unless he had attended drama lessons since their previous meeting, he seemed genuinely pleased.

"Yes, Sir. The father has assumed his paternal responsibility. I think any court in Britain would uphold his right to do so."

"Did you even try to execute my order?"

"No Sir, I did not. I left Willem in the custody of his father."

Van Zandt smiled. "What's another charge of dereliction of duty, eh, Sergeant? You've got a few already," he said with mild amusement.

Mark could not hide his frustration. "I'll accept any additional charges as a badge of pride that I helped a young boy to live a free life."

"You should be proud, Zonder. There will be no court martial," van Zandt said matter of factly. "Her Majesty is pleased. You and the American have concocted a great cover story that cannot be disproved. The boy can do no harm to the throne."

"I think it is quite the reverse, General. The throne can do no harm to Willem."

"Quite so," van Zandt said and closed the file in front of him. He got up, opened the door to his office and waved Mark out with one final word, "Dismissed."

EPILOGUE

ALEXANDER VON BECKE

Alexander was taken as a prisoner of war in 1943. He was released from Russian captivity in January of 1947 and returned to Nederland. Due to his service in the Waffen SS, he was barred from carrying on his profession as an architect. He and Paula changed their surnames to the Dutch spelling of Van Beek. He entered the construction business and created a company that became one of the most successful rebuilders of the country's ruined infrastructure. He became a wealthy man and lives today with Paula in a villa in Noordwijk along the North Sea Coast.

PAULA VON BECKE

Paula was forced to remain in Charet-sur-Loire, France until May of 1945. The village was liberated by U.S. forces in August of 1944 but it would be another nine months before Nederland was liberated by the Canadian Forces. She returned to Delft to live with her parents. She was able to frequently exchange letters with Willem and keep up with his progress. She was reunited with her husband Alexander in 1947 when he was freed from a Soviet prisoner of war camp.

FERENC KOLMAR

Ferenc married Marcy Skorczeny in December of 1941; three weeks after the United States declared war on Japan and Germany. He doted on his newfound son and extended all the privileges of wealth upon the boy. He slowed his pace as a soloist in favour of composing and conducting. In 1948 at the age of 40, he was named Conductor of the New York Philharmonic. In 1982 at the age of 64, he was contacted by Juliana's private secretary for the current name and address of Willem.

DIRK VREELINK

In May of 1945 at the surrender of the German Forces in Nederland, Dirk Vreelink surfaced as a Colonel in the Armed Resistance Force. He obtained the rank of Major in the restructured Netherlands Army and served with distinction in the Police Action in the Netherlands East Indies

(1948) and the Korean War (1952). Now retired, he lives with his wife and dog on a houseboat in one of Amsterdam's picturesque canals.

GARY GALLUCI

In December 1941, Gary Galluci enlisted in the U.S. Marines and served at the invasion Iwo Jima. In 1946, he joined the CIA and was later attached to the unit of Cuban exiles in the ill-fated liberation of Cuba. Colonel Gary Galluci had a lead role in the Bay of Pigs invasion.

GENERAL FRANS VAN ZANDT

While Queen Wilhelmina continued to place complete confidence in van Zandt, the many betrayals of Dutch agents dropped in Nederland caused Winston Churchill to suspect that van Zandt was being "played" by the Abwehr. The Queen was asked to remove him from her inner circle. The book *England Spiel*, published by a member of the Abwehr proved that he fell for their counter-espionage tactics. He died in 1961.

HENK VAN WEEREN

Van Weeren recovered quickly from his gunshot wounds incurred in Delfzijl. In 1942, his marriage to Jenny Bos ended in a divorce granted by a German military court on the grounds of his wife's desertion. He remarried immediately. In August of 1946, the Court of Justice in The Hague sentenced him to 15 years in prison for a 1945 murder of an unarmed civilian whom he suspected of being a member of the Resistance.

KIRSTEN VAN ZANDT

After the war, Kirsten van Zandt returned to Sweden to manage her father's business empire, leaving Frans van Zandt in London.

ALICE HEGT

Alice married an RAF Squadron Leader named Bryce Saunders in 1944. Retired Lieutenant General Frans van Zandt gave the bride away. The childless couple now live in Torquay on the southeast coast of England.

KURT STREICHER

In March of 1945 near Groesbeek, three kilometres from the German border, Canadian Forces captured Oberleutnant Kurt Streicher. Returned to his native Bavaria in 1946, he became a German Customs Officer at the Basel, Switzerland crossing. He retired in 1973 with a full pension and lives in Gleichen, Bavaria, a village of 800 people.

ALLARD OOSTERHUIS

In the summer of 1943, the Abwehr arrested Allard Oosterhuis in Delfzijl at *de Witte Zwaan* along with three of his Resistance workers. They were incarcerated in the concentration camp in Westerberg in

Northeastern Nederland. They were freed in March of 1945. Oosterhuis sold his shipping business, bought a yacht and sailed the seas until 1961 when his boat was shipwrecked off the coast of Ireland where he built a home and remained for the rest of his days. In 1970, the City of Delfzijl erected a monument in a tribute to its symbols of the Resistance: Allard Oosterhuis and *Restaurant de Witte Zwaan*.

WILHELM FRANZ CANARIS

In November of 1944, Hitler had Canaris arrested for working against the interest of the German Reich. Together with his deputy, Canaris was humiliated before witnesses and then executed a few weeks before the end of the war at the Flossenbürg concentration camp. By the time of his execution, Canaris had been decorated with the Iron Cross First and Second Class, the Silver German Cross, the Cross of Honor and the Wehrmacht's 12 and 25 Year Service Ribbons.

WALTER SCHELLENBERG

When it became clear that Germany would be defeated, Schellenberg went to Stockholm where he attempted to start peace negotiations. He was arrested in June 1945 and he saved himself from a long term in prison by testifying against other Nazis at the Nuremberg War Crimes Trial.

Schellenberg also provided information to Allen Dulles of the CIA on the Soviet Union. In April 1949, he was sentenced to six years in prison where he wrote his memoirs, *The Labyrinth*. He was released after two years because he was suffering from a serious liver condition. Walter Schellenberg died in Turin, Italy on March 31, 1952.

HEINRICH HIMMLER

In the last days of the war Himmler sought to present himself to the Americans as a defector, contacting Eisenhower's headquarters and proclaiming he would surrender all of Germany to the Allies if he were spared from prosecution. He asked Eisenhower to appoint him "minister of police" in Germany's post-war government. Eisenhower refused.

Unwanted by his former colleagues and hunted by the Allies, Himmler wandered for several days around Flensburg near the Danish border. He disguised himself as a sergeant major of the Secret Military Police. Himmler was arrested and scheduled to stand trial with other German leaders as a war criminal at Nuremberg but committed suicide by means of a potassium cyanide capsule before interrogation could begin. His last words were *Ich bin Heinrich Himmler!*

PRINCESS JULIANA

Three months after the end of the war Juliana and her three daughters (Beatrix, Irene and Margriet) returned to the Netherlands. In 1947, she gave birth to another daughter, Maria Christina who was partly blind, a fact the Princess blamed on having suffered scarlet fever during her pregnancy.

Queen Wilhelmina abdicated the throne in April of 1948 in favour of Juliana.

Juliana's marriage to Bernhard hit the rocks when she turned to faith healers for succor and became ever more devoted to the paranormal.

In 1951 Bernhard became the father of a daughter Alicia born to a French member of the aristocracy. In 1967, a daughter Alexia was born in San Francisco, the result of a liaison with a German female pilot.

The couple remained estranged until after her abdication in 1980 when reconciliation brought them closer together. The county's mores had become far more accepting with respect to children born out of wedlock. Therefore, in summer of 1982, Juliana acceded to Bernhard's wish that all six of his daughters should meet at the Palace. The meeting was to be both secret and private. Juliana, then 73, surprised her family by confessing she had a son from an affair prior to her marriage and insisted that he should also attend.

The gathering took place at the Palace at Soestdijk on September 15, 1982. The youngest child was Alexia Biesterfeld at 15; Willem van Beek at 53 was the eldest.

Juliana died in March 2004. Bernhard died eight months later.

WILLEM VON BECKE

Willem arrived in New York City on August 12, 1941 to live with Marcy and Ferenc Kolmar in the Gladstone Apartments on Fifth Avenue. To this day, the civil registry lists him as being born to Paula and Alexander von Becke, who are still alive – a fact that made it impossible for the Kolmars to adopt him formally. He attended nearby Lexington High School in New York City and became an American citizen upon reaching the age of 18. In 1948, after visiting Alexander and Paula during his summer holidays he followed their example and changed his surname to Van Beek.

In 1951, he graduated from Columbia University with a law degree. He joined the covert operations section of the Central Intelligence Agency (CIA). Because of his language skills, he was posted to Paris where he served among the vanguard of American officials who aided Western European nations as they created the North Atlantic Treaty Organization

(NATO). He undertook several undercover missions to prevent East Bloc infiltration into the Alliance.

He travelled widely throughout Europe on behalf of the Government of the United States and frequently returned to Nederland to visit Grandpa and Grandma Meunier who both lived until the age of 95.

MARK ZONDER

Because of his experiences in occupied Europe, Sergeant Zonder was exempted from further overseas service. In 1942, Mark and Jenny were married. Until 1943, he served in the Princess Irene Brigade as a trainer of survival techniques. During that time, he and his family lived in a charming cottage provided by Ferenc Kolmar in Hounslow, a suburb of London.

Through the influence of Ferenc Kolmar, the OSS, the fledgling American spy operation headed by "Wild Bill" Donovan, formally requested that Sergeant Zonder of the Netherlands Army be seconded as a training officer for their covert operations in Europe. His rank as First Lieutenant was immediately reinstated at a pay scale commensurate with the equivalent rank in the U.S. Army. He and Jenny were moved to Quantico, Virginia. During their seven years in the U.S., they spent many holidays with the Kolmars in New York.

In 1950, after the OSS was restructured to become the Central Intelligence Agency, Mark retuned to Nederland and joined the newly established CID while remaining a covert operative of the CIA.

Jenny gave birth to a son, Hubert Mark Zonder, in 1946 in Washington D.C.

In 1953, the Netherlands Army named Captain Mark Zonder to the Intelligence Section of the newly formed North Atlantic Treaty Organization (NATO) in Rocquancourt near Paris. Part of his responsibilities included the establishment and subsequent supervision of the NATO language school in Papendal near Arnhem in Nederland.

Made in the USA
Lexington, KY
25 September 2010